Also by Treasure E. Blue

A Street Girl Named Desire
Harlem Girl Lost

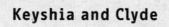

Keyshia and Clyde

Treasure E. Blue

Keyshia and Clyde

a novel

One World | Ballantine Books | New York

A One World Books Trade Paperback Original

Copyright © 2008 by Treasure E. Blue

Published in the United States by One World Books,
an imprint of The Random House Publishing Group,
a division of Random House, Inc., New York.

ONE WORLD is a registered trademark and the One World
colophon is a trademark of Random House, Inc.

LIBRARY OF CONGRESS CATALOGING-IN-PUBLICATION DATA
Blue, Treasure E.
Keyshia and Clyde : a novel / Treasure E. Blue.
p.   cm.
ISBN 978-0-345-49329-3 (pbk.)
1. African Americans—New York (State)—New York—Fiction.
2. Street life—Fiction.   I. Title.
PS3602.L85K49 2008
813'.6—dc22   2008008557

Printed in the United States of America

www.oneworldbooks.net

4   6   8   9   7   5   3

Book design by Laurie Jewell

James W. Sellers

To one of ALLAH's black angels who came on the
planet earth with a wonderful and beautiful spirit and
who shared it with whomever he came in contact. One of the
best examples of a black father that one could have. You are
truly missed, but will never be forgotten, for I know you
will live in our minds and our hearts. May ALLAH
bless your soul, black man—we love you dearly.

—The Family

Keyshia and Clyde

Prologue

Keyshia

Get ready to die, was the thought that ran through Keyshia Simmons's mind as she stared into the smeared, tiny bathroom mirror in the federal courthouse building in lower Manhattan. Suddenly, she lost it again and ran to the nearest toilet stall, where she fell to her knees and threw up violently. It took a few minutes to regain her composure and get back on her feet. Time was running out. Unsteadily, she walked to the sink, cupped a handful of water, and splashed it over her face and into her mouth, the cool water soothing her skin. Life, that day, had new meaning, a new zest, a new zeal. But Keyshia knew it would only be short-lived.

The beginning of the end was near, and Keyshia

knew it. She took a breath, looked down, and rubbed her growing stomach. As her pitiful life flashed before her eyes, she grew angry. But as suddenly as the anger came, it disappeared when she thought about the last years of her life with her man, Clyde Barker. Just moments earlier, she'd sat no farther than ten feet away from him in the courtroom as she awaited his fate—their fate. She loved Clyde more than life itself, because he told her she was beautiful when she couldn't find beauty in herself. She loved him because he taught her how to love herself when she never knew how. She loved him because through him, she now knew what true love really was and what it felt like to be loved and be needed. They'd made a promise that they would die together, and today that's exactly what would happen.

Using her sleeve, she wiped the remaining perspiration and water from her puffy eyes and forehead, exhaled deeply, and repeated, only this time out loud:

"Get ready to die."

The courtroom was outside the bathroom door, a hundred yards away. Once again, and for the hundredth time, it seemed, she tapped both weapons, fully loaded nine millimeters, which she had strapped securely on either side of her ribs. The only things that could keep her from reuniting with her man were three court officers, three guns, and opportunity. The odds didn't matter today. What did matter was to get her man out or die trying! The twelve jurors, one judge, and half a chance didn't offer favorable odds. So she was ready.

Keyshia glanced at her watch—time was up, and suddenly she felt dizzy. She used the sink to brace herself. She took a deep, deep breath and paused—she had to clear everything out of her mind for the mission at hand. She began to think optimistically; if things worked out, she and Clyde could slip out of the courtroom and be lost in all the panic that was sure to come. They might be able to pull it off. However, she knew it was more likely that she would go out down and dirty. So be it.

Life wasn't worth living that much anyway. She touched her stomach once again and smiled as she thought about what could have been. But Keyshia stopped such thinking because she had to be strong. Strong enough for both of them. She closed her eyes again and proceeded to will herself into combat mode, the will of survival, the art of war. Instinctively, her chest began to heave, pulse began to surge, teeth began to grind, nose began to flare, palms began to sweat, and then, there it was—a burst of adrenaline raced through her bloodstream. She let go of the porcelain sink and stormed out the bathroom door. She was ready. Ready to die!

Clyde

Someone was going to die today. Clyde Barker was that someone as he sat sullenly at the defendant's table awaiting his fate. Though he'd known from the very beginning that he hadn't a chance in hell, he could not help but hope it wouldn't go down this way.

Get ready to die! he thought.

The twelve jurors whisked by in single file without looking in his direction. This was not a good sign. Reading body language was a necessity in the world of Clyde Barker, because 90 percent of things he did in those streets was not said, it was almost a given. When he robbed drug dealers in their drug spots, the black gloves, ski mask, and shotgun spoke for itself. *Run that shit!* When he kidnapped a dealer's family member, they looked only for the ransom note, the time, and the place to drop off the loot. See, nothing else needed to be said. *Run that shit!* But now, Clyde's world was about to come to an abrupt end, as the shoe was now on the other foot.

Where was Keyshia?

Clyde thought back to the very first time he'd seen her beautiful face months ago when he pickpocketed her wallet—she couldn't stand his ass. But as fate had it, when love calls, love calls. There's nothing you can do. You can duck and hide, but there's no escaping it; when love comes knocking on your door, you got to let it in. Well, Keyshia didn't only knock, she kicked down the whole fucking door, and he loved the shit out of her for that.

"Has the jury reached a verdict?" asked the judge as he sat imposingly upon his bench.

"Yes, Your Honor, we have," stated the jury's forewoman. An overwhelming fear washed over Clyde at that moment. Not fear of being found guilty, but fear of his plan dissolving before his eyes. Where was Keyshia? He turned and eyed the door again, causing the burly court officer who stood behind him to turn and look at the door also. Be cool, Clyde thought as he tried to make it look as if he were looking toward his two family members in the benches behind him. His palms began to sweat as he questioned the letter that he'd sent her.

My Beloved Aihsyek

As you know, my trial date is scheduled for February 23, at the Federal Court Building on 40 Centre Street. I spoke to my lawyer and he feels I have a very good chance of beating this. I feel the same way. I know you are happy for me. I'm ready to live a brand-new life shortly after that and we can live together forever and ever, just like we talked about many, many times before. There should be only three charges that stand in my way, but I'm only worried about two of them.

You should give yourself about three hours' worth of time in case it is crowded. You may have to sit in the back. I want you to bring two cigars, not the cheap ones, so we can celebrate on our way out the door. Do you remember Mike? He said he can get us some of the best champagne to celebrate with, plus he will keep it on ice for us. Damn, I can hardly wait to be in your arms again. I'll write you plenty more as the days pass, so until then be well.

Love, Clyde

P.S. As soon as we hear those sweet words "Not Guilty," we going to celebrate like it's the Fourth of July.

Decoded, the letter read like this:

My Beloved Keyshia
     As you know, my trial date is scheduled for February 23, at the Federal Court Building on 40 Centre St. I spoke to my lawyer and he feels I'm going to blow trial and be found guilty on all charges, never to see the light of day again. I know this news is fucking you up. I don't want to ever live without you either. That's why I made up my mind, I'm not going out like a chump, so if you are down with the way we talked about, "in a rage making front page," we go out together. Only three court officers should be there at sentencing, I'll handle the one closest to me, you take the other two out. As long as you come fully loaded, we could take 'em with no problem. Make sure you sit right in front, and use two high-caliber weapons, brand-new so we know they won't jam. Get in touch with Spanish Mike, he could get the guns smuggled in for you, and you can trust him. I can't wait to see you in heaven so we can be together forever in

each other's arms. This will be my last contact with you, so be well. I think it adds to the drama and very smart. I prefer it to stay.

P.S. As soon as you hear the word "Guilty" it's on and blazing. Set it off!

Suddenly, the door to the courtroom opened, and there Keyshia was. A smile spread across Clyde's face as he watched his girl, his woman, his world, enter the courtroom. He could read her mind just by the expression she had on her face. She was ready, and he knew it.

"Have the jurors come to a unanimous decision?"

"Yes, Your Honor, we have."

Clyde did not hear the proceedings because his attention was on his baby. He was enthralled by her beautiful face and tunnel vision set in. He always knew it, but he realized even more so now, how fortunate he was to have found and known what true love felt like in his brief lifetime. Love was something that remained ever so elusive since his mother was taken away from him when he was little. In a short period, this beautiful woman gave him a lifetime of love.

A tear fell from his eye. He couldn't help but chuckle at how chunky his woman was getting. She must be stuffing herself because she misses me, he thought. He loved the way her boots clicked with each determined step that she took on the marble floor. She seemed to glide toward the front of the courtroom.

The jury forewoman stood to give the verdict, but Clyde was fixated on Keyshia. He hadn't seen Keyshia in the nearly eight months since his arrest, and he missed her.

Then Clyde's head tilted like a curious K-9 as he noticed how wide her hips had gotten. As she got closer, he noticed how big her normally small breasts had grown.

He watched her rub her stomach—her hard, protruding stomach, wide and round. He frowned slightly. Keyshia was so close now that he could see the red in her eyes, the flaring of her nostrils, and the grinding of her jaw. Clyde blinked rapidly, and then it finally began to register. Oh shit, is Keyshia pregnant? Body language.

"In the case of federal bank robbery, what has the jury found?"

Clyde watched in horror as Keyshia reached inside her blazer jacket with both hands. He froze.

"We find the defendant, Clyde Barker . . ."

Oh, shit, he thought.

"Guilty!"

Clyde rose to his feet and yelled, "No!" but he was too late.

The last word that could be heard throughout the room was "Nine!" Then the entire courtroom erupted into pandemonium!

Chapter 1

Keyshia's Beginnings

"Keyshia, get your lazy black ass up and start making breakfast for the boys before I come in there and get you up myself," yelled Keyshia's aunt Ninny. It was five-thirty in the morning, and sixteen-year-old Keyshia barely moved off the couch where she slept. She knew from years of experience that her aunt's warning was only an idle threat—for now—and that she had at least twenty-five more minutes before her aunt would come into the living room to make good on her promise; so she stayed just where she was. Keyshia had lived with her aunt Ninny for almost five years and was more than used to all her aunt's threats, intimidation, swearing, and plain old evilness. Ever since Keyshia had come up to New York from Charleston, South Carolina, at the age of twelve, Aunt Ninny had seemed to despise her.

Keyshia was exceptionally skinny and dark skinned, with the kind of short, close-cropped hair that black folks were taught to despise. Her facial features were strong—keen and sharp—and her country accent, the way she dressed, and her out-of-place behaviors caused her to be ridiculed by her classmates the moment she was asked to introduce herself in class. Keyshia had long accepted that she was "different" and adapted to the loneliness of being an outcast. She was born poor and fatherless to a mother who bore baby after baby, six in all, in an effort to find acceptance in her small life. Keyshia became only a number, a number that was forced to vie for attention and survive on her own wit or starve in the interim. But it wasn't only because Keyshia's mother had a hard time raising her children that Keyshia was sent up north to live with her aunt Ninny. It was also that Keyshia had got into "a situation." When a situation happened in the South, it was something that was not to be discussed. It was only to be dealt with, no questions asked. The Simmons household in the South needed relief from that situation, and the best way to handle it was to get rid of it.

When her uncle Polk, who had lived in New York for over fifty years, did the family duty of picking Keyshia up from the Greyhound, Aunt Ninny's eyes seemed to light up with excitement at the arrival of her sister's firstborn child. Keyshia stood wide-eyed and awkward as she held all her meager belongings in a pillowcase. Her aunt graciously whisked her in and said, "Come give your auntie Ninny a hug," as she squeezed Keyshia lovingly in her arms. She told her two boys, Eric and Andrew, to come and give their cousin a hug and a kiss. They did.

Afterward, she helped Keyshia take off her matted and too-small sweater. "Welcome to your new home, baby." As Ninny inspected the plaits in her niece's hair, she frowned and said, "First thing Auntie gonna do is take you to Wilma's on a Hundred Twenty-fifth Street and get that head of yours done."

Uncle Polk was in his seventies and was the first member of the Simmons family to move to New York back in the fifties. Settling in Harlem, he rented a small room and went out looking for work. Not long after he arrived, he landed a doorman's job at the premier Waldorf-Astoria in the heart of the city and became a permanent fixture at the hotel for the next forty years. He was good-natured and a very well-to-do black man for his time. He put his four kids through college and became the pillar of the Simmons family. Over the years, he became sort of a sponsor to the rest of the family, who wanted to move out of the dreaded South and find solace in the promised land, the big city, New York. He would pay the way for each and every family member to New York, find them a place to stay, and help them along until they got a job and were on their feet. The only thing he asked in return was that they help out any family who wanted to come up north just as he had helped them. His niece Ninny was one such that he'd helped to settle in New York. It was time for her to return the favor.

"Uncle Polk, take off your coat and let me heat you up some dinner."

He smiled and said, "No, I can't. Doris is waiting right now for me to pick her up from church, and you know not to keep ole Doris waitin' too long."

Ninny chuckled and agreed, "Yeah, I know how Auntie Doris gets when she waitin' too long; she liable to cuss you out soon as ya see her." They laughed as they walked to the door.

"Oh yeah, I almost forgot." Polk reached in his coat pocket and pulled out an envelope and handed it to her. "Just a li'l something ta help you out with some expenses."

"Oh, Uncle Polk, you ain't hafta do that."

"Child, please, it's my pleasure. We family gots to stick together." She nodded and walked him to the door. "I'll drop by at the end of the month," he assured Ninny, "and drop you off something again." Polk beamed down at Keyshia and said, "You in good hands now, you with family, li'l girl." He kissed Ninny one last time and was on his way.

Aunt Ninny hollered good-bye again and closed the door behind her. She turned around and walked up to Keyshia slowly. She inspected her from head to toe, then suddenly, out of nowhere, she slapped Keyshia across her face, causing the girl to spin around and fall to the floor.

"You black little heifer, how dare your black ass fuck my home up." Keyshia was speechless. "I want yo' li'l black ass to know right now, you gonna earn ya keep to stay here." Ninny scowled at her niece and yelled, "Bitch, when I talk to you I want you to answer me, do you understand?"

Keyshia, still holding her jaw, nodded as if her life depended on it.

Ninny yelled at her two boys, ages six and eight, and said, "I want both of y'all to go to the bathroom and wipe y'all face off and then change ya clothes. Y'all done hugged and kissed this black dirty heifer, and I don't want her spreading what she got ta y'all."

She turned her attention back to Keyshia and threatened, "And if you even think about opening your filthy little legs to any of my boys and offering them some of that stinkin' pussy of yours, I'm gonna make you wish ya funky little ass was never born. Now try me."

She stared Keyshia down and spewed, "I don't know why I agreed to let yo' black ass come up here. Yo' damn mother ain't shit! And don't think for a second you gonna be just lying 'round here to eat, sleep, and shit. No, ya black ass is gonna do some work 'round here!" Ninny stared down at her frightened niece with cold, sullen eyes and shouted, "Now pick up that funky bag of yours and let me show you where you be sleeping."

Keyshia followed her aunt and watched her open up a closet door near the living room. "Put your shit in there, 'cause this is where you will be sleeping, too."

Even though Aunt Ninny was just as dark as, if not darker than, Keyshia, she hated Keyshia's Negroid composition with a passion. Aunt Ninny was in her late thirties and did everything in her power to separate herself from her country Negro persona. She forced the country southern accent that she had out of existence and had Keyshia straighten her hair every single night with the hot comb before getting her hair relaxed with chemicals that burned holes in her scalp. She used skin-bleaching cream without fail until her skin pigmentation turned her a ghastly faded color. She even went so far as to pick her male impregnators by design. Only the lightest of light black men with soft straight or curly hair were worthy to mate with her in order to spare her children from a lifetime of ridicule, mockery, and persecution. And she adored her two boys because of their physical attributes.

Aunt Ninny made good on her promise over the years and made Keyshia a virtual slave. Keyshia did the bulk of the cooking, cleaning, and washing in the household. Her two cousins made it known to Keyshia that she wasn't shit. They would purposely fuck up the house and make her clean it. Once, one of the brothers ordered, "Hey, black bitch, come clean this leak up on the floor."

Keyshia came with the mop and asked, "Where is the leak?" Her cousins smiled and pulled out their penises and peed right there on the floor in front of her. Keyshia couldn't stand their arrogant little asses.

The early years at her aunt's were the worst because she was always lonely, scared, and nervous. But she grew to accept her position in life. Over the years, she learned how to hurt and manipulate them all, including her dreaded auntie. If things got too hectic around the house or the beatings became too much, she would fake sickness, as if she were about to die. Because Keyshia's body was riddled with whip marks and iron burns and appeared malnourished, her aunt dreaded taking her to the hospital—she feared her abuse of her niece would be exposed. Besides, over the years she developed a dependency on Keyshia and at that point couldn't function without her. In a matter of days following Keyshia's "illness," the whole house would turn upside down. The apartment would be a wreck, and the boys would complain that they were starving. In no time at all, they would take care of her by bringing her chicken noodle soup and waiting on her hand and foot as she recovered from the mysterious illness that had her bedridden. These were the moments Keyshia really enjoyed. The only other times she was happy was when she was alone and could watch television or put on DVDs and watch movies for hours on end. Her favorite movie was *The Color Purple* because she felt exactly like Celie, the character played by Whoopi Goldberg. Keyshia cried each and every time she saw the movie. She felt Celie's pain, her hardship, and her quest for freedom. Keyshia also felt she was ugly, helpless, and torn from her family down south and that nobody from there would come rescue her. She also loved the movie *Set It Off,* which starred Jada Pinkett Smith, Queen Latifah, and Vivica A. Fox. She loved the way the girls took control of their lives and went all out to get what they wanted by force. Keyshia would act and repeat everything the girls said while she watched them. I could never be so confident, she thought. Keyshia would get so caught up, so lost in the movie, that she would forget where she was at times. Whenever she acted out their parts, she spoke almost properly and just like the characters on-screen.

Chapter 2

Clyde's Beginnings

"Yo, what the fuck is this nigga's problem?" shouted the boy as he and his friend watched a bicycle skid to a stop. The two boys, Jeff and Dino, were drinking forties and macking to two young girls when Clyde whizzed by, just missing their sparkling jet-black Honda Accord by inches. The teens ran over to inspect their vehicle and then, satisfied that no damage was done, they turned their attention to Clyde.

"Yo, nigga," shouted Jeff, "if you would've hit my car, I would've hit that ass."

Clyde showed no emotion as he got off his bike and stared at them.

Emboldened by Clyde's lack of response and wanting

to show off for the girls, Dino jumped in front of Clyde and said, "Yeah, that's right, nigga, fuck around if you want to. You get that ass fucked up out here—" And he put his hand in his pocket like he was strapped with a weapon and was ready for him. Clyde looked him square in the eyes, then walked around him to go inside Johnny's to drop off his money from the delivery.

Johnny's Ice House on 118th Street between Manhattan and Eighth avenues delivered ice to various businesses in the neighborhood and sold bags of hot peanuts and the coldest sodas in Harlem. Johnson Gadson had been there for years, and everybody knew Johnny, or "Pops," as some called him, because of his genial personality. His colorful and animated stories would have people laughing for hours on end. The police department at the Twenty-eighth Precinct even made him an honorary member, which basically meant nobody was to fuck with him. Pops watched nearly everyone in the neighborhood grow from Pampers to adulthood, including many of the young boys who became gangsters, killers, and, sadly, dope fiends. Hell, he usually gave these boys—many of whom were poor, general hardheads, and misfits—their first job. Most of them didn't last a day. The job was hard work with meager pay, and boys didn't want to be laughed at for riding those boxy old three-wheeled bikes.

Most Harlem teens would never be caught dead working for Pops when they could sell dope and make a hundred times as much just by serving as lookout. Only the really desperate worked for Johnny's Ice House—like Clyde Barker, seventeen years old, who lived right around the corner on 117th and Manhattan.

Clyde looked like a darker version of Tyson Beckford and was thin in build, but his powerful arms and chest were chiseled like a superhero's. When he lifted the heavy blocks of ice to put on his bicycle, his veins would pop out and highlight his strength. Clyde was a strange individual. He'd worked for Johnny's Ice House for nearly four years, since he was thirteen years old, and he could care less about how people in the neighborhood regarded him. He didn't do the things that normal teens did, such as play basketball, hang out on the avenue, or get into drama. He was reserved and kept to himself. The other kids didn't know what to make of Clyde, so they stood clear and didn't test him. Well, some didn't test him.

Pops watched the entire exchange with Jeff and Dino go down from the window inside the store and was impressed, once again, by the measured wisdom and control Clyde had for his age. He would listen to Pops talk for hours on end about life. Clyde had a close bond with the older man because he never had a mentor in his life who didn't want anything from him but his well-being.

"You handled yourself good out there, Rocco," said Pops as he accepted the delivery money from Clyde, calling him by the nickname he'd given him.

Clyde only nodded.

"You know, young fuckers like them out there is stupid. They make gestures like they some big-time gangsters, when all they doing is tryna impress them young gals out there," Pops said as he chomped down on his dollar cigar while staring with disgust out the window. "If you remember one thing, you remember this—" Clyde jumped on one of the soda boxes and waited for Pops to drop him a jewel. "See, Rocco, the most valuable thing you can learn in life is learning people." Pops nodded, agreeing with his own words. "Once you've mastered the art of people's characteristics, it's like you can read anybody's mind." He stared at Clyde with his deep, dark eyes to ensure that he had got the point. "And you want to know what's the biggest giveaway?" he asked. "Their body language." Pops nodded at his revelation. "Anything you want to know about anybody, just look in their eyes, look at how they walk, how they gesture, how their body and eyes respond after you challenge 'em. Shit, I seen more niggas out here talk a good game. Yelling like a gorilla, cussin' and rantin' what they gonna do. And when a real man takes 'em up on their challenge, they shit their pants and start apologizing." Pops stared at the two boys and frowned. "And I tell you right now, them two bastards out there would need diapers if they fucked with a real man. That's fo' sho'."

Clyde jumped off the soda case, exited the store, and stared at the two boys as they told the two girls where to meet them for a date that night. Clyde never wore his emotions on his sleeve. He never allowed anyone to know what he was thinking.

When Clyde got home from work, he listened at the door before he entered. This was his usual routine. He wanted to know what kind of situation he was coming home to so he could get a jump on things. He heard nothing, so he figured Martha was in her room watching television or sleeping and he felt safe to enter.

Clyde had been avoiding Martha lately because she'd been dogging him about not going to school anymore. He knew that she wasn't too concerned with his missing out on an education, but rather that his not going put her at risk for losing her monthly government subsidies and stipends such as food stamps.

Martha was his mother's best friend, and she took him and his two older brothers in when that thing happened with their mother and father nearly fourteen years ago. That fateful winter night the neighbors heard a fierce argument and struggle, followed by a loud shot. When the police arrived at the apartment, they found a woman slumped on the floor with a single gunshot wound to the head, surrounded by her three sons begging and crying for her to get up. On the bed sat her husband, dazed and confused, with a .38 revolver nearby, repeating over and over, "I don't know what happened, I was drunk, I didn't mean to do it." Clyde's father was arrested and convicted of attempted murder and had been incarcerated ever since. Their mother survived the shooting but was in a coma for several weeks after. When she finally awoke, she was in a vegetative state, leaving the boys motherless, fatherless, and, finally, hopeless. But as fate had it, the boys weren't lost in transition. They were given to the closest next of kin the boys had, Martha Woods, who was their mother's lifelong friend and confidante. She raised the boys as though they were her very own and ensured that they had an ongoing relationship with their mother over the years by taking them to the hospital and encouraging them to spend time with her even though she didn't know they were there.

When Clyde entered the kitchen, he was surprised to see not only Martha, but his two older brothers, Ceasar and Sonny. Sonny was trying to console Martha, who was sitting at the table crying her heart out. When he entered the kitchen, all eyes fell on him and he immediately felt uncomfortable.

"Yo, where you been?" asked Sonny in his usual hostile tone.

"You know where I was," responded Clyde, matching his brother's mean scowl.

Sonny was the problem child of the family. He was barely nineteen years old and had already served two bids on Rikers Island on robbery charges. The tallest of the brothers, he would have been just another Pretty Boy Floyd with his light brown eyes if it weren't for the long razor scar right below his cheek. Sonny was nicknamed "Set-it" because he was a live wire with a quick temper and would set it off on anyone at any time. He was so moody and unpredictable that most people kept their distance from him. The older Sonny got, the more brazen he became as he began to rob numbers holes, drug spots, or even kidnap for ransom. If there was a major stickup in Harlem, everyone knew who did it, but Sonny didn't give a fuck. He'd tell you in a minute to "come get back if you think I did it" and bust his guns just for asking! He was the second oldest and fiercely loyal to Martha, because no matter what he did or how much trouble he got into, she stood by his side. She made sure that he was taken care of whenever he was away in police custody and always welcomed him home when he got out. As far as Sonny was concerned, Martha was his mother.

Martha was in her midfifties and had spent most of her early years as a barmaid in local bars throughout Harlem and the Bronx. In her later years, she began to work in numbers holes for some of the local betting spots. She and the boys' mother, Cathy, were inseparable in their younger days. They used to dress alike, stay over at each other's houses for days on end, and tell everyone they were sisters. They even lost their virginity the same night together by twin brothers. Martha was with Cathy the night she met Lamont Barker in the Baby Grand Bar on 125th Street one Saturday night. Lamont was a ladies' choice in the club that night because he was tall, dark, and handsome in every sense. He was a sharp dresser and had his own Cadillac and, most important, had a job. Though at twenty-nine he was much older and more experienced than the nineteen-year-old Cathy Bellows, they fell madly in love and married soon after. Martha, of course, didn't approve of her homegirl marrying the older man and the disruption of their relationship; however, she was the bridesmaid at her wedding.

"Well, you should have been here for Martha when she needed you," Sonny said.

Clyde was the only brother who still lived under Martha's roof, but he rarely saw her lately because he usually got home in the wee hours of the morning and was back on the street before Martha awakened. The only reason he was home so early tonight was to retrieve some things from his room for a job he had later.

Clyde shifted from one leg to the other impatiently. Sonny continued, "What you need to be doing is making sure Martha's all right instead of riding around Harlem on a fucking ice bike."

"Fuck you, Sonny, at least I got a job. I ain't sticking people up."

Sonny chuckled and said, "Nigga, please, you call that a job? You make what . . . twenty, thirty dollars a day at most?" He laughed again. "And don't think for a second that I don't know yo' ass, either. You just like me, but you afraid to admit it."

Martha had had enough. "Would y'all please stop arguing?" She stared at both boys as they put their heads down. Ceasar remained quiet and listened.

Ceasar was the eldest and most stable of the brothers. He was the shortest one at five feet ten and had worked as a bank teller for more than four years, ever since his senior year in high school. He was highly detailed, methodical, and an immaculate dresser. Extremely guarded by nature, Ceasar had had more than his share of beautiful young women in his life, but lately, he'd been working so hard with his day job at the bank and college in the evening that he hadn't much time to date. Since he was paying for college, he was struggling to keep up with his bills.

"Now," Martha continued, "what we need to be concentrating on is how I'm gonna manage my rent and bills now that they cut Clyde off my budget."

"Well, what do you want us to do, Martha?" Ceasar questioned. "It ain't like we can call those people up and make them give you money. You just gonna have to get a job or something."

Martha started crying even louder. Sonny was livid at his brother's lack of concern. "Come on, Ceasar, how you gonna say that? Have you forgotten who you're talking to, who raised us for the past ten, twelve years?"

Ceasar rolled his eyes and said, "Well, what could we do?"

Sonny walked over and said, "What you think? We could all chip in each week and make sure she straight. Or give her a lump sum and pay off the back rent and put some toward the future."

Ceasar said, "Chip in what? I got my own rent and bills to pay.

I ain't got no money to be paying somebody else's bills. Who gonna help me if I can't pay mine?"

Sonny jumped in, "All we have to do is chip in each week and give—"

Ceasar cut him off. "Chip in and pay what?" He sucked his teeth and continued, "Martha, did you expect to live off us for the rest of your life? You didn't think we would all grow up and you would have to find someone else to leech off of!"

Martha didn't say a word, and Sonny and Clyde stared at Ceasar and wondered how he could be so cold toward her. Ceasar had enough and went for his jacket.

Sonny knew he couldn't talk his older brother into anything and just let it go. "That's fucked up, Ceasar," he managed to say as he watched his brother head out the door.

"Well," said Ceasar as he exited the apartment, "so is hell for all the shit you doing, Sonny!" Before Ceasar left he assured his younger brother, "Clyde, you can stay with me if they try putting pressure on you to give up all your money." Ceasar slammed the door shut on his way out.

Sonny didn't like his brother's selfishness, but he always respected him for having his own mind. Sonny felt Ceasar didn't have the same temperament as he and his younger brother because he never got his hands dirty. Clyde, on the other hand, was a natural predator—a perfect stickup kid. Sonny should know, because he taught Clyde everything he knew. Clyde had instinct, something that couldn't be taught, and most of all, he had nerves of steel. He and Clyde had been doing stickups and robberies together since they were preteens. They started their careers robbing and strong-arming paperboys on Sundays in Washington Heights in upper Manhattan for their papers, money, and shopping carts. From there, they began robbing college students and professors at the City College campus. Pretty soon after, they stuck up residences in housing complexes, small-time weed

dealers, or anybody else who thought their shit was sweet. They
had some rules back then, a sort of "stickup-kid rule of honor"
that Sonny had made up and took very seriously.

1. No robbing old people or pregnant women.
2. No kids younger than themselves, unless they had a
   sweet ten-speed bike.
3. Don't hurt the vics if they give it up, but if they resist,
   do everything in your power to break their fucking
   jaw.
4. Always give a portion of earnings to the household.

"Fuck it," Sonny said as he locked the front door behind his
brother. "Don't worry about nothing, Martha. Me and old boy
here," he said while looking at Clyde, "we gonna handle this shit."

He tapped Clyde on the shoulder and gestured for him to follow into the bedroom. Sonny was already pitching his caper to
Clyde before he even took off his jacket. "Yo, I got word of this
sweet spot up in the Bronx." Clyde sat on the bed and remained
silent. He never knew who was giving Sonny the information on
stickup jobs, but they were always reliable. "Only one gun in the
place, put his ass down and everybody ready to give it up." He
stared at his younger brother to see if he would bite.

Clyde asked reluctantly, "How many we gon' need to pull it
off?"

"I say we would only need three niggas to take over the spot."

Clyde frowned and asked, "Who's the third?"

Sonny looked at his brother through the dresser mirror. "Me,
you and . . . Wolf."

Clyde jumped up. "Fuck, no," he said quickly. "I damn sure
ain't fucking with you if you bring that trigger-happy nigga along.
Hell, no. Find somebody else."

Wolf was Sonny's right-hand man in the stickup game. He

stood a mere five feet eleven and weighed only 170 pounds, and nobody fucked with him on the streets 'cause he was all heart. He and Sonny met in C-76, the juvenile ward on Rikers Island. On the island, young Brooklyn cats were the majority, so they ran the house. When Sonny and Wolf walked in, neither knew each other, and five Brooklyn cats stood by the gate and asked the eight new prisoners, "Where y'all niggas from? And y'all better say Brooklyn or y'all getting fucked up!" Almost simultaneously, Wolf and Sonny dropped their blankets, pillows, and sheets and said, "Harlem here. Now come get some!" From then on, they fought back to back until they took over the whole house together.

If Wolf didn't bust off his guns at a robbery, he'd find a reason to do so just for the fuck of it. Wolf had been shot so many times, he'd lost track of how many.

Sonny exploded, "Nigga, fuck you care 'bout who I bring along? All you doing is watching our backs."

"What, you think I'm stupid, Sonny?" Clyde asked with a twisted face. "You think I forgot that shit y'all pulled last time I got down with y'all? You and Wolf killed everybody in the fucking place and didn't even tell me. I had to read about that shit in the paper."

Sonny snapped, "Yo, you think I planned that shit to go down? Shit like that happens sometimes. It comes with the territory of our profession." Clyde remained silent. "We doing all the hard work and you still get an equal piece of the loot!"

Clyde smiled at him and said, "I would also get equal time if we get caught. Don't think I don't know if we got caught I be charged with the same amount of bodies y'all stack up." He shook his head. "Naw, fuck that, y'all go find somebody else to play pussy, I ain't with that killin' shit."

Sonny remained cool and said, "It ain't a problem. It's plenty niggas out here who wanna get this money, but you remember one thing, maafucker, if Martha don't get money for her rent and bills every month, you are assed out, too." He stared at his brother hard and long. "I'ma gonna pay the rent up for three months, so you gotta start pulling ya own weight around here and bring money to the table or you gonna starve and be living in the men's shelter." He stared at Clyde, knowing he'd struck a note in him. Despite Ceasar offering Clyde a place to stay, Sonny knew his little brother wouldn't take him up on his offer because he had too much pride. Clyde wasn't used to no handouts; he was a loner who did his dirt all by his lonesome.

Chapter 3

The windows of the black Honda Accord were so fogged up that no one could see in or out. Jeff was in the front of the car with his young vixen, and Dino was in the back with his. They were parked by the Hudson at the 125th Street exit. Both couples were going at it hot and heavy, oblivious to the fact that they were being watched.

"Come on, ma, take your pants off," Dino said to his girl from the backseat.

"For what?" asked the squeaky-voiced girl. "What you giving me?"

Dino responded, "Come on, ma, we take care of that shit later."

The girl up front was more direct. "Yo, fuck that, Lee-Lee. These niggas ain't even offering to take us to a motel or something and you expect them to hit us off?"

Both boys knew she was right but were duty bound to keep up the front. Jeff said, "Yo, check this out, me and my man ain't no chump-ass niggas, and don't get down with that punk shit. We just testing the water to see if it's worth it before we take y'all to our cool-out spot in Jersey with the indoor Jacuzzi."

The girls were young and fell for the older boys' game. "So, what you mean by test the water? What we got to do?" said the girl in the back with Dino.

Both boys looked at each other and knew they had the pussy. Dino said slyly, "All we want is a little sample right now, you know, a li'l bit, and we could bounce after that." He gave her a serious look, pulled out a wad of money, and showed it to them both.

Jeff sealed the deal when he said, "Yo, ma, real talk. I don't know what type niggas y'all be fucking with in the Bronx, but we Harlem niggas ain't about just talkin' 'bout it. We 'bout it," as he pulled out a thick wad of his own.

The girls smiled at each other and began peeling off their tops. Just as they were about to come out of their tight-fitting jeans, the driver's-side door flew open.

"What the fuck?" Jeff said with terror in his eye as he stared down the barrel of a twelve-gauge Mossberg.

"Shut the fuck up," the masked gunman said as he searched Jeff's body for a weapon. The gunman used the barrel of the weapon to knock out the overhead light in the car. "Where the heater at, nigga? I know you got one."

Speechless, Jeff couldn't do anything but stutter uncontrollably.

The gunman used the butt of the shotgun and whacked him

viciously across the jaw. "Nigga, I ain't asking you again. Where the gat at?"

Jeff pointed to the glove compartment, still too afraid to talk. The gunman turned the weapon on the occupants in the backseat, who were both shivering in tears, sniffling. "If any one of you motherfuckas move, I'm putting y'all brains on the carpet." The gunman told the girl in front to open the glove compartment slowly and hand him the gun. When the gunman felt the weight of the pistol, he knew immediately that it was a fake. He snarled at them and tossed the toy gun in the boy's face. "Nigga, run the money." He looked in the back and said, "You too, nigga, run it!"

The gunman collected both knots of money and looked at them closely. He stared at both boys in disbelief. He unfurled the wads, and stuffed inside between a couple of dollar bills was cut-up newspaper. He threw the money in their faces. "Y'all two fake-ass niggas."

The girls stared at the fake money flying everywhere and realized they were being played. Disgusted, the gunman snatched the seemingly platinum and diamond necklace and cross off Jeff's neck and examined it. The gunman looked up and ordered, "Get the fuck out the car." He thought for a second and said, "You two"—pointing the shotgun at Jeff and Dino—"strip! And I mean butt-fucking-ass-naked."

In seconds, both men were naked as the day they were born. He ordered one of the girls to pick up their clothing and put it in the car. She did. She stood with her hands up in the air, unsure of what to do next as she watched the gunman continue to stare at her. She nearly panicked when he approached her. Suddenly, he raised his hand to her face and snatched the gold chain and pendant off her neck.

The gunman got into the car and stared at both boys, who

were bending and covering their exposed penises. When he got half a block away, Clyde pulled off the black mask and gloves and laughed all the way to the chop shop. Pops was right, he thought as he remembered how both boys had been trembling from fear. Body language.

Chapter 4

It was springtime in New York City, and it seemed like every high school student in the city had taken off to play hooky. Keyshia was one of those students, but she didn't need a weather change to motivate her to take off a day. She didn't like school, and she had long stopped attending on a regular basis because she simply had no interest in being laughed at and ridiculed by her fellow students. Keyshia still had a thick, broken southern accent, and as soon as she opened her mouth her fellow classmates laughed themselves silly because no one could understand what she was saying.

Keyshia was sixteen years old and still in the ninth grade, having been left back three times. Every time she would be transferred to a new school or new class, she had to stand and identify herself to the class: "Hi's, I's name iz Keyshia Simmons." That would be the furthest she got before everyone bust out laughing at her, and she vowed each time never to open her mouth in front of anyone again, if she had her way. The cruel students never stopped taunting and teasing her in the hall and cafeteria, so she lost interest in being accepted and kept to herself.

Her aunt Ninny was cool as long as Keyshia had the whole house spick-and-span, food cooked and set on the table, dishes clean, and laundry washed every week. She even let Keyshia sleep on the couch because she had grown quite a bit and felt remorseful that making her sleep in the closet wasn't the "Christian" thing to do. But the school issue was another subject. Her aunt went to her schools a number of times and had her transferred until Keyshia found herself in a last-chance charter school designed for problematic and incorrigible youth. These particular schools were the worst of the worst both academically and socially. Most of the students had been to jail for infractions such as bringing concealed weapons to school, assault on other students or teachers, and in some cases rape and murder. Teachers didn't expect anything from these students, and the students expected nothing from them.

Keyshia would walk around midtown Manhattan for hours on end, looking into the windows of the most expensive and exotic stores in the world. She was amazed that all the white people lived the way they did. She would almost get dizzy as she walked around, staring up at some of the tallest high-rise buildings in the world. There were so many people walking so fast that she felt she would fall down and get trampled by them. On many days in the shopping district, Keyshia would imagine that she was rich and part of that society. It was only a matter of time before she conjured up the nerve to go inside the ultrachic and expensive stores such as Saks Fifth Avenue, Bloomingdale's, Macy's, Gucci, or Fendi. She would roam for hours on end, pampering and indulging herself with the most expensive perfumes in the world. She even got a makeover in the cosmetics section as she marveled at how different she looked with a simple highlight here or a smidgen of eyeliner there. She gained confidence with each brazen venture and even tried on sleek designer clothing. By now, she'd learned how to act and speak whenever suspicious salespeople or security guards questioned her presence in the store. She would talk like they did in the movies, with a snobbish air about her, and tell the questioner that she was in the store with her mother and their driver. They would smile and tell her to take as much time as she needed and simply call them if she needed further help. Keyshia would agree and turn around and giggle.

One day, on her way back home from one of her excursions in the makeup section at a department store, she ran into a boy from her school named Omar, who also lived in the neighborhood. Omar was sitting on his stoop with three of his friends when he jumped off and ran up to her and said, "Hey, Keyshia, what's up?" They had never spoken until just now. As a matter of fact, Keyshia was surprised that he knew her name. The boy repeated, "Yo, what's up, you can't speak back?"

Eyeing the ground, she answered nervously, "Hi."

He turned around and looked at his crew before asking her, "So, where you on your way to?"

Still eyeing the ground, she answered, "I's on my way home."

He noticed her shyness and asked, "Why you act like you afraid of me?"

Keyshia looked up for a second and answered, "I's not 'fraid of yous, I's just don't know who you is."

He quickly extended his hand and said, "Oh, my bad, my name is Omar. You don't see me in your class?"

She shook his hand quickly and pulled it back just as fast.

"Yeah," said Omar with an assured smile. "Sixth period, Ms. Wiggins's English class." She remained silent. He observed her closer, then asked, "Is that makeup and lipstick you got on?"

Keyshia blushed. She had forgotten she still had the makeup on her face and wanted desperately to hide now.

Omar picked up on her awkwardness and added, "You ain't got be ashamed. You look hot."

Keyshia looked up because she'd never received a compliment before, so she had to know if he was joking. Unsure what to do next, she said softly, "I's got ta get home now. My aunt don't like me being out if she ain't home."

Looking her over, he asked, "You don't live with ya momma?"

Growing edgy, she said, "No, my momma south, my aunt look afta me."

He asked, "So nobody home but you?"

She shook her head, "Till she come home and bring my li'l cousins t'night."

"Can I walk you home, then?"

Unsure what to say, she just shrugged and said, "If you want to."

He smiled again and offered to carry her book bag. As she led the way, he signaled to his three homeboys to follow.

Three hours later, when Aunt Ninny arrived home that evening, she found her apartment in complete disarray and screamed immediately for Keyshia. Keyshia came limping out of the bathroom, hunched over, arms wrapped around her shoulders as if she were holding herself together. With tears in her eyes, she muttered, "Dem boys done rape me," as Ninny and her sons stared at Keyshia in shock.

The four boys had raped Keyshia brutally that evening. This

kind of thing took place every day in the inner city, as boys saw a girl no longer as a person, but as an object—a piece of meat.

Keyshia sat on the couch trembling as she answered a barrage of questions for nearly forty minutes from the police officers, who grew weary and suspicious with each incomplete and unsure answer that young Keyshia gave them. Looking down at her with frustration, one officer stopped writing in his pad and asked, "So, young lady, you said that you invited"—he paused to look back into his notes—"Omar in as your guest and the other three boys came in later?"

Keyshia was barely audible as she tried to answer each question to the best of her ability through her tears and broken English. "No, I's only let one boy carry me home."

Both officers stared at each other. "So, you're saying you were only willing to let one of the suspects spend time with you?"

Shaking her head in frustration, she repeated, "No, they carried in by demself, thro da doe, wise da other boy was on top of me."

Shaking his head in frustration, the other police officer repeated, "So, three other boys came in, through the front door, while you and the first suspect were having intercourse?"

Keyshia was so dizzy and confused that she nodded her head and agreed.

The other officer immediately caught the inconsistency. "I thought you said that you only let the first boy take you home, you didn't say anything about having sex." Keyshia's head was spinning as she buried her head in her lap and began crying.

Her aunt interjected, "Officer, you got her confused and scared. She ain't too bright, either, so she may be a little afraid right now and can't think straight. She say four boys done pushed up in here and raped her, so don't you think you should be going out there and looking for them?"

The two white officers stared at each other, and the older one responded, "Well, ma'am, it's like this. We see a lot of cases like these, and unfortunately, many of them have no validity after we've investigated."

Aunt Ninny grimaced and asked, "So what the hell you telling me? My niece wasn't raped?"

"What we're saying," the older cop continued, "is that based on the information we received from the complainant, she basically allowed the boys an opportunity."

Appalled, Aunt Ninny retorted, "What the fuck do you mean, allowed them opportunity? Four little bastards break into my home and rape my niece and she gave them an opportunity? She done told y'all she tried to stop them and told them no. You got evidence that she was raped, now what else do y'all fucking need to go after those bastards?"

Both officers waited until she'd calmed herself down, then the other officer, on cue, pulled out a white washrag and held it up. "Ma'am, is this your makeup and lipstick on this rag?"

Aunt Ninny stared at the rag for a moment and shook her head no.

"Well, it matches the same cosmetic that appears on your niece's face." Aunt Ninny stared down at Keyshia, too shocked to speak, as the officer continued. "Now why would a sixteen-year-old young lady doll up her face with heavy makeup and lipstick if she wasn't expecting to impress or see someone?"

All Ninny could do was stare sullenly at her niece with anger and embarrassment. The police didn't even want to continue to make further efforts to take a report. They didn't even offer to take poor Keyshia to the hospital after the brutal assault on her body. Once again, and for the second time in Keyshia's short life, injustice was done to a poor little girl through no fault of her own.

After the police had left, Aunt Ninny gave her niece the beating of her life. She took off every stitch of Keyshia's clothing and whipped her till skin came off her body, till she was black and blue, to the point of exhaustion. She castigated Keyshia with every ill-gotten word in the book. "You bring li'l niggas in my house, you no-good bitch, you better have me some money when you finished.

"You little fucking slut, you got what you deserve.

"If your little funky ass turn up pregnant, you getting out my house.

"You ain't shit but a little whore.

"That's exactly why they didn't want your ass down south."

Nobody was ever charged or arrested for the rape, and Keyshia was never the same. Any innocence or happiness she'd had in her body left her that day. So she turned cold—cold and bitter against everything that society stood for. Instead of falling into a shell, afraid to live life on life's terms, she confronted it and everyone else with a brazen attitude and contempt. She now took to the streets and gravitated toward all the ill reputes, misfits, and general hardheads the cold Harlem streets had to offer. She now found a place where she fit in, and fit in she did. All her life she got into trouble because of the evil that men or boys do. So from then on, she vowed that she would no longer resist, she would give up her body so she wouldn't have to suffer as a result of them taking it. So much trouble, she thought. She'd make it easier for them from then on. She didn't want to make no more trouble.

Chapter 5

Winter had come, and because Johnny's Ice House didn't
need him during that time of year, Clyde's money was
running low. Clyde no longer could take living with
Martha. The more the city and state cut out her money,
the more desperate and angry she became, and the
constant harassment for money took everything out of
him. She would stand by the door no matter what time it
was with her hand out, then bicker and argue with him
about bringing more money home, forcing him to do the
things that weren't right—robberies and stickups. And
there was also Sonny to deal with—they fought about the
big caper that he had lined up and wanted Clyde to be a
part of. But Clyde wasn't a killer, and he detested his

brother for harming innocent people just for money. As a result, he began to avoid them both by staying in an abandoned apartment above the Ice House and by stealing from supermarkets to survive.

Keyshia's relationship with her aunt was now nonexistent. After the rape and then the beating by Ninny, Keyshia no longer had love or respect for her aunt because she beat every ounce of it out of her that fateful night. Keyshia was no longer her puppet on a string and didn't cater to her like she once had. No, those days were over. Even when Ninny tried to force Keyshia to do little chores around the house, Keisha spited her by not bothering even to respond, much less to carry them out. Her aunt tried to beat her the first time she refused, but Keyshia stood defiant and took every blow that she could dish out. From that day on, Aunt Ninny decided that if Keyshia wanted to be grown and no longer listen to her, she couldn't eat her food, so she padlocked the refrigerator and made only enough food for her and her boys. This didn't bother Keyshia one bit; it only made her resourceful and determined to survive by her wits and her will on the streets. Keyshia was willing to do anything to get what she wanted. Whether it was stealing from the store, pickpocketing a sucker, or straight fucking men for some dollars, she no longer gave a damn how she got it, as long as she got it. She hadn't any sympathy for the lame, either; if she caught anyone slipping, it was all she wrote, she wasn't taking all their shit. Keyshia didn't take any shorts from any men or women alike and would fight with anything she could get her hands on and try to take someone's head off in the process. She was slowly developing a reputation in the neighborhood as the dirtiest-hearted bitch in Harlem, and she enjoyed it.

• • •

Keyshia was in Marshall's department store on 125th Street, just off Lenox Avenue. She was inside browsing in the women's department to see if anything caught her eye when she happened upon a young dude, about her age, looking around suspiciously as he examined price tags on women's pantsuits. It was obvious to Keyshia that he was there to steal something because he stuck out like a sore thumb. Keyshia had long since learned the art of blending in and knew to be calm, never look around nervously, and simply act as if she belonged there. As she stared at the guy, he caught her eyeing him and frowned at her to tell her to mind her business. She chuckled at the boy's ignorance, wondering why out of all the sections in the store to steal from he'd choose the section he was most likely to get caught in because he stood out.

Though Clyde was a consummate stickup artist, he was never much of a booster. He looked once again in Keyshia's direction and saw her still staring at him. He knew she wasn't an employee because she looked too young, so he took her to be just a nosy patron. He put on his best evil-eye look and said, "What the fuck are you looking at?"

Keyshia just laughed at him and kept moving down the aisle as she continued her hunt. Minutes later, from the corner of her eye, she noticed a man dressed in casual clothes, speaking softly into a black walkie-talkie. She looked in the direction where the man was looking, and sure enough, he was dead-eyed on the suspicious-looking boy she'd seen minutes earlier. Keyshia remained calm and continued browsing as another man came along and conversed with the man with the walkie-talkie. He pointed at the boy and took his position at the exit. Keyshia wanted to stay out of it, but the allure of the action drew her into the mix. And besides, she thought, she felt sorry for the dumb boy.

Clyde sensed something was wrong when he noticed a man

shopping in another aisle. The chances of two men shopping solo in the women's department was unlikely. Seconds earlier, Clyde had stashed four female garments down his pants and was now looking for the exit. He knew that he could get away by jetting out the door with no problem in case the other male shopper was a store cop, so he decided to cut it short and leave now.

When Clyde walked off, he noticed that the man began to follow him. Clyde began to dump out the clothing, four pieces in all, as he continued walking. The man began moving in faster. Now only one aisle away, Clyde still had two pieces left to dump and decided to break for the door. Just as he was about to bolt, he was grabbed by someone as he came out of the aisle. It was the girl he'd spotted clocking him early. He stared at her as if she were crazy and tried to break free, but she held on tight. She said firmly, but in a whisper, "There's another guard waiting for you at the exit, so if you want to not get busted, you play along with everything I say, boy. You hear me?" Clyde stared at her as if she were a snake and decided to trust her for reasons he didn't know.

Keyshia stared back at him, then let him go and went into acting mode and put on a big smile and said loudly enough for all to hear just as the store detective arrived, "Brother, where have you been? I was looking all over for you."

Slightly out of breath, the store detective put his hand on Clyde's shoulder and said, "Excuse me, sir, but I need you to come with me."

Keyshia said loudly, with no trace of her country accent, "Excuse me, but what are you doing to my brother?"

"Ma'am, I've been following the perp for quite some time and I observed him pilfering various items."

· Keyshia hadn't a clue what he was saying but decided to play it up for what it was worth. "My brother didn't do any such thing. Now take your hands off him."

People started to gather, making the store detective grow nervous. To both Keyshia's and Clyde's surprise, he obeyed Keyshia's demand. "Now," Keyshia continued, "my brother didn't do anything, he was just lost."

The detective looked down and observed the items sticking out of Clyde's pants. He smiled and reached for the clothing and pulled it out, saying sarcastically, "Oh yeah, what is this, then?"

Clyde was just about to bolt, but then a second and third detective came over and stood behind them. He was fucked, he thought.

Keyshia sucked her teeth and said, "Oh, he do that all the time." They looked at Keyshia, perplexed, as she explained, "Oh, my brother is retarded." All three men looked at Clyde as if searching for a sign of his mental capacity. Keyshia continued smiling, not believing how lame the boy was, and put another spin on the lie. "He doesn't talk."

She gave Clyde a look indicating that he should play along, and Clyde finally reacted by saying gibberish: "Aaaah, whine ah corm."

He began to pull products off the shelves as Keyshia stopped him and hugged him tightly. "See, he don't know what he's doing." All three store employees didn't know what to do, so Keyshia began to work it.

"Look how dumb he is. Look at his little beady eyes." Clyde gave her a vindictive glare, but she kept on. "Look how big his head is." They all looked at him and agreed. Keyshia decided to flip it and make them feel guilty. "How do you think I feel to have to watch him day after day?"

They all began to feel sorry for her, and one of the detectives told her, "It's okay. I understand. Just keep a close eye on him, okay?"

Keyshia smiled widely and thanked each one with a big hug. She hugged the detective who had appeared on the scene last and pickpocketed his wallet in the process. Clyde watched her all the while. She said her final good-byes, then said to Clyde, "Come on, brother. We got to get home now."

She led Clyde outside. When they were a good distance away from the store, Keyshia said, "We all right now."

"Thanks for what you did for me back there."

Keyshia added jokingly, "Boy, better find yo'self another hustle, 'cause you ain't much of a thief from the ways I sees it."

Clyde shrugged and said, "Whatever, but listen, that's my bus, I got to go," and he gave Keyshia a hug for saving him. "Thanks again for having my back."

Clyde ran toward the bus and got on it. Keyshia watched him and felt great about gaming the store detectives. She smiled even wider as she thought about how much money was in the wallet that she'd lifted off the store dick. She looked inside her purse but didn't find it. She searched her jean pockets, and still it wasn't there, and she cursed and looked in her purse once again . . . nothing. She looked up at the bus and saw the boy she'd just saved from going to jail, smiling widely as he mockingly waved the wallet around in the air.

Keyshia was livid and took off toward the bus. Just as she got curbside, the bus took off, leaving exhaust fumes in her face as she screamed obscenities at the distancing bus.

Chapter 6

The last Sunday of the month was visiting day for the patients at St. Steven's nursing home, and for the past twelve and a half years, the Barker brothers, Ceasar, Sonny, and Clyde, had paid their monthly visit to their mother. Clyde hated these visits. Not because he didn't want to see his ailing mother, but because she seemed so helpless and feeble. His mother was unresponsive and always looking off in the distance. It killed Clyde, as well as his brothers, to see her like that. Clyde prayed that his mother would one day reach out and embrace him or say that she loved them all dearly and that everything would be okay. But he could only wish. These visits made Clyde grow cold and resentful toward the man who had put her there—his cold-blooded father—whom he secretly wished he could look in the eye and ask why he would shoot his precious mother. But Clyde didn't know if he could face his father without wanting to kill him. He dreamed many times about going to the prison, where he was serving twenty-five years, and confronting him without saying a word. Just to look in his eyes and see the man who took so much from him.

Because Ceasar was the oldest, he had more memories of their mother, so he was the closest to her, feeding her at mealtime, pushing her around in her wheelchair, or just sitting and talking to her. Clyde and Sonny stood off in the background, unable to show emotion toward a woman they had never known. Ceasar was happiest around their mother and was standoffish toward everyone else except for Clyde. He'd practically raised both brothers until they could do for themselves. He'd taught them how to play catch, basketball, baseball. He'd wanted them to grow up as normal as possible, and he'd done a good job until Sonny started to gravitate toward the ills of the streets and brought Clyde right along with him. Ceasar wanted Martha to support him by putting his brother on some type of punishment, but Martha tried never to come between Sonny and the streets. She would bail him out whenever he was arrested, lie for him whenever he faced the courts for a crime he committed and needed an alibi, or make an excuse for him if the police or his probation officer came looking for him.

Martha would tell everyone how she took the boys in and ensured that every month they saw their momma. Ceasar would call her a liar under his breath because he knew the deal. He knew Martha was a money-hungry lazy tyrant who never wanted to work and whose only reason for taking the boys in was so she could receive monthly checks as a foster parent. In the beginning, she never wanted to take the boys to see their mother, but after Ceasar complained to their caseworker that they weren't seeing her, Martha was told that as a foster parent, it was her obligation to make sure the boys had an ongoing relationship with their mother. Ceasar was the only one who knew that Martha was not what she seemed.

Ever since the rape, Keyshia had made her mark on Harlem as a chick who could put Superhead to shame. Unbeknownst to her, she was videotaped by some local drug dealers while getting it on with three men. The video was circulated in the neighborhood and played in different clubs. Keyshia had fallen in love with drugs, all of them—weed, cocaine, Ecstasy, angel dust, alcohol, even sex. She didn't care. As long as the drug took her outside of herself, she was down to experiment. It made her forget the shame, the humiliation, and it also made her feel loved. She became addicted to anything that made her feel good, so she stayed high all the time, never wanting to come down. She was only seventeen.

Keyshia didn't come home for days at a time. For the last few days she had been holed up in a hotel with a guy she'd met on her way home. He was driving by in a tan Pathfinder and honked at Keyshia, who was wearing a tight-fitting pair of capris. He was in his forties, which suited Keyshia just fine, so she decided to check him out and see what he was working with. She found out that he was a postal employee and had cashed his check and was looking to hang out and get smoked up. When Keyshia heard *paycheck* and *getting lifted,* she hopped in. At the motel on 112th Street, she was surprised to see the man pull out two pipes and some crack cocaine—she'd thought they were going to smoke some weed. At first, Keyshia was offended that he thought she was a crackhead and was about to curse him out, but she decided to chill and wait until he was fucked up and then rob him of everything he had. She pulled out a blunt and a bag of purple haze that she still had and began to split open the blunt. Keyshia was never around anyone who smoked crack and was amused to watch him smoke it.

"Yo, can I ask you a question?" she asked him. After he took a hit from the crack pipe, it seemed like he forgot she was in the room and was surprised to see her there. Sweating profusely, he blew out the smoke and nodded. "How do you feel after you take a hit?"

He seemed to be searching for an answer as his wild, dilated eyes looked at her. He said, "Imagine having the best orgasm of your life." He paused and continued, "Now multiply that feeling a hundred times and you got a crack high. No more worries, no more pain, no more fears."

He then extended the pipe to her, but Keyshia said, "Naw, I don't fuck with that pipe shit." Even though she sniffed cocaine once or twice, and even smoked some coke in a cigarette, she felt that was nothing near fucking with crack.

Keyshia was about to roll the haze when he said, "Why don't you try sprinkling some inside your smoke? It's less intense and would make you feel good."

Keyshia looked at him, tempted by the good feeling he described, and agreed against her better judgment. She watched him crush some of the rock inside a twenty-dollar bill and sprinkle some all over the weed before she rolled it up and lit it. When she sucked in the smoke, the taste was a little different, but when she blew out the smoke, she felt a rush unlike anything she had ever experienced. She looked toward the ceiling, and suddenly she felt no more worries, no more pain, and no more fears.

It was three o'clock in the morning when Keyshia finally made her way home. She was tired as hell and wanted nothing more but to sleep. As soon as she opened the door, Aunt Ninny was waiting to cuss her out.

"Where the fuck you been all these fucking days?" she yelled.

Keyshia stood there for a moment, sucked her teeth, and dismissed her altogether. Angrier, Ninny persisted.

"You hear me talking to you, little bitch? If I ask you a question, you better answer me, 'cause your li'l ass ain't grown yet."

Keyshia looked at her aunt and said with defiance, "Why the fuck are you worrying where I been? You don't take care of me."

Ninny flew into a rage. "Who the fuck are you to curse in my house? Bitch, if you curse in my house again, I'm gonna bust ya li'l ass!"

Keyshia had grown resistant to her threats, so she just shook her head at her and mumbled, "Yeah, whatever," and kept moving toward the bathroom.

This seemed to infuriate Ninny even more, so she grabbed Keyshia by her arm and swung her around to face her. "Bitch, don't be walking away when I'm talking to you."

Automatically, Keyshia removed the switchblade from her pocket and pushed her aunt backward until she fell on the couch. Keyshia put the pointed blade to her aunt's throat and spoke through gritted teeth: "Bitch, if you ever put your hands on me again, I swear on everything that I will cut your throat long, deep, and continuous."

As they locked eyes, Keyshia's aunt realized that she was dealing with a person she no longer knew. Ninny was sure of one thing and one thing only at that moment: If she said one thing wrong, she would surely lose her life.

Keyshia removed the knife from her aunt's neck and eased up off of her. She stood, still defiant, and watched her aunt get up and walk off in a daze as she held her throat, happy that it was still there.

Just as Ninny entered her room, she turned and looked at her niece as if to say that she was sorry for turning her into a monster, before slowly closing the door behind her.

Chapter 7

Clyde was dressed all in black as he staked out an uptown cat named Sugar Bear, who was from 142nd between Lenox and Seventh avenues. Sugar Bear's crew was clocking major dough 24/7 on the crack tip. He had an old-school Harlem mentality, which meant that he had to flaunt and floss at all times. In fact, he drove a different car every week. Sugar Bear was big, black, and built like a small sumo wrestler. If it weren't for his round midsection, he would have been considered muscular. He was especially nice with the hands and was known to knock niggas out with one punch. Fridays and Saturdays were his nights to trick, and he loved freaky, scandalous young girls, the nastier the better. His MO was to pick them up from bars or clubs and flash thick wads of money in front of them to entice them and then take them to a local motel for sex. He was very hard to please and would try to convince them to let him have anal sex as an incentive for more money. When they declined, he would force himself on them, which turned him on even more.

Clyde had already stolen a car for the job that night and was staked out in front of a club on 126th Street between Park and Lexington. As he waited, slumped over in the car, not an hour had passed before Sugar Bear and a girl who looked no older than eighteen emerged from the club. It was on, Clyde thought.

Clyde kept a good distance away from Sugar Bear's sparkling black Lexus coupe, as he drove at a steady pace uptown on Seventh Avenue. Just as Clyde thought he would do, Sugar Bear drove over the bridge and into the Bronx and headed toward Fordham Road to a motel near the Bronx Zoo. Perfect, Clyde thought, he didn't have to worry about any evening motel clerk getting a glimpse of his face. His only concern was the outdoor cameras.

When Sugar Bear pulled into the motel parking lot, Clyde slowed and parked on the street so the cameras wouldn't record him entering the lot. He watched as Sugar Bear emerged from his vehicle and went into the lobby of the motel to pay for the room. Clyde loaded his weapon with bullets and waited. About ten minutes later, he watched Sugar's broad body step out of the office and walk toward his car. Sugar had extra pep in his step as he walked, probably anticipating the young piece of ass that he was surely about to slay. Sugar motioned for the girl to step out of the car and then from the backseat pulled out what appeared to be a brown bag. Clyde decided to wait at least an hour to allow Sugar to dull his senses with the alcohol and catch him at his weakest.

Clyde had learned long ago to never sleep on a potential vic. He wanted to give himself any kind of edge over them so that it didn't turn out to be more than just a robbery; he didn't want it turning into a murder. After all, he was dealing with a big deadly street nigga, who didn't last this long in the game without learning a thing or two. Clyde had to be ready for anything.

Sugar Bear lay back lazily on the queen-size bed as he swallowed another cup of Rémy Martin's 1738 cognac. He was undressed and had one hand on the cup and the other in his boxers.

"Yeah, baby, let me see what that tight body look like. Take that shit off." He stared lustfully at Keyshia's firm body as she gyrated herself into a sexual frenzy. She put her fingers down her half-open jeans and pulled them out and licked them like a lollipop. She stared at him with her slanted eyes and played coy.

"Now, you know how this works, baby, " Keyshia said, and licked her lips seductively. "Money on the dresser makes this pussy wetter."

Sugar smirked and said, "Bitch, you ain't sayin' nothin' but a word." He scooted his three hundred—plus pounds off the bed and reached in his jeans and pulled out three fat wads of money neatly stacked with rubber bands. With the zeal of a king, he said, "So now what's up?" as he tossed the money on the bed. "I got enough money for you to suck the farts out of my ass if I want to, so what you wanna do?"

Keyshia frowned at his crass statement but looked at the money and went against her better judgment. He fell back on the bed and opened up one of the knots and flipped through it, ensuring she saw it all, and said, "Bitch, I'm a freak, and I pay lovely for what I want and how I want it." He stared at her so she would know exactly where he was coming from. Keyshia didn't bat an eye. "I might want some deep throat, I might want some pussy.

But if you a real bitch and wanna earn some real ends, you let me get some of that asshole, lick my nuts and my ass." He peeled off two hundred-dollar bills and threw it to her and said, "And it's more where that come from. You just say the word."

Keyshia attempted to pick up the bills, but he stopped her. "Oh, I forgot, one more thing." He opened his fist and showed her five vials of crack and tossed them on the bed also. "I heard about you for a minute now," he said as he observed her closely. "I saw you in the video fucking the shit out of my mans and them. I knew I had get some of yo' young ass."

He flashed a wicked smile as she took the money and crack vials off the bed. After pocketing the money, she began taking off her clothes. He smiled and pulled off his boxers, filled his cup, and got an instant hard-on as he stared at her thin, almost perfect, youthful body. He poured another drink and downed it in one gulp and urged her to smoke her shit. "See, I already knew you smoke crack. To each his own, that's how I look at it. You like what you like, and I like what I like."

Keyshia knew that the alcohol had relaxed him because he was becoming too talkative. He preached on, "But we all got our own turn-ons, and I got mines."

Keyshia barely paid him any mind as she busied herself gutting a cigar. She then dumped her weed inside the empty leaf and sprinkled crack over the weed. When she lit it, she immediately leaned back at ease and listened to his confession.

Sugar Bear was now transfixed in his own imagination and said, "But, what I really, really like when I'm getting down the most is that *boy pussy*."

Keyshia nearly choked on her blunt smoke. She stared at him to see if he was serious and all he was doing was smiling and reminiscing. "That boy pussy," he continued, "is the best thing out these days. If you want, I could call my li'l friend up and we could have a real party."

Keyshia was speechless and sure of one thing at that moment: She was definitely going to make him wear a condom!

Clyde checked his watch and was satisfied that he had given them enough time and reached for a small jar of Vaseline. He quickly wiped a thick amount over his face and eyes and then put on his ski mask and gloves. He checked his weapon and leapt from the vehicle and into the parking lot bushes. He waited in the bushes for another minute or two to scope out the traffic within the lot and ran as low as he could toward their room door.

Inside the room, Sugar was forcing his rather large genitalia in Keyshia's mouth, but she was choking from the pressure he was putting on her. "Come on, ma, I know you can do better than that," he said as his frustration grew. His dissatisfaction with her continued to grow until he finally stopped her and said, "Man, you ain't doing it right, let me show you how to do this shit!"

To Keyshia's horror and utter surprise, she watched the huge man contort his back and neck all the way down to his penis and put it into his mouth. She cringed as she watched him force and swallow his own penis into his mouth until it disappeared down his throat! When he pulled it out of his mouth, he sat up, heaving heavily, and smiled. "See, that's how I want you to do me. Put all this shit down your tonsils. If I could do it, you can, too."

Keyshia grew apprehensive and began shaking her head as she backed away from him. She knew at that moment he was a sick, sick man, and he scared her. "No, I don't want to do this no more. I's gives you yo' money back and I's just want to go."

Sugar Bear was furious. "Bitch!" he snapped. "You ain't going no fuckin' where!"

Keyshia froze as he flew off the bed like a raging bull, grabbed her by her hair, and tossed her back on the bed. "Now open your

fucking mouth and take all this shit just like I showed you!"
Keyshia struggled violently, but he was a brute and slapped her
each time she resisted.

Outside, Clyde made it to the door and listened to Sugar
Bear's booming voice.

"Oh, shit, young girl, that's right . . . take all this shit, that's
how the fuck you do it."

Clyde knew they were in a compromising position and decided to make his move right then and there. He held the shotgun
firmly in his hand, backed up a few feet, and kicked the door wide
open. He caught Sugar slipping something lovely as he was laid all
the way back on the bed with his hand on the back of Keyshia's
head, thrusting it rapidly on his penis.

"What the fuck . . . ?" Sugar said.

Clyde saw the terror in his eyes as he leveled the weapon at
his face. "Get the fuck on your stomach and put your motherfuckin' hands behind your head!" he yelled.

"Okay, okay, man, just don't shoot!" Sugar Bear said nervously, his voice several octaves higher than Clyde's.

The thin, naked girl scurried on the ground, covering her
head, sniveling tears of fear. Clyde looked at her and felt sorry,
'cause she appeared to be no older than fifteen and was obviously
living harder than the average girl her age, because her rib cage
protruded through her skin. But he couldn't show any compas-
sion at that point and yelled at her, "Get the fuck up off the floor,
bitch, and shut the fuck up!" She obeyed.

When she stood up, it was then that Clyde recognized her
face. She was the same girl who'd saved him in Marshall's a few
months ago. When she stood up, still frightened, Clyde got a full
view of her naked body. He wanted to turn away. She was skinnier
than he'd thought, almost as skinny as those Africans on the
UNICEF commercials. He grew angrier with Sugar Bear, wonder-

ing what the fuck in the world this grown-ass man, well in his forties, could possibly want from a child like her.

"Put on your clothes," he said to Keyshia. He walked slowly over to the side of the bed where Sugar's black, naked ass lay nervous and trembling in fear. Clyde stared down at him with disgust and unleashed a wicked blow to his head with the butt of the shotgun, causing the big man to squirm in pain.

"Please, man," he pleaded, "don't hurt me. Take the money, all of it. I ain't gonna give you no problems."

"Shut the fuck up and give up them rings and bracelets." Sugar obeyed while shaking uncontrollably. Clyde wondered if this was the same dude with the feared reputation. He was shaking so badly that he could hardly take off his rings or bracelets. Clyde delivered another vicious hit to his ear. "Faster, motherfucka. Faster!" Sugar shook like an epileptic. After he took off all the jewels, he stared at Keyshia as she shifted from foot to foot as if she had to go to the bathroom. Clyde stood over him and stuck the shotgun under his jaw and spoke in an eerie whisper: "You like little girls, motherfucka?"

Bear panicked and began to cry. "Man, I don't know what you talking 'bout, she . . . she told me she was eighteen."

Clyde hit him again, this time drawing blood from his ear. "Do she look eighteen, motherfucka? You think I'm stupid?"

He unleashed a barrage of blows to the back of his head while Sugar Bear pleaded for his life: "Please, man, I'm sorry, I don't want to die, please." Clyde looked over at Keyshia, who was almost fully dressed but still a nervous wreck, and stared at her as his chest heaved in and out. Clyde reached in his back pocket and pulled out a folded-up nylon laundry bag and tossed it on the bed toward Keyshia. Keeping an eye on Sugar, he said, "Put all his money and jewelry in the bag." He watched the girl scramble as she complied with his orders. "Put his pants and his kicks in the bag while you at it," he added as an afterthought. Clyde turned his attention back to Sugar and stuck the barrel of the weapon between his ass cheeks.

Sugar pleaded, "Aw, man, shit! Don't do this, please don't do this."

Clyde smiled and pushed the barrel deeper into his rectum. "Move again, motherfucka, and I'm gonna blow your asshole out!" Clyde twisted and turned the weapon all around his rectum, tearing it to shreds as he continued to taunt him. Keyshia couldn't stand to watch, too afraid even to move any longer. Just as Sugar Bear was about to pass out from the pain, Clyde began pulling it out slowly and said, "Now, the next time you think of fucking li'l girls, remember how it feels"—he shoved the shotgun up his ass again, and Sugar Bear screamed so high and loud, you would have thought he was a woman—"to have a shotgun barrel rip your ass apart, motherfucka." And pulled the shotgun out of his ass in one swift move. Sugar Bear cried out in relief.

Clyde looked up and almost forgot that Keyshia, who was still holding the bag, was in the room. He walked directly up to her and turned toward the table and saw the vials of crack and blunts and tobacco. He stared at Keyshia with disappointment as she put her head down in shame. Clyde snatched the bag from her and shook his head as he backed out of the motel room.

Outside, he ran to the bushes to assess his getaway and strip and stash his clothing and weapon. He saw the room door open and the girl yelling as she tried to walk out of the motel when suddenly Sugar Bear snatched her back in as if she were a rag doll. Clyde cursed under his breath and regretted not telling her to leave because he knew Sugar would try to take his frustration out on the closest person to him. Clyde wanted to leave well enough alone, but his conscience was pulling at him. He stared at the silhouette through the window shade of the two bodies in a violent struggle. He tried to walk off, but he was stuck. He looked at the window once more and cursed under his breath again.

"Get your fuckin' hands off of me!" Keyshia screamed as she tried to free herself from his powerful grip.

Sugar hauled off and slapped her viciously, sending her flying down on the bed. "Bitch, I know you had something to do with it!" he roared. "You and that nigga set me the fuck up. I saw y'all whispering in the corner, and you think I'ma gonna let you leave without you telling me where that nigga is from?" Keyshia was so heated that he had slapped her, she reached for her purse to get her knife. "Oh, no you don't, bitch," he said, and snatched the bag out of her hand before tossing it away. He grew angrier and grabbed her by her throat. "Bitch," Sugar said through gritted teeth, lifting Keyshia up off the bed, "if you don't give me a name and address of that soon-to-be-dead nigga, I'm gonna choke the fuck out of you."

Keyshia gasped for air as she kicked and flung her arms around. The whites of her eyes began to turn bright red. Just as she felt she would pass out, she heard a loud thud at the door, and seconds later her lungs filled with air. Gasping heavily, she watched the masked gunman beat down her molester with the weapon.

Rubbing her throat, Keyshia gained her composure and stood up and pounced on her assailant. "You fuckin' tried to kill me, you punk bastard!" she screamed, and began kicking and punching him.

Clyde pulled Keyshia's frail body off of Sugar, who then rose from the floor with the stealth and quickness of a black panther. All Clyde saw before a crushing blow landed to his head was a black streak of lightning. Clyde was down and dazed. Sugar Bear's three hundred—plus pounds were on top of Clyde as he rained down on his head with his fists for what seemed an eternity. All Clyde remembered before he passed out was stars.

When Clyde regained consciousness, he was facedown on the bed with his hands tied behind his back and his feet bound at the ankles. "Yeah, wake up, bitch." Clyde looked around in a panic and saw Sugar Bear, who was still buck bone-ass naked, standing over him and smiling wickedly as he pointed the shotgun at him. "Yeah, yo' bitch ass done fucked up royally, nigga."

Clyde tried to break free but realized that he was tied down. His eyes scanned the room, and he saw the girl on the floor in the corner. Sugar Bear walked over to his prey in victory. "Oh, nigga, me and you"—he paused to savor the moment—"we 'bout to get down and have ourselves a party." He then put his heavy body on top of Clyde and said, "Now let's see what you look like." Clyde could smell the alcohol on his hot breath. Sugar Bear slowly pulled off Clyde's mask.

Keyshia looked at him and squinted. She recognized him immediately as the boy who'd stolen her wallet. Clyde and Keyshia locked eyes, his pleading for help. Sugar said with excitement, "Oh, shit, you's some young pussy." To Clyde's dismay, he felt Sugar's penis grow hard on his backside. "Oh yeah," he salivated, "we gon' have ourself a good time." Sugar Bear looked at Keyshia and said, "Bitch, I'm gonna let you leave." He grabbed the stolen loot bag from off the floor and removed one of the wads of money and handed it to her. He clutched the shotgun in his hand and stared at her and gave her a stern warning: "Forget about everything you saw here. If I ever hear my name mentioned in the streets about this, I'm killing you and ya whole family."

Keyshia believed him and nodded rapidly. Sugar put the shotgun aside by the wall and pulled down the boy's pants as Clyde wiggled and struggled violently. Keyshia picked up her purse and watched the terror in the helpless boy's eyes. She watched Sugar fight and punch the boy as he stuffed a sock down his throat. Keyshia watched Sugar mount Clyde's backside till his entire body was nearly undetectable under him. Sugar Bear looked up at Keyshia, frowned, and said, "You ain't gone yet, bitch?"

She made her way to the door. She was relieved when she exited the door, using the wall of the motel as support. She gathered her bearings and started to walk off but stopped in her tracks when she heard the muffled screams of the boy who had saved her. She fought with herself to keep moving on, but she couldn't walk any farther. She cursed and opened up her purse and stared at the money. She cringed once again as she closed her eyes and reached in her purse and pulled out her knife. Turning on her heels, she ran toward the door and entered and saw the big man brutally raping the other. Sugar didn't even have a chance to react as he watched Keyshia run toward him at full speed and embed the knife deep into his right eye. Clyde hurriedly rolled off the bed as Sugar Bear screamed in pain, bouncing off the walls, holding his bloodied eye. Keyshia ran toward Clyde and tried to untie the belt around his wrist, but her hands were trembling so badly that she made little headway. Sugar Bear managed to get on his feet and charge at Keyshia, knocking her off Clyde and into the wall, nearly rendering her unconscious. Sugar landed on his stomach, and he probed the floor for Keyshia and found her leg and pulled it toward him. Keyshia kicked him violently in the head and face, but he refused to let go. Just then, Clyde got his hand free and began to untie his legs, eyeing the shotgun near the wall. Finally free, he ran and retrieved the shotgun and took aim at his rapist's wide body.

"I'll kill you, I'll kill you!" Sugar Bear cursed as he pounded on Keyshia.

Keyshia fought viciously to ward off the beast, but it was a losing battle. She spotted Clyde with the weapon and yelled, "What are you waiting on . . . shoot this motherfucka!"

Clyde waited for a good shot with Keyshia out of the way, but he couldn't get one; he aimed again, then lowered his gun in frustration. Clyde knew the impact from the shotgun blast would have torn them both to shreds. He gripped the shotgun tightly and hit Sugar with the butt instead. He pounded and pounded him until Sugar finally collapsed on top of Keyshia. Blood and brain matter was everywhere, including on Keyshia and Clyde.

Chapter 8

Clyde and Keyshia drove inside the stolen car in silence. Both were numb, because they'd killed a man tonight and the bloody evidence saturated their faces and clothing. Keyshia curled up and began sobbing softly. Clyde wanted to tell her that she was going to be okay, but he didn't have the words at that moment. He was scared, too. He didn't bother to ask her if she wanted him to drop her off somewhere, because he knew it would be in his best interest that she was in the proper state of mind before they separated. He decided to drive to New Jersey and stay at a hotel so they could get cleaned up and buy some new clothing, and most important, he wanted to make sure Keyshia wouldn't rat on him, although he wasn't too worried since she was just as guilty. Clyde didn't know any particular place in New Jersey to go, so when he saw a sign that read, ATLANTIC CITY, he said, "Fuck it," and took that course. He had a bag full of money and jewelry, so he felt confident he could hold it down out there for a minute.

After pulling into a hotel in Atlantic City, Clyde parked the vehicle far away from the front entrance of the hotel's parking lot. Twenty minutes earlier, he had stopped off at a gas station and removed his bloodied getaway clothes and washed his face and hands. He looked over at Keyshia, who slept like a baby and was still curled up in a near fetal position, and smiled. She looked so much like an angel compared with the wild woman she was last night. He still couldn't believe that the little girl next to him had saved his life, twice.

"Yo," Clyde said softly, not wanting her to panic from a loud sound. "Yo," he repeated.

Keyshia opened her eyes and looked around slowly, unsure of where she was at that moment. She looked at Clyde and asked, "Where we at?"

"Atlantic City."

Keyshia was confused and frowned.

"Jersey," Clyde explained.

"New Jersey?" she asked. "Why's we all the ways in anovah state?" For the first time, Clyde heard the thick country accent in her voice.

" 'Cause I ain't had nowhere else to take you," he said flatly. "Plus," he continued, "I didn't think you wanted me to take you home with all that blood on your body and clothes."

It was daylight, and for the first time Keyshia noticed that Sugar Bear's blood was all over her. Knowing the answer, she had to ask anyway. "He dead?"

Clyde nodded and said, "I think so." Keyshia turned and gazed out the window. Clyde was speechless. He didn't know what to tell her because he'd never killed before. "It's like this: I know how you feel about that. I feel the same way, and I ain't never killed nobody either." Keyshia turned slightly and glanced into his eyes. "But that big nigga was trying to kill you and me!"

Keyshia thought back to the pain and remembered how Sugar's hands felt around her throat. Clyde shrugged and said, "I'd rather be feeling guilty and alive than dead and stinkin' any day." Keyshia searched his eyes and knew he wasn't lying. Out of nowhere, she started to laugh to mask her fear.

Clyde said seriously, "Listen, I think it's best if we lay low for a minute to get our weight up." She stared at him, confused, and he rephrased it: "Get some food and rest." Keyshia nodded in agreement. "You think your mom would miss you if you gone a couple of days? 'Cause if so, you better make a phone call and let her know you all right."

Keyshia put her head down and said, "Naw, nobody that matters will be looking for me."

Clyde watched her for a moment and then said, "Okay, we good then."

Keyshia agreed. For some reason, she trusted her co-conspirator. Maybe it was his reassuring eyes and soft tone, his strange, bad-boy persona, or maybe it was the fact that he'd risked his life and came back and saved hers.

"I'm gonna pay for the room, so just chill for a minute and I'll be right back." He didn't even wait for a response before he was out the door. Clyde gave himself a once-over, and after making sure no blood was visible, he swaggered with authority toward the hotel's entrance.

When they entered the room, they both noticed how much bigger and cleaner it was than the motels they were used to in the city. This hotel room had two full-size beds, a bathroom, and a Jacuzzi. Keyshia walked over to the bathroom and peeked inside, obviously impressed, and then went over to the Jacuzzi and said,

"They musta made a mistake, 'cause they got two tubs, one in the bathroom and one right in the open."

Clyde didn't say a word. Keyshia walked over to one of the beds and was amazed at the size and the amount of pillows and sat down to test it. Lying backward, she melted from the comfort of the padded mattress and stared up at the ceiling, smiling all the while. "Dag, they got two tubs, two beds, a telephone, room service, and mad pillows. I could sleep forever." Clyde watched her act like a child's first time at Disneyland and smiled. She popped up suddenly and stared at Clyde and asked, "You ain't gonna try ta kill me or nuffin, are you?"

Clyde chuckled. "If I wanted to kill you, I would have did it in the car while you was snoring."

Keyshia smiled smugly and joked, "I's don't snore." They both smiled and stared into each other's eyes.

Clyde snapped out of it first and said, "But, yo, you could take a shower first. I already ordered housekeeping to bring up some robes and shit." He looked at his disheveled clothing and said, "Later, we can go to a mall or something and get me and you some outfits, 'cause we got to get rid of everything we got on—everything!" She nodded. Clyde shrugged and said, "What's your name, anyway?"

"My name is Keyshia."

"My name is Clyde."

Chapter 9

Keyshia awoke in a cold sweat. She was having a night-mare of the event that transpired nearly twenty-four hours ago. She jumped off the bed and cowered between the two beds. Her eyes searched the room for the enemy as she gripped the covers. It took her several moments to realize exactly where she was. Looking around, she noticed Clyde standing behind her with an expressionless look on his face. Finally, he held up two plastic bags and said, "I got breakfast. You hungry?"

Keyshia stood up and adjusted her bathrobe and looked around for her clothing that she knew she'd placed on top of the bed.

"I told you we had to get rid of our clothes, so I got rid

of 'em," Clyde said. A mean scowl came over Keyshia's face, but before she could respond he added, "Don't worry, I put your *crack*," he said, "and the other thing, if that's what you're worried about, on the table." Keyshia looked at the table, and everything that she had in her pocket was there. She felt relieved yet ashamed.

They sat on the bed and ate their food in silence until Clyde asked, "Yo, if you don't mind me asking, what the fuck was you dreaming about?"

Keyshia stopped chewing her food and hesitated before she spoke. "Like you don't know?" she answered. "I don't go 'round killin' people for a livin'."

Clyde smirked and took the slight on his chin and continued, "I don't either, 'cause I don't usually stick around long enough to catch beef, instead of playing 'captain save a ho.' "

Keyshia rolled her eyes. "Yeah, but this ho saved yo' punk ass from getting a black dick stuck up it. Right?"

"Yeah, but 'least I wasn't giving it up for free. I saw you enjoying that black dick down your tonsils when I busted in, though."

Keyshia stood up and flew into a rage. "Motherfucka, I don't give shit up for free, that was business, my business! And what yo' punk ass need to do is be thankful, 'cause I saved yo' ass twice— *twice,* motherfucka—so you just remember that shit when you look at this ho!"

Clyde stood up and gave her an icy stare and wanted to counter so badly that he turned red, but he knew she was right and simply yelled, "I'm fuckin' thankful!"

"You're fuckin' welcome!" she screamed back.

They both sat down and continued eating their pancakes and sausages in silence.

Earlier that morning, Clyde had gotten rid of all the clothing and wiped down the car in a 7-Eleven parking lot. He'd gotten some basic clothing such as underwear, shorts, T-shirts, and flip-flops in the hotel lobby store for Keyshia to put on until they got to the mall.

That afternoon, he called the front desk and requested the location of the nearest shopping center and a taxi. Keyshia stared out the window of the taxi as they passed hotel after hotel. Each one seemed to have huge electronic billboards advertising upcoming performers.

They rode in silence until Keyshia suddenly asked him, "How much did you take him for?"

Clyde was taken by surprise by the question, "What?"

"You heard me, how much did you take off of Sugar Bear?" she repeated.

Clyde looked at the driver, who seemed to be paying attention to traffic. He turned his attention back to Keyshia and whispered, "What the fuck are you asking me some shit like that where anybody could hear you?"

"Fuck him," Keyshia said as she gestured toward the driver. "I want to know how much money and jewelry you got off of him!"

Clyde wanted to kick her out of the cab right then and there, but he knew he wouldn't do it. He also knew that he couldn't outtalk her, so he relented, for the moment. "All right, I'll tell you, but keep your voice down." She folded her arms and twisted her lip at him. "He had three bankrolls with a total of two thousand dollars in each, so that's a little more than six g's in cash." Keyshia's heart jumped, but she kept a poker face as she listened to Clyde talk about more money than she'd ever seen in her life. "As far as the jewelry goes, I can only guess." Clyde frowned and began calculating, "Umm, he ain't have nothing but gold, it ain't like he was pushing platinum or something, that nigga was still old school. But it was quality and had good weight and some diamonds, so I guess I could get from my connect 'bout another three or four g's." He nodded more to himself and asked, "Why you asked about that, anyway?"

She put on her best sass face and said without hesitation, "'Cause I should get half!"

Clyde stared at her as she returned his look without so much as blinking. He thought about all he'd put her through, plus the fact that she'd come back to get in the mix with that fool when she could have bounced with the knot of money he'd offered her.

"I'll give you two thousand," he said, stone-faced.

"Three thousand, plus half the jewelry," she countered.

"Three thousand, cash money now, and another two when I get back to the city."

Keyshia paused and looked at his face for a moment, then agreed. "All right," she said slowly. She extended her hand and said as she rolled her eyes, "But money in hand is the best plan."

Clyde knew this girl was game tight as he reached in his pocket and counted out three thousand in front of her and put it in her hand. She took the money and put it in one hand and extended her hand once again. Clyde frowned as if she were buggin'. "Fuck you still got your hand out for? I told you I'll hit you off with the jewelry money later."

Keyshia looked him in the eye again and said, "Don't think I forgot the wallet you stole from me at Marshall's that day. It's time to pay the piper." Clyde could only envy her tenacity, and he chuckled.

Inside the huge mall, Keyshia looked around in awe; she had never seen so many stores under one roof. They walked together slowly, undecided about what store they should patronize first, until Keyshia spotted Macy's. Her eyes lit up and she turned to Clyde. "Oh shoot, they got a Macy's!"

Clyde didn't see what all the excitement was about. "So, you act like you ain't ever been to a Macy's before. You never went to the one on Thirty-fourth Street?"

Keyshia was still ogling the store and answered, "Yeah, I been there plenty of times, but this is gonna be the first time I went there with money!" She grabbed Clyde by the arm. "Come on!"

Clyde stood by and watched Keyshia try on pair after pair of shoes and one outfit after another. Every time she tried on a pair of anything, she posed for Clyde and asked his opinion, which he gave her. For some reason, he enjoyed seeing her pick out clothes and shop wide-eyed like a child, as if she'd never had an experience like this before in her life.

Glowing, Keyshia ran up to Clyde with yet another outfit on, waiting for him to give her his opinion. "Well"—she turned around—"how's do I look with this on me?"

Clyde noticed how whenever she was relaxed and calm, her country accent came out, but whenever she was angry, her language was straight out of the garbage can. He looked over Keyshia's shoulder and watched a security guard standing fifteen feet away, watching their every move.

Keyshia caught Clyde's eyes and turned to where he was looking. She noticed the security guard acting as if he were concentrating on the rack in front of him. She turned back to Clyde and said, "You worrying 'bout Po-po behind you?" She sucked her teeth and told Clyde, "You ain't got nothing to worry 'bout. We's normal today, and you got to learn to play the role sometime. Acting like you belong here is how you get over." She continued doing as she was and said, "Let that motherfucka look all he want, and ignore his ass. In the end he gon' wind up feeling stupid."

Boxes of shoes were scattered all over the area where Keyshia sat. Trying on the last pair of shoes, she called the sales manager for the umpteenth time, and even Clyde knew the lady was getting frustrated with her finicky ways. "Yo, why you keep bothering that lady like that? She gonna get tired of you after a while."

Clyde's statement didn't even move her to answer him. She simply stayed in character and said, "You want to know why, Clyde Barker?" Coming out of the last shoe, she continued, " 'Cause I know she ain't doing her job. I useta go downtown and spend hours just wanderin' around stores like these. I useta see white ladies buying up the store, and I saw how they got treated. They be yellin' to salesladies that they like this and like that, they carried it fo' them as they stood by waitin' ta carry another piece like they their own personal clothes carrier." She looked at Clyde. "If I'm gonna spend this kinds of money, that bitch gonna do her job to earn her commission."

The sales manager came over, frustration written on her face. "What can I help you with now, or did you finally find a pair that you like?"

Keyshia remained calm as her voice changed. "Yes, yes, I did, and would you be kind enough to have them rung up and packed for me?"

The sales manager scanned the dozen boxes of shoes and boots and asked, "Okay, which one do you want?"

Keyshia said, "Why, I want all of them, and I'm paying cash."

The saleslady smiled as she repeated, "You, you said you want all of them?"

Keyshia nodded. Clyde enjoyed watching her work the lady over. The manager let out a goofy laugh and said, "Well, all I got to figure out now is how to get all these boxes over to the sales register."

Keyshia suggested, "Well, there a big strapping-looking employee right over there." She pointed at the security officer who was stalking them. "And I'm sure that he may be more than willing to assist you."

She smiled at Keyshia and said, "Thank you, I think I will ask him." The saleslady raised her hand in the air and snapped her fingers in his direction. The security officer ran toward her at breakneck speed, knocking over a few items in the process. He was a huge, grim-faced man. By the time he got to them, he was out of breath and his barrel chest moved in and out, ready to rumble. The sales manager simply pointed to the floor and told him, "Carry all these boxes over to the register for our guest." She walked away.

The security officer stood there like a dunce, so Clyde jumped in and said, "You heard her, you peeping motherfucka, carry all our boxes to the register!"

After Keyshia paid the bill, she asked the saleslady to hold on to the boxes of shoes because she hadn't finished shopping. She was more than happy to oblige. Keyshia then turned to Clyde, smiling. Clyde scratched his head as he looked at the long white receipt in her hand and said, "I see that you are one of those expensive girls."

Keyshia unfolded the receipt and continued smiling. "You only live once."

Not convinced, Clyde said, "True, but when that shit runs out, what are you gonna do then?"

"I just worry 'bout that when it happens. It wouldn't be my first time or gonna be my last time I don't have shit."

"But still, jerking your money on material shit ain't the answer. You never gonna know when you gonna need it."

Keyshia dismissed him again. "You sound like you old. You worry too much. Clyde, you got to learn to live a little or you life gonna pass you by. I don't know how happy your life is, but nobody never gave me shit!" Clyde remained silent. Keyshia picked up on it and said, "Yo, I don't know 'bout you, but I ain't never shop like that before. I ain't ever have nobody ta do something like that for me. I watched other people do it, I dreamt about it, and I promised myself first time I get a chance, I'm gonna see how it feel." She grabbed his arm and looked in his eyes. "Because of yo' help, I's know how it feels ta be special."

Clyde nodded. "I feel you, nobody ever did that for me either. I always had to go out and take mines, so I guess I wasn't too concerned about that other shit." They walked to a bench and sat down.

Keyshia asked him, "You live with yo' momma and pa?" Clyde put his head down and shook it slowly.

"Where they at?" she asked.

Unable to look her in the eye, he stared at the floor and said, "My mother's been in the hospital since I was three, and my dad's been in prison about the same time."

Keyshia saw him growing uncomfortable and changed the subject. She put on an excited smile and said, "Guess what?"

Clyde began to grow fond of her childlike smile and said, "Oh no. What now?"

"I'm taking you out to a concert!"

Caught off guard, he asked, "What concert?"

"Lyfe . . . Lyfe Jennings," Keyshia said excitedly. "You heard of him before?"

"Hell, yeah, that's my nigga. He sings my anthem, 'Stick Up Kid.'"

"Well, I saw one of the billboards at a hotel we passed in the taxi on our way here saying he gonna be there tonight. You down?"

She stuck out her fist, and Clyde tapped it lightly and said, "I'm down."

Keyshia grabbed him by his arm. "Good, now come with me to get my hair did and then go find you something to wear for the show!"

Chapter 10

After Keyshia finished getting her hair done, she and Clyde fought each other tooth and nail about what Clyde would wear to the show. Clyde wanted to wear his regular urban city gear: sweatshirt, Timberlands, and jeans. But Keyshia had another vision for him.

"You ever seen the movie *Set It Off* with Jada Pinkett Smith and Queen Latifah? And when what's-his-name came and pick Jada up for a date, yo, he looked smooth in the suit, and plus y'all look something alike."

"So?" Clyde said quickly. "That ain't got nothing to do with this boring-ass suit you want me to try on. Naw, fuck that, that ain't my style. I'm a 'hood nigga, and I'm always gonna be a 'hood nigga!"

Keyshia would not back down, "Clyde, you's ain't in the 'hood right now, boy. All I'm asking you is to try something new, that's all."

Clyde seemed to calm down as he looked in her soothing eyes, but suddenly he snapped out of it. "No, fuck that! I ain't falling for that shit again. I ain't wearing no suit and that's that!"

By the time they left the mall, Keyshia had compromised and agreed to let him wear the Timberlands and jeans but said she would pick out the shirt and jacket. They both walked away happy. They'd stopped off in McDonald's to have a bite to eat when Keyshia told Clyde that she had to pick up one more important thing before they left the mall. She quickly ran into Macy's again while Clyde continued to eat his food. When she came back, happy-go-lucky as usual, she carried a small shiny Macy's bag in one hand and a larger bag in the other and said, "I'm straight now, let's bounce." They now had to haul all their bags outside to a cab. Keyshia, ever the resourceful one, spotted a group of young white kids at another table and asked them, "Any one of you want to earn twenty dollars?" All the boys' eyes lit up.

At the hotel, Clyde showered first and got dressed. An hour later, Keyshia was still in the bathroom when Clyde knocked on the door and said, "Yo, Keyshia, the show starts in forty-five minutes, we got to be out."

"I'm coming," yelled Keyshia. When she finally came out ten minutes later, Clyde was blown away. He had to look twice because he couldn't believe she was the same girl. Keyshia wore a sleek, body-fitting red dress that ended slightly above her knees, complemented by a pair of high-heeled boots in a matching color. Her makeup made her look totally ravishing and sexy, and her hair gave her that Halle Berry look. Clyde was speechless.

"Well," Keyshia said, arms spread out, mouth smiling widely. "How do I look?"

Clyde still couldn't find the words as he shook his head and blinked rapidly. Finally he stuttered, "You look . . . you look beautiful. Absolutely beautiful."

Keyshia was taken aback for a moment, because she'd just realized that was the first time in her life someone had ever told her that. Even more, she saw it in his eyes and believed him. She looked down and smiled and asked, "I do?"

He shook his head and said, "Yo, you look like a dime, and that's real talk! When you first came out, I had to look twice 'cause I didn't know that was you, for real." Clyde, now feeling underdressed, looked at himself and said, "I don't think I look good enough to go with you now. "

Keyshia walked toward him. She was inches from his face and licked her lips and said, "I'm glad you said that." She walked toward where all the shopping bags were kept and picked up two of them, one small and one larger bag. She set both bags on the bed and reached in the big one first and pulled out a stylish blue suit jacket. She undid the buttons and put it on Clyde. He looked into the mirror and nodded. Next Keyshia reached inside the smaller bag and pulled out what appeared to Clyde to be a glass case that read FENDI on the front. Clyde opened it up, more excited than he wanted to be, and a fresh pair of black Fendi shades were inside.

He looked at Keyshia and said, "You crazy."

She smiled even brighter and said, "Go 'head, put 'em on, and let me see how you look."

"Not bad, not bad," Clyde said as he profiled in the mirror. "I've got that Jay-Z, Usher thing going on. I can live with this."

She reached into the smaller bag and pulled out a brand-new box of cologne and handed it to him. Excitedly he smiled and said, "You got me some cologne, too?" He looked closely at the brand and said, "Sean John, eighty-five dollars. Damn, girl, you ain't have to buy me some expensive stuff like this, I would've—"

Keyshia stopped him and simply said, "You only live once." He smiled and thanked her. She shrugged and said, "Hell, the glasses cost me two hundred fifty, but you worth it, right?"

Clyde had never met anyone like her before. He was excited that someone had thought about him enough to buy him something. She urged him to put on the cologne.

He opened up the box and sprayed some of the expensive cologne in his hand like it was going out of style. Keyshia stopped him. "No, Clyde, you don't put this shit on your body like that shit from the ninety-nine-cent store. This is that good shit; you don't need a lot to smell it." She took the bottle and told him to extend his hands with the palms up so she could show him how to apply it. She then sprayed his wrists, his jugular, and behind his neck. She said, "And that's it. You good for the rest of the night and then some."

Clyde smiled at her and asked, "How old are you?"

She looked at him. "Why you wanna know?"

"'Cause you seem so smart, like you been around for years, and got mad wisdom."

Keyshia wanted to cry right there on the spot. Never in her life had anyone called her smart, only dumb. Clyde watched her put her head down. He took his hand and lifted her chin softly and asked, "What's the matter, I said something to offend you? If I did, I ain't mean to."

She said quietly, "You really think I'm smart?"

"Smartest girl I ever met." Clyde frowned. "You ain't ever know that?"

She gave him a huge smile and said, "I do now."

They stared into each other's eyes, at that moment unsure of what they should do next. It was gravity, and they were no longer in control of their lives from then on, and destiny was its course.

There were Adam and Eve, Samson and Delilah, and now there was Clyde and Keyshia, forever.

They snapped out of their momentary trance and suddenly realized another half hour had passed, and they were late.

Keyshia looked at the time and said in a panic, "Clyde, call the cab!"

Chapter 11

At the show, Keyshia and Clyde were having the time of their lives as they sang along to Lyfe's lyrics. Just one of many things they would soon learn that they had in common. Lyfe was at his absolute best that night—singing all his hits, "Smile," "Greedy," "Stick Up Kid," "Cry," "Made Up My Mind," . . . but he saved the best for last: "Must Be Nice." He then started singing the song, and it was as if he were talking directly to them.

Must be nice
Having someone who understand the life you live . . .

Lyfe instructed all the ladies to "grab hold of your man and look him in his eyes, and listen to this." Clyde felt Keyshia take his hand as she turned toward him and they gazed into each other's eyes.

After they had dinner at a fancy seafood restaurant on the board-walk, they decided to take a slow walk on the beach. The evening was incredible. Shoes off, they walked hand in hand as the moon shone down upon them. It was as if they were on another planet, far away from the urban jungle that they both inevitably would have to return to.

"You never answered my question," Clyde said softly as he admired the sand between his toes.

"What's that?" Keyshia asked.

"How old are you?"

"Seventeen. I be eighteen in three more months." Keyshia studied his face and asked, "Why. Does it matter any?"

Clyde pondered the question. "Naw, not really. I ain't nothing but eighteen myself."

Keyshia smiled and said jokingly, "Shit, I thought you was 'bout forty years old the way you act." He smiled. Keyshia searched his face, noticed he still had questions that needed to be answered, and offered him an out. She stopped and said, "Listen, Clyde, I ain't got nothing to hide, so you can ask me whatever you want. But I can basically tell you that I ain't have too much of a pretty life to talk 'bout. My mama from down south ain't want me, so they send me up to New York to my aunt Ninny. She ain't like me or want me there. I ain't too smart enough for them schools, got left behind plenty of times. I can't even read or write good. I ain't got no friends I could think of, and I'm always by myself." They walked up to the boardwalk and sat on a bench.

They sat face-to-face, and Clyde still had an inquisitive look on his face. He began to stare off into the ocean, and he said gently, "What about that, you know, that crack shit you be fuckin' with?"

Keyshia knew it was coming and was kind of embarrassed to discuss it, but he had a right to know what he was getting himself into. Above all, she wanted the relationship to be open and honest from the beginning. She thought about it hard and long before she answered, still unsure what to say, so she just got honest. Brutally honest.

"When I was eleven, I was raped a lot by my preacher from the church doing Sunday school. He tells me not to tell nobody, and if I did, God gon' strike me down with lightning. I's useta tell my mama I's didn't want to go to Sunday school no mo', but since the preacher help my mama out with groceries, he say just keep sending me to Sunday school so I can learn God's word. Few months later, my stomach start ta grow."

A knot grew in Clyde's stomach, and he continued to listen. "They carry me down to the doctor, and he confirm I's was pregnant. The sheriff come and everything, and they ask me did I trys ta force myself on him and I's tell 'em no. They turn silent, and the next thing I know they start making like it was my fault. Keep tryna make me say I throw myself at 'em and things like that. I tell 'em, I's never like what he was doing, him being on top of me, hot breathin' and all, but they still make like he the victim." Keyshia spoke almost robotically as she recounted the incidents that happened next. "They found out that I was too far gone to get rid of the child, so they carried me away ta stay with this old, old lady, and I's wait there all the while till the baby come." Keyshia closed her eyes, and a single tear rolled down her cheek.

Clyde squeezed her hand in comfort. "Keysh, you don't have to tell me the rest, I understand."

Keyshia shook her head. "No, I gots to do it. I never told nobody 'bout this." Clyde put his head down as his insides raged for her. "I had a baby girl." Keyshia smiled. "She much prettier than me, I remember." She put her head down and said, "Right after that, the old lady hand my baby off ta somebody and I ain't seen her since. They say I can't never have no babies again, 'cause I was so young and all." They stared far off at the ocean. Keyshia continued with a little more confidence. "Since I's was trouble, they sent me off to New York to live with my aunt Ninny. She couldn't stand me from first day. She always call me black and ugly looking, that I's was nasty." Keyshia rubbed Clyde's warm hands. He instantly took off his jacket and placed it around her. She thanked him and snuggled in it.

"Back then I was nothing like I am now. I was quiet and afraid of anything that moved. I was so country and country soundin' that I didn't open my mouth fo' nobody 'cause I was too shamed." She began rocking back and forth. "A year or so ago, I was coming home from playing hooky at one of them department stores downtown, and this boy . . ." Keyshia sneered when she mentioned his name. "Omar, he come up to me and asked me could he walk me home." She shook her head and fretted, "I, I didn't know what to say, I was scared and just say okay." She paused to get past the lump forming in her throat. "He follow me up to my apartment, and that's when I saw three of his friends coming up the stairs." Keyshia began to break down. "He punched me in the face and pushed me in the apartment and they locked the door and ripped my clothes off of me and took turns—" Keyshia couldn't go on any further as she hugged Clyde tightly and cried her heart out on his shoulder.

He kissed her tears and cheeks and reassured her that things would be okay now. He reached in the jacket she was wearing and pulled out a tissue to hand to her. Wiping her tears, she took a deep breath and continued, "When the police came to the house, they convinced my aunt that I basically brought it on myself because I brought him to the door. They got away with it, and my aunt beat the living hell out of me." Keyshia's jaws began to grind. "After that, I turned cold as stone and didn't have love or inno- cence left in my heart for nobody. No matter how many baths I's take, I's still dirty feelin'. I didn't care anymore, so I just get numb by smoking weed and stuff like that. But I found out that if I put that crack in it, I feel different. I don't feel so dirty no more, I don't feel so lonely no more, I don't have to feel, period." Misty- eyed and puffy, she looked at Clyde. "There it is, boy, everything in a nutshell about the ho called Keyshia, love me or leave me."

Clyde looked her in the eye and caressed her face gently with his finger. "You ain't no ho, you are a smart, beautiful young woman who didn't deserve what happened to her. But you are worthy to live the way God intended for you, and that is not the stuff you doing now. You much, much better than that." Keyshia stared deeply into his strong eyes and gripped his hands tighter. "As long as I'm alive, you will always have someone there for you in me. You saved my life and I'm forever thankful and loyal to you, Keyshia, and I mean that!" They searched each other's faces, and then Clyde said seriously, "If nobody ever told you that they love you, let me be the first to say it: I love you, Keyshia."

They embraced and kissed for the first time. Keyshia's body trembled uncontrollably, but this time it was not from fear, nor was it from hurt, and certainly not from pain. She shook because for the first time in her short, turbulent life, she felt the power of being loved.

Chapter 12

When they arrived back at the hotel, both of them were feeling joyous. Neither had had such a good time in recent memory as they sang Lyfe Jennings's songs one after another, laughing and even dancing as Clyde twisted and twirled Keyshia around.

Laughing, Keyshia waved him off when she couldn't take it any longer. "You are so crazy, Clyde! I gotta go to the bathroom, you got my bladder hurtin'."

They looked deeply into each other's eyes, unwilling to let the moment end. Finally, Clyde let go of her hand and she backed away toward the bathroom, never losing eye contact. She grabbed a Macy's bag and her purse be-

fore she entered the bathroom and told him she would have a surprise for him when she came out.

Just as she was about to close the door, Clyde said, "Yo."
Keyshia turned around and he said, "You ain't no ho. You had to
do what you had to do to survive at the time. You are smart and
beautiful and have no reason to live like that today, 'cause . . ." He
paused as he searched for the right words to say. " 'Cause," he
repeated, "I love you, and you never, ever have to feel alone
again."

Keyshia couldn't believe what she'd just heard. She could
hardly contain herself as her eyes welled up. She dropped her
bags and ran over to Clyde. They hugged each other tight.
Through hard tears, Keyshia had to ask once more, "Clyde, you
love me?"

Fighting back his tears, he nodded and said, "Yeah, Keyshia,
I do."

Keyshia could no longer hold it in as they continued to embrace for what seemed an eternity. "I love you, too, Clyde," she
said before going into the bathroom.

Keyshia felt warm and sexual after she took a shower. As she
dried off with a towel, she looked at her purse and got an urge to
take her mood to another level. She put on her robe and pulled out
her weed, blunt, and crack vials from her purse. Then she stared
at the drugs as an overwhelming feeling of guilt washed over her.
She attempted to open the blunt, but she couldn't. She then stood
up and walked over to the toilet, lifted the seat, and threw all the
drugs down the toilet and flushed. She was proud of herself and
felt like a whole new person. When she turned around, Clyde was
standing at the door, smiling. He pointed backward with his
thumb into the room and said, "I was wondering if you wanted to
get in the living room tub with me after you finished." He'd got on
her earlier for not knowing what a Jacuzzi was.

Keyshia smiled and said, "You funny!" She ran to him and jumped into his arms and wrapped her long legs around him. "Carry me, nigga!"

As Keyshia's bare body lay comfortably behind Clyde's inside the bubbling hot Jacuzzi, the couple embraced and enjoyed every minute of the fleeting night.

"Yo," Clyde said, "I noticed that when you speak in front of me you sound country as hell, but when you get in front of people, your accent is gone and you speak all proper and shit. Why you do that?"

Keyshia smiled. "'Cause whenever I'm feeling comfortable in front of somebody who I know won't judge me, I's tends to be relax. But when I'm in front of outsiders, I be actin'. You know, like they do in the movies. I could turn into anybody I want to."

Clyde joked, "So, I's guess you's feel comf'ble 'round me now?"

Keyshia slapped his knee and said, "I's gonna kick yo' ass, too, if you keep playin' wit' me 'bout how I talk, boy." They went back and forth the rest of the night, but the laughter was interrupted when Keyshia asked Clyde about his life and his parents.

Clyde grew a little tense, but he was willing to tell his girl about his past because she'd been strong enough to tell him about hers. He thought about where he wanted to start and felt assured as she took his fingers between hers and kissed them gently.

"I was about three years old when it happened. Me and my two older brothers awoke to my mother screaming. Next thing we know, we hear a loud boom and then a real long silence. We were so scared that we didn't know what to do. Then my oldest brother, Ceasar, finally got up and opened our room door and we walked down the hall to my parents' bedroom and looked and saw my father sitting on the bed like he was in a trance, holding a gun in his hand. We looked across and that's when we saw my mother's best friend, Martha, who stayed over at our house a lot, next to my mother slumped on the floor with blood falling from her face. Martha was crying as she held her in her arms and yelled to us, 'Call the police, your daddy done shot your momma!'" Keyshia felt his body tense as he explained, "None of us could believe what was happening. It was so unreal at the time, like a dream."

Clyde put his head down. "Martha took all three of us in and raised us till the checks ran out. Since I was the youngest and just turned eighteen, you know, I was next to go, so I got a li'l room. Actually it's an abandoned room I live in above where I work on a Hundred Eighteenth Street. It got running water, but it's officially an abandoned building according to the city.

"My middle brother, Sonny, he's a fucking beast. He's a stickup kid from hell. He was the one who taught me everything I know, but as he got older he started to change and got tired of short money he was getting and stepped up to the major leagues and started robbing banks and shit. Even when he wore a ski mask, they knew who he was, so he just stopped wearing them. He started robbing so many drug spots and numbers holes in the neighborhood, they just start giving it up on the sight of him. They figured they could make far more money than he could ever take if he spared their lives. Him and his man Wolf is just alike, psychos. So if you don't kill both of them bad boys, you better not kill just one, 'cause the other is coming back to massacre you and your whole family; your mother, father, sister, brother, kids, everybody. These niggas done it before, I'm telling you. Them niggas are seven-thirty straight up—crazy. That's the only reason them niggas are still alive today. That's the reason I don't fuck with my brother on jobs anymore, because they want to kill everybody if they feeling moody.

"My oldest brother, Ceasar, is nothing like us; he's been working legit jobs since he was fifteen. He never got into trouble and graduated from high school and everything. He even been working at the same bank since his senior year in school and now

is an assistant manager of the branch." Clyde smiled as he reflected on his older brother's doing well. "Yeah, he ain't nothing
like us, and I'm happy 'cause at least one of our mother's kids
turned out well."

Keyshia told him, "You got a good heart, you just do bad
things, like you told me. You real smart and you probably can do
anything you want if you want to, Clyde."

Clyde shook his head. "Naw, I peaked. My greatest gift in life
is doing stickups. The shit is in my blood. But you," he went on,
"you are the real gifted one. You got natural instincts and wit.
Some shit you can't learn, either you have it or you don't. And
Keyshia," he said seriously, "you got that shit."

Keyshia listened to every new revelation about herself with
disbelief. "But I can hardly read or write and been told by my
family and teachers that I's dumb."

Clyde quickly retorted, "And you believed them." He turned
her around toward him and said, "All that bullshit that happened
to you your whole life was occupying your mind for all those years.
You never concentrated on things schoolwise, because you
could've cared less. But now that you got that shit and you know it
wasn't your fault, you can move on and do you for the first time in
your life—and when you do, watch what happens.

"That first time we met in Marshall's, the way you got me out
the situation, the way you talked to three grown-ass men and
convinced them when it was so obvious I was there stealing, but
you convinced them anyway that I was innocent, and they believed you, and we walked out the door." Clyde shook his head.
"Hell, you even convinced me to give you half the loot on the robbery, and I'm one of the hardest niggas to ever want to come off
with my dough." He chuckled. "What you should do is concen-
trate on becoming a lawyer, 'cause you can talk and convince the
devil himself that you didn't belong in hell. You mad intelligent,
yo!"

Keyshia kissed him softly on his lips, and Clyde compli-
mented her with his tongue, and they kissed until they were in a
frenzy. Clyde and Keyshia rose as water dripped from their glis-
tening bodies. He picked her up with his tongue still connected to
hers and laid her on top of the plush bed. Keyshia had her legs
spread, welcoming him to her sanctuary, but Clyde continued to
explore her mouth and neck. His hands caressed her body, sending Keyshia into bliss as she began to beg him to enter her. Clyde
didn't hear her pleas as he continued exploring her body with his
mouth, tongue, and hands. Keyshia's eyes began to flutter and
she began to gasp louder, "Clyde, put it in! Fuck me!" as her body
trembled in anticipation. Clyde mounted her, and Keyshia began
to moan loudly over and over again. Suddenly she shrieked like a
madwoman, "That's right, take this pussy, take this shit! " The
zone was broken as Clyde looked down on Keyshia in astonish-
ment as she continued screaming, "Take this pussy! Fuck me,
motherfuckers! Take it!" Keyshia's face was scrunched up and
rabid, her eyes closed as if she were in another place and time.
She began forcing him by pulling his hips toward her.

"Keyshia!" Clyde yelled, grabbing her wrist. "Keyshia. Snap
out of it. It's me, it's me—Clyde!"

She suddenly opened her eyes and began to shake and cry.
Clyde told her it was okay and lay down next to her and wrapped
his entire body around her as she eventually fell asleep.

Chapter 13

The next morning, they packed up in silence. Clyde was originally going to take the bus back to the city but ruled it out because of all their baggage. Besides, he felt Keyshia didn't need to be around so many people at that moment. He wanted to protect her from that point on and ensure that she would never be abused again. He had developed a newfound anger and hate, and he knew that it would not be settled until the wrong was made right. A boy named Omar and a preacher from South Carolina had hurt his baby when she was weak and innocent and unable to defend herself. They'd scarred her for life and never suffered the consequences. But for every action there was a reaction, and Clyde would be the reactor. He knew one thing—they might not be dealt with that day, maybe not that week or that year, but they would be dealt with one day! He was sure of it.

The couple pulled up in front of Clyde's building on 118th Street at about six-thirty that evening. Clyde had to make two trips to bring all the packages upstairs and into the apartment. Keyshia was right behind him when he turned on the lights in the apartment, and that's when he saw his brother Sonny sitting in the chair and staring out the window. Clyde was caught even more off guard when he saw Wolf creep out of the kitchen with a .357 Magnum dangling from his hand. Clyde turned toward Sonny and yelled, "Yo, what the fuck are you doing in my apartment?"

Sonny said almost casually, "A few nights ago an old-school nigga from uptown named Sugar Bear was murdered inside a motel in the Bronx." Keyshia nearly lost her breath when she saw the cannon hanging from Wolf's hand.

Clyde clutched her tighter and said, "Don't worry, Keesh, that's my brother and his stupid-ass partner, Wolf." Wolf smiled and made a howling sound.

Sonny continued slowly, "Before he was murdered, his boys said they last saw him leaving with a girl on a Hundred Twenty-sixth between Lex and Park, in a local spot frequented by young tramps looking to get with a baller for the night." Sonny stood up and walked toward his brother.

"They described the girl as young, dark-skinned, and real, real skinny." Sonny looked Keyshia over carefully. "As it turned out," he continued, "Sugar Bear got caught with his pants down so to speak and caught a bad one." Sonny frowned. "They say that somebody or some two"—being sarcastic—"smashed that boy's head in like a watermelon. Smashed it so bad the cops even found some of his brains on the ceiling.

"Police said whoever done it was an expert, 'cause they didn't even have no witnesses, no fingerprints, no suspects, no nothing, other than a three-hundred-and-fifty-pound naked-ass body with his asshole ripped out." Sonny walked directly up to Clyde. "My guess it was with a shotgun." He took a deep breath as he scratched his head and started walking back and forth. "Well, it seemed that Sugar got some people who was interested in his well-being. And it also seems that he owed these cats a whole lot of money, not including the money he had on the street, but the money and drugs the police got from his apartment after they searched it after his death because it appeared to be a drug-related killing. Now these people could care less about a grimy undercover homo like Sugar, but they are, however, concerned about the lost drugs and money."

Sonny stopped pacing and asked, "You probably asking your-self, What does this have to do with you, Sonny? And that a good question that I'm about to answer. Well, not only did Sonny's name come up, but also his little brother, Clyde. My first reaction was to laugh, and my second was to blow this nigga's brains out for throwing my brother's name in the mix like that, 'cause I know my li'l brother don't get down like that and I know that not his MO and I know he don't be fucking with no stink bitches on a setup tip. He work alone when he does his dirt." Sonny chuckled. "But on the strength of keeping peace, I said that I would check with my brother and find out the deal even though I knew it was im-possible."

Sonny began to laugh even louder and said, "So, I wait for my li'l brother, and what the fuck do I see pulling up in a fucking black car?" He started to get heated. "My brother and a bitch stepping out with shopping bags full of shit like they fuckin' hit the lottery!"

Clyde tried to interrupt, "Yo, don't be callin' my girl a—"

Sonny cut him off quickly. "Shut the fuck up, Clyde, you ain't in no fuckin' position to be talking that bullshit right now, nigga!"

Clyde had never seen his brother this serious.

"Nigga, I don't know if you know it, but you and this bitch is about ta come up missing."

"Yo, Sonny, I told you that she is my girl, don't be calling her no bitch!"

Sonny threw up his hands and said, "Oh, my bad, let me rephrase that, but you and this slut is about to come up missing." Clyde hauled off and clocked Sonny in the jaw, catching him totally off guard. Wolf stepped up, but Sonny just shook him off and checked his lip for blood. He shook his head and said, "All right, I was out of line on that one. I didn't think you like her like that." He spat and shook his jaw. "But, check this out, and this is the bottom line. You got two choices now. You, me, and Wolf, we got to kill all them niggas before they kill you and your . . ." He looked at Keyshia scornfully and said, "Girl."

Keyshia could not bear to look Sonny in the eye.

Sonny continued, " 'Cause if I figured this shit out already, they did also. And I ain't having them niggas come after you! Naa mean?"

Clyde spoke in a near whisper and asked while he eyed the floor, "What was the other choice, Sonny?"

Sonny looked at his brother and said, "What?"

"You heard me, you said we got two choices. What's the other choice?"

Sonny and Wolf looked at each other and laughed. "This nigga want to know the other choice, Wolf." Wolf stared at Clyde like he was a cute five-year-old who had asked to drive his car.

"You heard me, what's the other fuckin' choice?"

Sonny looked at Wolf again and said, "Oh shit, this nigga is serious. All right, nigga. The other choice is to come up with these niggas' money. Can you handle that?"

Sonny and Wolf laughed their asses off until Clyde shocked them by saying, "Then I'll come up with the money!" Their laughter stopped, and they looked at him as if he were losing his mind.

"Fuck do you mean you'll come up with the money?" Sonny asked.

"Just like I said, I'll come up with the money."

Sonny got serious. "How the fuck are you gonna come up with that type of money?"

Clyde snapped, "Don't worry how I come up with the money, Sonny. Just tell them they'll get it."

"Man, that's the stupidest shit I ever heard. All we got to do is slam all them niggas and that's that. Them niggas ain't that serious. Smash 'em and take they whole stash in the process. Rest of them niggas will be heading for the border, they don't want it!"

"I ain't killin' nobody, Sonny, I told you."

"Nigga, fuck is you talking 'bout? That shit you did to Sugar wasn't no Cub Scout shit."

Clyde remained silent.

"Listen, we hit them niggas quick, one shot and that be that. You or your peeps here ain't got to worry about none of the niggas coming after you no more." Sonny smiled and said, "Or we could do a straight bank job, and the three of us, shit, we'd come off like the motherfuckin' mob. Nigga, what's up?"

Clyde looked Sonny in the eye again and said through gritted teeth, "I ain't doing no bank job and I ain't doing no killin', Sonny!"

Angry, Sonny simply shook his head. "All right, I'm gonna speak to them niggas and tell them that you gonna pay. But remember this, nigga, this my last time bailing your ass out! You hear me? My last time!" Clyde shook his head. Sonny stared menacingly at Keyshia and Clyde and said, "Pack y'all shit. You can't stay here no more 'cause they might come after you before I talk to his peoples. I got a lay-low spot for y'all to stay at on Two Hundred Fifth Street in the Bronx." He looked around Clyde's place and added, "It might be a step up from this place."

. . . .

The place where Sonny took them was a modest two-family house on a nice tree-lined block. Clyde and Keyshia occupied the basement apartment and lay low, waiting for Sonny to get back with them. The apartment was better than they expected, clean and spacious. Clyde was worried about the situation, but he didn't want Keyshia to know that he hadn't figured out how he was going to come up with that type of money.

Clyde took small comfort in that at least it wasn't about no revenge shit, only business. That's how cats in Harlem got down; they looked at the bigger picture for the most part and tried not to take shit personal. Sugar Bear's bosses, Clyde thought, were probably just a bunch of niggas that came up on the same block together from back in the day. When niggas start getting money they form their own little crew, consisting of niggas who been on the block forever. Out of that crew, they ran the entire block, depending on how strong or greedy they were. If they had both those attributes, they ruled the block exclusively with their product; nobody else could sell on that block. You could have several crews pumping crack in and out of that block, yellow tops, green tops, red tops, or black tops. But it would be the same people, pumping the same products, supplying the entire area.

Sugar Bear had his own crew and made the most money out of them all; he had better quality and more potent crack because he didn't cut it up with all the bullshit like the rest of the crews. The other crews hated him on the low-low, because he flaunted his riches and talked down to them 'cause he was getting more money. There were a lot of people happy to see his demise. On the block, Sugar tried to fuck everybody's girl, sister, or mother and was more than happy to tell everyone that he did the next day. Even the police were happy to see that he finally fucked with the wrong person. Sugar would not be missed.

After a couple of days, both Keyshia and Clyde were starting to feel a little more at ease. They even began going shopping for household goods. Since the apartment was cable ready, they bought a twenty-seven-inch television and DVD player. They even went to the supermarket, and Keyshia, who was already an excellent cook, began fixing Clyde home-cooked country-style meals that he enjoyed. Despite the circumstances that surrounded them, they tried to make the best of it and even grew closer in the process.

"Clyde," Keyshia asked one night while they lay in bed together, "did you ever wonder what you was good at? You know, what you was really meant to do with ya life?"

Clyde thought about it for a second and answered, "Yeah, I want to work for a bank one day, work real hard, and maybe become a manager, maybe even one day make it up to regional manager." Keyshia smiled and turned on her side, pleased to hear Clyde talk about his future. "And then," Clyde said enthusiastically, "after I make it to the top . . ." He paused and looked at Keyshia. "I'm gonna stick they fuckin' ass up!" He laughed and laughed.

Keyshia gave him a love tap on his arm for stringing her along with his joke. "You are stupid."

"Naw, for real yo, I won't even need a gun. I'll just walk in the vault and carry that shit out like they did in *Scarface*." He looked at Keyshia and asked her, "What about you? What was you meant to do in life?"

She thought for a moment and said, "To take care of you."

Clyde was flattered, but he asked, "For real, what would you do?"

"I am for real, boy, what do you think I should be?"

Clyde lay back on his pillow and said, "I'll get back to you on that."

. . .

They did this every single night. Talked and learned about each other and fell asleep snugly in each other's arms, waking up in the same position every morning. They hadn't made love the entire time they were there, until one night . . .

The moonlight coming through the window was the only light in the room as they lay facing each other, preoccupied with their own thoughts. Keyshia shook Clyde softly and asked, "What are you thinking about?"

He stared at her and smiled. "Nothing, just thinking."

"That's what I want to know, what you thinking," she joked.

He turned and lay on his back and stared at the ceiling. "It's just all this shit that's going down. I feel bad about putting you in the middle of it." He shook his head. "If only I would have minded my business, took his shit and be out, and—"

Keyshia stopped him. "And we would have never met."

He stared at her and said, "It just that, I'd die if something happened to you."

Keyshia was stunned. She still wasn't used to having someone care about her well-being, and each time he said something like this, the same indescribable feeling overwhelmed her.

She got on top of Clyde and said, "I love you, boy, I love you to death. I love you because I know you fuckin' love me, and I'm willing to ride and die with you and do whatever it take to see us through this." She sat him up and squared her face with his and spoke with dead seriousness. "I ain't talkin' no punk smooth shit, just to hear myself talk, I'm for real. Whatever you tell me to do, I'm gonna do it. If you told me to sell this body to get this money up, I'll do it. Anything for you, Clyde, you hear me? Anything. And if by chance, baby, we don't come up with the money, fuck it! If you have to die, we gon' die together, 'cause I ain't gon' let no motherfucka put they hands on you, 'cause I love you, boy."

A single tear rolled down the side of Clyde's face as he stared into hers. It suddenly occurred to him that he no longer had to think alone or act alone, because he had Keyshia. He felt stronger. In his heart he was now ready to conquer the world because somebody had his back and wasn't gonna let him fall.

He pulled Keyshia closer to his lips and they kissed slowly, then nature took its course as they entered each other for the first time and would not stop. Their bodies became one as they cried out and solidified their eternal love for each other, until death do them part!

Chapter 14

Keyshia and Clyde woke up early the next morning to a loud knocking on the front door.

"Who is it?" yelled Clyde, fully expecting his brother Sonny.

"It's me Clyde, Ceasar."

Clyde wasn't sure if he was hearing right and asked again, only this time he got off the bed and headed toward the door. "Who?"

"Clyde, it's me, Ceasar. Open the door."

Clyde turned toward Keyshia and said, "It's my other brother." He said, "Yeah, hold on for a minute," as he waited until Keyshia grabbed some clothes and went into the bathroom before he opened the door.

When he did, Ceasar walked in without so much as an invitation and said with a serious overtone, "Clyde, what is this stuff I'm hearing about you owing some gangsters some money? What did you get yourself involved in?"

Clyde stood at the door and closed his eyes. Ceasar was the last person he wanted to know what was going down in his life.

"What is going on, Clyde?"

Clyde walked over to the couch and plopped down, rubbing the tiredness from his eyes.

"Clyde, I'm not gonna ask you again: What did you get yourself into?"

"Nothing I can't handle," Clyde said, avoiding eye contact.

"You gonna handle yourself getting yourself killed, that's what you gonna do!" yelled Ceasar.

"Who told you that shit?" Clyde asked defiantly.

"Martha called me last week and said that she ain't heard from you and you ain't been home in two weeks. I called back last night, and she told me that Sonny told her you got yourself in some kind of big trouble. I then called Sonny's sorry ass, and I made him tell me what happened and where you were at."

Clyde sank further into in the couch.

"Now I heard that you owe some people some money, something about you killed a man?" Ceasar began to plead, "Clyde, look at me and tell me this stuff ain't true." Clyde tried to look up, but he couldn't face his brother. Ceasar immediately put his hand over his eyes and cried, "No, Clyde, no, you didn't!" Ceasar had to sit down because he was beginning to grow light-headed. Clyde wanted to say something, but he couldn't find the words.

They remained silent until Ceasar finally spoke up. "I never wanted you to turn out like Sonny, Clyde. I always wanted better for you. But I guess I failed." Clyde was so ashamed and knew by the way Ceasar's voice cracked that he was crying. Clyde felt even worse.

"Ceasar, it's not what you think." Clyde finally looked at his brother. "All I can tell you right now is that I got it under control and it's gonna be all right." He watched Ceasar wipe the tears from his eyes and continued, "I promise you that I'm not gonna turn out like Sonny. I got my own mind and my own plans. I don't like the things that Sonny do; you taught me better than that." Clyde knew that he'd hurt his brother deeply and stood up to give him a hug.

Ceasar whispered, "I want you to promise me that you'll be careful, and if you need anything," he stressed, "anything, I want you to call me and I'll be there no matter what."

Clyde nodded.

"I love you, Clyde."

"I love you, too, bro."

They pulled away, and to break the tension in the room, Ceasar changed the subject. "Where you been?"

Clyde smiled and said, "I been on a li'l vacation out of town with my friend." He blushed as he told his brother, "We went to Atlantic City for a couple of days."

Ceasar smiled and said, "Atlantic City, huh?"

Clyde continued to look like a child as he added, "Yeah, we went to see Lyfe Jennings and everything."

Ceasar was impressed. "Who is this somebody that got my li'l brother acting like he was five years old again?"

Clyde chuckled and began to blush even more. "You want to meet her?" he asked, hoping he would say yes.

"I surely would."

Clyde walked quickly over to the bathroom and tapped on the door. "Keyshia, come out here, I want you to meet my other brother." Keyshia timidly walked out of the bathroom. "Come on out," Clyde urged, "he's cool."

Standing tall and smiling proudly, Clyde said, "Keyshia, I want you to meet my big brother, Ceasar." Keyshia smiled nervously.

Ceasar looked her over and smiled and said, "Oh, Clyde, she's so shy . . . and beautiful." Keyshia immediately felt his warmth. "Clyde, she looks like one of those girls on *America's Next Top Model* with them long, sexy legs." Both Keyshia and Clyde blushed as if they were children. "Come here and give your brother-in-law a hug."

Keyshia walked over to him, and he gave her a genuine, loving hug. Keyshia closed her eyes and felt honored to be accepted by his brother.

After they chatted for a little while longer, Ceasar told them he had to go. He gave both Keyshia and Clyde a warm hug, and as they walked him to the door, he added, "Oh yeah, Clyde, don't forget Sunday is the end of the month and we gonna visit Mama, so make sure you ready, 'cause Sonny will be picking us up, and you know how impatient he is."

Clyde nodded and told him he wouldn't forget.

About an hour after Ceasar left, Sonny stopped by and told Clyde to come outside and talk. When Clyde came out, he wore a black hoodie, a pair of jeans, and an untied pair of Timberlands as they took a walk around the block.

"All right, listen," Sonny said in a low tone. "I spoke to that nigga's people last night, Black Sam and 'em." Clyde's heart skipped because he knew of Black Sam. Sonny, always paranoid, looked over his shoulder and continued, "They pretty much knew who it was that put in the work, but the reason them niggas ain't hit you up yet was because they knew I was your brother. They figure out of respect, they would come see me to let us know that they know all about that fucked-up shit that you did." He paused until a Mexican family had passed and then continued. "See, the last thing them niggas give a fuck about is that li'l bit of money that they lost—that shit is chump change to them. But they don't want niggas thinking they soft or look pussy if they don't react to the shit." He looked at Clyde. "Sugar Bear was part of they crew, and he represented Black Sam. So to them niggas you might as well have violated him."

Black Sam and his crew had been around Harlem pumping one form of drug or another since the seventies. Sam trusted nobody, but he treated all his workers well. He never got into street politics with the fiends and never hung on the block no longer than an hour. Black Sam wasn't a killer by any means, but he'd contract that shit out in a minute if he felt a reason to do so. He was a just person by nature, willing to work a problem out with a sit down, and only as a last resort would he conspire to have you murdered. He had the old-school mentality of take over the entire block and hire from within, that way the money would be recycled in the neighborhood and everyone would be happy. Black Sam knew that Sonny and his right-hand man, Wolf, respected him enough not to ever step on his toes. Above all, Black Sam did not want beef with the two natural-born killers and had his boys reach out to Sonny, so shit didn't get out of hand.

"So this is the deal," Sonny said, "a hundred and fifty thousand, plus Sugar's jewelry."

Clyde's face was blank. One thing Sonny envied about his brother was his smoothness under pressure. No matter what the circumstances were, Clyde would never let you know how he actually felt. He had the perfect poker face, emotionless. "They wanted to kill yo' bitch—" Sonny caught himself. "My bad, but they wanted the deal to include yo' girl come up missing." Sonny looked around again and said, "They had her building staked out for the three days. She was lucky she never came home. They wanted me to find her and kill her as part of the deal. But I told them no dice, she is not to be touched." Clyde was relieved. "So it's your call, B, what you wanna do?"

Clyde just looked him in the eye and said, "Okay, how much time do I get?"

"Two weeks," Sonny said. "Yo, if you think you can't handle it, I got a bank job lined up and we need a third man to pull it off."

Clyde shrugged. "Why don't you just find somebody else?"

" 'Cause I don't trust nobody else!" Sonny snapped. "This is a bank job, and you can't bring along just any knucklehead; a nigga got to be on point! That's why I need you, bro. So what do you say?" Clyde shook his head again, wanting no part of it. "Come on, man, we be in and out in eight minutes, eight fuckin' minutes, yo! You in or what?"

"No, Sonny, damn! If I wanted to get down with you, I'd say so. Stop pressuring me all the time with that shit."

Sonny backed off and said, "All right, kid, I feel you." Both stood by and watched a father and his three little sons on their way to the park to play basketball.

Clyde asked, "What if I don't make the deadline?"

Sonny turned toward him and gave him a glare that was undeniable. "Hell, we up in Harlem, baby boy. We got to get them niggas before they get us!"

Clyde knew exactly what he was now up against. Come up with the hundred and fifty thousand or participate in a massacre of an infamous Harlem gangster and his entire crew. He also sensed that Sonny would rather wipe out Black Sam. Clyde didn't like the odds and for the first time asked his brother for help. "Yo, Sonny, man"—Clyde fought with his pride—"you think if I come up a little short, you can front something to put towards this thing?"

Sonny responded coolly, "Bro, please, you think I got that kind of money?" Clyde suddenly wondered why he'd asked. "But, like I told you," Sonny continued with enthusiasm, "we need a third gun on this bank job to pull it off. If you get down on this one with us, you'll have enough money to pay them niggas back and move out of Harlem with yo' sweet li'l girl and live sweet the rest of your life, kid."

"Naa, I'll take my chances doing my thing," Clyde said.

"All right, suit yourself. You got enough heat to handle your business?"

Clyde thought about the question. He'd tossed the shotgun in the murder and hadn't given much thought about needing weapons until now. "Naa, not really."

Sonny looked at his younger brother and shook his head. He got into his SUV and said, "Yo, you better step up your game, son. You fuckin' around with your life, so you better take this shit serious." He went to the back of the SUV and pulled out a green duffel bag from under the wheel well and handed it to Clyde.

Clyde knew exactly what it was. "How many hot ones are on them?" he asked.

Sonny seemed offended that Clyde had asked how many people he'd killed with the guns he was giving him. "None, nigga. Them shit are clean as a whistle. You think I would do that to you?"

"Yo, I'm just asking, all right? You was the one who taught me to always ask that shit." Sonny felt a little proud. "Thanks," Clyde said to him.

"Hold up, I got something else for you." Sonny walked to the back-door seat and lifted the seat cushion. He told Clyde, "You gonna like this one." He pulled out a brand-new shotgun and showed it to him for a second. He saw Clyde staring hungrily at it and smiled, then commented, "Yeah, I know your style, nigga, I was the one who taught you." Then he dug deeper in the rear and pulled out two bulletproof vests and held them up,

"These those new shits, they can stop hollow points." He slid them all into the bag, pushed the bag into Clyde's chest, and said, "You got enough heat to bring down Fort Knox, so you shouldn't have no problem coming with that short money if you do yo' shit right."

Clyde sucked his teeth and said, "Short money, I gonna hafta put in work twenty-four seven to make them numbers. Fuck is you talkin' 'bout, Sonny?" Clyde hung his head down, and for the first time in his life he felt defeated.

Sonny leaned against his SUV and said, "You got options, my nigga. So whenever you want to stop fucking around with this chump change and make this real money, get at me, 'cause this job is going down soon."

Damn, Clyde thought, he ain't never seen Sonny this persistent about a job before. "You know my answer," he said.

"All right, All right," Sonny said, throwing his arms in the air. "Do you."

Clyde turned and was walking back toward the house when he heard Sonny call him.

"And yo—"

Clyde turned and gave him the evil eye.

"Don't forget to bring out the jewelry so I can drop it off. I'll drop 'em off tomorrow, and that'll give you an extra day."

Clyde continued toward the house.

Clyde felt a chill run through his body as he walked across the street to give Sonny Sugar Bear's jewelry. Though he'd never admitted to Sonny that he participated in the slaying, handing him the jewelry would be confirmation enough. Clyde knew Sonny would give him an "I always knew you were just like me" look, so he just threw the bag of jewelry in Sonny's lap as he sat in his SUV and walked away without saying a word.

As Clyde crossed the street, he heard his brother's mocking voice scream, "Oh yeah, one more thing, killer!" Clyde turned around to Sonny's sarcastic smile. "Don't forget, next Sunday we going to see Mama, so be ready!"

Chapter 15

Keyshia met him at the door and said, "What's up, Clyde, what did he say?"

Clyde slung the duffel bag off his shoulder and laid it on their bed. "Said I have two weeks to come up with a hundred and fifty thousand dollars."

Keyshia gasped as terror lines filled her face. "A hundred and fifty thousand in two weeks!" she yelled.

Clyde nodded and said as he rubbed his face, "Yep, two weeks."

"Clyde, how do they expect you to come up with that kind of money in two weeks?" she said, both angry and fearful.

Clyde shook his head. "I don't know, they just do."

Keyshia paused and looked at him with her arms folded. "Clyde, are you sure about this? You sure you can trust what your brother say about this?"

Clyde assured her, "One thing about Sonny, when some shit like this go down with anybody in the family, he don't play—especially when it comes to me or Ceasar." Keyshia shifted her weight to her other leg and listened as Clyde explained, "When we was coming up, me and Ceasar never once had a fight with other boys on our block because either Sonny jumped in and fought for us or the other boys refused to fight us because they knew who our brother was and got scared. Sonny didn't play that shit. It's like he's unable to see any of us hurt in any kind of way, it's crazy. Sonny loved fighting. I mean, he loved it. It was like when he was fighting somebody he came to life or something, you could see it in his eyes. One time, Ceasar's gym teacher made a joke about his shorts being too tight or something and all the students in the gym started laughing at him. Ceasar came home crying his heart out. Sonny was so angry that he ran all the way to Ceasar's school to defend his older brother's honor and went to fight the teacher. He stopped the teacher just as he was leaving school and asked him why he made a comment to his brother Ceasar Barker. The teacher laughed, dismissing Sonny, and walked away. Sonny pulled out a kitchen knife and started stabbing the gym teacher everywhere. Sonny was only eleven years old at the time."

Keyshia was stunned. "Damn, eleven!"

"Yeah, don't fuck with his family. I'm surprised Sonny ain't do nothing to Black Sam and them already, because he killed niggas for much less, I seen him."

Keyshia pleaded, "Then let's just take the money that we have left and move out of Harlem for good, at least we be safe."

Clyde looked at Keyshia, who had a hopeful look on her face, and debated whether he should tell her everything. "Your aunt lives on a Hundred Twenty-second and Second Avenue, in the Wagner projects?"

Keyshia was surprised. "Yeah, how'd you know?"

Clyde looked her in the eye and said, "Black Sam's people was waiting there for you for three days."

Shocked, Keyshia sat down. Clyde quickly assured her, "Don't worry, Sonny made sure they won't come after you no more."

"What about my aunt, and my li'l cousins?" she asked, panicked.

"They didn't bother them, they just wanted you." Keyshia was relieved. Clyde continued, "They also said if we don't come up with the money, they . . ." He grew silent, then said, "They said they was gonna execute your entire family." Seeing how distressed Keyshia was, Clyde said, "Don't worry 'bout nothing. We gonna come up with the money and pay them off, and that will be that, trust me."

Keyshia remained in a daze, and after a few moments she looked at Clyde with fire in her eyes. "Okay, okay, we just have to do this, baby. We just got to figure a way out of this shit."

Clyde picked up the duffel bag and emptied it out on the bed, and about eight large-caliber handguns, a shotgun, and box after box of ammo fell out. Keyshia was in awe at all the guns and picked one up slowly and handled it as if it were a venomous snake. The weapon seemed longer than her entire arm as she aimed it and smiled at Clyde, then asked, "When do we get a chance to test these babies out?"

Clyde looked at her in amazement.

Keyshia and Clyde hopped out of a cab on 118th Street between Eighth and Manhattan that afternoon. Pops smiled as his young protégé exited the cab with a duffel bag dangling from his shoulder and a girl at his side.

"Hey, Pops!" yelled Clyde, genuinely happy to see him.

"What's up, Rocco?" Pops said with a wide, toothless smile.

Clyde bent down to hug Pops. They pulled apart, and Pops turned his attention to the girl at Clyde's side. "Pops, I want you to meet my girl, Keyshia," Clyde said with a huge smile.

Pops turned on the charm and gripped her hand softly and kissed it. "Why, my, my, my, Rocco. What is this beautiful, charming young lady doing with an ugly big-headed boy like you?" He looked at Keyshia with a dirty old man stare and said, "Hey, beautiful, what do you say you toss this one aside and get with a handsome teenage boy like me?" Keyshia blushed, and Pops laughed so loud that he began to choke on his cigar. He patted Clyde on the back and said, "Come on in, come on in."

Inside Pops offered them some sodas and hot peanuts. After they short talked for a while, Clyde and Pops went into the back to talk privately. Clyde said, "Listen, Pops, I got myself in some trouble and I need a favor."

Pops frowned but listened in silence to every word that Clyde said as Clyde told him the whole story. After he'd finished, Pops asked, "So tell me, Rocco, what can I do to help you?"

Clyde smiled and said, "Well, I remember you telling me you used to go down into the basement and practice shooting your pistol in case a nigga ever got out of hand."

Pops nodded proudly. "Still can shoot a peanut off a rat's ass if I wanted to. This building was built in the 1800s; you can shoot an atom bomb down there and nobody would hear nothing on the outside." He looked at Clyde suspiciously. "Why, you got a bomb in that bag or something?"

Clyde smiled. "Naa, nothing that big, but I got some shit for a nigga's ass if they want it. I got to show old girl how to handle these big babies."

Pops's eyes lit up like a Christmas tree as he asked if he could see inside. Clyde opened up the bag, and Pops looked in and nodded. "Okay, okay, not bad, not bad." He hobbled over to the wall and retrieved a key. "Take that stairway in the back to the basement. Be careful of them stairs, they old, okay?"

Clyde nodded, and before he walked off, Pops added in a whisper, "I don't know where you meet that li'l girl at, but I can tell she love you and would fight tooth and nail for you, even kill for you."

Clyde stared at Pops and wondered how he knew that. Seeing the questioning look in Clyde's eyes, Pops said with a wink and a nod, "Body language, boy, I can see it in her eyes."

The basement was old, dark, and dank. If it weren't for Clyde guiding Keyshia down and through it, she would never have made it. Clyde had to turn on each lightbulb individually as they hung precariously throughout the basement. When they finally made it to the rear of the long basement, Clyde turned on a final lightbulb and Keyshia saw hundreds of green sandbags stacked to the ceiling against the far wall. Clyde brought a sawdust-ridden table over to Keyshia. He found an old piece of cloth and began wiping dust off the table. After he'd finished, he picked up the duffel bag and pulled out each and every weapon and laid them all out on the table. He pulled out three boxes of ammunition and took the cover off each one.

"Okay, you ready to get down?"

Keyshia chuckled, a little overwhelmed as she stared at all the black and deadly weapons laid out before her. "Yeah, I, I, guess so."

Clyde lifted up one of them and pulled out the clip. "This here is a Glock nine-millimeter. It holds seventeen bullets in the clip and one in the chamber." He held up the clip in front of her and slid back the chamber. Then he put the clip back in the weapon and showed her the safety.

"This here is called the safety. Now this is very important to remember." Putting it close to her face, he continued, "If you switch it to the red dot, that means it's ready to fire. If it's on the blue dot, it's on safety. You got it?"

Keyshia nodded and repeated, "Red, fire, blue, safe."

Clyde nodded and smiled at her. "All right," he said, "just put it in your hand to feel the weight for now and pull the trigger."

He handed it to Keyshia, who was amazed at the lightness of the huge gun and said, "Oh, shoot," holding it with both hands and waving it around.

Clyde immediately said with a smile, "Rule number one: Never point the weapon at your partner!"

Keyshia let out a goofy laugh and said innocently, "I'm sorry."

"It's okay, baby, you learning," Clyde said reassuringly. Keyshia pointed the weapon unsteadily at the sandbags and aimed. Clyde wrapped his arms around her, steadied the weapon in her hands, and said, "Always aim low or at the center of the body." She followed his instructions. "That's right, baby, never aim at the head, always low and centered to their body. That way you have a better chance of hitting something." Keyshia aimed at her target, and "click." They both smiled.

"All right," Clyde said. "It's time for the real thing." He pulled out bullet after bullet and placed them inside the long clip. He showed her how to load her clip until she could fill her own.

"Always respect your weapon and it will respect you," Clyde preached. "Never take for granted that your gun is empty." Keyshia hung on every word he was saying. "That's how most shooting accidents happen, someone assumes that the gun is empty. Always clear your weapon by cocking it several times like this." He then gripped the upper rear part of the weapon and pulled back several times and said, "See, it's all clear." She nodded. She looked at Clyde the way a kindergartner looks toward her teacher for guidance.

"All right," Clyde asked, "are you ready?" Excitement in her eyes, she nodded. He nodded back and said, "Okay, its gonna be loud and have a nice little jolt to it, so be prepared, okay?" She nodded again.

"I'll go first." Clyde lifted his arm and aimed at the wall of sandbags and fired ten steady bursts from the weapon. When he finished he looked at Keyshia, who was clearly eager.

"What you think?" he asked.

"Loud," she answered.

"Yeah, you ready?" She nodded, more excited now. "Get down, then," Clyde said as he moved behind her. Keyshia raised the weapon and closed her eyes and pulled the trigger. Nothing. She opened her eyes and Clyde said simply, "Safety switch?"

Keyshia smiled and switched the safety and said, "Red, fire, blue, safe."

Once again, Clyde stepped behind her and said, "Remember, keep squeezing the trigger." He showed her with his finger. "Bap, bap, bap! Okay, get down, baby." Keyshia flipped off the safety, raised the weapon, and pulled the trigger. *Bap, bap, bap, bap, bap, bap . . .* Clyde watched the sandbags twist and turn as sand leaked rapidly out of the bags. Keyshia continued to squeeze the trigger until the gun was empty and smoking!

"Goddizam!" Clyde exclaimed as he stared at Keyshia with utter surprise. "I thought you said you never shot a gun before?"

Equally amazed, Keyshia finally opened her eyes and watched the smoke rise from the gun, then saw the leakage of the sandbags, then smelled the acrid gunpowder. She suddenly felt invincible.

"Goddamn!" she cried as adrenaline coursed through her body. She looked at Clyde and asked, "Can I do it again?"

Clyde nodded, and they both rushed to the other guns, loaded them, and began blazing and bucking off rounds for the next hour. All the guns were broken in except for the massive shotgun left on the table. Keyshia looked at Clyde mischievously.

"Oh hell, no. Don't even think about it!" Clyde said with a smile. "That shit there ain't for no li'l girl."

Keyshia continued to approach, staring into his eyes all the while. "I ain't no li'l girl no more. I want to shoot it!" she said as she locked him in a corner.

"Hell no, Keysh, that shit will knock you on your ass!" Clyde's back was now against the wall. "You don't need to fuck with that bitch, you already—" Keyshia started kissing Clyde's neck. "No, don't do that, baby!" he began to plead.

"Let me shoot," Keyshia said in a low, sexy tone.

"You might get hurt," said Clyde as his voice became weak.

"I'll hurt you, then. Give me some!"

They started kissing and hugging when Clyde suddenly broke free and relented, "Okay!"

Keyshia smiled.

Clyde wondered if he would ever be able to tell her no. Keyshia watched carefully as Clyde filled up the shotgun casing with rounds. He looked at her and said seriously, "This bitch here ain't nothing like the nines, this shit got kick to it." He pumped the shotgun and said, "Hold your ears," and then the shotgun roared, *Boom! Boom! Boom! Boom!* Clyde's whole body jerked violently from each pull of the trigger. After he finished he yelled at the weapon in his hand, "Goddizam! Fuck!" He admired the powerful weapon for a few moments longer and then looked at Keyshia. "You sure you ready for this shit?"

A little intimidated, but still willing, she nodded. Clyde gave her the shotgun, and she was shocked by the weight of it. She looked at Clyde, who was still amped up, and he nodded.

"You can do it, baby, plant your legs firm, hold it real tight between your arms, and pull that shit!"

Keyshia nodded quickly and took a deep, deep breath.

Adrenaline started flooding her bloodstream, then suddenly she gave a bloodcurdling yell and pulled the trigger, and, *BOOM!* roared the mighty weapon, nearly causing her to fly into the wall.

"Goddizam!" she repeated as she stared at the shotgun in her hand.

She looked at Clyde, who was smiling wickedly. He said, "Squeeze that shit, baby, squeeze that shit!"

Keyshia obliged as she took aim and squeezed off round after round and didn't stop till she was out of ammo. Her mouth was open as if she had just run a hundred-yard dash.

Clyde was elated and hugged Keyshia, who was still in a zone, and he said, "Oh, shit, my baby look like Rambo in this piece! Yo, you ain't no fuckin' joke!" Keyshia, equally excited, hugged him for joy. They kissed and Clyde said, "Yo, let's start cleaning this place up to get ready for tomorrow." He began picking up each and every round, talking all the while.

"I ain't got no doubts now, we gonna handle our business, naa mean, baby?"

When Keyshia didn't answer, he turned and looked at her. She had unbuttoned her shirt, and her firm breasts and nipples were hardened. Clyde paused as he stood up with an instant erection. Keyshia walked over to him and said in a husky voice, "Make love to me, boy!"

Chapter 16

The sun was just going down when Keyshia and Clyde got home.

"Keyshia," Clyde said while he was packing the weapons, "do you love me?"

The question was so out of the blue that she frowned. "Yeah, Clyde, you know I do," she answered.

Clyde paused as he searched for the right words to say. "Well, I love you, too." He looked toward the far wall as if he were straining for the right words.

Keyshia began to grow worried. She walked over to him and grabbed his hand and said, "What's wrong, baby? Tell me."

Clyde looked deep into her eyes. "I . . . I just can't let

you go through this with me . . . I just can't." Keyshia saw the seriousness and dread in his eyes.

"I just don't know what I would do if you get hurt, I just can't." Keyshia put her head down. She'd known this moment would come.

"I never felt like this about another person, never knew this feeling existed. But I do now. If you love something that much, how could you ever put it in harm's way?" Keyshia searched his pleading eyes.

"I can do this shit by myself, yo, and afterwards we could get out of Harlem and live together somewhere where there's no drama, and be suckers and get jobs." He stood and continued, "We . . . we could travel down south and visit your family, who you ain't see in years. We can leave all this shit behind, make some change in our life for the better." Clyde began smiling as he imagined that it could all really come true. "We could one day find out what we are meant to be, like you always say.

"So what do you say, Keysh? I can do this shit solo, ma!"

She looked down and began rubbing his strong hands and said softly, "Boy, looka here, I's love ya and I's loves ya bad. All my life I been by myself and alone because nobody care much fo' me. My whole life they calls me ugly and calls me dumb 'cause I don't know much. They tells me I was a bald-headed, skinny, big-lip, big-nose, black bitch. They tells me I's was trash 'cause I was tampered with as a child and that nobody ain't gonna want me. My mammy gives me up and leave me to my aunt, who slapped me 'round so much I couldn't do nothin' but to accept it. After whiles, after so many beatin's and all the name callin', you can't help but feel like shit inside. Then being forced on so many times by grown men and boys and ta be blame for it, does sumtin' ta ya mind, to ya soul. I guess I's didn't want to feel no more so I get to the point I don't care no more 'bout me or my body. I use to travel 'round them department stores imagining I was somebody special, somebody important, like them white folks I use to see with they family, doing and buying what they want. Then I met you however that ways we did in a motel room between a man legs. Even though you saw me hows you did and smokin' them crack, you tells me I's was better than them drugs and you still look after me and never treat me like no ho. Then you up and tells me I's was beautiful."

Keyshia paused as she shook her head and thought back to that moment. "Me . . . you call beautiful." She looked at Clyde seriously and asked, "Did you know that was the first time I was ever called beautiful by somebody? Did you know how that made me feel? But you know what, that ain't even the sad part, the sad part is I's believed them when they told me I was ugly and wouldn't amount to nothin'. But when you told me I's was beautiful that day, and treat me like you do, and mean it, I looked at yo' face and looked in yo' eyes and I knew you was telling the truth! I's fell for you right then and there and knew I ain't never want to be with nobody but you fo' the rest of my life. I ain't got nothing going fo' me but you, and I ain't lettin' you go nowhere, boy. Now, I's done tells you once before and look into my eyes when I say this: If things gotta go down, we gon' go down together, that's fo' sho'. Now I's know you love me back the same and you can try to explain all you want after what I say, but remember this, and never forget, if I can't have you by my side, it ain't gon' be worth living, so either I's with you or I'm ready to die for you, boy!"

Clyde stared at her, expressionless, until he finally said, "Yeah, now for what you were meant to do with your life." Keyshia stared at him, perplexed.

"A lawyer."

Keyshia smiled and said, "You think so?"

Clyde nodded. "Hell, yeah, you convinced me. Every time I try to say no to you for something, you convince me otherwise. Think about it—the first time we met at Marshall's, you convinced three grown-ass men I wasn't stealing and caught red-handed with the shit hanging out my pants. The way you got them people in Macy's to respect you by knowing the right words to say. And don't forget the way you convinced me to give you half the loot on the robbery—half the take! That's the same thing them big-time lawyers do because they know the right thing to say and when to say it. I heard somewhere that the best lawyers are ten percent actors and ninety percent liars."

Keyshia frowned and threw a piece of tissue at him. "You saying I'm a liar?"

"What I'm saying is that you could convince the devil himself that he made a mistake of bringing you to hell if you wanted to. Shit, I would want you as my lawyer if I ever was in a fucked-up position anytime, that's fo' sho'!"

For the entire evening they spent their time plotting and scheming. Clyde taught her everything in regards to robbery, including where she should be positioned, what to look for during an actual robbery, and the three kinds of victims that can be a potential threat to a perfect jump-off. The first is the hero. Clyde warned her that in every bunch there is always one potential hero who can turn a simple robbery into a nightmare and that you have to make an example of these. For whatever reason, human nature tells one of these knuckleheads that they are duty bound to be a crusader and that they can really match the quickness of a loaded weapon. But, as many find out, right after they secure a hot searing bullet in their flesh, or hear the sound of the cracking of their jawbone when a weapon hits their faces, they are not comic book superheroes. These types you have to be able to spot immediately because you don't want to catch a body on a simple robbery. They are the ones who are constantly looking around with their head and their eyes, searching for a weak spot in their assaulter.

The second possible liability are what Clyde called the crabs, who feel that their jewelry is too precious to part with. Clyde heard everything from "I can't give you this, man, my momma gave me this before she die," to, "You might as well shoot me now, 'cause I worked too hard for this shit!"

Then there were the last, and possibly the worst: the sleepers. These are the ones who flop and fall out in fear from the robbery. They were easy to spot because they did their best Fred Sanford act feigning a heart attack before falling out, faking they were asleep or unconscious.

Clyde taught Keyshia that when she spotted these kinds to take them out hard and take them out quick. He told her to hit them hard on the bridge of their nose because that would cause them excruciating pain, making them forget all about being a hero, crab, or sleeper instantly.

Time is of the essence in any robbery. You want to be in and out in a matter of minutes, never giving the victims time to think. Never be greedy, take what's obvious—rings, necklaces, wallets, purses, watches, bracelets, and money clips. Anything above that is too time-consuming and you risk losing everything because of greed!

Put Vaseline around your eyes. It can make you look lighter or darker, depending on the lighting in the area of the stickup. It also makes you look sadistic, which helps out the robbery tremendously.

Always have a plan B. In robberies always expect the unexpected. Nothing happens the way you plan, so you have to be flexible.

The more noise the better. When you enter your robbery scene, cursing, yelling, and making threats will make it seem like twenty deranged psychokillers have invaded their space, scaring them half to death.

On the getaway, be as calm and poised as possible. Many thieves are caught directly after the robbery because they panic. Ninety percent of police never even have a description of the perpetrators, only the area in which it happened. What they look for is unusual behavior or body language, which can be dead give-aways.

Clyde decided that they would go out that night to give Keyshia a test run, something small.

"Keyshia," he said with a devious smile, "get dressed in your baddest outfit, we going downtown to get something to eat."

Chapter 17

Keyshia and Clyde sat in the upscale eatery on 40th Street in downtown Manhattan, feasting on New York strip steaks and having a ball. The eatery, Milo's, was a popular restaurant for many celebrities and athletes. Milo's was known for its pricey menu, but the food was good and the service impeccable.

Two couples in the far corner were enjoying themselves. They were having such a good time that they never even noticed the two pairs of eyes watching them. The two women looked like video bimbos and laughed at their suitors' jokes every five seconds. The men wore oversize diamond-laced jewelry like they were rappers in the making. It was obvious that the women would be their dates' desserts shortly.

The women excused themselves from the table and told their dates they were going to the ladies' room. The men stood up and let them exit the table first and then headed to the restroom right behind them.

Inside the men's room, their spirits were racing. "Yo, you see shorty's lips?" one said as he unzipped his pants and used the urinal. "She look like she could slob a nigga's knob something lovely by the size of them shits."

His man agreed as he checked himself out in the mirror. "Fuck that, you see the size of my shorty's ass? You know I gonna try my best to get all this dick up inside that shit."

His partner grinned and said, "Knock the dook shoot out of her, huh, man?"

"You damn skippy! Bang! Bang! Bang!" he responded, unable to contain himself. Suddenly, the masked Keyshia and Clyde burst out of the stalls and pointed their weapons at them.

"What the fuck?" shouted one man as he tried to zip up his pants. Keyshia immediately played her position by the door and locked it, concentrating on one of the men as Clyde attended to the other.

"Say another word and I'm blowing your motherfuckin' brains out, nigga!" They were instantly neutralized. "Now run them jewelry and your wallets!"

Both men complied quickly and willingly. Keyshia pulled out a bag and they dropped everything inside. Without a word, both Keyshia and Clyde raised their weapons and put them in their faces and said, "Strip!" While they were coming out of their clothes, Clyde recognized them and said, "Yo, I know you two. Y'all play for the fucking Knicks, don't you?" Still nervous, both men nodded. Clyde suddenly flipped out.

"I should shoot y'all niggas right now. I hate the Knicks!"

Both men began to plead. "Man, it's the coach, man, I don't even like him," said one man.

"Yeah!" said the other. "And the GM. We ain't got nothing to do with the plays, we don't even like 'em."

Clyde suddenly laughed and said, "Na, I'm just playing! I'm just playing! Now go inside the stall and count to one hundred when I tell you." He motioned to Keyshia to take off her mask and leave quietly. The he took off his mask and said loudly enough for them to hear, "Now, make sure these niggas count to a hundred, and when they get to sixty, you can leave." Clyde yelled to the men, "Y'all clothes will be on the sink if y'all be good. Now start counting."

"One, two, three, four . . ." counted the men. By the time they got to six, Keyshia and Clyde were already out the restaurant door and around the corner.

Keyshia and Clyde were in predator mode and were currently staked out across the street in a popular after-hours spot uptown called Bell's. Cats from all over Harlem, mainly dealers and hardworking city employees who wanted to relive their "player, player" days, stopped by and posted outside with their fly rides and kicked it with the many honeys who were also looking to have a good time. Keyshia was the first one to spot their target. He was standing in front of his forest green Range Rover with the twenty-three-inch chrome rims and DVD monitors in the back of the driver's and front passenger's headrest, playing a movie, though no one was in the backseat. He was on his cell phone, and each time a group of girls passed by, he hollered at them without fail. He was begging to get stuck, so Keyshia and Clyde set out to accommodate him.

Keyshia wore her tightest black jeans with a matching blouse and high-heeled, knee-high boots. With the five-inch heels, she stood a towering six feet one as she walked stealthily toward their potential victim. As she got closer, she sized him up quickly. He was handsome, in his late twenties, and wore a modest amount of jewelry, including a twenty-four-inch gold necklace and matching cross and two gold rings on both hands. He was kicking it on a Sidekick 3. The man was a pure dog, 'cause he would try to talk to one girl and when she didn't give him any rhythm, he would quickly try to kick it to her homegirl.

When he spotted Keyshia, he froze and eased up off his SUV and said, "Oh, shit!" He quickly told the person he was talking to on the phone, "Yo, nigga, I holla at you later. I got to catch up with this shorty." He ended the call and stepped straight to up Keyshia. "Yo, ma, can I ask you something?" Keyshia played as if she didn't hear him and kept walking past him. The man wasn't letting her get off that easy, however. Her body was too tight to let her go without pitching his A-game at her.

"Yo, ma, slow down. You dropped something." Now a good distance away from his Range Rover, Keyshia decided to play into his little farce and looked around on the ground. "What did I drop?"

He ran up to her and said smoothly, "You would've dropped an opportunity of a lifetime if you don't stop and let a nigga holla at you for a minute." He smiled and extended his hand. "My name is T, and I'm feeling you, ma, just that simple."

Keyshia stared at him through her white Chanel glasses and decided to act coy. "Well, T, my name is Kashaun, not K. Do you mind telling me what your mother named you?"

He realized he'd underestimated this young'un and switched gears. "Oh, my bad, forgive me for my impertinence, Kashuan. My name is Terrence and you got me kinda twisted for the moment, but if you give me a second, I can come out of this daze you got me in."

Keyshia smiled and wondered how many girls had fallen for

his bullshit in the past. He continued talking as Keyshia looked over his shoulder and watched Clyde make his way across the street and toward his SUV.

"But what I really want to know is if you want to come with me somewhere, maybe get something to eat or some drinks?" He turned and pointed to his ride. "That's my Range Rover right there," he said proudly. "That's to let you know you ain't wasting your time with a broke nigga."

Keyshia cracked a light smile and said, "I hope not." She followed him to his SUV, and he opened the passenger-side door for her. He nearly tripped over himself running to the driver's side, thinking all the while how he amazed himself with his wit and game on these young bitches.

He hopped in, oblivious to the unwelcome guest who lay in the backseat. He looked at Keyshia and thought how he should just take her to a motel and wax that ass instead of wasting time and money on her dumb ass when he already knew she was out trickin' so she could get some money to pay for her cell phone or something. He pulled off and turned down the loud music and said, "Yo, ma, let's talk real talk." Keyshia nodded as he continued, "Why play games when we know what this is all about? I'd be a fool to insult your intelligence like that."

Keyshia smiled and said, "I could respect that, keep talking."

"You young and fine as a motherfucker, and I want some. What a nigga got to do to feel them insides?"

Without blinking an eye, Keyshia said, "Two hundred dollars."

"Goddamn!" T said. "You ain't bullshittin', but why so expensive? I just want to hit them guts and be out. Shit, the hotel is gonna be another hundred."

Keyshia gestured toward the back. "Shit, let's just handle business in the backseat; it look big enough. It would save you from paying for a hotel."

T smiled, 'cause he would never have thought a young fine girl like her would want to get smashed outside. Shit, he figured, by the time he would have wined and dined her, he would have dropped two bills anyway and still wouldn't be sure if he was getting the pussy. This way he'd be coming out much cheaper and was sure of getting the ass.

"All right, that's a bet. We can go to Morningside Park or sumptin', and handle our business like that." Keyshia nodded.

When they pulled up on Morningside, he parked his SUV between 119th and 120th streets where it was always deserted at that time of night.

"All right, so what's up?" T said.

"The money, nigga," Keyshia said sarcastically. He reached in a stash compartment in the vehicle, pulled out a wad of dough, and peeled off four fifty-dollar bills and handed them to her. Keyshia slowly put the money in her purse and then folded her arms and stared through the front window.

T was baffled. "Okay, what did I do?"

Keyshia continued to stare out the window and said, "You forgot to pay my man."

T shook his head, thinking he hadn't heard her correctly. "What you say?"

Keyshia turned and looked him straight in the eye and said slowly and steadily, "I said, you forgot to pay my man!"

Suddenly, Clyde rose from the backseat and put the gun right under his nose. He looked at Keyshia, who had her weapon drawn and was smiling wickedly.

After they stripped T down to his underwear, Clyde got out of the backseat and pulled him out like a rag doll and hopped in the driver's seat and drove off, dropping his shoes, shirt, and pants out the window along the way, leaving him to pick up each behind them.

They pulled off several small stickups over the course of the evening, and after they made it from the chop shop and Clyde's jewelry connect to convert the jewelry into cash, they made it home by cab by four in the morning. After they counted that night's take, they had made a little over twenty thousand dollars. Not bad for six hours of work.

Though they were happy, they knew they still had a ways to go to come up with another hundred and thirty thousand. Clyde knew that was just a test run to get each other in sync, to know each other's instincts, each movement. They also knew that they had to step up their game to where the money was really at—drug spots—where it would become more dangerous.

Chapter 18

Keyshia and Clyde sat in a stolen Buick on the corner of 112th Street and Seventh Avenue. Clyde got the word that some young boys were pulling in major paper pumping crack 24/7 in front of the hotel on the corner. He favored sticking up the young ones because they weren't as organized as the older cats in the drug game. You could always catch them slippin' because they were more interested in talking to girls than they were in making money. From what Clyde saw, there were two major players who oversaw two other workers who did the actual hand-to-hand sells. They also had two workers who stood on the corner and watched the traffic flow and alerted them whenever they saw police coming through. After they finished work

about six-thirty, the two bosses hit off the workers and drove off
with the money to the East Side, where they apparently lived. This
was Keyshia and Clyde's second night watching and following
them. Just like always, they finished work and hit off each worker,
and then the two bosses, who were no older than nineteen, drove
off in their black Expedition. Following them uptown, Clyde
made sure that he stayed behind them at least a block away so they
wouldn't detect them. When they got to 137th Street, they made an
unexpected U-turn, causing Clyde to curse in fear of them sus-
pecting that they were being followed. Clyde held his breath and
continued driving past them without looking in their direction.
When he drove two blocks up, he made a quick U-turn, afraid that
he had lost them altogether. But when they passed 135th Street,
they spotted the shiny black SUV parked in front of an IHOP.
Clyde parked a block away and waited.

"You think they in there eating?" asked Keyshia.

"I don't know. Maybe," said Clyde as he looked through the
rearview mirror. "Let's just chill for a minute and see what happens." Keyshia turned and looked out the back window and nodded. After about ten minutes of waiting, Clyde said, "All right,
here's what we gonna do." He looked at Keyshia. "Go in there and
look around, order some food if you have to, and find out what
they doing and come back out so I can know what's up."

Keyshia smiled and gave him a kiss and said, "Yes, daddy."

Clyde returned her smile and said, "Oh, I'm no longer a boy,
huh?"

Keyshia smiled slyly. "Yes, you still a boy, but I got to switch
up on you sometimes, and keep you on point."

Clyde loved whenever he saw the twinkle in Keyshia's eyes.
"Yo," he said before she closed the door, "be careful and put on
your glasses, just in case." She nodded and pulled them over her
eyes and headed toward the IHOP.

As Keyshia approached the restaurant, she could see the two

sitting at a table, chatting and joking. She walked inside the store and decided to get a better look, maybe get a little information on their next plan. She saw two police officers sitting in the corner, drinking coffee while they appeared to be waiting on some food they ordered.

"Welcome to IHOP, ma'am. Seating for how many?"

Keyshia was a little startled by the unexpected cheerful greeting of the hostess. "Uh, no," she responded. "Can I have a take-out menu?" The girl smiled and pulled out a menu from behind the counter and handed it to Keyshia. Keyshia smiled and thanked her. She edged closer to the dining area where the men sat to get a better view and realized she recognized the faces of the men, but she hadn't known where from—then suddenly, as if a ton of bricks hit her, she realized it was two of the four guys who'd raped her at her aunt's house. Keyshia was suddenly overtaken by fear and had to get out of the restaurant. When she turned to exit the store, she bumped directly into a man's chest.

"Damn, baby, where the fire at?" said the man she'd bumped into. She was preparing to apologize when she looked into his face and saw that he was none other than Omar. Air seemed removed from her lungs as she simply stood frozen, unable to move, unable to think.

"You all right, sweetheart?" asked her rapist, not recognizing her while looking her over. "Or do you want to sit at my table with my mans and 'em so we can break bread and get to know each other?"

Keyshia put her head down and found the strength to walk around him and head for the door.

When she'd made it outside, she used the wall for support to keep her balance. She closed her eyes and breathed fresh air and then staggered uneasily toward the car. Clyde must have seen her the moment she exited the restaurant because he was already out of the car and at her side.

"Keyshia!" he hollered. "What happened?" Keyshia was still unable to get a grip on things and continued to gasp for air. "Baby, what's wrong? Somebody touch you?" asked Clyde with flames in his eyes.

Still unable to speak, Keyshia grabbed him for support and managed to say, "Get me to the car."

Clyde grabbed hold of her arm and got her to the car and sat her inside gently. He waited until she'd cleared her head and then asked her again, "Baby, what happened?"

Keyshia closed her eyes, breathed easier, and said, "Those are the guys that raped me."

"What, who!" Clyde stuttered angrily.

"The two guys we followed and the two guys that entered after them! Omar! I bumped right into him!"

Clyde reached under the seat and grabbed his pistol and scowled. "Which one of them was Omar?"

Keyshia cried, "No, Clyde, not like this!"

Clyde flew into a rage. "Fuck that, Keyshia, just tell me which one of them was Omar."

Keyshia had to throw her arms around him to prevent him from exiting the car. "Please, Clyde, don't do it, baby, not like this. The police is in there and everything, this is not the time."

It took every ounce of strength Clyde had to fight off the urge to go into the restaurant and start blasting away. He could taste his own blood in his mouth from biting down on his tongue. He began to think rationally, though, remembering the police precinct, which was just around the corner.

"Aaaahh!" he yelled, and hit the steering wheel, still reeling from not being able to act on his impulse. As Keyshia rubbed his face, he began to grow calm. She looked into his eyes and saw tears in them. "But they hurt you, baby. I just can't take them hurting you like that. I want to get them. I want to get them back for hurting you," Clyde cried softly.

"I know, baby, it's okay, it's okay, but not like this . . . we gon' get them. We'll get them in time, " Keyshia said, and laid his head on her chest.

Clyde shook his head and realized she was right, it wasn't the right time. They would get them back in time. "You right," he said as he wiped his eyes. "You right, this is not the way to do it." He looked at Keyshia and said, "I'm good now, baby, thanks."

Keyshia stared into his eyes and once again realized just how much he loved her. "Clyde, I love you . . . I love you!" They kissed and hugged each other, not wanting to let go.

"I love you, too, Keyshia." When they pulled apart, Clyde stared out the rear window and thought for a second. "Listen, you said the same four guys was all in there?"

Keyshia nodded. "I never gonna forget they face!"

"Do you remember what Omar was wearing?" Keyshia was a little apprehensive about telling him, but Clyde assured her that he was okay and handed her his gun to prove it. "No, I'm good now. I just thought about something and I'm just gonna watch and listen to him. I want to read his body language." Keyshia frowned and he said, "I gonna look for his weakness, his gestures, and what he sound like so I can use it against him one of these days." Keyshia still wasn't getting what he meant, so he simply said, "I'll explain to you later. What was he wearing?"

Clyde sat in the booth two tables away from the loud, unruly boys and watched them all the while. He paid specific attention to the one who wore a blue Yankees jacket and a blue Yankees cap with pants sagging so low, he looked like he had shit on himself. They were having discussions on everything from who was the best rapper to who had the most women and what kind of car they would be buying next. Clyde took particular interest in the apparent leader of the crew and absorbed everything that he said and how he said it. He was watching and listening to everything, knowing that it would come in very handy real soon!

Chapter 19

Tonight Keyshia was dressed like any junior high school teen in the city. Her hair was done in box braids by the Africans on 125th Street, and she'd had her nails done by the Koreans. Clyde wore brand-new Evisu jeans, sparkling white Uptowns, and a big-ass Rocawear belt buckle. To supplement the desired look of the evening, he wore the jewelry that he'd taken off T the other night, and instantly he looked like any other dope dealer. Keyshia also shopped purposefully that day at Dr. Jays and bought the latest street gear, giving her the perfect bubble-gum appeal. Clyde wanted them to play the perfect role for the company she would be keeping in apartment 4b in Washington Heights. The drug spot was just one of many on the block that sold cocaine by weight. They sold only eight grams or better; anything else was not worth their time. The Dominicans were very finicky about who they fucked with or served and didn't trust anybody but their God. And they were very deadly, too, and would kill you in a second if they even suspected that you were police or up to no good. On the surface they seemed like the perfect drug-dealing machine, but as with all, even the strongest have their weaknesses—and theirs happened to be pussy—the younger the better!

Keyshia knocked on the sturdy brown door, and before too long she heard the heavy squeaking of the floorboards as someone approached. She chewed her gum loudly, trying to remain as calm as possible. She heard the peephole latch raise and squared her face to it. After a few moments, a thick-accented voice asked, "Yeah, who dat?"

Keyshia said, "Yeah, I'm looking for Miguel. He told me to meet him here." She heard the person yell something in Spanish in the background.

More footsteps approached, and the eye latch closed and opened again. "Yeah, who you want?"

With her best sass, Keyshia responded, "I'm here for Miguel, and he told me to meet him at this door."

A second later, the door opened and an eye peered through the crack. After the man behind the door scanned the steps and saw that nobody else was with her, he opened the door and addressed her: "Who you looking for?"

Keyshia said with frustration, "I said I was here for Miguel. He told me to meet him here." The man suddenly noticed how young and pretty the girl was and began to look her up and down with lust in his eyes. "Well," said Keyshia, "is he in or what? This is the address that he gave me." She handed him the card with the address handwritten on it, and he read it.

Both men looked at the card until one of them said, "Oh,

mami, you got the wrong address. You suppose to be at a Hundred Forty-second Street, this is a Hundred Forty-first." He handed her back the card and stated, "You got the right building address, just the wrong block."

Keyshia rolled her eyes and pouted like a child. One of the men whispered to the other, and he nodded and said, "But you might be wasting your time going to see him." Keyshia gave him a confused look. "I know Miguel," the man lied. "De police come and arrest him last night, he gone." Keyshia just stared at them until the other man agreed, "He right, dey got him last night, dey go deport him, he not come back."

Keyshia sucked her teeth and cried, "Aw, man!"

"What wrong, he was yo' friend?" Keyshia nodded sadly. The other man said, "Don't be cry, we could be yo' friends now. My name Tony, dis my brother Alito."

Keyshia simply nodded, and they let her in. Clyde was on the upstairs stairwell all the while, listening to every word that was said.

Keyshia sat comfortably on the couch, looking like a thirteen-year-old, as both men smiled and offered her something to drink. "You want a cola or something cold to drink?" Keyshia declined and kept looking around the apartment shyly. She listened very closely toward the back room to hear if anyone was back there. She heard nothing.

Both men made small talk with Keyshia, all the while watching her thin, sleek legs cross each other. "Where you meet Miguel at?"

Keyshia continued her young, dumb act as she popped her gum loudly. "On my way to school. He stopped me and say I look nice and gave me his address. He said he was gonna take me shopping." Both men smiled, because this was how many Dominican dealers came on to young girls.

"What school you go to?" the same man asked.

"I go to high school, on a Hundred and Thirty-fifth Street and Edgecombe."

"What grade you in?" the other man said excitedly.

"Ninth grade," she answered.

The girl's youth excited them. Both men could no longer contain themselves as one stood up on instinct. They lowered their guard, and one of them asked her, "Do you get high?"

Keyshia looked up and smiled like she was guilty. "I smoke weed one time with this boy," she confessed.

Both men smiled gleefully, because they never would mess with a girl who smoked crack. They thought women who smoked crack were the absolute worst and could not be trusted or respected.

It was a wrap, and they no longer hid their motives anymore but got real open with her as one of them approached her and sat next to her on the arm of the couch.

"Listen, mami, do you know what me and my brother do?"

Keyshia innocently shook her head and looked confused.

He smiled and continued, "Me and my brother here are businessmen, and we do business with a lot of people and make lots of money." Keyshia's eyes lit up and she smiled. He smiled in return and said, "Come here, I want to show you something."

He helped her off the couch and took her into the bedroom. He cut on the light and Keyshia looked around the huge empty room. Inside was a large bed, larger than anything she'd ever seen. He gestured to her to have a seat, and she did. He smiled and went to the closet and pulled out a suitcase. He smiled at her again and threw the bag on the bed and began to unzip it. When he did, Keyshia's heart skipped a beat because inside it was nothing but stacks and stacks of cash. The man stood over the money proudly, sure that this little girl would give them anything they wanted now that she saw they were in the big leagues.

Just then, there was a knock on the door, and the moneybag

man closed the luggage instantly. He looked over his shoulder to his brother and nodded that it was okay. He put the bag back into the closet, escorted Keyshia back to the couch, and cut off the light.

"Who is it?" Tony asked as he looked through the peephole.

Clyde stood on the other side of the door with a stylish pair of sunglasses on, counting a wad of money. "It's me, my dude. Omar. Open up."

Tony opened the door, and in came Clyde, smiling. "Oh, shit, what up, Alito?"

He frowned and said, "I'm Tony."

Clyde continued counting his money and quickly said, "Oh, my bad, I always getting y'all niggas mixed up."

Tony locked the door and showed Clyde into the living room. When Tony saw how the young boy's pants sagged nearly down to the ground, he shook his head and wondered how these Americans could adopt such a foolish clownish look and think it looked fashionable. To him, they all looked the same. He dealt with hundreds of his kind on a daily basis and couldn't stand these types because they were so arrogant, but he tolerated them for business.

When Clyde reached the living room, he greeted the man standing at the table. Although he didn't know them from Adam, he greeted the man like he'd known him for a hundred years. "Oh, shit! What's up, Alito?" Clyde gave him a dap and a silly smile. He looked around and saw Keyshia, who quickly threw up two fingers, signaling to him that there were only two of them in the house. He turned back to Alito and continued to smile like a country boy who had a mouth full of gold teeth and shuffled the money around in his hand.

"Yo, nigga, business has been good, been good to a nigga. Nigga, yo, nigga Omar is out there clocking twenty-four seven on them niggas. Omar don't give a fuck about sleep, sleeping is for suckers. I'm tryna get this Diddy money, naa mean? And the bitches! Oh, my God, I got so many on reserve I'm gonna hafta get my own team. I'm 'bout this money, yo." Clyde busted a rhyme: "'I useta stand on the block, selling cooked-up rocks. . . .' That's that Kool G Rap shit, papi! He one of my top five rappers dead or alive. Biggie, number one, of course, that nigga Scarface, Ice Cube . . . but the old Cube, naa mean, my nigga G Rap, and . . . oh, shit, my nigga DMX! That nigga is gutter like me, kid. I like that old-school shit, when shit was real, naa mean? Jay-Z, my nigga Nas, holla!"

Tired of the young'un's voice and clowning, Alito cut him off. "Okay, okay, enough of dat shit. How much you need?"

Clyde faked like he was taken aback and frowned. "Damn, what the do, baby? Omar just tryna show y'all niggas some love."

Alito frowned again, tired of hearing his bullshit, and said, "Either tell me what the fuck you want or get the fuck out."

Keyshia watched his brother feel for the gun that he had in his back and slowly approach Clyde. Clyde looked at them and said seriously, "All right, man, let me get two ounces of powder. How's that?" Alito nodded to his brother, who went into the back room and closed the door behind him. They waited for what seemed like an eternity, and then Tony came out with a plastic bag full of white powder and handed it to his brother. Alito put it on the scale as Clyde watched it carefully until the scale registered the weight.

"Okay, two thousand dollars, papi."

Clyde looked at him as if he were insane. "Two thousand? Come on, man, an ounce is going for eight. How you gonna sell it to me at a grand an ounce?"

Alito handed the bag back to his brother and said, "Then go buy it for eight from somebody else!"

Clyde quickly backed down. "All right, man, I'll take it." Tony handed the bag back to his brother, and Clyde started counting out the money and put some on the table. "That's sixteen hundred." He reached in his back pocket and pulled out some more bills and laid them down, and then finally he reached in his jacket pocket and produced a gun. Tony's eyes lit up and he frantically reached for his, but he was too late.

Keyshia was already behind him with the gun to his head and said with an eerie wickedness, "If you move one motherfuckin' inch, I'm gonna blow your fuckin' brains out all over your brother! Now get that ass on the floor."

Tony spread his arms and instantly complied with her order. Clyde put his man down and pulled out the handcuffs and rope and cuffed their arms behind their back and tied both their legs together hog-style. He assured the men, "If any one of you motherfuckas even look like you gonna move, I'm gonna shoot the other one in the face before your eyes, you understand?" Both men nodded. Clyde quickly slapped them both and said, "Didn't I just tell y'all niggas not to move?"

Keyshia yelled to Clyde, "I'm going to get the money!" He nodded and kept a close eye on the men on the floor. Keyshia quickly turned on the lights and ran to the closet and pulled the suitcase into the living room and went back and searched the closet again. She saw two other bags and pulled them into the living room. She thought about going back again but remembered what Clyde had taught her—"Never be greedy"—and told Clyde it all was good. Clyde scooped up his buy money off the table and grabbed two of the suitcases. Keyshia took the third and they were out the door.

In the hallway, they kissed and went separate ways: Clyde up to the roof and Keyshia down the stairs. This was something they'd planned for safety purposes—they never knew who was watching traffic from an adjacent building.

When they met back at their designated rendezvous spot, Starbucks on 125th Street and Lenox, Keyshia was surprised to see that Clyde was already there, smiling as he watched her through the window. They sat together for half an hour, drinking coffee and laughing about the event that had just transpired. They took separate cabs and got home shortly after ten o'clock that evening. They couldn't wait to see how much loot they came off with. They threw each bag on the bed and smiled at the amount of pressure it took them to hoist it to the bed. Not a word was said. Keyshia stood frozen, palms sweating, when she looked up to Clyde, who nodded for her to have the honor of opening up the first bag. She reached for the zipper and unzipped it slowly. When she opened the flap, she gasped at the sight of all the money; there were thick stacks of cash. Their hands trembled as each reached inside and pulled out stacks of well-worn tens, twenties, and fifties. Keyshia jumped for joy and into Clyde's arms as he swung her around and kissed her on her lips. They regained their composure, realizing that they had two more bags to open, and again, Clyde gestured to Keyshia to open the other one. Just like the first, it had thick wads of cash, only this time it was all one-dollar bills. Finally, Clyde decided to open the last piece of luggage. He turned it toward him and looked at Keyshia, who was biting her nails. He slowly unzipped the heaviest of the three bags. When he flipped back the cover and revealed the contents, a large lump formed in both their throats.

"Oh shit!" was the only thing Clyde managed to say as he stared down at the drugs that had been stored in the luggage.

Wide-eyed, Keyshia stared at the pounds of wrapped-up drugs and muttered, "Clyde, is that what I think it is?"

Clyde didn't know what to say. He knew exactly what it was and wished that it weren't. Dazed and confused, he managed to say, "I think so." They both had the urge to sit down. Each went to a corner, sat, and simply stared at the bag in silence.

Out of all the drug spots they had to hit in Washington Heights, Clyde thought, they had to hit one of the safe houses. A safe house was one consolidated location that kept the drugs and money that is to be picked up or distributed to other locations in the neighborhood. The dealer could have over twenty locations, and all twenty would drop off money at the safe location and also pick up bundles of drugs to resell. That much money or drugs is usually not stored in the safe house for more than twenty-four hours at a time, so for whatever ungodly reason, and as fate had it, Keyshia and Clyde's timing was perfect. But under these circumstances, it could possibly turn around to haunt them, because this amount of money and drugs cannot just go down as missing or unnoticed. No, someone or some *two* would eventually have to answer for it.

Chapter 20

The grand total of the cash take from the Washington Heights job was eighty-seven thousand dollars, not including the drugs or the singles. After Clyde tested the product, it was determined that it was, in fact, cocaine—sixty-five pounds of pure uncut cocaine, to be exact, all finely wrapped in thick cellophane plastic wrap. Clyde sat up the rest of that night and kicked everything around in his head to see how he could uncomplicate the situation. It was bad enough that he was in debt to Black Sam and them, but to have the Dominicans after them also was bad!

Clyde knew he had to get the drugs out of the house. He had never associated himself with drugs because it was a dirty business, and he didn't feel comfortable with that amount of drugs around him. Second, and quite honestly, he didn't want the drugs around Keyshia because he knew that cocaine in particular was a cunning, insidious drug. He had seen many people change at rates unparalleled and do things so foul that it was as if they were no longer humans. He wasn't going to put Keyshia at risk like that in case she still wasn't strong enough to fight off the temptation. He thought about calling Sonny, then quickly ruled it out because Sonny wasn't a dealer and would only bring heat to them. So he made up his mind about where he could stash it at until he could find out what to do with it.

Clyde went to see Pops first thing the next morning as he was opening up the gate to the Ice House. As always, Pops was elated to see Clyde, and as always, Clyde didn't say a word, just took over the procedures of opening up the store, something he'd done for the last six years or so.

After everything was set up and ready for business, Clyde went over and retrieved the blue luggage bag. "Pops," he said, "I need to ask a favor from you." Pops chomped down on his cigar and looked at Clyde. Clyde turned away, unable to match his stare.

"What is it, Rocco?" asked Pops.

"I need something put away for me," Clyde said apprehensively.

Pops watched him closely and stared at the bag he held in his hand. He told Clyde to pull up a chair and have a seat next to him.

"Rocco," he said with a stern fatherly look, "many young boys worked for me right here in this shop. I seen 'em grow up before my eyes, plenty of 'em. Some of 'em went on to live a nice honest life." Pops didn't skip a beat and said, "But most of 'em fell to these here streets." He nodded over and over. "Some got into selling drugs, using drugs, turned into killers, in and out of jail, some never getting out again. But every time over the last forty years, I never got used to it when they family come tell me they done got themselves kilt." Pops paused as he reflected and then pulled out a cigar box from behind the counter and handed it to Clyde. Clyde took the box but was hesitant to open it.

"Go 'head, open it." Clyde opened it slowly, and inside it were plastic cards and funeral obituaries with pictures of young black males, some so old that they were turning yellow. Clyde could only stare at them, too afraid to ask who they were, knowing the answer. Pops didn't stop there but pulled out two more boxes and placed them on the table. Clyde was moved and kept his head down, fearing that Pops would see right through him.

"Rocco," said Pops, "from the time you came walking through them doors and asked for a job, I saw something special about you. You had a clean heart. But it was something different in your eyes." Clyde looked up momentarily as Pops continued, "A lot of pain. Pain that deep ain't suppose to wear on a young boy's eyes like yours, I thought. You hiding or fear something so deep, you afraid to face it, so you can't let go of it, boy. If you don't learn how to face it, you gon' change, and a lot of boys"—Pops pointed to the box—"changed, and you never know it, but they do. It's like you look up one day and they a brand-new person, like you never knew 'em. There's a saying, Rocco, and don't you never forget this: If you keep a cucumber marinating long enough, it will eventually turn into a pickle. The thing is, boy, you will never know when the change actually happens, you just look up one day and you just changed." Pops stared at Clyde hard and long. "You just remember, once you turn into a pickle, you can never, ever, go back to a cucumber again."

Clyde thought about what Pops said and thanked him. They talked for another hour or so and wound up laughing like the old days. Pops chose not to ask Clyde what was in the bag but told him that the bag would be safe and put away where nobody would be able to find it. Clyde thanked him and they parted with a big hug.

Later that evening, while Keyshia and Clyde were lying in bed, Clyde was silent for the better part of the night, thinking about everything that he and Pops had discussed that morning. "I spoke to Pops today," he said as he stared up at the ceiling. "He said something like, if a person don't face they fears, they would be stuck for the rest of their life."

Keyshia didn't know where all this was coming from. "What do you mean?"

Clyde thought for a moment. "You see how you act when you saw Omar and them niggas that did that shit to you?" He sat up and continued, "That was fear, baby. You could hardly breathe. You was walking around all these years with pain that you didn't even know existed, and when you saw them it all came out."

Keyshia nodded.

"Think about it. You told me yourself that after all that shit happened you changed, and Pops told me you never know when you change from a cucumber to a pickle, and once you a pickle, you could never go back to being a cucumber."

"So you saying that I'm scarred for life and that I'm a pickle now?" asked Keyshia.

"No, I'm saying that if you stay carrying the fear and not address it, it's a pretty good chance that you will turn into a pickle." Keyshia lay back in silence.

Suddenly Clyde turned toward her and asked, "Baby, can I ask you a question?"

Keyshia turned to face him and said, "Yeah, maybe."

He moved closer. "For real, yo, you got to be dead honest."

Keyshia knew he was serious and answered, "Yeah, but only if you answer the same question." He nodded.

Clyde paused as if he were thinking of a way to form the question. "What is the biggest fear that you have and are afraid to confront, and what would you do when you finally faced it?"

Keyshia was blown away by the depth of the question and took a moment to think about it. Suddenly, she looked at Clyde and asked with a sneer on her lips, "Do you really want to know?"

Clyde sat up and nodded. Keyshia stared at the wall and spoke slowly and measuredly. "I'd go down south and see the man who raped me and took my baby. I'd wait and hunt him down, and at the right moment I'd go to his house, the same place he used to carry me, ring the doorbell, and wait for him to answer." Keyshia's jaw began to grind. "Then I'd look him right in the eye until he remembered who I was, and when he do I's gonna shoot his fuckin' dick off!"

Clyde asked, "You serious?"

Without blinking, Keyshia said, "As a heart attack!"

Clyde lay back down, put his hands behind his head, and stared at the ceiling.

"What about you?" Keyshia asked.

"I ain't got none," Clyde answered casually.

"Come on, Clyde, that's not fair. I told you one, now you got to tell me," Keyshia pleaded, and than flipped it on him. "Clyde, did you see how you reacted when I told you that those was the guys that raped me?" Clyde just stared at her. "The shit that went down with Sugar, you put a shotgun up his ass, Clyde." Clyde put his head down. "It's like you unable to see somebody who's weak get taken advantage of, it's a reason for that. It's a reason why you feel you have to rescue somebody. Could it be that you trying to make up for somebody you couldn't save, Clyde?"

Clyde was stunned. He turned his back and paused before he started speaking.

"Over the years, whenever I went to see my mother in the hospital, I would get so depressed. She just sits there and stares like she saw something so horrible that she can't snap out of it." Keyshia slid over to him and slowly rubbed his shoulder. "Every time I go, I just wish I would walk in and she is cured, show a smile, say something, anything. But like clockwork she's sitting in the same old chair, staring at a wall or something." He turned and looked at Keyshia and said, "I leave out of that hospital each and every time angry at the world and want to hurt something." He fought the wells of tears in his eyes. "I don't even know how it feels to be comforted by my own mother." He turned toward Keyshia and lost the battle of holding back his tears. "All I want her to do is hug me and tell me everything gonna be all right now."

Keyshia instantly felt her man's pain and said, "Oh, Clyde," and hugged him and kissed his tears gently.

Clyde sneered as he talked about his father. "That mother-fucka took everything from me, and I hate him for it. You hear me: I hate him." He wiped the remaining tears from his eyes and said, "Yeah, I have a fear. A fear of what I'm gonna do to him when I see him. I just want to look him in the eye and ask that heartless bas-tard why, why would he do that to my innocent mother?" He looked at Keyshia. "Why would he do that to her, Keysh? Why would he want to do that?" he repeated over and over.

Keyshia embraced him and said, "I don't know, baby. I don't know, but it gonna be all right, you'll see."

Clyde pulled out of her arms and said with a weak smile, "Yeah, it's gonna be all right, 'cause I been thinking over the years of paying this nigga a visit, right, and just look him in his eyes, then asking the bastard, Why? Why he do it?" Clyde shook his head and continued, "Then, then I'm gonna give him a choice to make things right." He nodded again. "I'm gonna sneak in a cyanide pill and slip it to him without saying a word and tell him either he could die now or wait until he get out and die later at the hand of his own son." Keyshia stared at Clyde; she realized that his pain was much deeper than she had known. Flames were in his eyes when he looked at Keyshia. "You right, I got to own up to this fear, baby; we both do."

Keyshia nodded and said, "You wanna?"

Clyde nodded back. "Let's do this shit, baby. Let's go down

south and handle yo' business and come with me to handle mine!"

They both began to smile, and Keyshia said, "No pickles here!"

Clyde smiled back and agreed, "No pickles here, either. After we take care of everything with Black Sam, we head out of town to do our thing, bet!" he said with an extended fist.

Keyshia smiled and looked at his fist, tapped it, and said, "Bet!"

Chapter 21

Keyshia and Clyde were on day six and seemingly on target for obtaining all of Black Sam's money. They had one hundred and twenty-seven thousand dollars and were feeling pretty good about how things were going. Not one shot had been fired, and most important, no one—including themselves—got hurt. But Clyde still didn't know what to do about the sixty pounds of drugs or the situation with Omar and his crew. He deliberately dropped Omar's name during the drug heist, but he wanted the other three in Omar's crew as well. He began to speed up the process so he and Keyshia could head out of town.

Clyde retrieved the package from Pops and then went uptown to the bodegas in Washington Heights to purchase thousands of bottles and caps, which are traditionally used to seal up drugs. Clyde bought the large quantities to ensure the word got out.

Packing the powdered cocaine inside all the bottles wasn't an easy task. It took them nearly six hours. When they finished, well after midnight, they packed up the product and headed to Harlem. When they pulled up to 116th Street and Eighth, the fiends were out lurking and hustling, trying to find the means for their next hit.

Clyde parked on the downtown side between 117th and 116th and said to Keyshia, "Just chill here and I be back in a second."

Keyshia nodded and said, "Be careful." Clyde nodded and removed a black plastic bag and left.

As soon as he got to the corner, several fiends pitched at him, "What's homey, I know where that butter shit is at."

"Yo, they got them fat nickels around the corner."

Clyde said smoothly, "Naw, I'm good, but check this out, I got some samples I'm giving out, and I want you to spread the word."

The two fiends stood there salivating, not believing their ears. "You giving out samples, bro?" Clyde reached in the bag and pulled out a handful. The men's eyes bulged at the size of the bottles, and they instantly had their hands out.

Clyde said, "Now what I want you two to do is hand these out. I'm gonna be standing right here watching you, and tell everybody this . . . this is Omar's shit from a Hundred and Twelfth in front of the hotel." The men nodded rapidly. "You got that? Omar from a Hundred and Twelfth will be selling these as dimes of powder." Clyde lifted one up and they stared at the size of it as sweat formed on their foreheads. He reached in the bag and gave a fistful to each man.

"When y'all two finish, I'll give y'all twenty bottles apiece." They nodded. "Now hand them out and come back to me when you run out. Remember, Omar from a Hundred and Twelfth

Street." They nodded and went right to work. In a matter of seconds a crowd so large had formed that Clyde had to hire more fiends to keep them from causing a riot. "Samples, y'all. Omar samples from a Hundred and Twelfth in front of the hotel, y'all!" screamed the distributors.

Since Omar and his partners had two spots, one on 112th and one on 129th and Lenox, Keyshia and Clyde drove over and did the same thing on 127th and Lenox Avenue, handed out bags and bags of cocaine there also. "Samples, samples, y'all!" screamed the fiends. "This is Omar shit from a Hundred and Twenty-ninth, y'all!" They screamed this over and over until the word spread throughout Harlem that a dude named Omar would be selling pure cocaine the size of Now and Laters for only ten dollars.

Just like usual, Omar and his crew knocked off at six-thirty and headed over to the IHOP on 135th Street to have breakfast and discuss business. Keyshia and Clyde watched both cars pull up minutes apart and the crew enter the restaurant. Clyde and Keyshia made their move with the Slim Jim, black gloves, and opportunity to make things right. Keyshia and Clyde hadn't had time to sleep and went into the next phase to ensure everything worked according to plan.

It was three-thirty, and kids were coming home from school when Clyde stepped out of the car in front of the Grant projects on 125th Street and Amsterdam Avenue with a black plastic bag in his hand. He surveyed the area and reached in the bag and yelled at the top of his lungs, "Free money!" and tossed a handful of single dollar bills high in the air. He immediately caused a frenzy as children and old people alike were on their knees scrambling for the money. "Compliments of Omar!" Clyde repeated over and over again as he emptied the shopping bag.

He went to several other projects in Harlem and did the same thing. Then he and Keyshia sat back and waited to see what that cat would bring in.

Word around Harlem about a dude named Omar spread fast. It spread even faster in Washington Heights as word got back to two brothers, Tony and Alito, that a young Negrito by the name of Omar was selling pure coca in his neighborhood dirt cheap and that he brought Christmas early to people in the projects by giving away money—his money—like it was going out of style. They knew what had to be done and called up several of their associates to rally up a hit squad. Someone had to answer for the robbery, and all would be settled that night!

When Omar's people showed up on 112th Street, they saw a mob of fiends lurking around as if they were expecting government cheese or something. And when one of them spotted the boys' SUV, they all began to rush toward it.

"Yo, what the fuck is going on?" asked one of the boys.

Frowning, the other said, "Fuck if I know. It looks like they all waiting for us to set up."

"Goddamn, yo, they must be a shortage or some shit. Park this motherfucka and let's get this money, nigga."

When they got out of the truck, they were swamped by hundreds of fiends pulling at them and holding out money in their hand.

"Yo, calm the fuck down!" screamed one of the dealers. "Y'all niggas are gonna get served, so make a line! Make a fuckin' line!" When he served the first man in line, he asked, "How many?"

"Gimme two." The boy handed him two dimes of crack, and the fiend protested, "Naw, I want the powder."

The boy sneered at him and said, "We don't sell powder, only cook-up."

"No," said the fiend, "I want that shit y'all was giving out last night!"

Growing agitated, the young dealer said, "Get the fuck out of here, man, this the same shit from last night."

The fiends in the back began to protest also. "Bullshit, your man Omar was giving out samples last night on a Hundred and Sixteenth and said that's what y'all be selling from now on."

"Yo, I don't know what the fuck you talking 'bout, so either fuck with these dimes or step the fuck off." The fiends began to grumble and walked off. Both teens watched them walk away cursing under their breath.

"Yo, give Omar a call and tell him 'bout this shit." The boy pulled out his cell phone and dialed Omar.

After a couple of rings, Omar picked up. "Yo?"

"Yo, O, this Rodney, yo. Some of these fiends is saying you gave out some samples of those things last night and came for that shit today."

"Yo," said Omar, "the same shit is happening 'round here. Mad niggas rushed me talking 'bout some powder shit."

"So, what's up? What you gonna do?"

Omar scratched his head and said, "I don't know. Shit don't sound right." He paused and looked at his man arguing with the fiends and said, "Yo, pack that shit in for the night and meet up at the spot on one three five."

Rodney nodded. "Awright, I see you there in fifteen minutes."

Rodney nodded to his partner and headed toward the SUV and drove off. Minutes later, Omar hopped into his truck and headed toward their meet-up spot also. Unknown to both parties, they were being watched closely and followed. Both trucks pulled up curbside and parked illegally right in front of the IHOP.

Tony, Alito, and the two other men inside the car watched the four men exit their trucks. When they spotted Omar, who had his pants sagging to the ground, their eyes lit up and they pointed quickly.

"*Mira*, that him, that him!" said Tony. Alito nodded. "Yeah, that's that motherfucka!"

They all watched as the four young black boys gave one another five and entered the restaurant. Tony asked his brother, "So what we gonna do, wait till they come out or hit them now?"

Alito stared at all the parked police vehicles in the block and said, "No, not here, de precinct is right in de block. We wait." He nodded. "Call Paco, and tell him where to park in case both cars split up again." Tony got on the phone and called his cousin, who was parked directly behind them.

Keyshia and Clyde were parked one block away and watched as their plans unfolded before their eyes.

While the four boys discussed the events that had happened earlier, one of the boys noticed that a squad car had pulled up in back of their illegally parked vehicles.

"Yo, police is giving us a ticket." Rodney and his partner jumped up and were heading out to the truck to move it before they got a ticket.

"Yo," Omar yelled to them, "y'all dirty?" Both men nodded no. "What about the inside?"

Rodney said, "Naw, we left everything in the mailbox in the building." Omar nodded and they ran outside to catch the police before they wrote the ticket.

Omar looked at his partner and said, "Here." He tossed him the keys to the truck and said, "I ain't got my license on me, drive it around the corner and I'll order the food." The boy nodded and left.

Omar watched his boys argue with the police, who still, despite the boys getting there before they wrote the ticket, continued writing, not giving them a break. He watched Rodney, who he knew despised police, continue to argue with them.

Tony and Alito watched another police car pull up behind the boy's truck, and Tony asked, "What the hell is going on?"

Alito shook his head. "I don't know."

"What the fuck is wrong with this nigga, just take the ticket," Omar said to himself.

Seconds later, he watched another police car roll up and get out and assist the two officers, and before he knew it, he watched his boys be ordered to put their hands on the car as their names and driver's licenses were run for warrants. Omar closed his eyes and shook his head. When he saw the officers who checked their names in the computer order the other officers to handcuff them, he knew that he would have to be down in court for the rest of the night bailing them out. The police pulled stacks and stacks of money out of each man's pocket and laid them on top of the patrol car.

Moments later, Omar watched as another police car came by and stopped—it was the K-9 unit.

"No," Clyde said excitedly as he watched the dog hop out of the patrol car. "This can't be happening, it's too perfect."

Keyshia assured him, "Yes, it is!"

Omar watched as the dog sniffed inside the vehicle. Omar wasn't worried that they would find anything because they never rode around with drugs in the vehicle. But then the dog started barking loudly and the police opened the rear door of the vehicle and stripped everything out of the trunk. Omar's jaw nearly hit the floor as he watched the officers pull out a thick cellophane-wrapped product that looked like bundles of cocaine.

Alito took off his glasses and strained his eyes, unable to believe what was happening. "What the . . ."

Tony gritted his teeth and said, "They had our coca right in the fucking trunk!"

Omar watched them go to the trunk of the second vehicle and pull out several more bundles of dope from his vehicle. Omar panicked, looked for the back exit, and ran through the kitchen and out the back door.

Alito was too livid to watch any further. "Let's get the fuck out of here!"

Tony quickly said, "But this Omar is still in de store."

Alito took a deep breath and asked, "Do you see him at the table anymore? He fucking took off out de back exit or something." He took a hit of coke up his nose, sniffed loudly, and said, "We catch Omar, soon. Real soon."

Chapter 22

After having been on their feet over twenty-four hours, Keyshia and Clyde were in a deep sleep when they heard pounding on the door.

Clyde forced himself out of bed and walked to the door and yelled, "Who is it?"

"Wake your ass up and open the door!" It was Sonny, and he was the last person Clyde wanted to see at that point.

"It's me, too, Clyde. You ready to go see Mama?" Clyde closed his eyes because he'd totally forgotten about his monthly visit to see his mother. He opened the door and peered out.

Sonny instantly threw up his hands and said, "I told you this pussy-whipped-ass dude wouldn't be ready."

Clyde wanted to protest but didn't have the strength to argue with Sonny at that moment. "Y'all can come in. I'll be ready in a second."

Sonny declined and said, "Man, I'll be outside. Just hurry the fuck up!"

Ceasar decided to enter, and Clyde led him to the living room. Keyshia peeked out the bedroom and waved to Ceasar. He smiled and waved back to her and asked, "Keyshia, you gonna come with us so you can meet our mother?"

Keyshia looked at Clyde, who hadn't given it much thought. He asked her, "You wanna go?" Keyshia was flattered and said she would love to.

Keyshia and Clyde took a shower together to save some time and were dressed in a matter of minutes and out the door. When Sonny saw the three together, it was obvious that he was displeased with Keyshia being there. Ceasar picked up on it and said quickly as they piled into his vehicle, "Sonny, don't do that. She is Clyde's girl, and you respect her like she family, you hear me?"

Sonny gave him a dumb look and said, "I ain't even said nothing."

"You better say hello."

Sonny snickered, but he followed his big brother's command, gave Keyshia a slight smile, and said, "Hello . . ."

Ceasar quickly snapped, "Keyshia!"

Sonny followed suit and repeated, "Hello, Keyshia."

"Hi, Sonny," Keyshia said meekly.

Happy, Ceasar said, "Now let's go see Mama!"

•   •   •   •

When they arrived at the nursing home, Keyshia was nervous. Many girls who meet their boyfriend's mother for the first time have a good reason to feel butterflies in their stomach because their worst fear is that the mother won't approve of them. In Keyshia's case, Clyde's mother wouldn't know what or who she was anyway. But it was still a challenging event. When they walked into her room, she was sitting in a chair staring out the window just like Clyde had told her she would be. If you didn't know her, you would expect her to turn around any second and greet her visitors, but she didn't even flinch. She had long, luxurious black hair flowing down her back with beautiful gray streaks right in the middle. Her skin was almond brown and seemed untouched by age except for the slight wrinkles forming at her deep eyes.

Ceasar and Sonny walked directly up to her and gave her a kiss on the cheek and said, "Hi, Mama." They looked at Clyde and Keyshia, who both walked over to her and said hello and planted a soft kiss on her face. She barely moved.

At a closer view, Keyshia could see the hideous scar right under her right eye on the cheekbone where the boys' father must have shot her. Keyshia also noticed that Clyde would barely look at his mother. She squeezed his hand gently, and he smiled lightly.

They took a seat in the corner of the room and watched Ceasar carry on a conversation with his mother like she could understand him. She then watched Sonny pull up a chair next to her and do the same thing. After a few minutes, he got up and gestured to Clyde to talk to her. Keyshia could tell that Clyde didn't want to do it, but he did it to make everybody happy.

When he sat down, Ceasar came over and sat next to Keyshia, smiled, and said, "They say that when you talk to a person in an altered or comatose state, they can understand everything you say. They just can't respond, so we been doing this for years to let her know that she is loved and not alone." They watched Clyde say a few words in her ear and get up and walk toward them. Ceasar looked at Keyshia, smiled, and said, "Why don't you go over there and introduce yourself."

Keyshia looked at Ceasar and blushed. "I can't do that, she don't know me."

Ceasar said reassuringly, "Girl, you are family. Now go over there and introduce yourself to your future mother-in-law." He smiled at her and took her hand and led her over.

Before Keyshia sat down, she looked at all the brothers' faces. Even Sonny seemed not to mind her sitting down to have a conversation. She sat down slowly and didn't know what to say. Ceasar told her, "Just tell her how you feel about her son." She nodded and scooted the chair to face her. She was nervous but spoke real low as she introduced herself.

"Hi, Mrs. Barker, I's name is Keyshia . . ." She closed her eyes and apologized for speaking broken English. "I mean, my name is Keyshia, and I . . . I'm your son Clyde's girlfriend."

Keyshia paused and watched as the brothers left them alone. Still a little nervous, she continued, "You don't have to worry about me hurting your son, I would never do that." She put her head down and said, "I know you his mammy and all and want ya son to always be happy, and I can do that, 'cause I really, really love that boy and would never do nothing ta hurt him. He tells me he love me back, and ma'am, I believe him, that's why I love him so." Keyshia explained, "I's gonna be truthful with you, ma'am: We got ourself in some trouble, but we almost out of it. After we do what we got ta do, we plan on going back ta school and live right. I'm gonna guarantee you that. He tells me the other day how much he love you and wish you could hug him. I's tell him that one day you will come 'round and give him plenty hugs. So until then, I make sho' yo' son get plenty nuff of them hugs till you ready to give him some on your own." She smiled and thought of something Clyde had said. "Your son taught me that the eyes don't lie, so I want you to see my eyes when I say this." She lifted Mrs. Barker's head and looked her straight in the eyes and said with great intensity, "I love him so much, ma'am, that I would die fo' him!" As she stared at Clyde's mother, she could have sworn that she saw her nod her head like she was acknowledging her. She gave her a kiss on the cheek. Clyde walked back into the room and sat next to Keyshia as they all held one another's hands.

Outside the room, Ceasar and Sonny were in an intense argument. Sonny told Ceasar how much money Clyde owed Black Sam. Ceasar flipped out. "How in the world did you expect him to come up with that type of money, Sonny? Have you lost your mind?"

Sonny countered, "I offered to take care of it, but he refused and said that he could come up with the money. What else do you want from me, Ceasar?"

Ceasar said, "And you believed him? You believed he could come up with that kind of money without putting himself in harm's way?"

Sonny shrugged. "Clyde ain't no li'l boy no more. And he ain't as innocent as you think."

Ceasar rolled his eyes and said, "What do you mean by that?"

"You know exactly what I mean." Sonny gave him a knowing smile. "That li'l boy murked a nigga, that's what I'm saying!"

Ceasar turned his back on Sonny, refusing to accept the truth. "Well," he said, "the man probably had it coming. I know Clyde—he ain't gonna just go around"—he lowered his voice—"killing people."

Sonny agreed, "Yeah, you right. But the fact of the matter is he's a grown-ass man. I offered my help, he declined. Now what was I to do, C?"

Ceasar said, "Sonny, please, for me, make sure you see that nothing happens to Clyde." Ceasar suddenly began to get choked up. "I won't be able to handle it if something happens to him, okay?" Never wanting to see his brother in pain, Sonny agreed.

After they kissed their mother good-bye, Ceasar suggested that they all go out to dinner at Amy Ruth's or Manna's in Harlem. Everyone agreed except Sonny, who had something to take care of, but he offered to drop them all off.

When they exited Sonny's truck, Sonny called out to Clyde, "Yo, Clyde, come here."

Clyde walked over to Sonny. "What's up?"

Sonny countered, "Fuck you mean, what's up? How you doing with that thing?"

Clyde nodded and said, "I'm doing all right."

Sonny smiled. "How much you got so far?"

Clyde, never the one to tell lefty what righty was doing, said, "Don't worry about it, as long as I come up with the money, right?"

Sonny looked at Clyde, said, "Yeah, right," and took off.

When they finished eating and the check came, Ceasar reached for the bill and offered to pay, but Clyde wouldn't allow it. "No, Clyde, I got this."

Clyde insisted, "No, Ceasar, for real, I got it."

Ceasar simply said, "What you need to do is hold on to every dime to come up with that hundred and fifty thousand."

Clyde was surprised that he knew how much he owed. "Who told you, Sonny?"

"Who do you think?" Clyde sat back in the chair and frowned. "What?" Ceasar said. "I shouldn't know what's going on with my li'l brother's life?" He looked around and asked, "Clyde, do you really expect to come up with that kind of money?"

Clyde just stared at him and said, "Can I be honest with you without you getting upset?"

Ceasar nodded. "Yes."

Clyde was not satisfied. "No, say, 'I promise I won't get pissed.'"

Ceasar turned his head and took a breath. "I promise I won't get pissed."

Clyde smiled and edged closer. "We already came up with a hundred and thirty thousand."

Ceasar gasped and said rather loudly, "A hundred and thirty thousand!" He caught himself and looked around for a moment, then continued in a lower tone, "Clyde, where the hell you get that kind of money from?"

Clyde shrugged. "We earned it."

Ceasar's voice began to rise. "Who's 'we,' Clyde?"

Clyde reminded him, "You said you wouldn't get mad, C."

Ceasar shook his head and repeated more calmly, "Who is 'we'?"

"Me and Keyshia."

Ceasar looked at Keyshia, who had her head down, embarrassed. "Oh, Lord." Clyde looked toward Keyshia and gave her a quick smile. Ceasar turned and stared at the wall to gather his thoughts, then said, "Okay, I'm not gonna ask no more questions. Now if you really have the money, that means you need only twenty thousand dollars more to pay that Sam guy back, right?" Clyde nodded. "So here is what I'm gonna do, Clyde, I'm gonna give you the rest of the money." Clyde was taken aback for a moment. He had no clue his brother had that kind of money available. "But you got to promise me, both of y'all, promise me . . ." He looked at them like an older brother should and said, "That y'all gonna stop doing what y'all doing from this moment on and stay out of trouble, okay?" Clyde looked at Keyshia, and they both agreed with a smile.

Satisfied, Ceasar looked at them both and shook his head. "You two were definitely meant to be together—Bonnie and Clyde, that's what y'all are."

Clyde confided in his brother, "Listen, Ceasar, me and Keyshia will be going out of town soon, so can you do me a favor?"

"Yeah, both of y'all need a vacation, I'm sure. Where are y'all going?"

Keyshia answered, "Oh, we going down south and visit my family in South Carolina."

Looking at Clyde closely, he asked, "Where else?" Keyshia looked at Ceasar and knew he knew something and didn't want to lie to him and remained silent.

"Clyde," Ceasar repeated, "you know I know you. Any time you freeze up like that, it means you're holding back something. Where are you going?"

Clyde lifted his head and said, "I'm going upstate." He paused and then said, "to see our father."

Ceasar was taken by surprise and was speechless momentarily. He recouped quickly, deciding not to touch the subject. He cleared his throat and asked, "What is the favor?"

Clyde edged closer and said, "I need you to hold the money until I get back."

Ceasar nodded and said, "I can put it in a safe deposit box on my job." Clyde nodded.

Chapter 23

That same evening, Keyshia and Clyde packed for their weeklong journey. They still had over ten thousand dollars in reserve, which would take care of all their expenses.

They decided to hit upstate to visit Clyde's father first and then head down south to see Keyshia's people. Clyde contacted a childhood friend of his named Miguel to help him rent a car.

Miguel had been Clyde's best friend since the seventh grade. He was a pretty boy who was half black and half Puerto Rican, with deep curly hair, and because the girls liked him, other boys would hate him and want to fight him. Though he fought back, he would always lose because of the number of guys that pounced upon him. One day during a fight or slaughter, he got help from an unlikely source, a quiet young boy named Clyde, and from that day on, Miguel no longer got jumped on because he now had backup, and they'd been best friends ever since. Clyde even got him a job working with Pops, but the work was too hard for Miguel and he didn't last two days before he quit. Miguel wasn't suited for hard work, he was more of a people person, and as they got older everybody knew and liked him. If anybody needed anything, "Mike" could make it happen. He always knew a friend who knew a friend to get the job done. Other than Sonny and Keyshia, Mike was the only person in the world who knew what Clyde did and was capable of doing. They were closer than friends, they were brothers indeed.

Before they left for the trip, each had to make one stop.

It seemed like a lifetime had passed since Keyshia last walked into the Wagner projects. When she got to her former building, she pulled the door and was surprised that it was locked and finally fixed for a change. Since she didn't have any keys, she waited until someone exited the building, which wasn't too long. When she stepped into the elevator, she smelled the stale acrid scent of dried urine. There was a time when she wouldn't have flinched from the smell, but she had been away for a few weeks and the smell was nauseating. She was relieved when she stepped off the elevator and took a deep breath to clear her lungs. She paused as she gave herself the once-over, ensuring that nothing was out of place, running her fingers through her long braids. Today, she wore an expensive blue Donna Karan suit, with a matching pair of high-heeled shoes, giving her a conservative, professional look. Above all, she wanted to prove to her aunt Ninny that she could survive without her, and most important, that she wasn't the greasy, grimy bitch that she always called her.

Her body tensed as she stood at the door. This was the moment she'd dreamed about ever since she was younger: how she
would stand before her aunt a success and rub it in her face. She
had the envelope full of money to give to her little cousins in her
Fendi purse so she could watch their faces and tell them to buy
whatever they wanted. Yes, she had something to prove, she
thought. After all the horrible things she was called, after how she
was told she would turn out, how she was told that nobody would
want her because she was molested as a child—it was only right
that she throw it in her aunt's face and prove her wrong. Today
was the day of reckoning. She could hear movement inside the
apartment—the boys playing, the scent of dinner being cooked—
perfect timing, she thought.

Keyshia lifted her hand to knock on the door, but she
stopped. She raised her hand again, same thing. She put her head
down and reached inside and pulled out the two envelopes that
had her cousins' names on them and slid them under the door.
She stood up, smiled, and walked away.

Still unable to break old habits, Clyde listened for movement in
the apartment before he entered, and as always, the house was as
quite as a mouse. He walked to the kitchen and saw nobody was
there. He walked toward Martha's room and tapped on the door
before he opened it and saw no one was home. He breathed a sigh
of relief because he was happy that he didn't have to go through
the motions with Martha and could just put the money he had for
her on the kitchen table and leave.

Clyde decided to go into his old room just to see if everything
was still intact—it was. He sat on the end of the bed, and for some
reason his former sanctuary seemed much smaller. He surveyed
the room and smiled as he looked at the torn-out sports figures
that he had taped all over the walls of his room. He looked on his

dresser and saw a picture of him and his two brothers when they were much younger, smiling widely as they wore their Sunday-best outfits; they all seemed so close and innocent back then. Then he picked up another photo of his mother smiling bright and wide in her teenage years. She was so beautiful, Clyde thought. For a boy to live a lifetime and never know the feeling of a mother's love was unnatural. Unless proper attention is given, the boy's heart would turn into a stone. He'd never learn how to feel, he'd never learn how to give love, and he'd never learn how to receive love. He would always find that true love was elusive and hard to find and never realize that he need look in only one place—the place he never searched: within himself. Until he'd met Keyshia, Clyde never had a girlfriend, no one that he was even remotely interested in. But he was fortunate; he'd found a kindred soul. A one-in-a-billion match—someone who not only loved him for who he was, but someone whom he could actually love back. When something like that happens, there's no power on this great earth that can separate them. Not only would they live for each other, they would die for each other!

Clyde fell asleep cradling his mother's picture in his hand until Martha woke him.

"Clyde!" Martha said as she towered over him. Clyde popped up and blinked his eyes rapidly, not sure where he was at. "Clyde, baby, you home."

Clyde stared up at Martha, realizing where he was, and stood up, kind of embarrassed that he'd fallen asleep. "I'm . . . I'm sorry," he said as he straightened out the wrinkles on the bed.

"Boy, you ain't got nothing to be sorry about," Martha cooed. "This is your home."

Clyde gave her a light smile and nodded. They walked out of the room, and she quickly started complaining about money.

"I'm just coming back from the supermarket, and I could barely afford to buy something 'cause everything so expensive."

When they got to the kitchen, Clyde helped her unpack the groceries and she started digging into him.

"I ain't seen you in God knows when, Clyde. Why you just up and left your auntie? You know I'm concerned about you," she chided.

Clyde shrugged. "I don't know. I been kinda busy lately."

"Too busy to even call to let me know how you doing? And who's this girl I hear you running 'round with? You ain't been with them no-good girls. Why start now? And what's this stuff about you getting yourself in trouble? Boy, you ain't doing right." Her mouth was running a hundred miles an hour, and Clyde grew impatient. He couldn't stand when she threw the guilt trip on him, and he decided to cut it short.

"I'm sorry, Martha, but I'm in a little rush. I'm going out of town for a few days, and I promise I'll talk to you when I come back." He reached in his pocket and pulled out a roll of money and handed it to her. "That's a thousand dollars; I wanted to make sure you was okay."

Martha's frown instantly turned into a smile. She gave him a hug and thanked him several times. "You know, you looking more and more like you mother every day. Yep, I remember it was just like yesterday, me and your mother dressing up for the weekend like twins." She smiled and said, "See, nobody on earth could love your mother more than me, and nobody ever will, that's for sure. That's why I do what I did for you boys." Clyde had heard this a million times before.

She walked him to the door and said, "Sonny comes 'round here all the time to check on me. Make sure I'm okay, to see if I need anything. You know they done took you off my budget and I ain't got much coming in?" Clyde wanted to tell her to get a job and stop complaining like Ceasar had said, but he could never tell her that, he thought. But it was the truth. It seemed that she thought they were in debt to her for life since she took them in as

kids. But she'd received a good penny from the state and government to keep them, so they should be even like Ceasar always
said. Martha was just plain greedy and strived to make them feel
guilty every chance she got.

At the door, Clyde turned around to give her a quick kiss and
bounce, but she stopped him. "Clyde, now you know it ain't none
of my business, but I talks to Sonny and he said that he need your
help with something, but you ain't willing to help him out." Clyde
was surprised to hear her mention this and frowned.

"Now you know I stay out of y'all business on what you do, but
you should really think about helping him 'cause he your brother
and you gots to stand by each other." Clyde didn't say a word and
just listened. Did she know exactly what Sonny had in mind? He
was sure she knew what Sonny did for a living because of the
amount of times she'd helped and defended Sonny over the years
whenever he got himself in trouble.

"Just think about what I said, okay? And I see you when you
get back."

Clyde nodded and backed out of the door with a bad taste in
his mouth.

The last place he stopped off before he went home was to see
a brother from the neighborhood by the name of Jimmy. Jimmy
was a local guy who practiced holistic healing with herbs and vit-
amins. People sometimes called him the mad scientist because
he concocted various capsules that you could take for whatever
ailed you. As always, Clyde caught him on 127th Street and Lenox
at the outdoor flea market next to Sylvia's restaurant in the lot
owned by Mr. Smalls, who sold hats, T-shirts, and other items to
the tourists who came by the busload to eat in the restaurant.

"Jimmy!" Clyde yelled, and waved for him to come over. He
was a smooth cat who seemed not to rush for anyone. He ac-
knowledged Clyde with a nod and continued with his conversation.

He strutted over five minutes later and greeted Clyde like a lost brother with a hug and a bright smile. "Brother Clyde, long time no see."

Clyde smiled and said, "Good to see you, Jimmy."

"So what can I do for you, young brother?"

"Well, I need something special today and maybe you can help me."

Jimmy smiled and said, "You know I got what you need. Lay it on me."

"I need some pills that would take you out."

"Sleeping pills?" He frowned.

"The permanent ones, and I need them in an hour."

Chapter 24

The notorious Sing Sing state prison in Ossining, New York, was huge and intimidating. Clyde's mouth went dry and his palms started to sweat as he and Keyshia waited for his name to be called for his twenty-five-minute visit. Keyshia held him close to absorb as much of his pain as she could, for her man would soon come face-to-face with a man he knew so little about yet who had caused him so much pain.

Finally, he heard his name called: "Clyde Barker."

Electricity shot through his body as he stood to face the inevitable. Keyshia stood up with him and grasped his hand. She looked him in the eye and assured him that everything would be all right and that she would be there for him upon his return. They hugged each other as if their lives depended on it, until Clyde finally had the courage to break free, nodding to Keyshia that he was okay.

Inside the bowels of Sing Sing, Clyde sat and waited at the table and stool that was in the visitor/inmate area. Sweat drenched his body and clothes. Then he heard the echo of an opening mechanical door, causing excitement among the visitors as they stood up from their metal chairs, peeking and peering about. Easy, he continued to repeat to himself, be easy. Suddenly, the first line of men appeared, all looking around the room and beaming. All the men wore the standard prisoner visiting garb of bright orange jumpsuits and shower flip-flops. Each guard pointed to where each prisoner's guest was sitting. One by one, the prisoners rushed over to their loved ones in joyous fashion, and all hugged and kissed as if they hadn't seen one another in years. Some hadn't, Clyde thought, but he was sure that this prisoner would not be greeted as such.

Clyde searched each face, unsure of how his father looked, until one face appeared awfully familiar—the spitting image of his oldest brother, Ceasar. Clyde's heart skipped when the CO pointed over in his direction. Tunnel vision set in as he watched this man walk toward him. Clyde stood up, not wanting the man to think for a second that he was superior to him. Clyde's insides were a raging storm; he wanted to scream, yell, curse, but he couldn't, so he braced himself for anything. The man had all the elements of a Barker male: smooth, almond brown skin, muscular broad shoulders, thick, powerfully sculptured arms, and deep, discerning eyes. Face-to-face now, Clyde stood in equal height to this man who was obviously his father.

Neither knew what to say or what to do. Finally, the senior Barker managed to utter the first uncomfortable words: "Hello, son."

Clyde refused to answer him, or maybe he was unable to respond. His father seemed to understand and sat down. Clyde remained standing and eyed this man who was his father, who tried to make small talk and smiled. "I always thought that Ceasar or Sonny would be the first one to visit me, but I'm just as happy to see you, Clyde." He beamed in admiration at his last-born son. "You know, your mama named you after her grandfather, who was once a great blues singer from New Orleans, Clyde Waters." He lost his bluster when he saw that Clyde was not the least interested in his banal short talk. He knew Clyde was there for answers.

"I know how hard this must be for you, son, and I understand if you don't know what to say." The senior Barker rubbed his hand over his eyes and continued, "Whatever the reason you came here to see me, it took a lot of courage to do so, so what I'll do is relieve you of having to ask certain things which I'm sure you may want answered." Clyde remained silent and allowed him to speak. "I knew this day would someday come, and I thought about it a million times, and even to this point I still don't know what to say." He turned and stared off for a moment to gather his thoughts. "Son, I love your mother more than life itself and would never, ever lay one finger on her pretty head." Clyde turned toward him and gave him an icy glare. "We never even had so much as a argument, much less me putting my hands on her. Your mother was strong, strongest woman I've ever known, and she would never tolerate any form of abuse on her or you boys." His father's face flushed. "The day everything happened, I was so stoned and drunk that I honestly don't remember anything about that evening. The only thing I remember was making love to your mother, and the next thing you know I hear screaming and woke up with my gun in my hand and your—" He couldn't finish and became too emotionally overwhelmed to go on. Clyde sat down finally and watched his body language. He was at least happy to know that he wasn't the bastard without feeling Martha had told them he was. Clyde watched his father's face become drenched in tears and got stronger each time he squirmed in pain, but for some reason, he began to feel sorry for him as well.

Finally Clyde spoke. "If you loved my mother so much as you say, just answer this question: Why did you shoot her?"

His father kept shaking his head over and over again, unable get a single word out of his mouth. "Son, I don't know, I really don't know." He cried, "I fell to my knees when I saw her on the floor. I cried out to God for Him to take me and to spare her life." Through bloodshot eyes he spoke in utter despair. "And then I took that same pistol and put it to my head and I pulled the trigger! I cried even more because there were no bullets in the chamber to put me out of the misery that I was feeling at that moment. I searched the room for some bullets and found them, but by then . . . by then, you and your brothers were standing in the doorway and I just couldn't do it. I didn't want to do it in front of my boys so y'all didn't have to go through any more mental damage!" He strained as he looked at his son. "The only reason I'm still living right now is to see the day one of you come looking for some answers so I could tell you the truth, the God's honest truth!"

Clyde stared somberly at the graying older man. He dismissed the idea of giving him an ultimatum of putting himself out of his misery. To call his bluff, he said coldly, "Now that you told one of your boys the truth, you no longer have a reason to go on living, do you?"

The older man shook like a wet, timid puppy as he listened to his son's cold, disparaging words. He wiped the snot and tears from his face and shook his head. "If that's what you want and if that's what it would take for me to have redemption, so be it. I have nothing but you and your brothers and the beautiful memories of your mother." He began to smile and thought back in time to when he was with his wife and said, "Nobody on this earth could love you more than me, and no one ever will!" Those words echoed in Clyde's ears, because they were the same words Martha said she and his mother used to say to each other.

"What did you say?" asked Clyde.

"Oh, that is something me and your mother used to say to each other. That was our personal saying we had between us. Why'd you ask, son?"

Clyde only stared at him and shook his head. "Nothing."

"Clyde," his father said softly, "can I ask a favor of you?" Clyde shrugged, and his father continued timidly, "Can you tell me a little something about you and your brothers? You know, that's if you up to it, of course."

Clyde figured since the man agreed to put himself out of his misery, he could at least give him insight on what he'd missed out on. "Well, Ceasar works as a bank manager." His father beamed with admiration on hearing about the success of his elder son. "He's been working in the same bank on a Hundred and Twenty-fifth Street since he was in high school. He's shorter than me and Sonny and looks almost exactly like you. He's real neat and clean and did a good job at raising us." They talked for the remainder of their time, and Clyde could see that he was enjoying everything he was telling him from the way he smiled.

He offered Clyde a bit of advice. "Son, I don't know how you feel about Martha, but I have to tell you that that woman is sneaky and no good. I appreciate how she took you boys in and kept y'all together and all, but she ain't never wanted to see me and your mother together. All I'm saying is don't put too much trust in the woman. I'm only telling you that 'cause I love you."

As soon as he said that, the correctional staff made an announcement that visiting time was over. They sat and stared at each other until the prisoners were asked to stand. Clyde stood with him, and his father said, "Son, I'm gonna keep my word on what I promised you, and when it's over I want you to take my ultimate sacrifice as a gesture of the truth." When Clyde nodded, he stared at his son, who seemed rigid and cold, and offered, "Clyde, I spent many years in these prisons and I saw a lot of things, and if there's one thing I could give you to carry out of here, it would be this." Clyde folded his arms and listened. "Holding resentment towards somebody is like taking poison and expecting them to die!" Clyde pondered the words deeply and stored them to memory.

His father turned and watched the families hugging and got desperate. "Son, since this is the last time I'm going to see you, do you think I could . . . have one hug from my son?"

Clyde's mind said no, but his body craved differently. His lack of response prompted his father to walk toward him, and he put his arms around his son for the first time in nearly fifteen years and began breaking down and hugging him tighter. Clyde suddenly felt remorseful for the pitiful, tear-ridden man and slowly hugged him back as tears began to fall from his eyes as well. They pulled apart and each wiped the tears from their eyes and nodded. Clyde watched his father's back as he walked away for the last time and was overwhelmed with feeling.

Just as his father was about to round the corner, Clyde yelled at the top of his lungs, "Daddy!"

His father stopped in his tracks and turned around. "Yes, son, I'm here!"

"Don't do it, we need you!"

As if a million pounds had been removed from his shoulders, his father nodded. "I'll be here, son. I'll be here!"

.   .   .

When Clyde walked back into the waiting area, Keyshia was already standing by the door. When he spotted her, he could no longer hold back the tears and ran straight into her arms and hugged her as tight as he possibly could, not ever wanting to let her go.

Chapter 25

Clyde and Keyshia drove along 95 South in silence. Clyde's head was in a whirl as he thought about the visit with his father. Forgiving the man he'd hated and feared throughout most of his short lifetime lifted a heavy burden from his heart. Something in his father's voice, something in his eyes, caused him to believe that his father really loved his mother. Clyde was able to understand the undying love a man could have for a woman because he felt it in his heart for Keyshia. Clyde would kill himself at a moment's notice if he somehow caused Keyshia any harm. Something about the night his mother was shot just didn't add up, and everything pointed toward Martha, who might have some answers—he was sure of it.

Keyshia didn't ask Clyde any questions about what went on between him and his father. She knew it must have been tough for him to look his own father in the eye and say, "Either you kill yourself, or I'll kill you later." She knew that whatever happened, Clyde was a different man from the one who had entered the prison only a few hours ago, and she was even more eager to settle up with the preacher.

Clyde drove for nearly seven hours, and Keyshia stayed awake with him the entire time. When she noticed his eyes getting droopy, she told him it was time to rest and get a good night's sleep. Clyde declined and said that he could manage, but Keyshia put her foot down and said, "Clyde, you had an extremely rough and stressful day, and it's okay to rest properly and proceed in the morning."

Clyde looked at Keyshia and said, "Why you sounding different?"

Keyshia blushed and said, "What do you mean?"

He looked at her knowingly. "You sounding all proper and stuff, that's what I'm talking about."

"You got me. I'm just preparing so when I get down south I'm gonna show everybody that they done made a mistake in sending me off and I come back a success, despite all the things they said and did to me."

"It sounds like you got something to prove to somebody."

"You damn right I got something to prove, Clyde. I got something to prove to my mama, my brothers, my sisters, and that whole sorry-ass town. I want revenge!"

"Keysh, listen: The only person you got something to prove to is yourself, nobody else. You don't really know the whole truth if you only get half the information. The only way you can get the other half is from the horse's mouth, and when you do, you can come to your own determination."

Keyshia persisted, "I understand what you are saying, and I

hope you understand why I hold a deep resentment towards my family, especially my mother."

Clyde nodded. "I understand how you feel, and until recently I would have agreed with you, but I want you to listen to this and never forget it: Holding resentment towards somebody is like taking poison and expecting the other person to die. You only be hurting yourself and yourself only, so you got to learn to let go if you want to move on."

Keyshia stared at Clyde because the words really hit home and made sense. "Where did you learn that from?" she asked.

Clyde looked at her and said proudly, "I learned a thing or two from some people."

Clyde finally stopped in Washington, D.C., so they could rest their heads. The next morning after checking out of the hotel, Keyshia reminded Clyde of his promise to take her to see the Washington Monument. Clyde got lost in downtown D.C. and ended up in front of George Washington Hospital at Foggy Bottom. He pulled over to get directions and got out of the car to ask one of the street vendors. Keyshia got out of the car and spotted a hot dog vendor and told Clyde she was getting them something to eat and drink. He nodded.

Clyde walked over to a gentleman who was selling books in front of the hospital to ask him directions to the memorial.

"Excuse me, brother, can you tell me how I get to the Washington Monument?"

With a welcoming smile, the tall, slim man said, "Sure, soldier." After he told him the direction, he asked Clyde where he was coming from.

"New York," Clyde responded.

The man smiled with a perfect set of white teeth and said,

"New York, huh? I got a lot of people up there that I know from Harlem."

Clyde smiled and said, "That's where me and my girl are from." He pointed toward where Keyshia was at the hot dog stand.

"I was up in New York last year for a book signing for Terri Woods at Justin's, P. Diddy's restaurant."

Clyde nodded.

"I also got a couple of homeboys. They're writers from Harlem named Treasure E. Blue, Kwan, and Hickson. You heard of them?"

Clyde shook his head. "Naw, I don't read too much."

The vendor frowned and said, "Black man, the only way you ever gonna grow is if you read. Years ago they used to string a black person up by the neck and hang them if they even picked up a book!" The vendor suddenly turned into a fireball as his voice dripped with passion. "Do you know why they didn't want us to learn how to read?"

By then Keyshia had joined them.

"Because they knew power lay between words. If you don't know any words, then you have no voice, and to have no voice means you have no power." The book man asked them both, "Name any famous black man or black woman that you know of."

Clyde shrugged and answered, "Malcolm X."

The book man immediately responded, "Was he a powerful speaker?"

They both nodded.

"Give me another one, young lady."

Keyshia thought and quickly said, "Martin Luther King."

The book man nodded and said, "Jesse Jackson, Angela Davis, Marcus Garvey, the Honorable Elijah Muhammad, Louis Farrakhan, and many others. But one thing they all had in common was they were all well-read, and it wasn't a coincidence that they all rose to prominence and became powerful leaders. So remember this, you have a choice of staying in the dark for the rest of your life or being in the light. Where would you two rather be? Many of these young'uns are in the dark. That's why Washington, D.C., is the murder capital of the world. Here they all walk around carrying these nine-millimeters and thinking that gives them the power." He shook his head in pity. "But your mind, your mind is a million times more powerful than any weapon man can make. So always let your mind be your nine!"

Keyshia and Clyde were so overwhelmed by his powerful words that they were struck silent. They had never heard anyone put reading to them in that way. The man seemed to grow taller as he explained to them their history, but then he suddenly returned to his joyous, bright, smiling self and extended his hand to them both. "They call me the Bookman, and I got something for you both." He turned around and searched his table and picked up two books. "This one, soldier, is for you."

Clyde accepted it and read the title on the cover: *The Autobiography of Malcolm X.*

The Bookman smiled and said, "That is a powerful book written by Alex Haley, and it's about change. That book will save your life, soldier." He turned to Keyshia and handed her a book. "Sister, for some reason I can look in your eyes and see a lot of pain that people inflicted upon you." Keyshia looked at him as if he were reading her mind. "But don't you worry about none of that. Don't allow your past to carry into your future because someday you are going be a powerful speaker, a savior to somebody who's going to need you, who believes in you, so you got to prepare yourself for when that time comes." He seemed to stare right through into Keyshia's soul.

"I want you to read that book, and you will get some understanding of the evil that some men and women do, so you can live and become the person that you are destined to become." He smiled and said, "That book is by a good brother of mine from the same place you're from. His name is Treasure, and he wrote that book about you; it's called *Harlem Girl Lost.*"

Keyshia and Clyde were genuinely appreciative and thanked him and offered to pay for the books.

"You can pay me back by reading those books and living righteously."

They nodded and said that they would and shook hands.

After they walked around the Washington Monument, they took a short break and sat on one of the benches. Keyshia still had the book in her purse and decided to look through it. After a couple of minutes of reading it, she turned the first page and on to the next and so on, until she got to a part that hit her. "Clyde," she said with excitement, "listen to this:

> It's not your fault if you were molested like I was, beaten like I was, or homeless and abandoned like I was! And it's definitely not your fault if you developed some dreadful disease or addiction. Whether it's an addiction to drugs or alcohol, sex or crime, it really doesn't matter, because it's not wholly your fault—and believe that!"

Keyshia looked up at Clyde and he said, "Damn, Bookman was right, that sounds just like you."

Keyshia agreed. "He seemed like he could see right through me, Clyde, all by just looking in my eyes."

Clyde nodded. "I guess if you read a lot and get to meet so many people in your life, you kinda get the sense of what they been through. Pops can do the same thing. He was the one who taught me about a person's body language, so I guess he was right. And that thing the Bookman said about the mind is more powerful than any weapon, damn, that shit fucked me up!"

Keyshia added, "Your mind is your nine."

Clyde smiled and repeated, "Your mind is your nine."

As they continued their journey down south, Keyshia stayed stuck into the book the entire time, reading certain passages from the novel that she thought Clyde should hear. She was so enthralled by the book that Clyde caught her shedding a tear or two because the novel had hit so close to home.

It was turning to dusk when Keyshia and Clyde finally made it into the state of South Carolina and pulled into a Motel 8 in Charleston. They figured that they could get a shower and a good night's sleep and head out to see the bad preacher first thing that morning and take care of the business.

Lying in bed after they'd both showered and eaten, Keyshia still had her head in the book, unable to put it down. She began to yell, "That's right, Silver, tell her ass off!"

Surprised, Clyde asked her, "What was that all about?" Amped up, Keyshia quickly explained, "See, this girl named Silver was raised by her mean grandmother, who used to beat her 'cause she reminded her so much of her mother. Silver was an A student and everything, and her grandmother didn't let her go to her own prom, but she went anyway." Clyde smiled as he watched her explain without even taking a breath.

"So," Keyshia continued, "her grandmother wind up busting her at her prom and marched her home to beat her, and then when they got home her grandmother began cursing her out and told her to get out of her dress and bring her the extension cord to beat her with. Now just as she about to beat her, she had enough and said she wasn't gonna let her beat her no more and took it out of her hand. Her grandmother got mad and told her to get out, and when she walked out the house she started yelling that her mother was a no-good ho and that she was happy she was dead and that she was gonna turn out like her. That was it! Silver ran up on her, real, real mad, and guess what she did?"

Surprisingly interested, Clyde said, "What? She beat her down?"

Keyshia smiled and said, "Nope, she kissed her on her cheek."

Clyde frowned and said, "Hold up, her grandmother beat her for years, talked about her mother like a dog to her face, kicked her out of the house, and called her everything but a child of God, and all she does is kiss her on the cheek?"

Keyshia nodded and explained, "Yep, that was the point. She told her . . ." And she began reading from the book:

"My mother used to say, 'For your worst enemy you don't have to do or wish them any harm that they aren't already putting on themselves.' She told me that instead of hating your enemy, love them, and that would kill them quicker than any bullet ever would.

"And then she walked away, leaving her grandmother fucked up!"

Clyde shook his head and reflected on the powerful words that she had read to him. "That shit is deep. I could understand what she was saying."

Keyshia looked at him, incensed. "Get the fuck out of here! I would have fucked that bitch up, and you would have, too, Clyde."

Clyde shrugged. "I don't know, maybe before, but—"

Keyshia cut him off. "But what, Clyde? You think you could forgive a motherfucka just like that if they did fucked-up shit to you for years? What do you think we doing now? Paying mother-fuckas back."

Clyde sat up and paused for a moment before he spoke. "I don't know, it's just that maybe things ain't always what they seem."

"So what are you saying?"

"I'm saying I didn't give my father the pills. I forgave him."

Keyshia stared at him, astonished.

Clyde explained, "All these years I had nothing but hate for this man, nothing but hate for what he did to my mother. I had in my mind even as a child that when I got big enough and strong enough I was going to kill him. But when I was waiting to see him I began to get scared, Keyshia, real scared." Clyde's eyes pleaded for her to understand. "And when I saw him for the first time, he didn't look like the monster I had imagined he was, he looked just like Ceasar." Clyde put his head down. "He went on to explain everything that happened. How he woke up and saw my mother shot and how he loved her so much that he put the gun to his own head 'cause he didn't want to live any further."

Clyde stood up. "I still didn't give a damn what he was saying and even went as far as to tell him that I still wanted him to die. Keyshia, he looked at me and said that if that's what it takes to prove that he was telling the truth, he would do it. I could see in his eyes that he was telling the truth. He said something that him and my mother used to say between them, something like 'Nobody loves you more than me and nobody ever will!' "

Keyshia shook her head and said, "So?"

"Every time Martha used to tell us stories about her and my mother in they younger days, she said that that's what they used to say to each other."

"So, you saying this to say what?"

"I'm saying that my father said that Martha never liked them together and that we shouldn't trust her because she was sneaky and no good."

"And you believe him?"

"Keyshia, she is sneaky and no good—that's the point. Ceasar said that about her, like he knew something we didn't."

Keyshia nodded. "Baby, I understand, but I'm still gonna do what I have to do."

Chapter 26

The country air in Charleston was fresh, clean, and crisp
when they checked out of their motel room. Keyshia felt
rejuvenated as the heat from the sun bathed her skin,
something she hadn't realized she'd missed. Clyde, on
the other hand, wasn't as used to the heat and cringed at
the thought of staying outdoors too long.

Keyshia felt a surge of energy with each familiar sight
that they drove past: the stores, the schools, the gas station, and the church. Keyshia didn't want to waste any
time in completing her mission for fear that Clyde would
try to talk her out of it. Keyshia's body flinched when she
spotted the small dilapidated church where she had been
molested. She gripped the weapon she held in her hand

for a sense of security. Clyde stared at her, sure that she was ready to do what she set out to do with vengeance. She was ready. A late-model car was parked in front of the church, so Clyde drove around to the back and stopped.

When they parked, Keyshia looked intensely at the old church as if she were in another space and time as her mind raced with each passing second. Clyde touched her hand in support, but she recoiled, snapping out of her deepest thoughts.

"You sure you ready?" Clyde asked with concern.

Keyshia inhaled quickly, nodded, and placed the weapon in her handbag. They exited the car, and Clyde looked around. The area was quiet, and not a soul was around. When they entered the church, it was dark and humid, and the only signs of life were the flickering candles peppered throughout. They walked toward the front of the church, and were startled when they heard a voice behind them.

"Can I help you?" They turned and saw a man wearing a robe and grasping a Bible. Clyde looked at Keyshia and saw the glint in her eyes and watched her clutch her bag close to her and reach for the gun. Clyde had his head down as he walked slowly behind her, and once again the man asked, "Is there anything I can help you with?"

Keyshia picked up her pace and walked directly up to the man, then stopped when she saw his face. It wasn't him. Both Clyde and Keyshia let out a breath.

"Don't let me disturb you in your prayer," said the pastor.

Keyshia recovered quickly and said, "Thank you. Me and my family grew up in this town, and I used to attend this church when I was younger."

The pastor smiled. "Welcome home."

She nodded and continued, "Well, back then our pastor was Pastor Green. Is he still here?"

The pastor put his head down immediately and cleared his

throat. "I'm sorry, my dear, but Pastor Green is no longer with our church."

Keyshia hid her disappointment and kept smiling. "Oh, that's too bad, I really wanted to see him."

The pastor looked at Keyshia more closely. "If you don't mind, can I ask you the reason you would like to see Pastor Green?"

"Like I said"—Keyshia smiled—"he was my pastor since I was a little girl."

The pastor began to look her over and then at Clyde and asked suspiciously, "I'm sorry, I didn't get your name."

Without missing a beat, Keyshia quickly extended her hand and answered, "My name is Debra . . . Debra Washington, and this is my brother Darrell."

The pastor smiled and said, "And I'm Pastor Wyatt T. Baker." There was a moment of silence until the pastor cleared his throat and spoke seriously. He nodded uneasily and rubbed his chin. He put his hand on Keyshia's small shoulders and asked, "Young lady, may I ask you a question?" Keyshia nodded. The pastor said, "To be quite honest with you, Pastor Green was removed from this church three years ago because of some horrible acts that he forced upon some vulnerable church members, mainly children." Keyshia's face showed nothing as she listened to the pastor.

"Many of these deplorable acts went on unnoticed for years, until the family of one of his victims insisted on justice being served. He was finally arrested for the act and brought to justice and had a trial. It is unfortunate, but Pastor Green was a very popular person and this is a small county and everyone knew one another. He was found not guilty by his peers, but not by the board of directors here at the church, and he has since been removed."

Both the pastor and Keyshia stared at each other for a moment, but she remained silent.

"Over these last few years, many young victims, all young girls, have been coming forth and expressing that they, too, had in fact been a victim of Pastor Green's sick acts, but no one had the courage to bring him to justice again for fear of being outcast." The pastor gave Keyshia an earnest and sincere fatherly look. "Were you one of the pastor's victims who was caused great pain?"

Keyshia's smile grew faint and she said, "No," as she shook her head.

The pastor gazed at her a little longer and smiled. "Good . . . good." He took a deep breath. "I'm sorry I had to tell you the bad news, but I'm sure you can understand my asking."

Keyshia nodded and said that she understood. She and Clyde shook the pastor's hand and thanked him for his time. Keyshia suddenly wanted to leave the church, and she walked out as fast as she could. When she got outside she bent over and started vomiting. Clyde helped her steady herself. When she finished, her eyes were bloodshot and her jaw was clenched as she said to Clyde, "Let's go to that motherfucka's house!"

When they entered the well-maintained, tree-lined neighborhood, Keyshia recognized the former pastor's modest white colonial home and pointed it out to Clyde. Clyde made a U-turn at the end of the block and parked across the street from the house. They stared at the home for quite a while until Clyde finally asked Keyshia, "Keysh, you don't have to go through with this if you don't want to. The pastor seemed to be saying that you could still bring him to justice and they would believe you now since it's in the open."

Keyshia shook her head. "No, this is something I got to do."

Clyde felt torn, but he would stand by her no matter what. "Okay," he said softly.

Keyshia got out of the car, and Clyde was right behind her. Keyshia's eyes were set on the house, and Clyde's quickly surveyed the entire area. As they stood at the door, Keyshia pulled out the weapon from her bag. She looked at Clyde and warned him, "Clyde, no matter what happens, let me handle everything, okay?"

Clyde watched her grip the Glock 9-mm, nodded, and offered one thing: "Remember, your mind is your nine." Keyshia was ready to confront the man who had caused her so much suffering and pain. The man who'd stolen her innocence, who had ensured that she would never have any more kids, and ultimately, the man who had taken from her the most precious thing on earth—her only child. Clyde played his position on the side of the door, and Keyshia took a huge breath and then knocked as she held the gun behind her back. Seconds later the door swung open and Keyshia stood face-to-face with the man who had molested and impregnated her over six years ago.

"Yes, can I help you?" the man said in a thick country accent. Keyshia froze and stared at him through her Chanel sunglasses. The man smiled again and repeated, "Yes, can I help you, young lady?" Clyde stood menacingly on the side, unsure how Keyshia would react. Suddenly, she lifted the ugly black weapon straight to his face and pushed him inside. Terror filled the man as Clyde appeared from the side, causing him to throw his hands in the air and plead for reasoning.

"What is this about? I think you got the wrong place." He jumped when he heard the door slam loudly behind Clyde, who produced his own weapon, causing him to tremble.

"Please, young lady," he pleaded to Keyshia, "you got the wrong man, I tell you. I'm a pastor and—"

Keyshia cut him off. "Look at me!"

His eyes widened as Clyde approached both of them. "Wha . . . what?" he stammered.

Keyshia cocked the weapon back and repeated, "Motherfucka, I said look at me!"

He turned toward his intruder's face, squinting his eyes to recognize her. Slowly, Keyshia took off her sunglasses, revealing her tear-ridden face. It took him seconds to recognize her. "Oh, my God," the man gasped as he lost his balance and fell to the floor.

"Don't ask for God now, motherfucka!" said Keyshia with vengeance. "You didn't ask for Him when you were between my fucking legs, did you, motherfucka?" She suddenly unleashed a brutal kick to the man's face, causing him to cower in pain. Keyshia continued to kick him with everything she had. "Did you call on God when you tore my fucking insides up, motherfucka?"

The former pastor curled himself in a ball to protect his face, and Clyde walked up to him and pointed the weapon at him and kicked him viciously. "Sit the fuck up, you son of a bitch!"

Keyshia shook her head and cried, "No, I got this!" She wiped her tear-soaked eyes and said to him, "Do you really have a clue about what you did to me? Do you know what you took from me?"

"I'm sorry, I'm so, so sorry!"

Keyshia kicked him again. "Was you sorry when I begged you to get off top of me? Was you sorry when you got me sent out of town for the shit you did? Was you sorry when they took my baby from me?" She grew angrier with each passing second.

"Please, the baby—"

"Shut the fuck up!" This time Keyshia slapped him viciously across the face with the weapon. A million things raced through her mind as she stared down at the man cringing in pain from the sickening blow she delivered to him. Clyde saw the glint in her eye and knew it was over for the man, and deservedly so, but he couldn't help but wish it hadn't had to go down like this. He wanted better for her.

"You fucked my whole life up, is what you did!" Tears continued to fall from her eyes as she aimed the gun at him, ready to end his life.

"And . . . I'm here to make sure that you pay for this shit!" She took aim and screamed, "I'll see you in hell, motherfucka!"

Suddenly, a pretty young girl about five years old came running into the living room, screaming, "Don't hurt my daddy! Don't hurt my daddy!"

Both Keyshia and Clyde immediately put their weapons behind their backs and watched the beautiful little girl wrap her tiny arms around her father and fall to the floor to protect him. Keyshia's eyes began to blink rapidly as she saw a faint similarity in the little girl's face and frightened eyes. Then she gasped, turned, and ran out the door and didn't stop till she got to the car. Clyde was right behind just as she nearly collapsed in the street and had to be carried to the car. He started the engine and took off.

Keyshia cried and cried through the rest of the night. *Could it be?*

Chapter 27

Keyshia could not hold any food down and refused to get out of the motel bed over the next two gloomy days. Clyde tried to get her up and about, maybe to go visit her relatives, but she didn't have an ounce of strength to move. Seeing her daughter was just too much for her to handle, especially with him. Never in a million years would she have thought that she would ever see her daughter again.

Clyde waited on her hand and foot, giving her massages, feeding her soup, and even carrying her to the bathroom and bathing her. He constantly asked her if she wanted to talk, but she told him that she wasn't ready.

To keep her mind off the events that had transpired,

Keyshia sought refuge in *Harlem Girl Lost.* The more she read, the more she began to grow inspired as the main character in the book went through insurmountable pain and injustice yet rose to the occasion again and again. By the time she completed the novel, the first one she'd ever read, Keyshia seemed to have purpose, a new meaning to life despite what she'd been through.

By the third morning, when Clyde awoke, he was surprised to see Keyshia standing over him, smiling and dressed to a T. "Get up, sleepyhead, we got some shopping to do and some family to see."

Clyde chuckled and said, "Glad to see you back, baby."

Since Keyshia was the oldest—she had four younger brothers and one sister she hadn't seen in over six years—she wanted to go shopping at the mall and surprise them and her mother with gifts. She racked up on video games, toys, basketballs, and other sporting goods for all her brothers, and dolls, a CD player, and various games for her sister. For her mother, she bought some expensive perfume and jewelry. After they'd purchased everything, she was ready to see them.

Even though the area in which Keyshia's family lived was considered the city, Clyde couldn't help but think differently. He passed by many homes that still had outhouses, and many of the children were tattered-looking and outside playing barefoot. Keyshia assured him that many children in the South chose not to wear shoes when they were playing. He had to also get used to all the people who waved and said hello to him as he drove. Keyshia had to explain that this was traditional and everyone was being friendly.

"Goddamn, Keyshia, I ain't used to all this waving."

"That's just that southern hospitality." Keyshia smiled.

"I mean, they don't even know me and—" Someone pulled up

to Clyde at the stop sign and suddenly waved. With a fake smile, Clyde waved back at them. "See what I mean? If they did this shit in New York, people would give them the finger."

Keyshia laughed. "Well, get used to it, buddy, 'cause this how they get down in the South."

When they finally reached Keyshia's family's home, there was no driveway or anything. It was a shabby-looking house that sat on a plot of grass surrounded by thick vine oak trees. The area was nothing like downtown Charleston; it was more backwoods and open. Clyde knew that her family was dirt poor. Keyshia looked around nervously, not spotting a soul, when suddenly a little black face appeared at the screen door. He had on a pair of shorts but no shirt or shoes.

Keyshia smiled and put a hand over her mouth. "Oh, my God, Clyde, that's my youngest brother, Damon."

As soon as she said that, another boy, much older, rail thin, and tall, peered out the door, but this time opening it. He squinted and put his hand over his eyes to see who was in the car. Keyshia opened the car door and stood face-to-face with her closest brother, who was only eleven months younger than she. He recognized her instantly and asked in a thick southern drawl, "Keyshia?"

Keyshia nodded and said, "Kevin?"

He yelled at the top of his lungs and jumped off the porch and embraced her tightly and swung her around. The loud commotion caused everyone in the house to come outside, and when they realized who it was, they began yelling also and running up to her and giving her tight-wrapped love. All her siblings jumped all around, as jubilant as if she had just come home from the war, all calling out her name.

"Keyshia!"

"Sister, welcome home!"

"We missed you!"

The last person to come out was her mother, who had one arm wrapped around herself and the other one covering her mouth. She was already emotional. Keyshia looked up and saw her and walked to the porch and up the three steps. She stood face-to-face with her mother, who was now much, much shorter than she, saw the tears in her eyes, and said, "How you doin', Mama?"

Her mother's lips began to tremble, and tears exploded from her eyes. "I's okay, chile. I's miss you much!"

They embraced, and Keyshia closed her eyes, feeling for the first time in six years the comfort only a mother can give. The whole family came to the porch and surrounded them and joined the family reunion hug. They wiped their eyes and laughed heartily as they pulled themselves apart. Keyshia turned around and waved for Clyde to come over. He walked up the steps with a cool New York swagger, and they all beamed bright and proud at their sister's guest.

"Everybody, I want you to meet my boyfriend, Clyde Barker." Everybody submerged him and gave him equal love. Keyshia looked at all the faces and said with great pride, "Guess what?" All eyes lit up like a Christmas tree in anticipation. "I got gifts for each and every one of y'all." They all jumped up and down joyously, making the porch feel like it would collapse.

"The stuff is in the car, and all I need is help." Each sibling jumped off the porch and ran toward the car, waiting for their early Christmas presents.

Keyshia watched her brothers and sisters tear through the bags and scream with excitement. She personally handed her mother a white box.

As her mother held the box, she blushed and said, "You's got this fo' me?"

Keyshia nodded proudly. "It's for you, Mama. Now open it."

Like a little girl, she blushed again and untied the red ribbon around the box. When she lifted the cover and saw a gold necklace with a cross pendant, her hand flew over her mouth. She repeated, "Dis fo' me?"

Keyshia nodded again. "It's all for you, Mama! Let me help you try it on." She fastened the necklace around her mother's neck. Her mother looked down at the necklace and felt it. She giggled and thanked her daughter with a hug. They stared at each other, and both knew that a lot of wrongs had to be answered for, but now was not the time.

Her mother's smile grew big and she said to Keyshia and Clyde, "I's hope you all ain't eaten none, 'cause I's 'bout to feeds y'all a sho-nuff hearty meal ta fill them bones you carryin'." She wrapped her arms around Keyshia and Clyde and led them inside.

Clyde was surprised when he entered Keyshia's family's home. Though it looked small and dilapidated on the outside, inside it was spacious, clean, and well maintained. While Keyshia, her mother, and her little sister were in the kitchen preparing the meal, the brothers were in the living room showing Clyde the family photo album. He saw pictures of Keyshia when she was in her newborn, toddler, and preteen years. They all got a kick out of showing Clyde their sister at her best and worst.

It was as if Keyshia had never left as she fell right in step with her mother and they busied themselves inside the kitchen. They made homemade biscuits, fresh ham, sausages, bacon, pancakes, eggs, and grits. The entire family got a kick out of watching Clyde's reaction when their mother brought all the food over to the table. Clyde had never seen so much food before. Keyshia told him that this was how they cooked in the South whenever someone had a guest or family over. She said it was a tradition.

When all the food was set up on the table, they joined hands and were led in grace by Keyshia's mother.

"Lawd, thank You fo' blessin' us wit' this food we 'bout ta receive, fo' You are the Provida of our ration. I's also likes ta thank Ya fo' bringin' my baby gurl back ta me spite the hardness I's know she been through and not comin' back with a heavy heart. Bless her mista friend, Clyde, and hope that they stay awhile." Keyshia and Clyde peeked at each other, knowing she was giving them a hint. "Amen!"

Everyone repeated, "Amen," and ambushed the food before them.

They ate and had fun talking about the past and telling Clyde how Keyshia was a tomboy coming up and how she was so skinny the called her Olive Oyl from the *Popeye* cartoon.

All through the meal, Keyshia's little sister, Kenya, eleven years old, was eyeing and smiling at Clyde. She suddenly asked him, "Clyde, are you gon' marry my sista?"

The question caught Clyde totally off guard. Everyone got real quiet and awaited an answer.

Clyde cleared his throat and said, "Kenya, me and your sister never talked about marriage. Us bein' so young and all." They hung on every word he was saying because they were very big on marriage in the South. Clyde saw all the eyes still staring and added, "But when the time is right, I'm gonna find the biggest, most expensive ring I can afford, then I'm gonna bring her back down here, in front of her whole family, and get on my knees." Clyde looked at Keyshia, who sat across from him.

"And I will ask the loveliest, most gorgeous woman in the world, the only woman that I ever loved, would she have my hand in marriage so I can spend the rest of my life with her."

Everybody turned their attention to Keyshia, who was ready to erupt in tears of happiness; she couldn't hold them back and ran out of the kitchen.

All her brothers laughed, and their mother reprimanded

them, "You boys hush!" She threw her napkin on the table and followed behind her daughter.

Kenya stared at Clyde and said, "Well, she look like she don't want to marry you, Clyde, but I will!"

"Shut up!" all her brothers yelled in unison.

Chapter 28

Keyshia and Clyde had planned to leave Charleston on Friday morning but decided to stay until the weekend because Keyshia's mother told them about a gathering. They had until Monday to get back to New York and give Black Sam his money. All Clyde had to do was hook up with Ceasar to get the remaining twenty thousand dollars and give everything to Sonny to square things up. Keyshia's mother insisted that they stay at the house for the night in Kenya's room.

The time had come when Keyshia and her mother were alone inside her mother's bedroom. Both women were uneasy and made small talk.

"So, Keyshia, it looks like ya auntie Ninny done a fine job in raisin' ya."

Keyshia hesitated, fighting every muscle in her face not to reveal the truth, then nodded. "Yes, Mama, Auntie done take good care of me."

Her mother beamed proudly. "I's knew I could rely on Ninny ta take good care of my baby."

Keyshia wanted so badly to tell her the truth, but she knew her mother had enough guilt on her plate and this would surely push her over the edge.

"You look just like them people on TV, and ya speak just like 'em, too." She giggled. "And you got so tall, I's now have ta look up ta ya."

Keyshia smiled. There was a long pause, and then Keyshia finally broke the silence. "Mama . . ." She looked down as she gathered her thoughts. "I know how hard everything must have been on you, and you don't have to feel bad anymore. I since moved on, and I hold no grudges against anyone, especially you."

"But I's still feel bad 'cause I's put you in harm's way. I's suppose ta be the one who care fo' ya, protect ya, 'stead I's let that man tamper with you. I's shouldn'ta been such a fool, being so trustin' and all and stupid."

Her mother put her head down in shame, but Keyshia lifted her chin and looked her directly in the eyes. "Mama, you ain't stupid or a fool. All you wanted was the best for me and to learn the word of God. That man and that man alone violated me, and he's the one who has to answer to God for his crimes." Keyshia's mother looked at her in awe and wondered how in the world she'd gained such wisdom at such a young age in spite of all that happened.

"I's always knew you was special, Keyshia. I's knew that from the very first time I's lay eyes on you. You always been the determined type, and I's know you would always be some kinda doctor or one of them lawyers or something."

"You really thought so, Mama?"

"Yes, chile, ever since you were li'l, and useta try ta do somethin', you didn't stop till ya master it." She laughed. "You 'member the time you learn how ta ride a two-wheel bike?" Keyshia shook her head.

"Well, you ain't nothing but four or five years old, and you keep tryin' and fallin' down, cryin' each time, scrapin' yo' knee, hands, chile, everything. We's try ta get you to stop, but ya kept at it. Later that day, ya comes in here screamin' and hollerin', all bloody on ya forehead, arms, and, chile, yo' knee's was so scrape up we thought they was gonna fall off, but you came in here screamin' top of yo' lungs, sayin', 'Mama, I did it, I did it,' and carry me by my hand outside ta show me." She smiled, "Then you gets right back on that bike and rides that bike just like the wind. You couldna stop you from smilin'!" Keyshia blushed.

"Yeah, chile, you was always some kinda special. I's know you gots ta be doing well in the big city with them fine clothes and them expensive gifts ya bring us."

Keyshia grew uneasy. Feelings of guilt arose inside of her. She knew all along what she was doing when she walked in the house portraying that she had her life together, speaking properly and bringing everyone gifts like she was rich. She'd dreamed about doing this for years, and when it finally happened, she was dissatisfied about the person she portrayed herself to be.

"Mama," Keyshia said as she shook her head, "I's not everything you thought I turn out to be. I's drop out of school, I's got myself put out of Ninny's house, and I was involved in them bad drugs on them streets." She searched her mother's face for a reaction but saw none. "I's got teased a lot by them folks in New York because of hows I's look and hows I's talk and make myself blend in by talking like 'em. I's lied ta you 'bout Auntie Ninny, too. She treated me horrible from the time I's came near. She beat me all the time and called me trash and worked me like a slave." Keyshia's mother's eyes began to grow cold and icy. "It got to the point where's I's was tired of all the name callin' and whuppin's that I's finally snap and pulled out a knife and put it ta her throat and warned her that if she ever lay a hand on me again, I's surely would cut her throat." She looked deep into her mother's eyes and said, "And I's would have, too." Her mother nodded, and Keyshia asked sullenly, "You mad at me fo' handlin' ya sister like that, Mama?"

"Mad?" her mother said, appalled. "You shoulda done it, if ya ask me. She had no right treatin' you like a dog like she did after all them years I's raised that chile."

Keyshia felt a burden had been lifted off her shoulders, because despite her aunt's treatment of her, she still felt that she was wrong to fight back the way she had.

"You ain't got ta feel shame 'bout nothin'. Ya did right, and when I's see Ninny it gon' be a whole lot of furniture movin' 'round in this house here."

Keyshia snickered, because in the South that was how they said there was going to be some fighting in the house. She took a big breath, relieved, but she still had something on her mind. Her mother picked up on it and inquired, "Ya still got somethin' on yo' mind, chile, tell ya mama what it is."

Keyshia lifted her head and gazed deep into her mother's eyes. Her mother nodded knowingly.

"You want ta know about ya's baby." She squeezed Keyshia's hand and continued, "Her name is Christina, and she is the most beautiful chile ya ever want to see. She smart and bright just like you."

Her mother spent the next hour telling Keyshia as much as she knew about her daughter, answering question after question. Her mother told her that she got a chance to see her daughter about twice a year, including Christmas. She told Keyshia that when she first found out that the pastor had her granddaughter, she made a valiant effort to gain custody of her by taking him to court. But being uneducated and poor prevented her from pursuing the case any further. She had even consulted a lawyer, who advised her to drop the case because the pastor would be more suitable to raise the child financially, and that if she really loved her granddaughter, she'd let her be raised in a better environment than the one she lived in.

"I's did everything I's could, but them courts would never give that chile ta me 'cause I's weren't prepared ta raise her. I's was barely able to raise the chillens I's have already; that's why I's had ta send you away. But, don't you worry 'cause—"

They were interrupted by Kenya, who was pounding on the door. "Mommy, I's ready to go ta sleep. I's tired!" Since Keyshia and Clyde were sleeping in her room, Kenya was sleeping with her mother tonight.

Keyshia's mother looked at the clock and said, "Let me let that chile get some sleep. You should do the same and get yaself some sleep 'cause we gots ourself a big day tomorrow, lotta peoples gonna be here." Her mother opened the door, and Kenya pounced right into the room and into Keyshia's arms as she sat on the bed.

"Mama," Keyshia inquired, "you ain't say nothing about family joining us tomorrow."

Kenya said as she played with her big sister's braids, "What do ya mean, Keyshia? Tomorrow the family reunion. A lot of people always show up ta the reunion."

Keyshia looked inquisitively at her mother, who smiled. "I's thought that was the reason y'all done come down here and all. Ninny ain't tell ya? She comin', too."

. . .

When Keyshia entered the bedroom, Clyde was already settled in and lying in the bed reading the book he was given by the Bookman.

"Clyde, tomorrow's my family reunion and I didn't even know it."

"Huh?" Clyde answered, not looking up from the book.

"I said we having a big family reunion tomorrow."

Clyde nodded his approval. "Oh, that's cool, you get a chance to see your family you haven't seen in years."

"Guess who gonna be here tomorrow, too? My aunt Ninny!" Keyshia said enthusiastically. "And I told my mama everything, and she said it's gonna be a whole lot of furniture moving around tomorrow, if you know what I mean."

"Oh, shit! It's gonna be on tomorrow, then."

"Yep, sure is." Keyshia sat next to him and kissed him. "What are you doing?"

"Reading this book, *The Autobiography of Malcolm X*. Malcolm was no joke when he was younger."

Keyshia looked at what page he was on and asked, "Clyde, you already on page eighty-six?"

He nodded. "Yeah, why?"

"'Cause you can read your ass off. I never knew you could read like that."

"Well, this is a interesting book. Did you know Malcolm X's mother was in a mental institution?"

Keyshia shook her head.

"Yeah, and that turned him into a thief and burglar." Clyde shook his head. "Damn, all this time I thought I was the only one who goes through this shit."

Keyshia listened to him and smiled. "We all gotta go through things, baby, some go through more than others, but you definitely gonna go through it. But even if you got to go through painful things, don't let it define who you are."

Clyde looked up at Keyshia with an amazed expression on his face. "Goddamn, Keysh, where you learned deep shit like that from?"

She giggled and said, "Reading is fundamental."

Clyde smiled and grabbed her and began tickling her. "Oh, you want to be smarty pants, huh? You want to be hee hee hee how, huh?"

Keyshia began to laugh hysterically. "Clyde, stop, you know I'm ticklish."

"Tell me how much you love a nigga?"

"I love you, just stop." She laughed.

"How much?"

"I love you to death!" she shouted.

Clyde stopped tickling her and with a serious face asked, "Till death do us part?"

Keyshia stared up into his eyes. "Till death do us part, boy!"

Clyde looked deeply into Keyshia's eyes and saw no uncertainties. He knew beyond a shadow of a doubt that she would surely do just that.

"Clyde," she said, "you's is my world, and I want to be with you till I die. I's think I go crazy if something ever happen to you, that's why I want to tell you we got to stop doing what we doing so no harm will come to the both of us. The thought of not having you is too, too much for me to bear, so you got to stay out of trouble, and if you do . . ." Keyshia's eyes began to harden, and she spoke with urgency. "It ain't nothing you or nobody can say to stop me from getting you out of trouble. Do you understand me, Clyde? If we got to go out, we go out together, and I so mean that! Now promise me, promise me that we will, 'cause I'm never letting you go, boy!"

"Till death do us part, baby!" Clyde said, accepting the eternal pact.

They sealed it with a long kiss. That night, they made love like it would be their last time as they both professed their eternal love for each other.

Chapter 29

Bang . . . bang . . . bang!

The pounding sound woke Keyshia and Clyde.

"Mama said it was time ta get up so we could prepare fo' the reunion!" Kenya yelled on the other side of the door. *Bang, bang, bang!* "Get up!"

"All right, Kenya!" Keyshia yelled and they both collapsed back on their pillows.

"Don't lay back down! Mama said now!"

They both sat up and looked at each other, wondering how Kenya could tell what was happening through a closed door.

Keyshia's mother had stayed up most of the night cooking and preparing the food for the cookout. Keyshia chided her mother for not asking for her help. Her mother told her that it wasn't a problem and that she was used to cooking big meals by herself.

By eight o'clock, Keyshia's other aunts arrived with food and to help with the arrangements. They could hardly believe their eyes when they saw their niece, whom they hadn't seen in years. They all marveled about how tall and beautiful she was, and when she opened her mouth to speak, they commented on how she talked like them "white folks." They made a big fuss over Keyshia, telling her that she needed to come stay over at each of their houses so they could put some meat on her bones. Keyshia's mother pulled aside her three rather large sisters and told them what Ninny had done to Keyshia, and they grew livid. Since Ninny was the youngest of the five sisters, they had all virtually raised Ninny after their mother and father passed away when Ninny was seven years old. The sisters had sacrificed everything for their baby sister, working hard to put her through school and send her to New York. When she got a great-paying job and was on her feet, she turned her back on her southern upbringing. When she did visit, she tried to make her sisters feel as though they were ignorant because they spoke "geechi," a thick South Carolinian dialect.

Kenya had bugged her big sister all morning to borrow something that she could wear to the reunion. Even though Keyshia towered over her little sister by at least five inches, they were the same clothing size. So Keyshia went in her bag and found something for her to wear and even gave her a pair of coordinating sandals and brought out the old-fashioned hot comb to straighten her little sister's hair. After her sister was fully dressed with her hair done, Keyshia looked her over and thought Kenya needed one more thing and brought out her makeup kit. When she finished with her little sister, she looked exactly like an African princess. Even her brothers, who joked with her endlessly, told her how nice she looked. Her mother put her hands over her mouth when she saw her baby model and show off her new look.

"How do I's look, Mama?"

"You's looks absolutely beautiful, baby, beautiful, I's say!"

"Thank you, Mama." To be sure, Kenya ran to find Clyde, on whom she had developed a crush. When she found him in the room playing the Xbox that he and Keyshia had brought them, she said, "Clyde, how do I's look?" She smiled widely as she pranced back and forth like a top model.

"You look just like them models I see on television, Kenya, just like them."

Her eyes lit up. "You think I can be a New York model, Clyde?"

Clyde nodded. "Hell, yeah. You still got some growing to do, and if you grow anything like your sister, which is most likely, you definitely can be one." Kenya smiled from ear to ear. She ran up to Clyde and gave him a big kiss on the cheek and ran out of the room with high hopes.

Family members by the dozens began to arrive in cars and trucks. All their smiles were wide and happy each time any familiar face— or unfamiliar face, for that matter—showed up at the reunion. Clyde grew amazed at all the genuine love that Keyshia's family gave him—it was almost as if he were their blood family. He was even more happy for Keyshia, who was holding court with all her young female cousins, who asked her question after question about New York City.

"Do you know any rappers?"

"How much it cost ta get your hair did like that?"

"You think I's can get a boy like you got if I's comes to New York?"

"How'd you get ta sound so white soundin'?"

"Can you take me back there wit' ya?"

Keyshia answered each and every one of their queries, separating fact from fiction and telling them that they shouldn't believe everything they see on television.

Within the next couple of hours, the family reunion was in full swing, and the back and front yards were congested with over a hundred black faces. The men of the family all rallied together and set up nearly twenty barbecue grills and had the place smoking with hamburgers, franks, and, of course, spareribs. The women laid out the tables with huge plastic bowls full of potato salad, macaroni salad, macaroni and cheese, collard greens, turnip greens, cabbage, deviled eggs, rice and peas, lima beans, and more. They even had a huge pot of boiled crabs. Beer and alcohol flowed freely, and there was even a batch of homemade corn liquor.

Children ran around playing, and the teens were content to play video games. All was happy and joyous.

Suddenly the announcement was made: "Food is ready, line up for yo' plate!" With that, people lined up at the table, plates in hand, to fill their stomachs with savory food.

Keyshia sat on Clyde's lap as they listened to music and watched everyone dance and have a good time. New York and all their problems seemed a million miles away, as neither could recall in recent memory a family event being so fulfilling. In fact, this was Clyde's first experience at any kind of family function, and he realized what he had missed. But now that he had Keyshia and her family, who accepted him as one of their own, he knew that this one would not be his last.

"All right," the DJ said as he cut the music, "y'all know what time it is now . . . it's stepping time with R. Kelly. So I want everybody, and I mean everybody, to get up and 'Step in the Name of Love'!"

With that everyone got up and got in line and began the dance that went along with R. Kelly's song. Keyshia stood up and pulled Clyde by the arm and tried to get him to join in, but he protested.

"Naw, Keysh, you know I'm a gangster, and gangsters don't dance."

Still pulling at his arm, she joked, "You ain't no gangsta no more. Remember, that mean you normal now."

Clyde wasn't budging. "Come on, Keyshia, you know I don't know that shit."

"Then I'll show you," she offered.

"Naw, that's all right."

Keyshia called to her mother, and Mrs. Simmons came strutting over doing the damn thing, and Keyshia said, "Ma, Clyde said that he want to dance with you."

Her mother smiled and said, "Okay, come on and let's do the thing with yo' old mama-in-law, son."

She grabbed him by the hand, and he couldn't say no to her. As Keyshia watched her mother show Clyde how to do the dance, she smiled so hard that it hurt, and she put her hands over her mouth because she couldn't contain her happiness. Keyshia looked off in the distance and saw a man by a car holding a little girl by the hand. The little girl wore a colorful dress with red ribbons in her hair, and even from afar, Keyshia could see how beautiful she was.

Keyshia's mother saw that something was wrong with her daughter and followed her eyes to where she was looking. Mrs. Simmons touched Clyde's hand and walked over to where the man and child stood. Not a word was exchanged as the little girl took her grandmother's hand and followed her. The music stopped playing, and all eyes were on the older woman and child. The closer they got, the more Keyshia's insides began raging and growing tense. Her mind began growing cloudy and gray. Could it be? she thought.

The huge, silent crowd parted as Keyshia's mother and the little girl approached her. Clyde was emotionally overwhelmed, and tears welled in his eyes. Keyshia didn't know what to do as she stared down at the most beautiful little girl who looked so much like her. In her hand, the little girl had a brown teddy bear, and she raised it up to Keyshia and said, "My name is Christina. Is you my mama?"

Still speechless, Keyshia simply nodded.

"Well, my daddy say this is for you."

Keyshia accepted the teddy bear, which read, "I love my mommy." Keyshia fell to her knees and embraced her child for the first time. Then she pulled herself together and looked in her daughter's eyes through her tears. She said, "Yes . . . yes, baby, I's your mommy and I's love you."

Her daughter threw her arms around her and said, "I love you, too, Mommy."

Love never fails.

Keyshia picked up her daughter and carried her into the house to spend some quality time with her. As she walked toward the house, she watched Christina's father, who had bandages and bruises all over his pitiful face, nod, back into his car, and drive away.

After Keyshia entered the house, a car pulled into the driveway and two boys jumped out of the backseat and ran toward the gathering. "Don't you boys go far. And don't get your clothing dirty, and let me see the food before you eat it! You hear me?" The boys nodded and continued on. Everyone watched as Ninny exited the car. She frowned as she stepped uneasily through the spotted grass and dirt. She was dressed very conservatively and looked as if she were going on a job interview. When she noticed all her folks staring at her, she asked sarcastically, "My God, who died? I thought this was a family reunion." The crowd parted, and there stood her four older sisters with their arms folded, staring at her grimly.

Ninny smiled and waved and looked around at everyone's faces, "Hey, Sissy, hey, Carol, Marie, Mary. Why is the music not playing and everybody looking at me like this?"

Sissy—Keyshia's mother—approached her and said coolly, "Hey, Ninny, we got to talk."

Surprised, Ninny asked, "Talk about what? Girl, I just got here, driving for all them hours."

Her sister Mary said, "Oh, chile, it ain't gonna take but a second."

Marie interjected, "Yeah, we just going in the house, that way you can rest a li'l."

Ninny smiled and said, "Yeah, that sound nice, I do need to change into some slippers. My feet are killing me. Let me just tell my boys to be careful out here."

Carol, the oldest and biggest sister, said, "Now, Ninny, dem boys is just gon' be fine. Let 'em be boys, I's keep an eye on 'em."

Ninny nodded and joked, "I see you guys is still speaking country as hell. When are you going to learn proper English?" All the sisters remained silent as the five of them walked into the house.

Clyde watched everything unfold and smiled.

When they got in the house, the four surrounded their sister as they shut the door and locked it. Perplexed, Ninny suspected something wrong and asked, "What is this about, and why is everyone looking at me that way?"

Sissy said, "Ninny, you's gots ta answer ta Keyshia!"

"What?" Ninny stammered as she feigned ignorance. Just then Keyshia and her daughter exited out of one of the bedrooms. Ninny's eyes widened as a huge lump formed in her throat.

Sissy nodded and said, "Yeah, you do remember my daughter Keyshia."

"Our niece!" Carol said loudly.

Sissy walked up to her face and questioned, "You made my daughter sleep in the closet and put your fucking hands on her?"

"I . . . I . . . ," Ninny stuttered.

"I, what?" Sissy asked. "She's a black dirty bitch, and she ain't going to amount to shit? Nobody gonna want her?" The sisters stared at Ninny, incensed.

"Ninny, we raised you and raised you well," Sissy said angrily. "I quit school ta take care of you when Mama and Papa die, put you through school, and sent ya ta New York fo' a job and everything, and you pay me back by treating my daughter like a dog?" The more Sissy spoke, the angrier she got. "Keyshia, take the baby out of here, 'cause I's about ta show yo' aunt some of this here furniture. Excuse me . . . I'm sorry, that's not proper English, is it, Ninny? Allow me to rephrase myself: Please excuse us, Keyshia, because we are about to kick your aunt's ass!"

"Ooh, Mommy, Grandmommy cursed," Keyshia's daughter said.

Keyshia smiled, picked up her daughter, and exited the house quickly.

Chapter 30

Keyshia and her daughter, Christina, were in their own little world, laughing and playing and trying to make up for the time they'd missed together. They couldn't keep their hands off each other, hugging each other for what seemed like the thousandth time. When Keyshia introduced her daughter to Clyde, they seemed to hit it off immediately. The three looked like a family as Keyshia and Clyde swung Christina from their arms.

The reunion started unwinding at about ten o'clock that evening as family members hugged and kissed. It was about the same time that Christina's father pulled up to take her home. Christina pleaded tearfully with her newfound mother to come home and live with her.

"Mommy, why don't you and Mr. Clyde just come home and live with me and my daddy and we can all be together?"

"Christina, that would be real nice, but that is not possible."

"Why, Mommy?"

Keyshia could not answer her. All she could do was look in her daughter's precious, innocent face.

"Then can I come with you, Mommy?" she asked excitedly.

Keyshia could only tell her the truth. "Christina, right now your mommy can't take care of you the way Mommy wants to. For right now, it is best that you stay with your daddy, until your mother gets a job, maybe a house, and gets on her feet a little. When that happens . . ." Keyshia smiled widely. "You can come stay with Mommy as much as you want. How does that sound?"

Christina smiled and said, "Sounds great, Mommy!"

Keyshia stared at her daughter. "How did you get to be so smart?"

Christina shrugged and answered, "I don't know."

They embraced for the final time, and Keyshia said, "I love you, Christina. Always remember that Mommy loves you to death. Now go ahead to your father." She stood and watched her run into her father's arms and waved until they were out of sight.

Clyde walked over and asked, "You okay, baby?"

Keyshia threw her arms around Clyde for a long hug.

By noon the next day, Keyshia and Clyde were packed and ready for the fifteen-hour drive to New York. All of Keyshia's family were saddened to see them leave, especially her mother and little sister, Kenya. Keyshia and Clyde hugged each of her family members who lined up to see them off. Keyshia hugged her mother last and whispered in her ear, "This is for you and the boys and Kenya." And she slipped her mother a thousand dollars.

Her mother shook her head. "Keyshia," she began, but Keyshia stopped her.

"I know what you gonna say, Ma, but just accept it for me; it would mean the world to me." Her mother stared into her eyes and nodded. They embraced again, and Keyshia pulled away and entered the car because she didn't want to break down in front of everyone.

Kenya ran to the passenger side of the car, and Keyshia smiled as she looked into her little sister's big doe eyes and asked her, "What's wrong, Kenya?"

"I want to go with y'all!" she said.

Keyshia rubbed her smooth dark skin and said, "Baby, there's nothing in the world I would like better than to bring you back with me, but right now, me and Clyde have to take care of some important things." Kenya put her head down, dejected.

"But . . . ," Keyshia said.

Kenya lifted her head as Keyshia continued, "I promise that the next time we come down here you can come back with us to visit. How does that sound?"

Kenya's face lit up and she leaned in and kissed her sister and said, "You promise?"

Keyshia nodded. "I promise."

Clyde honked his horn and everyone waved good-bye and didn't stop until they were out of view.

They arrived at the George Washington Bridge just before seven in the morning and decided to get a head start and take care of everything that morning. Since the bank opened at eight, Clyde decided to head there and pick up all the money from Ceasar. He had been calling Sonny since last night to ask where to meet him to drop off the money, but he'd got no answer, so he decided to call Martha to see if Sonny had left a message for him.

"Hello, Martha, this is Clyde."

"Hey, Clyde, how is your trip turning out?"

"It was okay, but I'm back now and—"

"You back, since when?" she asked.

"I just pulled into the city and I'm looking for Sonny. You heard from him?" The phone went silent, and Clyde asked, "Martha, you still there?"

"Yes, I'm here."

"Well, did Sonny leave a message for me?"

"Umm," Martha stammered, "I ain't heard from him since two days ago."

Clyde frowned. "Okay, if you hear from him, can you tell him to call me? It's important."

"What's the matter? Can I help you with something?" she asked.

"Naw, it's not that important," Clyde lied. "Listen, I gotta go. I'm about to meet Ceasar at his job."

"Clyde," Martha said, "uh, you think you can stop over here first?"

"I'm sorry, Martha, I got to take care of something real important."

"Please, Clyde, stop by here first. I need to see you about something."

"Martha, what's wrong? Is everything all right with Sonny?"

"Yes, far's I know, but—" Just then he lost signal on his cell phone.

Keyshia asked, "What was that all about?"

Clyde shrugged. "She probably needs more money or something." He sucked his teeth and said, "We just go to a Hundred and Twenty-fifth to see Ceasar, and I'll see her later."

When they got to 125th Street and Lenox, traffic was unusually heavy. When they finally arrived at the bank, Keyshia double-parked. Clyde looked around and saw traffic cops all over the place and told Keyshia, "Listen, we can't double-park here, so drive around the block or something and come back so we don't get a ticket." Keyshia nodded.

As Clyde got out of the car, he heard Keyshia call, "Clyde!" Clyde turned around. Keyshia smiled and said, "I love you, boy."

Clyde smiled like a little boy and said, "I love you, too, girl!"

Keyshia watched him walk to the curb and enter the bank. She drove off and after a few blocks ran smack into traffic. She peered out of the driver's-side window and saw a funeral procession. She couldn't even do a U-turn because it was so congested. After ten minutes of waiting, she stepped out of the car and watched a convoy of high-end cars follow a black hearse. Curious onlookers on the sidewalk watched the nearly fifty-car procession pull out one by one. Keyshia overheard a conversation between two drivers next to her and asked, "Whoever died must be pretty important to cause this much traffic. I wonder who it was?"

Both drivers looked at her, and one said, "You don't watch the news or read the paper?"

Keyshia smiled and said, "I was out of town for a week."

They nodded and the other said, "Well, it was hell up here in Harlem last week. Black Sam and his entire posse got wiped out! They say it was the worst killing since the St. Valentine's Day Massacre." He held up the *Daily News,* which read, HARLEM'S GANG BOSS BLACK SAM LAID TO REST TODAY.

Shocked, Keyshia quickly got back into the car and pulled over to park it. The men looked at her as if she had gone mad. Keyshia jumped out of the car and ran the two long blocks down 125th Street toward the bank as if her life depended on it.

When Clyde entered the bank, he looked for Ceasar but he didn't spot him. He observed a security guard watching him closely, so he walked over to an older female employee who was sitting in a cubicle and asked, "Excuse me, ma'am, I'm looking for my brother Ceasar Barker?"

She smiled and walked toward him and said, "You look just like your brother, only taller. I'm Mrs. Williams, your brother's supervisor. I just hung up with Ceasar and he said he will be a little late. You can wait for him over there, if you like." She pointed to a seating area in the rear.

Clyde thanked her and said that he would. He took a seat, and no sooner did he sit down than three men burst through the bank door and announced a robbery. Clyde couldn't believe this was happening. The men, who held shotguns and handguns, quickly rounded up everyone.

"Put your fuckin' nose to the floor, and if one of you mother-fuckas moves, I'm gonna blow your fuckin' brains out."

Clyde immediately recognized the voice. One masked man came to the back and pointed the weapon in Clyde's face and ordered him up front. When he got to the front, the masked man with the shotgun paused and stared him in the eye. Clyde recognized him instantly—it was his brother Sonny. Clyde knew enough to play everything cool and obeyed the man's order to lie on the floor. Clyde heard Wolf's voice as he grabbed the older lady he was speaking to earlier and ordered her to open the door to where the tellers were. She screamed in fear, and Wolf whacked her with his handgun and pushed her to the door, telling her all the while, "Shut the fuck up, bitch, and get them keys out!" Clyde didn't know the third man, but he appeared to be very nervous and shaky, which was a bad sign.

The security officer who was lying beside him reached toward his ankle.

Damn, Clyde thought, Sonny's slipping by not watching his hostage. He began to panic when he watched the security guard pull the pistol out of his leg holster and begin to rise. He saw the glint in the security guard's eye and read his body language: He wanted to be a hero, and Clyde knew he was going to kill his brother, who had his back to them. Clyde rose quickly to his feet, grabbed the man's hand, and wrestled with him for the gun.

Pow . . . pow . . . pow! Shots flew everywhere as the security officer squeezed off round after round. The third gunman panicked and ran out of the bank. Sonny and Wolf joined in the struggle and bashed the security officer in the head with the shotgun, causing him to go down instantly. The hostages began to cry and scream for their lives. Sonny, Wolf, and Clyde ran out of the bank, but as soon as they had exited, they were swarmed by police cars and cops pointing weapons at them. They knew it was a no-win situation, and all three fell to their knees.

When Keyshia got to Lenox Avenue, she panicked when she saw the bank surrounded with police cars. She ran at top speed and got there just in time to see the police handcuff Clyde and walk him to a squad car. Keyshia lost all feeling in her legs as she collapsed at the sight of seeing her man arrested. "Clyde!" she yelled.

Clyde looked up and saw Keyshia, and he was totally helpless. "Clyde, no!" she screamed over and over. She tried to get to him, to just touch him, but she couldn't. The burly cops wouldn't allow it. Just then, Ceasar came up behind her and hugged her as they watched both his brothers be led into a police car.

Chapter 31

Ceasar drove Keyshia home. Though he was saddened by the fact that both his brothers had been arrested for armed bank robbery, he couldn't help but feel violated because his brothers had committed the act at his place of employment. Keyshia told Ceasar that Clyde was innocent.

"You're wrong, Ceasar. Clyde didn't have anything to do with that bank robbery," she pleaded tearfully. "We just came back from South Carolina when I dropped Clyde off to meet you to get the money you were gonna give him to pay off Black Sam."

Ceasar asked, "Why would Clyde want to pay Black Sam his money back if he was dead?"

"Clyde didn't know, Ceasar! We just pulled back into New York! When I heard I ran to tell Clyde!"

Ceasar's mind was processing all this as he stared at the floor. "Did Clyde ever tell Sonny that he came up with all the money?"

Keyshia shook her head. "I don't think so. He was trying to contact Sonny for a while to let him know where to meet him to pay Black Sam his money."

As Ceasar stumbled to the couch, Keyshia caught him just in time. "Ceasar, what's the matter?"

Spooked, he looked into Keyshia's eyes and said, "Sonny killed Black Sam for Clyde."

Equally horrified, Keyshia asked, "How do you know Sonny did it?"

Ceasar's face collapsed as he said, "Because I told him to." He explained, "You remember when we went to see my mother at the nursing home that Sunday?" Keyshia nodded. "This was before you guys told me how much money you came up with. I was talking to Sonny about Clyde getting involved with Black Sam, and Sonny told me how much money he owed him." Ceasar shook his head. "When he told me how much, I panicked and told him that Clyde couldn't come up with that kind of money and that he should get him out of it. No," Ceasar said with emphasis, "I ordered Sonny to get Clyde out of it by any means necessary." His voice cracked, as he turned to her and said, "Oh, my God, I didn't think he would kill all them people for Clyde!"

Keyshia tried to assure him that it wasn't his fault, but it didn't matter. He felt like he was just as involved with the murders as Sonny. Ceasar began to fall to pieces, crying hysterically. "Listen, Ceasar," she said, "we got to think. We can't afford to buckle right now." She looked him straight in his eyes, and he admired her strength. "Clyde and Sonny need us right now, and we are their only help." Ceasar began to pull himself together and sat up straight and nodded.

"Now," she continued, "the best thing we could do for them right now is hire a good lawyer, right?" Ceasar nodded. "Do you still have the money that Clyde gave you?"

Again Ceasar nodded. "Yes, I left it in my safe deposit box I have at my job."

"Okay," said Keyshia, "that's a hundred and thirty thousand right there. Now all we got to do is find them a good lawyer, and I think that's where you have to come in, Ceasar."

They talked strategy for nearly two hours.

"I just wish I was there when Clyde walked in the bank." Ceasar said. "Maybe none of this would have happened."

"Ceasar," Keyshia asked, "you wasn't inside the bank when Clyde walked in?"

"No, I called in to work an hour late. Martha wanted me to stop by that morning. She said it was an emergency, but when I got there, nobody answered the door."

Keyshia told him that Martha was home when Clyde talked to her that morning and that Clyde told her he was going to see Ceasar at his job that morning.

Ceasar shrugged it off and quickly changed the subject. He looked at his watch and said, "Ooh, it's getting late. What I'm going to do is go to the bank and get the money so we can find them a lawyer. I want you to give me a call in the morning." He handed her his card. "That way, we could meet up and go and find one together."

Keyshia smiled and nodded, but she still felt uneasy. He gave her a light hug and kiss and assured her things would be okay.

Keyshia tossed and turned all night. Unable to sleep, she stayed up and stared at the walls. Everything was just moving too fast for her to comprehend, and she didn't know whom she could trust. She tried not to think the worst and hoped that the truth would come out, but she couldn't help thinking how everything had gone down.

At last it was six-thirty in the morning and Keyshia couldn't wait any longer. She decided to call Ceasar.

"Hello," responded the voice on the other end.

"Ceasar, this is Keyshia."

"Keyshia, I got some bad news." Keyshia immediately grew tense. "I got fired yesterday because they found out that both my brothers were part of the robbery and they think that I'm somehow a part of it. I'm under investigation by the police."

He paused for a moment before he continued. "Keyshia, they froze my funds and sealed my safe deposit box with the money."

Keyshia flipped. "What!" she yelled. "No, Ceasar, don't say that, don't say that!" She began pacing the floor.

"I'm sorry, Keyshia."

"Ceasar, please tell me this is a fucking joke?"

"Keyshia, these are my brothers' lives we talking about. I wouldn't joke like that."

"Ceasar, if you got something to do with this shit—"

He interrupted her, "Keyshia, I know how much you love Clyde, and you're not thinking right, but watch before you say something you might regret. These are my brothers, my fucking blood, and you think I had something to do with this shit?"

Keyshia would not back down. "Remember what I said, Ceasar—if I find out you had something to do with this shit, I'm coming after you, that's my word, I'm coming after you!" She heard a click on the other end of the line and threw her cell phone at the wall, smashing it to pieces. Suddenly she felt sick and fell on the bed. She folded herself into a ball and cried and cried until she fell asleep.

She was alone again!

Keyshia waited downtown at Manhattan court for sixteen hours until they finally called Clyde's name, along with Sonny and Wolf, to be arraigned. Ceasar was there also, but he sat on the other side of the court several rows behind her. Keyshia sat up when the three men walked into the courtroom. Clyde looked tired and disheveled but otherwise okay.

Clyde turned around periodically, nodding to Keyshia that everything would be all right, but it pained her to see him hand-cuffed and helpless as he stood before the judge.

Keyshia hadn't a clue about the legal jargon the lawyers were exchanging, nor did she care. The only thing she hoped for was that Clyde would be released, because she knew that there was surely a mix-up. But her world came tumbling down when the judge announced bail of two hundred and fifty thousand dollars each. She couldn't comprehend what was happening as the court officer began to escort Clyde and the two other men right back where they had entered.

"No!" she said, standing up. "Clyde, no!"

Clyde stopped in his tracks, turned back toward Keyshia, and yelled, "It'll be all right, baby!" over and over as they led him out the courtroom door.

A week later, Keyshia made her first visit to Clyde at Rikers Island. She was so excited to see him that she didn't sleep for two days leading up to the visit. Ever since the arrest, she had barely eaten and was a nervous wreck. She called ahead to ensure she had the proper identification and paperwork. She even found out what inmates could and could not have on visits and the maxi-mum amount of money she could leave in his commissary ac-count. She wore her best outfit the day of the visit and had to use extra makeup to hide the worry marks under her eyes to give Clyde the impression that she was holding up.

Clyde, along with Sonny and Wolf, was housed at the Beacon, a maximum-security prison on Rikers Island. Keyshia found some small comfort in the fact that he was housed with his brother and would at least be safer. While being processed, she overheard a young woman telling the officer that she was there to see Sonny Barker. Keyshia introduced herself, and the woman said her name was Cheryl. Cheryl had a bright smile and seemed very mature and educated, so Keyshia wondered how she and Sonny had gotten together. But Keyshia knew good girls always like bad boys, and Sonny was as bad as they came. Their common grief made the entire experience a lot easier on Keyshia because Cheryl had been through this process with Sonny before, so she knew what to expect and filled Keyshia in on everything.

Finally, they were permitted through the last phase of the process and entered a room with numbered tables, which were assigned to each inmate and his visitor.

"Barker, S, table six." Cheryl smiled at Keyshia, walked over to table six, and sat down.

"Barker, C, table twelve," barked the corrections officer, pointing. Keyshia followed his finger and made it to the table and sat down. Not much later, the mechanical door opened and men in gray jumpsuits and flip-flops entered the room.

Clyde was the first one to enter, and he immediately spotted Keyshia. Keyshia could hardly contain herself and shot to her feet. They embraced as if they hadn't seen each other in years. Keyshia didn't want the feeling to end as she closed her eyes and imagined they were back on the outside instead of behind steel gates. When they finally forced themselves apart, Keyshia looked in horror at Clyde's swollen and bruised face.

"Clyde, who did that to you, baby?" she cried, covering her mouth. One of Clyde's eyes was black and purple and closed shut. His lower lip was so swollen that it hung limp and was caked with blood.

"Fucking police!" he answered. "Right after that courtroom drama, they beat the shit out of me, Sonny, and Wolf." Clyde nodded. "But them punk motherfuckas had to do it with us hand-cuffed!"

"Did you see a doctor? Did you tell somebody?"

Clyde shrugged and said, "Naw, I'm all right, don't worry about it." He tried to smile. "You looking good, baby, I miss the shit out of you."

Keyshia blushed. "I miss you, too, baby. I can't even sleep." She put her head down and started crying, something she'd said she wouldn't do, but all bets were off.

"I know, baby, but don't do this to me now. I won't be able to take seeing you like this."

Keyshia tried to suck it up and apologized. "I'm sorry, I'm sorry, Clyde."

He helped her rub her tears away. "You ain't got nothing to be sorry about. It's just that I'm powerless in this bitch, and it ain't nothing I can do right now but think ill shit, you understand?" Keyshia nodded and took a deep breath.

Clyde looked around and lowered his voice. "You know I ain't had nothing to do with that shit, right?" Keyshia nodded and said she knew. "Sonny and Wolf planned that shit, and it just happened that I was in the wrong place at the wrong time. The only way I got caught up in the mix was because Sonny had slept on the security guard and I caught him pulling a gun from his ankle holster and stopped him from shooting Sonny." Clyde kept looking around for unwanted ears as he continued, "All we got to do is hire a good lawyer to separate me from all this fuck shit and I think I'm good." He looked around again and asked, "Did you hear about Black Sam and his people?" Keyshia looked around nervously and nodded.

"You know what went down?" he asked again. She nodded. He moved closer to her and said, "So that means that we ain't got to pay him." He gave Keyshia a crazed smile and continued, "We could now use that money on a lawyer for me and Sonny!" He nodded as if all his problems were solved. Keyshia put her head down, not wanting to destroy his hopes. Clyde immediately saw that something was wrong. "What is it, baby, what's wrong?"

Keyshia lifted her head and faced him. "Ceasar said that the feds confiscated the money."

Clyde shook his head as if he had heard her wrong. "What?"

"The police found out that he was your and Sonny's brother and the bank launched an investigation on him, too, and fired him."

Clyde closed his eyes as all hope seemingly disappeared. He put his hand on his head and began to rock back and forth, unable to believe what he'd just heard. When he lifted his head, Keyshia saw his tears and felt even worse for him. She didn't want to tell him about the argument she and Ceasar had got into or what she thought. She felt that he already had enough on his plate and any hint of betrayal would definitely push him over the edge.

"Didn't Sonny tell the police that you ain't have nothing to do with it?" Keyshia asked.

"Sonny and Wolf told them I wasn't part of it from the first time they arrested us, and they said they would sign statements saying so, but these motherfuckas ain't trying to hear that shit," Clyde answered, defeated. "I'm fucked!"

"Clyde," Keyshia said, "we'll work something out."

He snapped, "Work what out, Keyshia? We ain't got no money. What kind of lawyer I'm gonna have now?"

Keyshia was shocked. She'd never seen Clyde lose his cool like this before. He must have known something she didn't. "Clyde, is there something you're not telling me?"

Clyde closed his eyes and shook his head. "I'm sorry, Keysh, this place just got me stressed out. I'm not built for this shit. It's like the walls is closing in on me, yo."

Keyshia stared into his eyes and saw something worse than fear there—she saw death!

"Clyde," she said in desperation, "you not telling me every-thing."

Clyde knew he couldn't lie to her and told her flat out, "They offered us ten years to cop out."

Keyshia gasped, losing the air in her chest. Clyde continued, "Our lawyer said that we could get hit with a minimum of twenty-five years if we blow trial. The lawyer said he guarantees that we would be convicted since they caught us dead stinking in the act. Sonny and Wolf said they gonna take the deal." Keyshia was speechless. Clyde looked around again and edged closer and said with more seriousness than she'd ever heard before, "I ain't doing ten years, Keyshia. I'd rather die first!" His one good eye was aflame as he stared deep into Keyshia's eyes.

"I ain't gonna be having these motherfuckas touching me and telling me what to do, 'cause I'm gonna wind up killing one of these punk-ass cops or they gonna kill me. I refuse to live on my knees. I'll die before I do that!"

Keyshia searched his face and knew that he meant it. She pulled herself together and took a deep breath and shook her head. "I'm with you, Clyde. I'm with you and ready to die with you!" she vowed.

Clyde nodded and sat back with a smile. A smile came over her face as well, and they just stared at each other, relieved of all the pressure they'd felt earlier.

Chapter 32

Keyshia went to see Clyde nearly every visiting day in the two months that he was incarcerated. During most of their visits, they planned and strategized everything for the coming trial. Clyde decided to fight it out in court, and hopefully the truth would come out. But if not, they were willing to let the chips fall where they may and go out in a blaze. Even though Keyshia saw him three times a week on visits, that didn't stop her from writing every day. Clyde warned her not to write anything incriminating in the letters because his mail appeared to have been tampered with and read, so he taught her how to write in a code that only they would understand. This wound up being more effective than they could have ever imagined later on. Clyde began to grow suspicious of the relationship between her and Ceasar because neither spoke to the other, nor would either tell Clyde why. He decided to let his questions go because he had too much on his plate as it was.

Keyshia was running low on funds, and her biggest expenses were transportation to see Clyde and rent. Everything else she could manage, such as food, because she ate little. She didn't want to tell Clyde, but she had no choice; she was going broke. When she finally told him, she was surprised how quickly he solved the problem. He told Sonny, and the next thing she knew, his girlfriend, Cheryl, was at her door with groceries and enough money to pay the rent for six months and then some. Keyshia thanked her, and Cheryl assured her that it was Sonny's money and to call her when her money got low.

One morning Keyshia woke up sick and nauseated and ran to the bathroom to throw up. She paid no mind to it initially, but the symptoms became more consistent and problematic. She recalled having the same feeling at one point in her life, but she didn't want to believe it was possible. She bought one of those home pregnancy tests, and to her horror and surprise—it came back positive. She was dazed. She didn't know what to do and had to be sure, so she went to the health station, and sure enough, she was three months pregnant.

Keyshia was now torn by the news and couldn't believe her growing misfortune. She was alone and cried till she had nothing left. She didn't know how she was going to break the news to Clyde and came to the decision that she would keep everything to herself and let nothing come between her and her man's fate.

. . .

Keyshia arrived on Rikers Island to visit Clyde but was informed by one of the administrating officers that he was no longer allowed visits. The news caught her off guard, and she asked to see the person in charge. After waiting nearly an hour, a captain came out and spoke to her.

"Ms. Simmons?" the captain asked.

Keyshia nodded and said, "Yes, I'm Ms. Simmons, and I'm here for Clyde Barker." He put on his glasses and checked his chart, mumbling to himself as he searched for his name, "Barker, Clyde, Barker, Clyde . . . okay, Clyde Barker, yes, ma'am." He took off his glasses and said, "Yes, Ms. Simmons, Mr. Barker had to be placed in segregation. It appears that Mr. Barker attacked an officer, and when an inmate exhibits violent behavior, he is placed in segregation and all privileges such as visitation are taken away."

Keyshia was heartbroken. "When will his visitation privileges be restored?"

"Well, to be quite honest with you, this has been Mr. Barker's second infraction of committing a violent act on an officer. His privileges are removed indefinitely." The officer seemed sympathetic. Keyshia was numb as she stared at the floor, not knowing what to do next. The officer asked, "Ms. Simmons, are you okay?"

Keyshia snapped out of her momentary shock and said, "Yes, but do you think I can visit his brother Sonny Barker? He's in the same house."

The officer nodded. "Yes, come with me." The captain escorted Keyshia to the visiting room and even went into Sonny's wing and escorted him back.

When Sonny entered the room and saw Keyshia, he put his head down and walked over to her slowly. Keyshia stood and looked him in the eyes without saying a word. Sonny said, "Hey, sis."

A tear fell from Keyshia's eyes, and he quickly embraced her.

They sat down, and Sonny explained everything that had gone down with his brother inside the walls.

"Clyde just ain't built for this shit. I mean, me and my man Wolf been doing li'l skid bids all our life, we could eat them ten years, but Clyde, he seems like he can't do none. I mean, he ain't a punk or nothing, he just, I don't know what it is." Sonny kept shaking his head. "It's like he just changing, like he's losing his mind," Sonny tried to explain. "It's like, it's like he just turned cold, like he lost the will to live or something. First he wouldn't talk to the police, then he just stopped talking to everybody— including me." Sonny gazed at the walls as he continued, "Then he really started bugging, and that's why they put him in deep seg. He started refusing to do anything the police said, then out of the blue, he beat this officer down just because he asked to see his ID card, yo." Sonny shook his head. "Clyde just attacked him like he was crazy, and when the other duty officer came to help him . . ." He looked at Keyshia before he said, "He bit a piece of his fucking ear off, yo!" Keyshia put her head down.

He shook his head and tears began to fall from his eyes. He looked at Keyshia and said, "I never wanted to get Clyde stuck like this. It's all my fault, 'cause I was fucking greedy." His eyes pleaded with Keyshia. "I would gladly take his years for him, Keyshia, you got to believe me. I would never want to see my baby brother like this. I'm dying inside because of it, you hear me, dying! I never should have tried to rob that bank, that ain't my fucking style, I don't know what I was thinking." Sonny clenched his jaw. "I should have never listened to her fucking greedy ass in the first place!"

Keyshia frowned and thought back to what Clyde had said about Martha right before they got to the bank that morning when he called her greedy. "Who are you talking about, Sonny?"

Sonny shook his head and waved off his comment. "Nothing, it's not important."

They made small talk, and Keyshia told him about the trip they took upstate to see his father.

"Y'all did what?" Sonny said with surprise and anger.

Keyshia explained to him about why Clyde wanted to confront his father. "He actually went there to confront him and make him answer for your mother. Clyde was gonna give him an option of killing himself or waiting till he got out and then he was gonna kill him." Sonny's eyes burned with intensity as he listened. "Clyde even smuggled in some pills that was laced with poison to give him."

"So what happened?" Sonny asked quickly.

"He didn't give them to him."

Sonny was livid. "Why not?"

" 'Cause he changed his mind. He didn't think that he shot your mother."

Sonny rolled his eyes and gripped his seat tightly to prevent himself from standing up and throwing the chair. "And he believed that lying bastard?"

Keyshia shook her head. "Sonny, one thing I learned about Clyde is that he's a good judge of character. He knows how to read people, read people's minds. He could tell if they were a friend or enemy, lying or telling the truth, reliable or untrustworthy, just by watching their body language."

Sonny nodded. "Yeah, he always been like that." He chuckled. "That li'l nigga wouldn't say a word, just watch you. And when you think he wasn't looking, he would tell you about yourself if you tried to put one over on him."

Keyshia said, "That's why he forgave your father, Sonny, because he knew he loved your mother too much to ever hurt her."

Sonny folded his arms and thought about everything she said. "Well, somebody did. That bullet ain't get in her face by itself."

After their visit was over, they hugged and said their good-byes. "You make sure you take care of yourself out there and don't worry yourself to death, awright?" Sonny said like a big brother. Keyshia smiled and said that she wouldn't. She turned and was walking away when Sonny yelled out, "Yo, Keysh!"

Keyshia turned and watched him eye the floor like a child. "Yeah, Sonny?"

He looked up and said, "I'm glad to have you in the family."

Keyshia smiled and said, "Thank you, Sonny."

They walked away, and again Sonny called out to her: "Oh, yeah, happy birthday!"

Keyshia frowned for a moment and suddenly realized that it was in fact her eighteenth birthday and she hadn't even remembered it because of everything that was going on.

Sonny smiled and said, "Clyde was mentioning your birthday so much, the date never left my head."

It had been more than six months since Clyde was put into deep segregation, since Keyshia had heard or spoken to him. Unable to see him, she turned miserable and reclusive. She no longer came outside other than to drop letters to Clyde into the corner mailbox. Her world consisted of their one-bedroom basement apartment. The outside world no longer mattered to her as resentment and anger festered within her. The pregnancy was hard on her as she endured both physical and psychological pain throughout the day, and it was even harder at night. Many days she just wanted to end it right there, but she knew she had a mission to do before dying. But each time she felt her growing stomach, she couldn't help but wonder—what if she could turn back the hands of time? What if Clyde were there with her and she were in his arms as he caressed her stomach? What if they were having a boy? What if this were just a demented nightmare?

Even though Keyshia wrote Clyde faithfully every day, he no longer wrote back. She stayed in contact with his public defender to try to get an update on his case and court dates. He seemed to be overworked and too busy to speak to her in depth, which always pissed Keyshia off, but she tolerated it just to get even a bit of information. After their indictments were handed down and Clyde pleaded not guilty, all Keyshia could do was wait till his trial date, which he said would be anywhere from six months up to a year.

It was February 14, Valentine's Day, when the letter arrived, eight months from the day he was arrested—it was from Clyde. She read the letter over and over again:

> *My Beloved Aihsyek*
>
>   *As you know, my trial date is scheduled for February 23, at the Federal Court Building on 40 Centre Street. I spoke to my lawyer and he feels I have a very good chance of beating this. I feel the same way. I know you are happy for me. I'm ready to live a brand-new life shortly after that and we can live together forever and ever, just like we talked about many, many times before. There should be only three charges that stand in my way, but I'm only worried about two of them. You should give yourself about three hours' worth of time in case it is crowded. You may have to sit in the back. I want you to bring two cigars, not the cheap ones, so we can celebrate on our way out the door. Do you remember Mike? He said he can get us some of the best champagne to celebrate with, plus he will keep it on ice for us. Damn, I can hardly wait to be in your arms again. I'll write you plenty more as the days pass, so until then be well.*
>
>   *Love, Clyde*
>
> *P.S. As soon as we hear those sweet words, "Not Guilty," we going to celebrate like it's the Fourth of July.*

Keyshia knew beyond a shadow of a doubt that it was now the beginning of the end for them, and she was relieved. The mental duress of being away from Clyde was just too much for her to take any longer.

On Clyde's first day in court, on Wednesday, Keyshia was already seated in the front when they brought him into the courtroom. He wore an off-color brown suit that looked two sizes too small for him. He also had on a funky old-fashioned brown tie that looked as though someone had attempted to fix around his collar but had given up. His normally well-groomed hair was now a short, matted Afro with ragged sideburns that made him look like he was reliving the sixties. He looked so innocent and helpless as he sat in the defendant's chair, turning around periodically to get a glimpse of her. She wanted to cry! Keyshia wanted to hug him, to kiss him, or even touch him, but she knew it would be impossible. She turned suddenly and spotted Ceasar, whom she hadn't spoken to since the day she'd accused him of wrongdoing. She knew by his expression that he was equally appalled at his brother's appearance. Ceasar nodded, and she nodded in return and turned around.

When the judge entered everyone was told to rise. Keyshia vowed that she would do everything in her power to prevent Clyde from seeing her condition. She didn't want that issue to enter his mind and cause him unnecessary worry and pain. She hid her body from him by ensuring that she would always be in the courtroom before he entered and exit only after he was gone.

Pretrial jury selection had already taken place, and this was the first day the DA would present evidence to the jury. Keyshia hadn't heard a word of what was said by either attorney. The only thing that mattered was seeing her man Clyde, who was a mere ten feet in front of her.

The prosecutor vowed to the jurors that this was an open-and-shut case and that they had videos, they had fingerprints, and they had eyewitnesses. By the time he finished his opening argument, you would have thought Clyde was the Antichrist.

After two days of presenting evidence, hearing from witnesses, and watching the incriminating videos, the prosecution and defense gave their closing arguments and rested. Clyde never took the stand.

The jury was adjourned until Monday morning, when a verdict would be rendered. Keyshia was sure that it would be a long weekend.

Chapter 33

It was five-thirty in the morning when Keyshia sat up painfully in bed. She hadn't been able to get out of bed for three days now, not even to eat. She suddenly felt a need to get on her knees and pray to God, something she hadn't done since she was twelve years old and He didn't answer her prayers to have the pastor stop doing bad things to her. But this morning was different, and the urge was overwhelming to ask Him to give her the strength not only to complete her mission, but to shower, dress, and make it downtown in spite of her awful sickness. She rolled onto her knees and prayed. Prayed like she never did before as she cried out to God.

"God, I know You and me ain't communicate in a

while. And You should also know the reason why I ain't been talking to You is because You ain't been there for me like they say You would. I ain't do nothing to deserve what You been giving me. And when I do find happiness, why You don't see fit to have me keep it instead of taking it away, Lord?" Keyshia began to grow angry. "They say You suppose ta take care of fools and babies. Well, Lord, I am both—when are You going to start taking care of me for a change!" she screamed at the top of her lungs. She shook her head as if nothing mattered anymore. "Lord, I'm tired of crying. I'm to the point that I ain't got no more tears to cry, and all I want from You is to give me strength to get out of here and save the only man that ever loved me." She looked up and said, "Please, God, I ain't asking for much, please."

Keyshia closed her eyes and took a deep breath and used her elbows as support, lifting one leg at a time as she labored to rise off the floor. When she was on her feet, she closed her eyes in relief and thanked God silently before she waddled off into the bathroom, where she took a much needed shower.

Keyshia dressed slowly, looking at her body in the mirror all the while. Even though she carried small, her pregnancy was still noticeable. She rubbed her stomach ever so gently in a circular motion. She had long gotten over the guilt of putting her present circumstances in jeopardy and assured herself that this was her fate. She no longer had any options; it was get Clyde out of jail—or die trying.

Fully dressed in all black, which matched both the occasion and her mood, she felt the color would signify that this was their day of reckoning—a point of no return. She wore her black leather coat, black leather skirt, and high-heeled, knee-high black leather boots. She looked once again in the mirror—she was ready!

She waited until she could get to a pay phone to call Mike. She was about to commit a crime and didn't want Mike to be implicated by being the last person she'd made contact with before the shit went down.

"Hello?" said the man, who had obviously just awakened.

"Hello, Mike, this is Clyde's people," Keyshia said.

More alert, he said, "Hey, hey, I been waiting on your call. Everything is in place and ready to go. I'm on the job personally to hand you off them two sandwiches so you can eat. What time you gonna be there so my girl and me can meet you?"

"I'm getting there first thing."

"Cool, just tell me what you wearing so we recognize you."

"Black leather from head to toe."

"Okay, ma. I got you!" And he hung up.

Keyshia stood on the corner and checked the time. She was still nearly two and a half hours early. She turned and looked across the street at the diner. The baby was moving and turning violently; it was hungry because she hadn't eaten anything but crackers for three days. She rubbed her stomach and decided to go to the diner and give the baby a hearty breakfast, then head downtown.

When Keyshia arrived, the line into the courthouse was already starting to form, so she fell in with the rest of the blacks and Puerto Ricans who either had an appearance before the judge that day or were there to support their incarcerated loved ones.

By the time Keyshia made it to the fourth floor, she was beginning to feel dizzy. As soon as she got off the elevator, she ran to the bathroom, clutching her stomach, and then keeled over in pain. She finally reached the bathroom and ran into the nearest stall, where she threw up the morning's breakfast. She panted heavily as she fought to regain her composure when she heard a voice call her name: "Keyshia, you all right?" It was a Spanish girl about her age with a sympathetic expression on her face. Keyshia wiped the bile from her mouth and nose with her sleeve and nodded.

"I'm Lucy, Mike's girlfriend. He sent me in here to see if you was okay." Still on her knees, Keyshia nodded. It was obvious to anyone with eyes that she was not okay, so Lucy offered her a hand.

"Let me help you get on your feet."

On her feet, Keyshia nodded and said, "Thanks a lot."

In full view, Lucy looked Keyshia over and knew, even through her coat, that Keyshia was pregnant, but she remained silent. She snatched a paper towel from the wall dispenser and wet it with cold water and said, "Here, wipe you face and mouth with this. You'll feel better." Keyshia wiped her mouth and face, and Lucy handed her a fresh wet paper towel.

"Now wipe this over your forehead and the back of your neck." She did. Lucy smiled and said, "See, you looking better already." Keyshia thanked her. Lucy smiled and asked, "You sure you okay?"

Keyshia stood up straight and said. "Yeah, I'm good now, thanks."

Lucy turned around and asked, "You with Clyde, right?"

Keyshia nodded, and Lucy handed her a Louis Vuitton shoulder bag. "Mike told me to give this to you. You know what it is, right?" Keyshia nodded.

"The two sandwiches already got everything on it. There's a strap that come with it so you won't be detected. He told me to help you put it on." Keyshia was somewhat confused, and Lucy smiled and said, "Don't worry, sister, I got you covered." She led Keyshia into the stall and closed the door behind them and helped Keyshia take off her coat. After she secured the shoulder harness on Keyshia, she placed both handguns in them.

"You make sure you practice pulling them out because it can be a little stiff at first," Lucy warned her. Keyshia crossed both her arms and pulled out the weapons. It felt a little jerky to her at first, but as she practiced it became easier. Lucy helped her put on her coat again, and they exited the stall. The girl inspected Keyshia one final time and smiled. "Perfect, you don't even look like you carrying." Keyshia looked in the tiny mirror and agreed. They locked eyes, and Lucy gave her a long hug.

"Be safe, sister," she said.

Keyshia took a deep breath and nodded reassuringly. "I will, I will. Tell Mike I said thank you." Lucy forced a smile and said that she would and exited the bathroom.

The courtroom was nearly empty when Keyshia entered it. Her footsteps echoed loudly as she made her way to the second row on the right. As she sat waiting for what seemed like an eternity, she tapped her arms on the weapons that lay securely across her ribs for a sense of security.

After a long wait, the courtroom started coming alive as stone-faced court officers, court clerks, and aides busied themselves shuffling paperwork in preparation for the case at hand. Keyshia studied them all, but her main focus was on the two armed court officers who stood between her and her man. The district attorney and Clyde's court-appointed lawyer entered the courtroom.

Minutes later, the courtroom chamber door opened and in walked Clyde followed by a court officer who led him to his chair. A huge smile came to his face when he spotted Keyshia. Keyshia smiled back and noticed that today he had on a brand-new blue pin-striped suit and a fresh haircut. She marveled at how different he looked from the first time she'd seen him in court. She figured that Ceasar must have somehow got him the suit. Keyshia continued to make eye contact with Clyde, who smiled gleefully as he sat next to his lawyer. She stared at his face and watched him mouth, "Are you ready?" She nodded. She watched Clyde's eyes search the courtroom; she knew he was looking for Ceasar, who had yet to arrive.

Suddenly, the judge entered and the court officer barked for the courtroom to rise. The judge moved quickly toward his seat and waved them off to continue sitting down. Once the judge was in his seat, he asked the bailiff if the jury was ready.

"Yes, Your Honor," said the bailiff.

The judge nodded. "Bring them in."

The jurors filed into the courtroom and went to their seats. Keyshia watched Clyde stare at them all as if he were reading their thoughts, and when he turned to Keyshia he looked concerned.

The judge welcomed the jurors and explained to them the process of deliberation and coming to a verdict. After he was satisfied they understood, he dismissed them and reminded them that they had to come to a unanimous decision. They then followed the court officer to the jurors' room.

Keyshia sat on the hard courtroom bench for nearly three hours and began to grow sicker by the minute. The pregnancy and anxiety from the trial had taken their toll on her. At moments she felt as if she would pass out in the hot, unventilated courtroom as sweat drenched the inside of her leather outfit. But nothing was worse than the bile that kept rising in her esophagus, causing her to run to the bathroom and throw up painfully. She prayed for the jurors to come to the right decision quickly.

Just as she felt she would pass out, the court officer yelled, "Court come to order. The Honorable David N. Klein, presiding." The judge came out of his chambers holding a thick folder and took his place on the bench. Keyshia didn't even bother to rise. The judge cleared his throat and removed a piece of paper from the folder and looked it over. He stared down from his throne and asked, "Where is the defendant?"

One of his officers yelled, "The defendant is coming in now, Your Honor."

The judge nodded and continued shuffling through the papers before him. Finally, Clyde came through the door with the burly officer right behind him.

Keyshia came alert as the door opened and one by one the jurors began to file in. She watched every juror look straight ahead without so much as a glance in Clyde's direction—this was bad.

Now satisfied that everyone was in place, the judge nodded to the stenographer, who commenced typing. "Okay, ladies and gentlemen of the jury, it is my understanding that you have finished deliberating and are ready to render a decision." Keyshia noticed the DA was jovial and alert and that Clyde's lawyer was much more somber. She suddenly remembered him mentioning to her that the longer a jury deliberated, the better the chance the defendant had.

She began to hyperventilate and suddenly got sick in the worst way. She felt a sharp, stabbing pain in the pit of her stomach as bitter foam rose in her throat. In an instant, she was on her feet, holding her hand over her mouth to keep from vomiting on the floor and seats. Her prompt exit caused all eyes to shift in her direction, including the three court officers who now stood strategically behind Clyde and his lawyer. Clyde sat bewildered as he watched Keyshia's retreating back exit the courtroom.

Don't lose it now, Keyshia, he thought.

Keyshia rushed toward the bathroom, nearly knocking over several people in her way. She didn't make it as she threw up violently on the bathroom floor. She fell to her knees in front of the toilet bowl and prayed to God to take her out of her misery quickly.

Inside the courtroom, there was a deafening silence. Clyde scanned each juror's face and knew that it was truly about to go down. He cursed silently because a small part of him actually believed that he had a chance. He hated himself for believing such a notion, no matter how small the chance was. The time had come.

. . .

Get ready to die, was the thought that ran through Keyshia Simmons's mind as she stared into the smeared, tiny bathroom mirror in the federal courthouse building in lower Manhattan. Suddenly, she lost it again and ran to the nearest toilet stall where she fell to her knees and threw up violently. It took a full two minutes for her to gain her composure and get back to her feet. She had to—time was running out.

Unsteadily, she walked to the sink, cupped a handful of water, and splashed it over her face and into her mouth. Never in the past, it seemed, had she appreciated the vibrancy of cold water soothing her skin the way it did now. Life, it seemed, had new meaning, a new zest, a new zeal. But Keyshia knew it would only be short-lived. The beginning of the end was near, and she knew it.

She took a breath, looked down, and rubbed her growing stomach. All at once, her pitiful life seemed to flash before her eyes—she grew angry. But as suddenly as the anger came, it disappeared as she thought about the time she'd had with her man, Clyde Barker. She loved Clyde more than life itself, because he told her she was beautiful when she couldn't see beauty in herself. She loved him because he had taught her how to love herself when she never knew how. She loved him because through him, she now knew what true love really was, what it felt like to be loved and needed. They had made a promise that they would die together, and today that's exactly what it was coming to.

Using her sleeve, she wiped the remaining perspiration and water from her puffy eyes and forehead, exhaled deeply, and repeated, only this time out loud:

"Get ready to die."

The courtroom was just outside the bathroom door. Once again, and for the hundredth time, it seemed, she tapped both weapons, fully loaded Tech 9's, which were strapped securely on each side of her ribs. The only things that kept her from reuniting with her man were three court officers, three guns, and opportunity. The odds didn't matter today. What did matter was getting her man out or dying in the process. Twelve jurors, one judge, and half a chance didn't equal favorable odds. So she was ready.

She glanced at her watch—time was up, and she suddenly felt dizzy. She used the sink for support to brace herself. She took a deep, deep breath and paused. She had to clear everything out of her mind for the mission at hand. She began to think optimistically that if things worked out, they could slip out of the courtroom, be lost in all the panic that was sure to come. They might even be able to pull it off. However, playing devil's advocate, she ultimately knew that if she had to go out down and dirty, so be it.

Life wasn't worth living that much anyway. She touched her stomach once again and smiled and thought about what could have been. But then she stopped such intrusive thoughts from entering her mind. She had to be strong, strong enough for the both of them, she thought. She closed her eyes again and processed combat mode, the will to survive, the art of war. There it was: A burst of adrenaline raced through her bloodstream. Instinctively, her chest began to heave, her teeth began to grind, nose began to flare, palms began to sweat. She was ready. Suddenly, and without haste, she let go of the porcelain sink and stormed out the bathroom door.

She was ready to die!

Though he already knew the verdict, Clyde had but one thing on his mind at that point: Where was Keyshia?

He thought back to the very first time he'd seen her beautiful face. He couldn't stand her ass—but as fate has it, when love calls, love calls. There's nothing you can do. You can duck and hide, but there is no escaping it; when love comes knocking on your door, you got to let it in. Well, did Keyshia knock! She kicked down the whole fucking door, and he loved the shit out of her for that!

"Has the jury reached a verdict?" asked the judge as he sat imposingly and grim-faced upon his bench.

"Yes, Your Honor, we have," stated the jury's forewoman. An overwhelming fear came over Clyde at that moment. Not fear of being found guilty, but fear of having his plan dissolve before his eyes. *Where was Keyshia?* He turned and eyed the door again, causing the burly court officer behind him to turn and look at the door also. Be cool, he thought, and tried to make it look as if he were staring at his two family members in the benches behind him. His palms began to sweat as he questioned the letter that he'd sent her.

Suddenly, the door to the courtroom opened, and there she was. A smile came across Clyde's face as he watched his girl, his woman, his world, enter the courtroom. It was as if he could read her mind just by the expression she had on her face. She was ready, and he knew it. Body language.

"Have the jurors come to a unanimous decision?"

"Yes, Your Honor, we have."

Clyde could not hear the proceedings going on in front of him because his attention was on his baby.

He was still enthralled by her beautiful face. Tunnel vision set in. He always knew it, but he realized even more now how fortunate he was to have found her and to know what true love felt like in his brief lifetime. Something that had remained elusive since his mother was taken away from him when he was little. This beautiful woman in a brief and short period had given him a lifetime of love. A tear fell from his eyes. He couldn't help but chuckle at how chunky his normally ultrathin woman was getting. She must be stuffing herself because she's missing me, he thought. He loved the way her boots clicked with each step that she took on the marble floors. She seemed to glide with each determined step toward the front of the courtroom. Body language.

Oblivious to Clyde, the jury forewoman stood to give the judge the verdict, but Clyde was too fixated on Keyshia. He hadn't seen Keyshia since their visit so many months ago, and he missed her dearly.

Then his head turned like a curious K-9 would when he noticed how wide her hips had gotten. As she got closer, and for the first time, he noticed how big her normally small breasts had gotten.

With great, great surprise, he looked at her hard, protruding stomach, wide and round. He began to frown slightly. Keyshia was so close now that he could see the red in her eyes, the flaring of her nostrils, and the grinding jaw. He blinked rapidly as it all started to become surreal, as it finally began to register.

Oh shit, is Keyshia pregnant? Body language.

"In the case of robbery, what has the jury found?"

He watched in horror as Keyshia reached inside her blazer jacket with both hands.

"We find the defendant, Clyde Barker . . ."

"Oh, shit," he stammered.

"Guilty!"

As if everything were a demented nightmare, he watched Keyshia unbuckle her coat with vengeance in her eyes.

Clyde rose to his feet and yelled, "Nooooooo!" as Keyshia reached for the weapons. He watched the court officer turn around and reach for his weapon. Clyde felt helpless, and all he could do was yell, "Your mind is your nine! Your mind is your nine!" But Keyshia could not hear him. It was too late!

"No!" he screamed.

Out of nowhere, Ceasar came rushing down the aisle and grabbed Keyshia tightly before she could pull out her weapons. By then the officers had Clyde on the ground and their weapons pointed at Keyshia, who was struggling to be released from Ceasar's clutches. The entire court had hit the floor, including the judge and jury, as pandemonium filled the room!

"It's okay, Keyshia!" Clyde yelled as the officer put his knee in Clyde's back. "I'm okay, baby."

Keyshia suddenly lost her bluster, and when she did the pain in her body became excruciating. "Oh, God! I'm sorry, Clyde, I'm sorry!" she repeated. She was barely able to stand. Ceasar held her unsteadily in his arms, and that's when he noticed streams of liquid flowing down her legs. The officers pointed their weapons at them and yelled for them both to get on the ground.

"She's going into labor," Ceasar explained. "Her water burst. She's got to get to the hospital!"

The two officers, still on edge, eyed them suspiciously. After noticing a puddle of liquid underneath Keyshia, they put their weapons away and one rushed to the telephone as the other helped Keyshia to one of the benches. Keyshia screamed in pain as they laid her on the hard bench. The jurors and judge finally stood, sure that they were out of danger as word of the woman in labor spread fast.

Keyshia's eyes were bloodshot as she pulled Ceasar close to her face and whispered through clenched teeth, "I got two guns on me."

Ceasar turned around and saw one of the officers standing over them and yelled, "Why are you still standing here? My sister is about to have a baby! Go find a doctor!" Between the panic and Ceasar's authoritative tone, the officer scampered out of the courtroom to find help. Keyshia quickly undid the guns, and Ceasar stuffed them in his coat.

"Oh God!" she yelled as her eyes widened. "Ceasar, help me. I feel the baby coming!"

Ceasar stood up and yelled to anyone who could hear, "Somebody help, she's having the baby right now!"

Suddenly, one of the female jurors jumped out of the jury box and yelled, "Judge, I'm a registered nurse!" The judge, who was caught up in the excitement, nodded for her to aid Keyshia. The lady sprang into action and asked for help getting Keyshia to the floor.

The two officers pulled Clyde, who was now in handcuffs, onto his feet and were taking him out of the courtroom, but he pleaded, "Please, that's my girl. Please, don't take me away yet. I won't do nothing. I just want to see that my girl is all right." He looked both officers in the eyes as he begged someone for the first time in his life, "Please, man."

The officers felt sympathy for him and looked toward the judge, who had heard Clyde's plea and granted him permission to stay. Clyde, as well as everyone else in the room, was on edge as they all watched the party on the floor working intently. Suddenly, the gurgling sound of a baby's cry filled the courtroom. Everyone began to breathe easier and applauded. Even the judge felt an overwhelming sense of relief that everything had worked out. Clyde was near tears and was still worried about Keyshia. The paramedics arrived and quickly placed Keyshia and her newborn on the stretcher. As they lifted her and the baby, who was now wrapped securely in a blanket, she yelled to them that she didn't want to leave until the baby's father could see his child. The jurors, the office staff, and even the normally robotic officers looked toward the judge for approval.

With all eyes upon him, the judge thought back to how he'd felt when his first child was born over thirty years ago. He nodded and said, "Let the man see his newborn child." Once again the courtroom erupted in applause as the paramedics wheeled Keyshia and the baby forward. The court officers removed the handcuffs from Clyde as he walked timidly toward Keyshia and the baby.

Crying, Keyshia said, "Clyde, meet your son . . . Clyde Junior."

Clyde couldn't believe his eyes; he blinked rapidly as he tried to focus on his boy, whom she cradled in her arms. He kissed her and told her he loved her. Keyshia gestured for Clyde to hold him, but Clyde was too afraid. He looked up at the judge, who said, "Go ahead, son, hold your baby."

Clyde smiled and picked up his son with the gentleness of a lamb and cradled him in his arms. The world suddenly felt brand-new to Clyde as the heavens began to open up and blessings rained down upon him. He had a strong urge to live as he caressed his son in his arms and whispered in his little ear, "I will always be there for you, Clyde."

Chapter 34

Clyde Barker Jr. was a beautiful and healthy six-pound-five-ounce baby boy. Ceasar was so thrilled with the birth of his nephew that one would have thought he was the father, the way he came to the hospital every day and fussed over him. Keyshia had to stay in the hospital for over a week because she had lost a lot of blood during the birth. By the time she was due to be released, Ceasar insisted that she and the baby stay with him in his two-bedroom apartment. Uncomfortable with his generous offer, Keyshia declined. Ceasar knew that she didn't have a chance on earth to provide his nephew with decent housing, clothing, and food, unless she got on public assistance, and that would take time. In overcrowded New

York City, she would not be able to get an apartment until welfare found her and the baby one in the housing projects. She might have to go through the shelter system and wait months, maybe years, until she qualified and received section 8 vouchers to aid with the rent. Ceasar refused to take no for an answer. He knew Keyshia was proud, so he told her that he would be giving the room to his nephew, but he needed someone there to take care of him. Keyshia smiled and got his point and said that she would, but she would contribute to the household all the same when the baby got old enough and she could find a job and pay her way. Ceasar smiled and said:

"Okay, you pay your share and help me with the rent 'cause I could barely pay it by myself now; my new job as a teller at a credit union doesn't pay as much as my position at the bank. In the meantime, you can pay your way by doing chores around the house."

Keyshia nodded and said, "Well, I think that's pretty steep, but I think you got yourself a couple of roommates." She and Ceasar hugged.

During the two weeks that Clyde awaited his sentencing hearing, he had a one-hundred-eighty-degree change in attitude. Having seen and touched his child—his son—made a world of difference. He now had a purpose. He wanted to give his son something he never recalled having—a father. If Clyde had known that Keyshia was pregnant, he would have given serious thought to the ten years that they offered him. Now he was guaranteed a minimum of twenty years. But the sting was not as bad because his baby boy gave him comfort and strength.

Keyshia, Ceasar, and the baby were in the courtroom the day of Clyde's sentencing. They had prayed the night before in hopes of a modern-day miracle.

"Will the defendant rise," said the grim-faced judge.

"Clyde Barker, you were tried and found guilty by a jury of your peers. You are hereby sentenced to twenty years in federal prison."

Keyshia sobbed and shook her head, unable to believe what was happening. Clyde quickly turned around and stood tall to let Keyshia know that he was strong, but his weary eyes told another story.

To make matters worse, Clyde was remanded to Leavenworth, a federal penitentiary located in Kansas, diminishing all Keyshia's hopes of having regular visits so he could get to know his son. Keyshia and Ceasar stood and watched the officers handcuff Clyde. With tears in his eyes for his baby brother, Ceasar hugged Keyshia and nodded and yelled to Clyde that his family would be taken care of and not to worry.

Life for Keyshia would never again be the same.

For weeks, Keyshia remained locked in her room, coming out only to fix the baby's formula or give him a bath. Ceasar knew that if Keyshia didn't snap out of her funk, she would risk losing her sanity and her will to live. He knew firsthand about living in misery because he and his brothers had lived like that for most of their young lives. He didn't want his nephew to grow up under the same circumstances. So after nearly a month of her seclusion and solitude, Ceasar finally decided to confront Keyshia and knocked on her door.

"Keyshia, can I come in?" He heard the bed squeak, but she did not respond. So he knocked again. "Keyshia, it's Ceasar, I'd like to come in."

He heard Keyshia cough, and then she said, "Come in."

Ceasar turned the knob slowly and peeked in. "You dressed?"

Keyshia sat up and cleared her throat and said yes. It was

dark inside the room, and if it weren't for the moonlight coming through the window, it would have been impossible to see her.

"How's the baby?" he asked as he eased into the room and over to the bassinet where the baby slept.

She cleared her throat again and said, "He's good. His appetite is picking up. He had six bottles today already."

Ceasar nodded his approval. He looked down at Keyshia, and even though the room was pitch-black, he could still see that she was a mess. Her hair was wild and frayed, and her eyes looked as if they were sucked back into her sockets. And then there was her body. Even in the darkness Ceasar could see that she was nothing more than skin and bones. He was sure she was under one hundred pounds, and he was devastated and could no longer hide his dissatisfaction with her worrying herself to death.

"Keyshia," he said as his voice cracked. "Baby, you can't keep going on like this, staying in your room and not eating." Keyshia grew conscious of her body and pulled the sheets over her as he talked. He sat at the edge of the bed and continued in a soft, gentle tone. "I miss Clyde like you do, but I know that I got to live, and you got to live and survive without him." He stared at her, hoping he would get through.

"If you don't find a reason to live, then all you're going to do is worry yourself to death, and that won't do Clyde or the baby any good." He paused and edged closer to her and rubbed her hand. "I'm going to tell you this story. It's called 'Footprints in the Sand,' about a man who lost hope but had the courage to go on. One day this man was lost in the desert and was walking miles and miles with no water and no hope. Anyway, it was like a hundred and twenty degrees in the shade, but he kept walking and walking. After a day or so, he became weak from the lack of water and was ready to pass out, but he knew if he did, he would die, so he called out to God for help. He looked up toward the beaming sun and called out and said, 'God, please help me, I'm not sure if I can make it any longer and I need Your help.' Then suddenly, a pair of footprints appeared next to him, and he knew it was God guiding him in the right direction, giving him the will to go farther. So after a day or two of walking, he noticed that he no longer saw two sets of footprints in the sand, only one, and he became angry with God. This went on for days, and then finally, over the horizon, when he was sure he could no longer make it, he saw a community where people dwelled and knew that he'd made it. And just then, the second pair of footprints appeared again, and he yelled out to God his displeasure, 'God, You said that You would never leave me when I needed You most, but when I was in the desert almost dying, You left me, 'cause I didn't see Your footprints anymore.' God spoke and said, 'Son, I never left you. When you saw one set of footprints in the sand, that was me carrying you.' "

Ceasar looked at Keyshia and said real serious, "Keyshia, when you think you have no more hope, call on God and ask Him for hope, ask Him to give you a purpose to go on, and He will carry you." Keyshia stared at him, smitten by his words of wisdom. Ceasar knew he had grown to love Keyshia because of how much she loved his brother. He gave her a warm embrace and said good night.

Keyshia sat up the remainder of that night thinking about all that Ceasar had said. Then suddenly, Clyde's words popped into her mind, and she repeated, "My mind is my nine." She repeated these words aloud for the rest of the morning until they took hold of her. Then just like that, she had a purpose, a reason to move on and live.

That morning, when Ceasar got up to go to work, he was surprised to smell bacon. When he walked into the kitchen, he saw Keyshia standing over the stove, cooking. He looked at the table and saw it was set with two plates with scrambled eggs, biscuits, and orange juice.

Ceasar smiled and said, "What is going on here? Looks like somebody rose from the dead."

"Yeah, you were right about me isolating myself, it ain't good for me or the baby. Sit down and let me serve you some breakfast," said Keyshia as she brought the plate of bacon to the table.

Ceasar was impressed and said with a mouth full of food, "Damn, Keyshia! I didn't know you knew how to burn."

Keyshia smiled. "Boy, you didn't know? Where you think I'm from?"

He nodded and said, "I know that's right," as he ate the last bit of food on his plate.

"Seconds?" Keyshia asked. "I made more than enough." Before he could answer, she was already putting more food on his plate.

As they ate, Keyshia said, "Ceasar, can I ask you a question?"

He stopped chewing and wiped his mouth. "You know you can ask me anything," he told her.

Keyshia tilted her head to the side, searching for the right words to say. "When you spoke to Clyde last week, how did he sound to you? What did y'all talk about?"

Ceasar cleared his throat and thought back. "We talked mainly about you and the baby." He shrugged and added, "He was just concerned about y'all two being all right. He thanked me for taking y'all in and said that he owes me. I told him he doesn't owe me anything, but to take care of himself because we will be all right. That's mainly it."

"Did he sound sad or depressed or anything like that?"

Ceasar frowned and said, "No. As a matter of fact, he didn't even sound like he was locked up. He sounds more like a person who was on vacation or something."

Keyshia nodded. "That's exactly how he sounded to me. He

does that so he can relieve us from worrying, but he is really miserable. I know Clyde." Ceasar knew she was right.

"Like with y'all father," Keyshia pointed out. "You never would have imagined that Clyde harbored so much deep feelings of hate towards your father and that he dreamed for years about wanting to kill him, would you?"

Ceasar shook his head. "No. In a million years I would have never imagined that because we never talked to him about it. Clyde never allowed us to know if he was in pain his whole life. So he was always a walking time bomb waiting to explode. He always would talk and act like everything was okay, and we had no choice but to believe him."

"Ceasar, we got to do something to get him out of jail or he gonna die!" Keyshia said.

Ceasar grew concerned and threw up his hands. "What could we do? They already found him guilty, and there's nothing else for us to do. The feds don't even give time off for good behavior, so he got to do a flat bid twenty years straight." He watched Keyshia put her head down and felt bad. "I'm sorry I had to say that, Keyshia, and I know how much you love my brother, but you got to look at the reality of it all and move on—for you and the baby's sake."

After a long silence, Keyshia lifted her head defiantly and said, "Ceasar, the reality is that Clyde is innocent and I can't help but hold on to that. He always told me that for every problem there is a solution." She looked Ceasar directly in the eye and said, "Now my man got a problem and I'm gonna find him a solution." She stood strong and said, "All I got to do is find it."

"Damn, sis, I really believe you going to do it. You convinced me. Hell, you should have been Clyde's lawyer instead of that sorry-ass one he had, you would have got him off." Ceasar thought back to the case. "That sorry bastard didn't even put Clyde on the stand." He began turning red. "Shit, I wonder how many other mistakes his dumb ass made that we don't know about."

He looked at Keyshia and said, "Now, if there was any way to get Clyde off, it would lie in how many mistakes his damn lawyer made, and we could get a new trial going."

"Ceasar!" Keyshia said. "What do you think of me going back to school?"

Chapter 35

Five years had passed, and Keyshia was in her final year as a student at the John Jay College of Criminal Justice.

After the conversation with Ceasar, she'd found an alternative high school designed for teenage mothers. She'd taken on her studies with a vengeance, excelling academically to levels that surprised even her. She'd graduated at the top of her class with honors and was even featured in one of the city's newspapers as a student who had overcome many obstacles. Keyshia had received a number of scholarships and used them to help her along in college.

Keyshia and Ceasar had been holding Clyde down over the years by sending him letters and making sure he always had money in his commissary account. Along with Clyde, Jr., they visited him more than a dozen times so he could watch his son grow up. Each time they visited, it felt like Christmas, because they were able to spend the entire day together, hugging, kissing, and holding each other. But each visit left Keyshia with a bittersweet feeling inside, because even though she could touch Clyde and kiss him, she knew it was only temporary. Moments like these made her even more determined to get him out. She never told Clyde her plan, though, and he was happy just to know that she was still there for him and doing well for herself.

Ceasar became Keyshia's biggest cheerleader. He would pick up the baby after work and take care of him until Keyshia got home from school at ten o'clock at night.

Keyshia was a B student and maintained a 3.0 GPA. Math and philosophy kept her from being at the top of her class, but she wasn't mad because she figured that she was working three times as hard as the average student: In addition to being a full-time student, she had a full-time job and was a full-time mother.

During Keyshia's law studies class, she would find herself in the middle of sometimes nasty and heated debates about such issues as abortion, government regulation, homeland security, freedom of speech, and the war. She studied both sides of the issue at hand before committing herself to an opinion so she could slay her opponents by backing them into a corner and then using what they said against them. She learned she was a natural at this because the skills she needed to debate law issues were not so different from those she had used to survive on the streets—

with both, it was a matter of attitude and knowing what you were talking about.

After one of those heated debates, her professor stopped her before she left the classroom. "Ms. Simmons, may I have a word with you?"

Keyshia tried to hide her displeasure, because she was sure the professor would have something arrogant to say to her. This was the second semester she had Professor Akills, and they never saw eye to eye. Keyshia thought that he always tried to embarrass her whenever she raised her hand to give her opinion or that he would purposely call on her when there was a tough question that needed to be answered. He did it so often that the other students in the class began to notice and would often ask Keyshia for the answers. This forced Keyshia to learn everything early on her syllabus or for a particular case or issue so she could be prepared if the professor called on her. Then one day it happened: Keyshia caught him slipping and nearly had him at a loss for words, and he conceded that she was absolutely right. At that point, Keyshia felt she had won the biggest victory in her life, and that moment changed her. But the assault did not end there, because Keyshia became his personal punching bag many times afterward. She never got used to the feeling of defeat, so she stayed sharp and on point at all times when she was in his class.

"Yes, Professor?" Keyshia asked now, expecting him to say something sarcastic.

"Ms. Simmons," he asked sternly, "have you decided what law school you will be attending yet?"

"What?" Keyshia was taken aback by the question and wasn't sure how to answer it.

He said impatiently, "Come on, it's a simple enough question. You're not normally this speechless in class, Ms. Simmons."

Still flabbergasted by his comment, she said, "I was planning on becoming a paralegal."

The professor raised an eyebrow and said mockingly, "Ms. Simmons, you can't be serious. A paralegal? I'm talking about obtaining your law degree."

"I don't know. I never gave it much thought, to be honest with you."

"Well, you should, because I intend to recommend you to the law school advisory board for a full scholarship, given to students who show a particular inclination and merit for law studies. Only three students are recommended each year, and you are to be one of them, Ms. Simmons. You would make a good litigation attorney because you could argue yourself out of a paper bag. I should know, you've embarrassed me this semester more times than I care to admit."

Though Keyshia was basically the same age as most of her fellow college students, she felt much older because they seemed so lax when it came to their education, while she was a lot more willing and determined to get what she wanted in a hurry—her degree. She worked in a law office during the day and went to school at night. She was like a sponge in school and at her job, soaking up everything and doing whatever needed to be done, such as typing, taking memos, filing, or data entry tabulation.

At Hemmingway, Adorno, and Shaw, a law office that specialized in criminal cases, she learned about the inner workings and jargon of the law. Her manager, Ms. Hemmingway, was a black woman. Coworkers often mistook Keyshia for her, they looked so similar. Ms. Hemmingway was fond of Keyshia, because she reminded her of herself when she was coming up and working hard during the day while attending law school at night. She often had private talks with Keyshia, urging her to become a lawyer, but Keyshia thought she was just flattering her, and besides, she had no time to commit to several more years of school; her man was rotting away in jail, and she needed to find a loophole or mistake that had happened during his trial.

One day at work, Keyshia was asked to pull a file on one of their newest clients, a case in which Hemmingway, Adorno, and Shaw had won an appeal because of improper counsel. This particular case caught Keyshia's attention because not only was it a federal case like Clyde's, but it was an embezzlement case, which in the court's eyes was just as bad as a bank robbery.

On Keyshia's lunch break, she studied all the briefs on the case and learned that evidence that would have helped Clyde had been omitted from his case. She could not believe how negligent the defense had been with his trial and highlighted each and every infraction that she thought would apply to Clyde's case.

Keyshia filed paperwork to obtain transcripts from Clyde's trial, and in the meantime she contacted his public defender and learned that he had filed an appeal within thirty days after Clyde was found guilty and that it was still pending after all these years.

"Hey, Ceasar," Keyshia said as she walked through the door.

Ceasar was on the couch half-asleep when she walked in, and he yawned as he asked, "Oh, hey, Keyshia, how was school tonight?"

"We had a test in philosophy and it kicked my butt, but I think I passed."

"Good," said Ceasar as he stood up and stretched.

"How was Clyde, Jr. today?"

"Oh, his teacher said he told her off today because he didn't want to take a nap because he preferred to finish coloring."

Keyshia chuckled and said, "What am I going to do with that boy?"

"He's just doing the same thing Clyde used to do when he was little, because he was afraid to go to sleep thinking he was gonna miss something." They both laughed.

"Anyway," Ceasar said, "he had his dinner and bath, so I'm going to sleep."

"Thanks, Ceasar," Keyshia said as he walked toward his room.

Ceasar snapped his fingers suddenly. "Oh yeah, a package came for you today. It's heavy as hell, too. It's on the dining table. I'll see you in the morning."

"Night, Ceasar."

Keyshia knew that it was the transcripts and waited till he'd closed his room door to pick up the package and run to her room. He was right, she thought, that package weighed a ton. She put it on her bed and looked over at Clyde, Jr., who was sound asleep in his bed. Clyde, Jr. was growing fast, and it was evident he was going to be as tall as his daddy. She turned on the desk light and ripped open the package, then pulled out the mounds of paper and began reading each one.

Keyshia stayed up all that night underlining sections of the briefs with yellow and red highlighters. She made notes on anything disputable and was happy to see that even to her unskilled eyes, there were several questionable and dubious items. She knew she had her work cut out for her and wasn't the least bit daunted by it all.

Every night and all weekend for a month straight, Keyshia spent time picking the case apart one page at a time. Ceasar noticed the amount of time she was spending on the "project" she was doing for school and became interested in her clandestine task.

It was Saturday afternoon and he was standing at Keyshia's

room door with little Clyde's coat in his hand. He and his nephew had just come back from the matinee at the Magic Johnson Theatre on 125th Street.

"Keyshia, what are you doing?" he asked.

Keyshia jumped. "Damn, Ceasar, you scared me half to death."

Smiling, Ceasar walked closer and watched her put her hands across the papers she was working on. "I'm sorry, but I'll ask again. What are you doing that's so important that you can't spend time with your family no more?"

Keyshia gazed at him for a second and answered, "I'm working on this project—"

Ceasar quickly cut her off. "I know, you're working on a project for school, but what is it about?"

Keyshia decided to come clean, so she searched the papers and handed one to Ceasar to read for himself. He stared at it and looked at Keyshia before he began reading.

"*United States v. Clyde Barker.* . . . You just don't get enough, do you?" Ceasar said, giving her a sly smile.

Keyshia shrugged. "I got to try to save my man."

Ceasar melted and walked over to hug the girl who loved his brother more than she loved herself at times. He released her, wiped the tears from his eyes, and asked, "Well, what can I do to help?"

She smiled and began showing and explaining everything to him.

Later that night, Ceasar and Keyshia sat on the couch relaxing after going through all the paperwork.

"Do you really think what you found could get Clyde's case reopened?"

Keyshia nodded slowly. "According to the law and other cases similar to Clyde's, yes, it can. All we have to do now is get a lawyer to file an appeal and hope that a judge will grant it.

After that, he would go through the entire trial process all over again and we would pray that a jury would see things our way this time."

Ceasar asked, "What does Clyde think of all this?"

"I didn't tell him. I don't want to get his hopes up too high."

Ceasar thought about that and agreed. "Why can't we just go to a lawyer now and see if you're right, see if he got a chance?"

Keyshia looked at Ceasar and said, "Do you have any idea what it would cost to have a lawyer go through these files, Ceasar? It took me over a month just to come up with what I got, and that's exactly what they would have to do just to get to the crux of this case. Do you have any idea what lawyers bill by the hour these days? And they don't even do the research! They get some lowly intern or prelaw student to do the bulk of the work and bill the client two hundred dollars an hour. I know, 'cause that's how they do it at my job." Keyshia paused to let Ceasar process it all and then continued, "This way, we can file the papers and necessary documents now, and if his decision gets overturned, we could hire a lawyer to try the case."

"What makes you think this time will be any different?"

Keyshia edged closer to him and said, "That's where you come in, Ceasar."

He was taken aback for a moment. "What could I do to make a difference in his case?"

Keyshia took a breath and threw caution to the wind. "I think Martha had something to do with the bank robbery, Ceasar."

Ceasar looked at her and then laughed. "Come on, Keyshia, you're stretching it now. How could Martha possibly be part of Sonny and Wolf's shit?" He scratched his head and laughed again. "Martha the bank robber."

"I'm serious, Ceasar. I thought it was silly when I first thought about it, too, but everything points to her."

Ceasar tilted his head and asked, "How did you come up with this?"

"Well, when I went to see Sonny that time I couldn't see Clyde at Rikers, he slipped up and said he shouldn't have ever listened to her." She stared at Ceasar and continued, "When I asked him who he was talking about, he said nobody."

"And?" Ceasar said.

Keyshia asked quietly, "Where were you the morning of the bank robbery, Ceasar?"

As if a bolt of lightning struck him, his eyes widened and his mouth opened.

"Exactly," Keyshia said, "and it doesn't stop there. Clyde called her right before we got to the bank to ask if she'd heard from you or Sonny. She said she hadn't heard from either of you. Now if she knew you was coming over to her house that morning, why did she tell Clyde she hadn't heard from you? She even tried to get Clyde to stop over at her house after he told her he was going to the bank and see you."

"That bitch. She told me she wanted to see me and that it was an emergency. But when I got there nobody answered the door, so I left and went to work."

"That was the dummy move, Ceasar, to get you out of the bank so you wouldn't recognize Sonny!" ·

Ceasar stood up and began pacing the floor, fuming. He went to the closet to get his jacket and said, "I'm going to see that bitch right now!"

Keyshia jumped up and stopped him. "No, Ceasar, you can't!"

He looked at Keyshia with flames in his eyes and said angrily, "Oh, yes, I can!"

"If you do, Clyde won't have a chance to get out of the penitentiary." This stopped him cold, and he turned to look at Keyshia.

She explained, "We got to let her keep thinking she's safe, Ceasar, if we have any chance of getting him out. She's his ticket out."

He took off his jacket and hung it back in the closet. He took a seat to finish hearing her out. Keyshia put her head down and said sadly, "Ceasar, there's something else I got to tell you, but you got to help me out and tell me everything that you know."

Chapter 36

It took almost a year, but a hearing to determine if there were grounds for appealing Clyde's case was finally scheduled at the federal district court in a month. But Keyshia was concerned. She had used her firm's information to process the appeal forms and found out that they had to be present at the appeal hearing.

Keyshia was now in her first year of law school at Fordham University, which was not far from John Jay, where she often went by Professor Akills's office to talk law and get his opinion. One day he asked Keyshia to come see him, and when she walked into his office he got right to the point: "Ms. Simmons, I recommended you to an old colleague of mine from law school, Conrad

Coffield, who is now the local U.S. attorney for the eastern district, for a three-year internship. It's grunt work, it's working with the government enforcement agencies such as the U.S. District Attorney's Office, the FBI, the ATF, Secret Service, and the Treasury Department. It's quite a coup for a young, up-and-coming law student like yourself. It's on the table if you want it."

Keyshia thanked Professor Akills for considering her and told him that she would keep it in mind and try to give him her decision soon.

Keyshia's classes were tough enough, and with the burden of news she'd just received about Clyde's representation for the appeal, an internship was the last thing on her mind. She didn't see how she would be able to handle an internship so early in her law career, even though she knew she would eventually have to intern as a requirement for her degree. She was already striving hard to keep up with her fellow students, whom she found cutthroat and competitive in their quest for the top spot. Keyshia even had to stop working full-time during the school year with Hemmingway, Adorno, and Shaw, because the classes were so demanding and rigorous, opting to work part-time during the school months and full-time during the summer. She remained especially close with Ms. Hemmingway, who was proud of her and became one of her biggest supporters.

The hearing was exactly one month away, and if she and Ceasar hired someone other than the firm she worked for, they would have to start the process all over again. If she went to her boss, she would risk losing her job if they found out she'd forged the firm's name on the appeal forms. So Keyshia decided to do the unthinkable and represent the case herself.

Though Keyshia knew the case now like the back of her hand, she had to learn about the federal appeals process. She spent every

waking hour reading and studying. She wasn't about to leave anything to chance, so she went to Professor Akills, who was once a
fierce criminal defense attorney who tried cases for both government and private agencies.

She visited his office one evening and asked if she could
speak to him about something.

"Have a seat, Ms. Simmons. I hope this is about you accepting the internship position, because it won't be on the table forever." It had been a couple of weeks since he'd first mentioned it
to her.

"Yes, Professor, I'm thinking about it," she lied. "But I'm
here for something else."

He stared at Keyshia, amused, because it wasn't often she
came to him for advice. "Well, what is it?"

A little embarrassed, she said, "Well, I have this friend, you
know, who's been in jail and needs some help, and I said I'd help
him." Professor Akills observed her closely and listened to her
stumble over her words. He had seen this many times in his career as an attorney. He knew automatically that she was hiding
something and let her know it.

"What you're really asking me, Ms. Simmons—and correct
me if I'm wrong—is that your boyfriend has been arrested and you
need me to help you with the case. Yes?" Keyshia wondered if she
was that obvious. Her silence confirmed that he was right.

"What else, Ms. Simmons?"

Happy at least that he hadn't made her admit he was right, she
quickly told him the rest. "He has a hearing regarding his appeal
in a couple of weeks, and I wanted to get your input on the case,
procedures, and stuff like that."

"What grounds is the appeal based on?"

"Inadequate representation, exculpatory evidence that was
ruled inadmissible by the judge that was clearly mishandled by
his lawyer. The resulting charges against him were incorrect, and

the U.S. attorney pursued armed robbery charges when at most he was guilty of assault."

"I see. Another convicted criminal who feels that he got rail-roaded by his own lawyer."

Keyshia was angered by his statement, but said nothing.

He smiled and said, "Just the cases that I like, Ms. Simmons, because we do have a lot of incompetent lawyers out here. That's why I became a professor; I detested being around them." He looked at the folder on Keyshia's lap and asked, "Is that the case there?"

Keyshia nodded. "It is."

He said, "Well, you can leave it on the desk. You said his appeal hearing is in two weeks?"

Keyshia nodded again.

"You'll be hearing from me." He turned his back on her in his swivel chair, and that was her cue that her time was up.

With a three-day weekend ahead of them, Ceasar and Keyshia decided to get away for the weekend, but they had no particular place to go. Keyshia suggested that they go upstate and visit his dad. Initially, Ceasar rejected the idea, but then he remembered Clyde's change of heart regarding their father and decided to judge him for himself. Unknown to Ceasar, Keyshia had another reason to see their father—she wanted to ask him some questions that had been bugging her and about some facts that didn't add up in her mind.

They rented a car that Friday evening and stayed overnight in a motel near the prison. Clyde's father had been moved to a medium-security prison, which was fortunate for Keyshia because it meant she could visit him even though they weren't blood relatives.

Inside the waiting area, which doubled as the cafeteria, Ceasar was nervous but ready. Even though he had better memories of his father than any of his brothers, he still knew nothing about the man.

When the inmates began to file in, they had no escorts and all were dressed in regular clothes. A familiar face that was the spitting image of Ceasar stepped out of the crowd and began walking in their direction. Even from a distance, the similarities were eerie, and as Keyshia looked at Ceasar, she could tell that he felt the same as he watched his mirror image approach him. When the man got close enough to see who his visitor was, he stopped in his tracks.

Ceasar was his firstborn, his first son, and he had a closer affection for him. The elder Barker began to slow his steps the closer he got to his son, from fear and from happiness. As they stood before each other, eyes watering, neither was sure what to do. But then their natural instincts took over and they hugged each other as if their lives depended on it. The father grabbed hold of his oldest son and cried out loud, with no regard for anyone around him, and he would not stop. Keyshia stood back, holding Clyde, Jr. and became overwhelmed with tears herself as she watched the emotional moment unfold.

"I miss you, son" was the only thing his father could say.

After the reunion, Ceasar wiped the remaining tears from his now red eyes and introduced him to Keyshia. "Dad, I want you to meet Keyshia, Clyde's girlfriend."

His father smiled and gave her a hug. They pulled apart, and he beamed at her proudly. Keyshia saw where Clyde got his physical build from. Though she knew his father was in his late fifties, he was still fine-tuned and muscularly built and looked as if he were in his early thirties.

"So, you're Keyshia? Clyde told me all about you. You're even prettier than he said you were." Keyshia blushed. "I knew he was in love with you because every time he mentioned your name his eyes lit up."

Ceasar moved closer to Keyshia and announced proudly, "Dad, I want to introduce you to your grandson, Clyde, Jr.!"

His father's eyes widened and he paused as he looked down at the young boy. "That's my . . ."

Ceasar smiled broadly and nodded. "That's right, he's your first grandson!" He looked at Keyshia and she nodded also.

He slowly approached Clyde, Jr. and knelt before him and gathered him up in his strong arms and said softly, "Hey, Clyde, I'm your grandpa and I love you."

Amazingly, Clyde, Jr. said, "You my real grandpa?"

He nodded. "Yes, I'm your real grandpa."

Clyde, Jr. suddenly wrapped his arms around him.

They were allowed out on the grounds and sat at a table outside to eat. Two hours later, Clyde, Jr. fell asleep, and Keyshia gave father and son time to get to know each other. It seemed to her that Mr. Barker was telling his son the same things he'd told Clyde years earlier, because they did more crying and hugging instead of talking during most of their conversation. After their private time, Ceasar called Keyshia back over to discuss family issues and to give his father the bad news about his sons.

His father was deeply hurt when he found out about both his sons being arrested and convicted. When they told him they suspected that Martha may have been involved somehow, Keyshia thought that he would explode right there, because his blood was boiling so bad that veins began protruding from his forehead. He had to get up for a moment and walk around in order to calm down. He sat back down, and with his head hung low, he asked, "How much time did they get?"

Keyshia looked at Ceasar with uneasiness. "Sonny copped out to ten years," said Ceasar. There was a long pause.

"And Clyde?" he asked. There was a longer pause, until his father stared Ceasar in his eyes for an answer.

"Clyde took his case to trial and lost, and they . . ." Ceasar cleared his throat and said, "They sentenced him to twenty years."

His father went limp and looked as if he would have a heart attack right then and there. He let out a loud moan and cried, "No . . ."

Ceasar looked at Keyshia and said quickly, "But, Dad, that's one of the reasons we're here. We're trying to get him out, but we need your help!"

He slowly lifted his head and took a deep breath and wiped his eyes. "What can I do to help my sons?" he asked.

Ceasar edged closer to his father. "Keyshia is a law student now, and she's going to ask you some questions that will help out Clyde with his appeal hearing that's about to come up." His father nodded.

Keyshia was back in school that Tuesday and had just finished taking a test. She was completely spent and wanted nothing more than to get home and rest. Maneuvering through the crowd of students, she heard, "Ms. Simmons." She turned around to see Professor Akills motioning her over to him. Surprised to see her old professor in her school, she walked over to him quickly. In his arm, he carried the yellow files that she had given him the previous week.

He waved for her to follow him into a professor's office. Keyshia walked in and looked around. She watched the professor hastily throw the file on the desk and stare at Keyshia in dismay. Disappointment began racing through her head as she cursed herself for bringing it to him in the first place. She stood in front of the desk, unsure if she should speak, so she just waited for him to say something.

"Have a seat, Ms. Simmons," he said sternly. Keyshia bit down on her bottom lip, thinking the situation was growing tenser by the minute.

"Ms. Simmons, I took the liberty of reviewing the entire case this weekend." Keyshia thought he was lying because it had taken her an entire month to figure it out, until he began stating the particulars of the case.

"In my thirty years of practicing law, I have never seen such an inept and shabby job of preparation for a federal trial as your boyfriend's lawyer did. He did absolutely nothing to disprove or dismiss the U.S. attorney's claim that he was involved in the bank robbery. The bank's videotapes clearly show that Mr. Barker entered the bank at eight-fifteen on the morning of May 24—unmasked, mind you—and clearly, according to a statement by . . ." He referred to a his notes and read, ". . . Mrs. Williams, assistant bank manager, stated that he was there seeking his brother, I believe his name was . . ." He looked at his pad again. "Yes, Ceasar Barker."

Keyshia, excited, nodded with him.

"Now, if a person was going to rob a bank, or even be part of a robbery, for that matter, would he seek out a bank employee and let them know his name?"

Keyshia wanted to burst.

"And it doesn't stop there. According to the trial transcripts, he had just arrived from out of town. Is that correct, Ms. Simmons?"

Keyshia nodded. "Yes, we were together and had just pulled back into New York about seven-thirty that morning, coming from my family in South Carolina."

"Trips like these have recorded documents. Cameras at every

pit stop that would prove this, receipts, even tolls, but the lawyer didn't even bother to check on these things?"

Before she could answer, he said, "No, he did not!" The professor stared at Keyshia and said smugly, "Your boyfriend, Ms. Simmons—and it is only my opinion—will have his sentence reversed. All of the exculpatory evidence should be gathered, cataloged, and summarized as the core basis of the appeal. I'm not sure if this will overturn the verdict, but it will at least get you a new trial, if a competent lawyer presents these developments to a judge." Keyshia was too dazed to react.

"Your lawyer's job now is to gather as many of these documents as possible." Keyshia remained silent.

"Ms. Simmons, did you hear what I said, for Christ's sake? Your boyfriend has an excellent chance of having his sentence overturned!"

Keyshia suddenly jumped to her feet and ran over to her professor; she hugged him and gave him a huge kiss on the cheek.

"Thank you, Professor, thank you so much!" She backed away and had nearly run out the door when he called to her, "Ms. Simmons, don't forget your files."

Keyshia scooped up the packet and thanked him again.

Chapter 37

The hearing was scheduled for ten o'clock that morning with Judge R. L. Fenton, and Keyshia was more nervous than she had ever been in her entire life. What she was doing was unprecedented, and she was gambling not only with her career, but with Clyde's freedom, so she knew she had no room for error. Ceasar came with her to the hearing for moral support and posed as one of her assistants. Keyshia wore a nice conservative two-piece combination, the kind that Ms. Hemmingway wore every day at the office and whenever she had to appear in court, and she even had her hair rolled up in a bun like her. Keyshia also wore an atrocious pair of bifocals that made her appear older than her twenty-four years.

As they approached the federal court building, Keyshia wondered if she had bitten off more than she could chew. She and Ceasar took a deep breath and plunged forth. Keyshia took the employees' entrance and flashed her identification to the officers and held her breath.

"Thank you, Ms. Hemmingway," said the officer. He let her pass, and she put her bag and files on the conveyor belt leading through the X-ray machine. She waited by the elevator for Ceasar, who was being scanned thoroughly with metal detector wands, and watched the officer wave him through.

They stepped inside the elevator with a herd of lawyers who all looked stone-faced and seemed pressed for time as they checked their watches. Keyshia followed suit and checked hers. Ceasar tossed her a sly smile when she did. They rode up to the sixth floor in complete silence. When they got off the elevator, they went directly into the counsel's office to sign off on their docket for the day's proceedings. Keyshia had done a test run earlier and gone to the federal building and the counsel's office and explained to them that she was a prelaw student doing research on a day in the life of an attorney. She'd learned everything from A to Z about procedures, and it was paying off today.

While Keyshia sat and waited for the judgment after the oral argument for the pretrial motions, she struck up a conversation with an Asian girl who also happened to be a law student and was working as an intern for the U.S. Attorney's Office.

"So," Keyshia asked, "how do you like interning at the attorney's office?"

"Oh, I love it. It has a lot of perks. Whenever I tell anyone I work for the U.S. Attorney's Office"—the girl's eyes lit up—"they roll out the red carpet for me. I get access to every file, document, cases, everything. I might as well be the lawyer prosecuting the case because I know everything they do, because I'm the one who helps put it together!"

Keyshia's head suddenly began to spin as the girl continued to talk. One thing and one thing only was on her mind at that point: She was going to see Professor Akills as soon as she left the building.

Keyshia sat nervously as she watched the circuit judge shuffle through the paperwork and briefs he had before him. Her stomach churned as he looked at Keyshia with his cold, grim eyes. She was unsure if she'd pulled off the oral argument properly and began questioning if he knew that she was merely an amateur who was bamboozling the court.

After the hearing, Keyshia ran out of the federal building in a hurry, causing Ceasar to grow alarmed.

"Keyshia, what happened in there?" Ceasar asked as he followed her. Keyshia continued her long strides without saying a word. A hundred things were running through her mind at once, and she was trying to think.

"What happened? Did you get caught?"

"Ceasar, I won the appeal." He jumped up in the air with excitement and then noticed that she wasn't as joyous. Keyshia continued walking in silence until she stopped suddenly and said with exhilaration, "Ceasar . . . I got it!"

Ceasar grimaced and said, "You got him out?"

Keyshia moved down to Ceasar's face, and her smile widened. "Better!"

Ceasar was confused. "What could be better than getting Clyde out of jail, Keyshia? Stop playing!"

Keyshia looked at him and said, "Revenge!"

Ceasar looked into Keyshia's eyes and knew that she was dead serious.

"Now, Ceasar, I might have to quit my job in order to do it. Do you think you could swing the bills by yourself for a couple of months?"

Ceasar looked apprehensive, but he trusted Keyshia and said, "Yeah, I guess I can, but why do you have to do that?"

Keyshia smiled and said, "Because I'm going to be an intern, which means I'll be working for free."

Keyshia knew that she had won only a battle and that the real war had just begun. Her first stop would be to Professor Akills to see if the government intern position was still available. When she arrived at his office and told him she was interested in the position, he immediately got on the phone and spoke with the director.

"What day would you like to start, Ms. Simmons?" Professor Akills asked as he placed his hand over the phone.

The next day, Keyshia waited impatiently for her boss to arrive. She had brought her boss's favorite morning treat: Dunkin' Donuts coffee and crullers. When Ms. Hemmingway finally arrived, she was in a solemn, dark mood, but when she saw the crullers, her demeanor changed. Keyshia began pouring her a cup of hot coffee and said, "Two Equals, no milk, right?"

Ms. Hemmingway eyed her closely as she munched on a cruller. "What's on your mind, Keyshia?"

Keyshia feigned innocence. "Nothing, I'm just helping my boss out. Can I help you carry this to your office?"

Ms. Hemmingway picked up another cruller and turned without a word toward her office. Inside she placed her crullers and coffee on her huge oak desk and took off her coat. Keyshia assisted her and hung up her coat for her. Ms. Hemmingway took her seat and again eyed Keyshia suspiciously as she looked around the office without saying a word.

"Two dollars," Ms. Hemmingway said flatly.

Keyshia looked at her with confusion. "Pardon me?"

"I said, two dollars is the amount I'll give you as a raise." Ms. Hemmingway gave her a rare smile. "I know how much you have contributed to this office, and it's about time you got a raise."

Keyshia shook her head. "Ms. Hemmingway, I'm not here for a raise, I'm here to resign."

Ms. Hemmingway's smile disappeared. "You're joking!"

Keyshia shook her head. "No, Ms. Hemmingway, I'm not."

"Why would you want to leave, Keyshia?"

Keyshia hesitated but told her the truth. "I did something ethically wrong." She put her head down. "I used the firm's name to file an appeal for my son's father, who is incarcerated for federal crimes." Ms. Hemmingway said nothing.

"I even went to court yesterday and argued the hearing . . ." Keyshia paused and came out with the worst part. "And I won." There was a long period of silence, and Keyshia was unable to meet Ms. Hemmingway's eyes.

"Continue," Ms. Hemmingway managed to say.

"My son's father, Clyde Barker, was arrested six and a half years ago, for bank robbery." Keyshia's eyes pleaded, "Ms. Hemmingway, it was impossible for him to rob the bank because we had just arrived back in town from visiting my family. I just drove around the block, and he was handcuffed with two other men, one of whom was his brother and—"

Ms. Hemmingway challenged, "I don't listen to hearsay, Keyshia, only fact. What motivated you to pursue this matter in the first place?"

Keyshia knew she had no excuse for what she did, so she simply stated what came to mind. "The law clearly states, in Section

3731 of the U.S. Code, in a criminal case an appeal by the United States shall lie to a court of appeals from a decision, judgment, or order of a district court dismissing an indictment or information or granting a new trial after verdict or judgment, as to any one or more counts, or any part thereof, except that no appeal shall lie where the double jeopardy clause of the United States Constitution prohibits further prosecution."

Ms. Hemmingway was surprised and proud of her, but she didn't let it show.

"He's innocent, Ms. Hemmingway. I was with him."

"I want to hear what you argued, nothing more, Keyshia," said Ms. Hemmingway.

"I argued for the appellate court on the grounds of abuse of discretion. According to the trial de novo or the appeal on the record, Ms. Yolanda F. Hemmingway of Hemmingway, Adorno, and Shaw won the argument of proceedings with a body of evidence that his lawyer in fact committed reversible error, that is, an impermissible action by the court that he did not act properly. The evidence I also presented proved that the attorney acted erroneously by instructing the jury on the law applicable to the case, permitted serious improper argument by attorney, excluding evidence improperly."

Ms. Hemmingway rocked back and forth in her huge leather chair and finally said, "So that means I have two options." She looked up at the ceiling, then continued, "I could report this matter to the bar and authorities, and your boyfriend—who could in fact be innocent, but his appeal decision was just won because his girlfriend decided to play lawyer—would get his appeal null and void because of fraudulent and, how did you say? erroneous representation . . . or I can risk my practice and go ahead and represent Mr. Barker and break every ethical oath in the book to save face and you going to jail?"

Keyshia put her head down in shame. She knew that she risked putting Ms. Hemmingway in a compromising position, but love will make a human being do some stupid things.

Ms. Hemmingway swiveled around in her chair as she pondered and searched for an answer, then suddenly said, "Keyshia, I will accept your resignation, at which time you will not be able to work for Hemmingway, Adorno, and Shaw until after a decision has been rendered in this case, which we will represent pro bono." Keyshia's frown turned into a smile. She wanted to scream for joy, but Ms. Hemmingway stopped her.

"I ask that you leave all pertinent documents that you may have and . . ." They stared into each other's eyes, and Ms. Hemmingway smiled. "Congratulations on your first legal victory. You're going to make a fine lawyer one day." Keyshia smiled and thanked her.

Keyshia went to work as an intern the following week in the U.S. Attorney's Office, which tried federal cases. Her job consisted of assisting investigators with gathering evidence, obtaining records, researching decisions, and processing and organizing pretrial motions and appeals.

Keyshia could not believe how much access she had to every file, record, and case. Her first course of action was to pull Clyde's appellate case and ensure that it made its way to the top of the list. Clyde's case would now be approved by a judge for trial, and notice of preparation would be given to both parties for a pretrial hearing to schedule a trial date. Once the date was established, the case would be treated like a fresh case in the appellate court and would be heard by a new judge and jury.

Within two weeks after Keyshia arrived, the pretrial dates were scheduled. The prosecuting attorney was T. Bernard

Williams, a tenacious lawyer who was building a reputation for a future in politics by hanging criminals. Though he was a married man, T. Bernard flirted with Keyshia on more than one occasion. She didn't let it bother her, and she had actually flirted with all the attorneys; one of them would be prosecuting her man's case, she knew, and she had wanted to stay in good standing with everyone in case she needed a favor.

T. Bernard personally requested Keyshia to be part of his investigating team. He knew that the case before him didn't have any teeth because the evidence was in the defendant's favor despite the earlier conviction. T. Bernard hated losing and told his investigators and interns to find anything they could to ensure that he got a conviction. He had them go to Martha, talk to Clyde's neighbors, and they even found out about Pops and interviewed him.

Keyshia learned a thing or two about gathering information and decided to take a chance on a theory that she'd always suspected but now had the power and resources to investigate. She wanted to see the bank videotapes for the week before the robbery. Keyshia learned that it was very rare to rob a bank without first casing it. In the original investigation, neither Sonny, Clyde, nor Wolf was shown in the tapes prior to the morning of the robbery, so Keyshia assumed that Sonny and Wolf must have had a spotter, because they knew exactly which manager had keys and specific locations that only a person with prior knowledge of the banking operations would have. Since Keyshia had never met Martha before, she asked Ceasar to get a picture of her so she could check for her on the videotape.

There were five bank tapes in total, and each tape had sixteen hours of footage. Keyshia sat through hours upon hours of footage and was nearly ready to give up all hope when she came to the last tape and a middle-aged woman who fit Martha's general description walked in. She zoomed in until she got a good view of the person's face and held the picture up to the monitor and realized that it was a perfect match. She released the pause button and continued. Keyshia's jaw nearly dropped to the floor when she saw Martha and Ceasar in the bank together.

Keyshia stormed up the stairs to her apartment, and when she opened the door she was livid. She slammed the front door shut, causing Ceasar and little Clyde—who were in the living room playing a game on the Xbox—to jump. As she stared maliciously at Ceasar, she said to her son, "Clyde, go into your room, now!" He quickly got up and scurried to his room without hesitating. Keyshia waited until she heard his door shut and then held up several photos and asked, "Ceasar, what the fuck is this?" He was speechless and stared at the photo with his mouth agape. Keyshia waited for an answer, but she got none.

Keyshia's eyes turned into a river of tears as she shook her head, not wanting to believe it. "Ceasar, tell me you didn't have anything to do with this robbery. Tell me you didn't."

As she watched Ceasar hang his head in shame, she knew once and for all that he had in fact been part of the crime that put his two younger brothers—including her man—away for years. Keyshia didn't want to believe that it was true, but his actions at that moment spoke volumes—he was guilty!

"Just tell me why, Ceasar? Why would you do that to your own brothers when you said you loved them?" Ceasar's head hung low, and he still didn't answer.

"Ceasar, I'm fucking talking to you, answer my goddamn question!"

"Because I didn't want anything to happen to Clyde, that's why I did it!" Keyshia was stunned as Ceasar looked at her with pleading eyes. "I found out who that Black Sam was and got scared, so I had to do something to protect Clyde, Keyshia."

"But you said that you had the rest of the money to cover us. You lied?"

Ceasar nodded shamefully. "Sonny brought the idea to me earlier when I went to him about that Black Sam mess. He told me the only way they could come up with that kind of money was to do a bank job. But I looked at him like he was crazy. Then Martha started calling me, telling me that these gangsters was coming by the house looking for Clyde, which wound up being a lie, and I got scared." Keyshia shifted from foot to foot because she still felt a certain amount of guilt about being just as much to blame for the incident.

Ceasar continued, "She was the one who was telling me about Clyde running around doing petty robberies and risking his life in the process and that it would be impossible to come up with that kind of money. She said he was too proud to say anything. That's when I went back to Sonny and told him that I was willing to"—Ceasar turned his head uncomfortably—"help him rob my bank."

There was a long silence. "Did you have anything to do with Black Sam and his people getting murdered, Ceasar?" Keyshia asked softly.

Ceasar lifted his head slowly and stared at her. "No, but I found out the real reason Sonny and Wolf killed them. When I went to see Sonny on a visit, he told me that he killed them for you!" Keyshia began to grow weak in the knees and sat down. "Sonny said when he had the sit-down with Black Sam and his people, the deal was only for Clyde's life. They told Sonny that after they finalized the deal by getting them their money"—he put his head down—"they were going to kill you and your family." Keyshia was emotionally drained from hearing how close she and her family had come to dying, and she began to shake.

"But," Ceasar continued, "Sonny found out how much Clyde really loved you, and that's when he decided to kill all of them."

"Then why would you still want to rob the bank, Ceasar? You could have just kept the money we had for Black Sam if that was the case."

"I did!" Ceasar said with vigor. "I was going to give the money back to you and Clyde, but Martha must have found out, and since she wasn't getting nothing out of it, she must have convinced Sonny to still do it. And that's when she set me up and called me to come to her house that morning, claiming something had happened to Sonny and to get there quick." Keyshia felt exhausted from all the new information she had just received after all these years.

"Keyshia, what happens now? Does it affect Clyde's case or . . . ?"

She looked at him and knew he was wondering if he would be involved now. She shook her head and said, "I don't know. I mean, it doesn't affect him getting out or nothing because I'm the only one who knows that you had anything to do with it." She saw Ceasar take a relieved breath.

"It does mess up my plan for getting Martha tied to the case like I wanted to do. I can't put her on the stand now that I know she might get you involved with this bank shit to save her neck."

"I'm sorry for not telling you about this earlier, Keyshia. Martha fucked me over and I just had to accept it. Now we can't even pay her ass back."

She placed her hand on Ceasar's and said, "That's okay, we just have to find another angle to tie her into all of this, that's all."

"How? I might have blown our chance," he said, disgusted with himself.

"Not really. We just have to get Sonny to implicate her as an accessory to the robbery."

Ceasar frowned. "Keyshia, I'm telling you right now that will never happen. Sonny would rather do fifty years before he told on Martha. She is the closest thing to a mother he ever had, and

Sonny is fiercely loyal to family. In his eyes, Martha can do no wrong."

"Ceasar, when you pull the wool off a sheep's eyes, what they are going to see are wolves. All we got to do is get Sonny to see her for who she really is."

"How are you gonna do that?" asked Ceasar.

Keyshia smiled. "Clyde taught me a long time ago to always have a plan B. It's a long shot, but if my female intuition is right, she will get a rise out of the entire courtroom."

Chapter 38

After the appellate court determined errors in the proceedings of the lower court in Clyde's case, he was
granted a new trial. Keyshia spent countless hours at the
office preparing for it. Jury selection was in two weeks,
and opening statements would take place soon after.

Keyshia continued to work not only on the case, but
on T. Bernard, who began to take a special interest in his
new, hardworking intern. He no longer looked at Keyshia
as a lowly young intern that he would try to bed; he began
to respect her for her work ethic and passion for law. He
would see Keyshia in the research room when he got to
work in the morning and would see her when he left well
into the night. Unknown to him and everyone else in the

office, Keyshia was on a mission: Get her man out of jail or die trying. Instead of using weapons this time, she would use her mind—her mind was now her nine!

The trial was in one week, and T. Bernard Williams had gathered his team to discuss strategies. All the investigators presented background information on everyone affiliated with the case, such as witnesses, bank employees, coconspirators, and so on. These people would receive subpoenas. Keyshia smiled when she saw Ceasar's name. She knew that the government had confiscated the hundred and thirty thousand dollars and would use it as evidence. The money had been introduced as evidence in Clyde's first trial, and because neither Clyde nor Ceasar was able to explain how they had come by it, it had ultimately helped to seal Clyde's fate. Keyshia anticipated this problem would arise again and had already made plans to offset it, but she would need help.

She saw that Sonny had not been subpoenaed because he was considered a hostile witness. This was a problem because she needed Sonny on the stand to admit that Martha had been the mastermind and architect behind the robbery, even though she would need to figure out how to force Sonny's hand to get him to do so.

"Mr. Williams, may I have a word with you?" Keyshia said as she peeked into his office.

"Come in, Ms. Simmons," he said, taking off his glasses.

"I believe there is another conspirator in the Barker case."

T. Bernard rubbed his eyes and leaned back in his leather chair. He knew from experience that many up-and-coming interns became overzealous, and he wondered how he was going to tell Keyshia, his star intern, to leave the courtroom theories to the seasoned professionals. He liked Keyshia and didn't want to de-

flate her enthusiasm for hard work and her vigor, so he indulged
her.

"What proof do you have?" he asked, trying to appear interested.

"We could get the brother who is incarcerated to tell us who
else was involved."

T. Bernard began to laugh aloud. "His brother is almost in his
seventh year of a ten-year sentence with only three to go and you
think he will rat on his brother after all these years? I don't think
so."

"I didn't say anything about him ratting on his brother; I'm
talking about the person who set everything up—his stepmother."

T. Bernard was thrown off guard, and Keyshia knew she had
him rattled. "That's right, I found out through a reliable source
close to the defendants that Martha Woods, who raised both boys,
was the actual ringleader of the bank robbery."

T. Bernard stared at Keyshia grimly and asked, "Does this reliable source that you mentioned have a name?"

Keyshia paused to build up his anticipation and then said,
"Ceasar Barker, their oldest brother!"

T. Bernard leaned back in his chair and rubbed his beard.
Keyshia knew she had him on the ropes and dropped the bomb:
"Here are pictures dated five days prior to the robbery of her entering the same bank where the robbery occurred." She handed
him the pictures.

He studied them silently, then tossed them on the desk. "Circumstantial; it doesn't prove anything. She could have come there
to visit the brother who worked there."

Keyshia was prepared and threw another folder on his desk.
She smiled and said, "She has priors. She's been arrested on
racketeering charges in both 1968 and 1971, but was never
charged because of lack of evidence. She was also arrested on embezzlement and credit card fraud in 1974, for which she served

four years of an eight-year sentence in prison after she agreed to assist the government and testify against her coconspirators. And then"—Keyshia savored the moment—"in 1981, three years after she was released from prison, she was arrested for, you guessed it, conspiring to commit federal bank robbery." Keyshia proudly handed him the entire folder, and T. Bernard flipped through each page.

"Her boyfriend at the time was"—Keyshia opened up another file—"Rodney Walters. He and three other men were charged with robbing twelve other banks in the county of Manhattan over an eleven-month period. During the last robbery, the men fatally shot a security guard. Ms. Woods, once again, was offered an out since she was only the getaway driver and was granted full immunity if she testified against the men, who all received life sentences with no possibility of parole."

T. Bernard simply sat and stared at the folder on his desk. "There's no way to tie her into this case," he finally said. "Unless . . ."

"Unless," Keyshia said quickly, "one of the defendants testifies against her."

T. Bernard stood up and shook his head. "It won't work because Ceasar Barker was never charged in the robbery, and only one of the defendants would be able to connect her to the case, and that is very unlikely and puts us back at square one."

"Sonny Barker will testify against her," Keyshia said compellingly.

T. Bernard just scratched his head and said, "How?"

He listened to everything Keyshia told him and was impressed at how thorough she had been as she showed him documents, records, and police files. He had to admit that it was a long shot, but he was willing to take a chance to serve justice. He stared at the mound of evidence that Keyshia had piled on his desk and began to process it.

"How do we get her to take the stand? We can't subpoena her and ask her about her past; the judge won't allow it."

"If she is called to the stand by the defense and asked to be a character witness, you can. According to his last transcripts, she testified as a character witness at Barker's trial, and they are calling her again." Keyshia presented him with the defense attorney's witness list.

He stared at the list. Then he gave her a sly smile and said, "Looks like we are ready for court, Ms. Simmons."

It was Sunday and one day before the trial. Keyshia's stomach churned as she took the train upstate to visit Mrs. Barker at the nursing home. Over the last seven years, she, Ceasar, and little Clyde had been visiting her regularly, and they had grown close enough that Keyshia would feel her grip her hand from time to time, a sign that she always kept to herself because she didn't want to give Ceasar any false hope. Keyshia spent many visits painting her nails or braiding her hair to try to make her feel better. Even when Ceasar was unable to make it, she still went on her own to visit and read to Mrs. Barker from her favorite book, *Harlem Girl Lost.*

Keyshia told Ceasar that she needed to make this particular visit alone and asked if he could watch Clyde, Jr. for her. Ceasar agreed. He knew whenever Keyshia went on what seemed to him a baffling quest, it was always for the good of others—mainly for his brother Clyde—and that's why he loved her so.

As always, when Keyshia walked into her room, Mrs. Barker sat in the chair by the window, staring earnestly toward the heavens. Keyshia forced herself not to break down as she approached her and greeted her as she always did.

"Hey, Ma, how you been doing this week?" Keyshia rubbed her hands and gave her a reassuring smile. She looked at Mrs.

Barker's frayed corn rows and said, "Oh, it looks like you are due for a touch-up."

Keyshia went into her bag and pulled out a jar of grease, a brush, and some combs and began to undo the braids. As Keyshia greased her scalp and braided her hair, she talked about everything under the sun, from Mrs. Barker's grandson, to her three sons, to current events and even the weather. Keyshia had spoken to her like this for years even though she was unsure if Mrs. Barker understood her. Then one day as Keyshia was preparing to leave, she had asked Mrs. Barker if she was going to be okay. To Keyshia's surprise, Mrs. Barker had given her a faint smile and nod. Keyshia had turned around to see if Ceasar had seen it, but he was busy with his nephew. Keyshia had stared back at Mrs. Barker and smiled. More and more, little things began to happen, and Keyshia just let it flow and was simply honored to have a "thing" between them.

After Keyshia finished her hair, she pulled out *Harlem Girl Lost,* which seemed to be Mrs. Barker's favorite novel also. Keyshia began reading it. She came to an emotional part of the book and couldn't continue reading any further; she began to break down. All the pressure that she had been carrying on her shoulders for years had become too heavy, and she burst. She fell to the floor and buried her head in Mrs. Barker's lap and began telling her the tearful truth.

"I can't go on anymore, Mrs. Barker, I just can't! Everything is so bad. Tomorrow is Clyde's trial, and I'm scared that if we don't win this time he will be hit with even more time because I want to act like a damn lawyer!" Keyshia began to grow hysterical. "If he loses, what am I going to say? What am I going to do? They already took him from me for over seven years now, and I miss him, Mrs. Barker, I miss him so bad!" Keyshia lifted her head and looked at her future mother-in-law through a puddle of tears. "You are the only chance he got, Mrs. Barker, his only chance." Keyshia gritted her teeth and yelled, "That damn Martha ruined both your sons' lives, Mrs. Barker. They need you, they both need you. I need you! Please, please help me. I miss your son so, so much, and I don't think I can go on if he loses at trial! I don't think I could take it." Terror was in Keyshia's eyes as she pleaded on bended knees with Mrs. Barker. Keyshia looked for a sign from her, but she continued to stare blankly and remained silent. All hope was lost, and Keyshia squeezed her hand and cried as if life would surely end.

But then she looked up, and what she saw amazed her.

Chapter 39

It killed Keyshia to miss the first day of trial, but out of
respect for Ms. Hemmingway she opted to wait until it
was in full swing before she snuck into the courtroom.
Ceasar was there, however, and during the recess,
Keyshia waited inside a nearby coffee shop for him to fill
her in on everything that went on. She was especially
happy to hear that Clyde was in good spirits.

The day ended as expected, and Keyshia knew that
opening statements would begin the next day. She didn't
leave anything to chance and went straight to her office,
making a last-minute call to ensure everything and
everyone was in place.

• • •

Later that night, Ceasar stayed up late with Keyshia as she went over the last-minute details of the case. Keyshia noticed that Ceasar was not himself.

"What's wrong, Ceasar, you been quiet all night. What's on your mind?"

Ceasar looked at Keyshia and hesitated. "I don't know. I'm starting to feel guilty from seeing Clyde on trial today." He grimaced. "I mean, he didn't have anything to do with none of this, but I did, and he's been suffering for over seven years and I'm free." Keyshia took off her reading glasses and listened to him share his feelings. "Here I am, guilty, and I let my little brother take the damn weight, Keyshia. What kind of man am I?" Keyshia tried to interject, but he stopped her. "No, hear me out!" he snapped. "I'm tired of feeling afraid and guilty. I can't take it any longer." Keyshia realized that he had been carrying the burden of Clyde's incarceration for years. He looked at her and said, "Keyshia, I want you to tell them people that I was involved in the robbery so Clyde can come home."

"Ceasar, you don't have—"

"Keyshia!" Ceasar screamed as his voice cracked. "Listen to me!" He paused and looked in her eyes so she could get the message. "I want you to tell them people that I was involved and I'm ready to testify." Keyshia stared at him as he assured her, "If you don't do it, I'll go to them myself, but I know I can no longer go on knowing I didn't do anything for my brother." Tears began to stream down his cheeks as he nodded to Keyshia with a smile and said, "I'm ready, sis."

Keyshia hugged him. When they pulled apart, she had her head down because she knew that she would be losing him and couldn't do anything about it. She loved Ceasar just like a brother and asked him, "Ceasar, do you trust me?" Before he could answer, she reiterated, "I mean, do you really trust me?"

He nodded. "Yeah, you know I trust you, Keyshia, but I'm standing by what I said."

"Okay, and I respect you for that and I won't stop you, but can you just do me one favor and give me two days? Two days—and if you're not sure that Clyde will get off by then, I'll rat you out myself on the evening news if I have to, okay?" Ceasar shook his head and smiled at her silliness.

"Okay?" she asked again, but this time she nudged him in his midsection, causing him to giggle. "Okay, now let me see those pearly whites."

Ceasar smiled and yelled before she tickled him again, "Okay, Keyshia! But I'm serious. If all ain't over in two days, I'm doing what I said."

"Is counsel ready to proceed?" asked the judge as he looked down from his bench at the prosecutor.

"Yes, Your Honor, the government is ready," said T. Bernard as he rose from his seat and stood poised and tall and gazed at the jurors.

"Good morning, ladies and gentlemen. Let me introduce myself. I'm T. Bernard Williams, representing the United States of America in this important case." He paused to let them feel the effect of his words. He appeared relaxed and confident as he approached the jurors to continue his sermon-style delivery. "My intention this morning is to help you foresee what you will hear over the next few days or weeks as you listen to evidence. I merely want to give you a general idea of the government case against Clyde Barker and thank you in advance for your patience and undivided attention. Your willingness to serve is a true reflection of your sense of civic duty and commitment to serve justice." He was a master at seducing his audience when needed. "Let me say right up front that the government is aware of the burden of proof we bear in this case, and we are confident that by the end of the trial you will be able to see that we have more than met that burden. That is my promise to you. You will see from reliable testimony and hard evidence presented that the defendant had motive, opportunity, and means to commit the crime. In addition, we have firmly established the identity of the criminal offender to be that of the defendant in this case through evidence.

"Now, you will repeatedly hear the defense say that the government's case rests on circumstantial evidence, implying that because the defendant didn't enter the scene with the other men convicted of this crime, they weren't in concert. But in the law of our land, planning a crime is equal to doing the crime. But the defense will use terms like 'innocent victim at the wrong place at the wrong time' or 'victim of circumstances,' and basic common sense will serve you in seeing that this was merely his excuse for being in a place that happened to be the place of employment by someone so close to him—a bank!" As if it were a comedy performance, T. Bernard threw up his hands and said, "And it doesn't stop there, ladies and gentlemen. The person who was actually robbing the bank happens to be someone equally close to him."

T. Bernard observed their eyes closely as he chuckled. "The evidence is going to be so overwhelming, ladies and gentlemen, that the defense"—he pointed in their direction—"will try to insult your intelligence by somehow making you believe that he was . . ." T. Bernard snickered sarcastically. "In the wrong place at the wrong time!" He ended his opening statement like that and swaggered back to his chair.

It was the defense attorney's turn to make an opening statement. "Defense, are you ready to proceed?" said the judge. Ms.

Hemmingway sat back without saying a word, then rose suddenly and smiled.

"Yes, Your Honor. The defense is ready."

She walked directly up to the jurors and gazed at each and every one of them and said in a soft yet confident voice, "Ladies and gentlemen, we are here today because a tragedy has occurred. An innocent young man, an innocent young father, an unsuspecting individual, was the victim of a senseless act. You and I could just as easily have been in the situation leading up to the event that brought us here today. But there is a second tragedy in this case, ladies and gentlemen." Ms. Hemmingway's face turned mournful as her voice turned sorrowful. "My client, Clyde Barker, not only saved the life of an overzealous, thrill-seeking security officer, but possibly prevented the potential bloodbath of many others by standing up and saying no, putting his life in harm's way. In the process, the only gain he would receive was knowing he'd done the right thing. But today, he stands here before you wrongfully accused of a crime."

Ms. Hemmingway walked over to where Clyde sat and pointed. "But before your very eyes, look where he sits." All the jurors stared at Clyde, who still looked eighteen. "He is sitting before you in the fight of his life!"

Ms. Hemmingway walked with her head down all the way back to where they sat, as if she were exhausted and nothing made sense. She stretched out her arms. "Try to imagine, if you will, what it feels like to be falsely accused of the things the prosecutor wants us to consider. How would you react if you were in the same predicament, how would you react if this were your brother, your father, your son?" Ms. Hemmingway paused purposely to allow them to absorb the words. "What Mr. T. Bernard Williams failed to tell you, ladies and gentlemen, is that there is no real evidence linking my client, Clyde Barker, to the robbery other than being related to the real robber, who has already been charged and convicted for the crime. We cannot assume that because he is related to an individual who happens to be a career criminal, he should be convicted as well, nor should we depend on the kind of shoddy police work you will see exposed in the government case. Please keep asking yourself the hard questions, and remember there's always another side to every story. Mr. Williams is right about one thing so far: I will use terms like 'wrong place at the wrong time' and 'victim of circumstances.'" Ms. Hemmingway said earnestly, "But I will promise you, ladies and gentlemen, that I will not insult your intelligence, because I'm sure you can separate the truth . . ." She paused and looked over her shoulder at T. Bernard and said sarcastically. "From . . . and pardon my expression, the bull!" Many of the jurors laughed. Ms. Hemmingway had drawn first blood, and T. Bernard knew it and stewed in his seat.

"Ladies and gentlemen, promise me you'll listen to the whole story and prevent another tragedy from occurring—the wrongful conviction of an innocent person. Thank you," Ms. Hemmingway said. She nodded to the judge as she walked back to her chair and put her hand on Clyde's shoulder.

"At this time, ladies and gentlemen, there will be a fifteen-minute recess," said Judge Denton. "Remember, nothing pertaining to the trial is to be discussed amongst yourselves at this time."

Keyshia and Ceasar quickly slipped out the door to ensure she didn't attract anyone's attention.

"Mr. Williams, is the government ready to proceed?"

"We are, Your Honor."

"Very well, you may call your first witness."

T. Bernard stood and said in a booming voice, "The government calls Mrs. Clara Williams."

The bailiff went to the witness room to bring out Mrs. Williams. He led her through the door and escorted her up to the witness chair, where she was sworn in and took a seat. Clyde immediately recognized her from the bank. T. Bernard walked over to where she sat and welcomed her.

"Can you state your name and occupation?"

"My name is Mrs. Clara Williams, and I work at the First Bank of Savings as a branch manager."

T. Bernard smiled and asked, "Where is the bank located?"

"It's located on West One Hundred and Twenty-fifth Street in Harlem."

"On the morning of May 16, 2001, do you recall where you were?"

"Yes, it was a Monday, and I was at my job."

T. Bernard nodded. "Do you recognize anyone in this courtroom who was in the bank on the morning in question?" When she nodded. T. Bernard said, "Can you point that person out?" She looked at Clyde and pointed in his direction.

"Now, can you describe if the person is male or female and what they are wearing?"

"He is a male wearing a blue suit, white shirt, with a red tie with blue stripes."

T. Bernard looked at the jury and said, "Let the record reflect that Mrs. Williams pointed at the defendant, Clyde Barker, who is wearing a blue suit, white shirt, red tie with blue stripes." He turned his attention back to Mrs. Williams. "Now, Mrs. Williams, do you recall anything significant that happened at approximately eight twenty-five that morning?"

Mrs. Williams closed her eyes and took a deep breath. The jurors watched her every move. "Three masked men suddenly came through the door waving guns and ordered everyone on the floor." Mrs. Williams began shaking as she thought back to the incident.

"Do you need a moment, Mrs. Williams?"

"No, I'm okay."

T. Bernard stared at the jurors. "Were you confronted by one of the masked bank robbers?"

"Yes, one of the men came directly up to me and told me to open the door to the tellers."

T. Bernard smiled at the jurors. "How many customers and employees would you say were in the bank that morning, Mrs. Williams?"

She thought back for a moment and said, "I guess about fifteen or maybe twenty at the most."

T. Bernard had his back toward her and asked as he looked at the jurors, "Mrs. Williams, you mean to tell me that out of the entire fifteen or twenty customers and employees, the bank robbers came directly up to you and asked you to open the door to the teller room?"

She shrugged and said, "Yes."

T. Bernard nodded and asked, "The defendant that you pointed out, his name is Clyde Barker. Do you know anyone he is related to?"

She leaned forward to the microphone and said, "Yes."

"And who would that be?"

"Ceasar Barker, the defendant's brother."

"And can you tell us who is Ceasar Barker?"

"Yes, he was an employee at the bank."

T. Bernard watched the jurors' surprise and decided not to let go. He nearly raced to his table and lifted up a folder and announced, "Let the record reflect that in my hand I hold sworn testimony that one of the men who pleaded guilty to robbery of the bank in question is named"—he walked directly up to the jurors and held up the paper so all the jurors could see—"Sonny Barker!" Clyde cringed in his seat as all the jurors' eyes seemed to bore holes through him.

"Nothing else, Your Honor." T. Bernard thanked Mrs. Williams and walked over to his table, satisfied that he had drawn blood.

"Cross-examination, Ms. Hemmingway?"

Ms. Hemmingway stood and greeted Mrs. Williams. "Mrs. Williams, may I ask you, how did you come to know Clyde Barker?"

"Well, he came into the bank and introduced himself as Ceasar's brother."

Ms. Hemmingway frowned. "He told you this through his mask?"

"Oh no. He wasn't one of the men who came into the bank to rob the place. He came earlier looking for his brother."

"So he had nothing to do with the bank robbery?"

"Objection!" T. Bernard shouted. "Defense counsel is leading the witness."

"Sustained," said the judge.

Ms. Hemmingway smiled. "Sorry, I'll rephrase the question. Was the defendant, Mr. Clyde Barker, one of the three men who came into the bank with masks on and waving guns?"

"No," said Mrs. Williams.

Ms. Hemmingway stared at the jury. "Did he participate in any capacity in the robbery itself?"

"No," Mrs. Williams said calmly.

"Did he threaten any of the customers or employees with a weapon?"

"No," she answered.

Ms. Hemmingway folded her arms and said, "Let me get this straight: The defendant entered your bank, introduced himself by name, and he neither participated in the robbery nor did he threaten anyone that day. Is that correct?"

Mrs. Williams hesitated for a second and then answered, "Yes, that's correct."

"No further questions, Your Honor," said Ms. Hemmingway as she smiled at the jurors.

"Redirect, Mr. Williams?" asked the judge.

T. Bernard stood quickly and said, "Yes, Your Honor." He stared at his notes and asked Mrs. Williams, "Now, Mrs. Williams, does the First Bank of Savings employ a security officer?"

"Yes, we do."

"On the morning in question, was there a security officer on duty?"

"Yes, there was."

"Can you tell me, madam, if the officer on duty got into any altercation during the robbery?"

Mrs. Williams looked at Clyde and said, "Yes."

"With whom?"

"The defendant, Mr. Barker."

"Were any weapons involved?"

"Yes, they were struggling for a gun."

"No further questions, Your Honor." T. Bernard stared at Clyde and then at the jury.

"Defense, any redirect?"

Ms. Hemmingway said, "Yes, Your Honor." She approached the witness. "Mrs. Williams, do you know whose gun was involved?"

"No, I assumed it belonged to the defendant."

Ms. Hemmingway walked over to her table and removed a piece of paper and asked, "What is the name of the security officer who was on duty the day of the robbery and who was involved in the confrontation?"

She thought for a second and said, "Mr. De La Cruz."

"Mrs. Williams, I have one more question for you."

Mrs. Williams nodded, and Ms. Hemmingway continued, "Does the First Bank of Savings have any protocol or guidelines for employees in case of a bank robbery?"

She nodded. "Yes, we have a strict policy."

"Would it be safe to say that one of those guidelines is to not resist during the course of a bank robbery?"

"Objection, Your Honor, she is leading the witness again."

"Sustained."

Ms. Hemmingway apologized and said, "Mrs. Williams, in your own words, what is the bank's policy in the event of a bank robbery?"

"It instructs us to not resist whatsoever for the safety of our customers and employees."

"So did the security officer violate the strict guidelines and put not only himself in jeopardy, but the public and employees?"

"Yes, yes, he did," she answered.

"Does that same officer still work at your bank?"

"No, he was removed from the bank for not following the branch guidelines."

"Thank you, Mrs. Williams. Your Honor, I have no more questions."

T. Bernard called various bank employees to the stand to confirm that Clyde was at the bank, and each time Ms. Hemmingway cross-examined them, they all stated that they saw Clyde there and struggling with the security officer and that was it. After calling seven bank employees and three customers to the bench to testify, the judge announced a recess until two.

Keyshia and Ceasar had lunch together and sat and talked about the case.

"So, how do you think the case is going?" asked Ceasar.

"As well as expected," Keyshia said.

"Your boss is a motherfucka. He's really trying to stick it to Clyde. You're not hurt by what he's saying? 'Cause it kills me every time he paints him in a corner."

Keyshia sipped her iced tea and thought about what he said. She told Ceasar point-blank, "He has to do it, that's his job."

Ceasar frowned at her. "You sound like you're on his side."

Keyshia stared at Ceasar and said, "No, he's actually helping."

Ceasar frowned again and said, "Helping us? Keyshia, have you lost your mind? It only takes one juror believing that he is a monster."

Keyshia gave him a defiant glare and said, "You ever heard of the lesser of two evils?"

Ceasar nodded. "Yeah, so what's your point?"

She smiled and said, "By the time all this is over, Clyde is going to look like a Cub Scout going up against the Devil."

The next witness T. Bernard called after lunch recess was the security officer, Jorge De La Cruz.

De La Cruz was sworn in by the bailiff and took his seat in the witness box with an air of confidence.

"Afternoon, Mr. De La Cruz," said T. Bernard.

De La Cruz edged close to the microphone, and his voice boomed throughout the courtroom: "Afternoon to you, too, sir."

T. Bernard winced at the sound and said in a low tone that he didn't need to speak too loudly. Then he asked, "Mr. De La Cruz, can you tell us where you were on the sixteenth of May?"

"Yes, sir, I was employed in the capacity of security officer at the First Bank of Savings between the hours of oh seven hundred and fifteen hundred."

T. Bernard hated these types and had warned De La Cruz previously to keep his answers short and to the point. Now he began to wonder if he'd made the right decision to have him testify.

"Thank you." De La Cruz nodded. "Do you recall seeing the defendant, Clyde Barker, enter the establishment?"

De La Cruz stared grimly at Clyde and said, "Yes, sir, I observed the perp as soon—"

"Objection, Your Honor," said Ms. Hemmingway. "Witness is characterizing my client with his opinion."

"Sustained," said the judge, who then instructed the witness to not form an opinion and to address him as the "defendant."

De La Cruz nodded and continued, "I observed the defendant enter the establishment at exactly oh eight twenty-five and quickly noticed his erratic and unusual behavior."

"What did you do then?" asked T. Bernard.

"I immediately began making a mental note in my head of his full description and kept a close eye on him during his duration in the bank."

T. Bernard nodded. "Then what happened?"

"Within fifteen minutes after the defendant entered the bank, three heavily armed men in masks with high-powered handguns came in and announced a robbery."

"Then what happened?"

"One of the robbery suspects pointed a weapon in my face and ordered me to lie facedown behind the customer service counter."

"Where was the defendant at this time?"

"Lying down next to me."

"Did you notice anything unusual at this point?"

"Yes, I noticed that the defendant and one of the masked gunmen were making eye and head gestures like they knew each other."

"Objection, Your Honor. Witness is expressing his opinion again."

"Sustained," the judge said.

"No more questions," T. Bernard said.

"Cross, Ms. Hemmingway?"

"Yes, Your Honor." Ms. Hemmingway walked directly up to the witness, and De La Cruz knew he would be in for a handful from the eager-looking black woman.

"Mr. De La Cruz, you said you noticed the defendant acting suspiciously as soon as he walked into the bank, correct?"

"Yes, ma'am," he said confidently.

"In your opinion, what makes a person appear suspicious?"

"Well, he walked in looking around."

"I see. So anytime a person walks into a bank and looks around, in your opinion he is deemed suspicious, Mr. De La Cruz?"

"No, but he seemed different."

"Different how?"

Suddenly Mr. De La Cruz was at a loss for words. "I . . . don't know, it was something about him."

"Come on, Mr. De La Cruz, it was something that made him look—and these are your words—'erratic and unusual.' " De La Cruz was speechless, and Ms. Hemmingway moved on. "You mentioned that when the gunmen entered the bank, you were ordered to lie down on the floor and observed the defendant and one of the gunmen making some kind of gesture? What kind of gesture?"

"A gesture like they knew each other. Like he was part of the robbery."

Ms. Hemmingway nodded and walked over to her table and retrieved a handgun in a plastic bag with a tag on it. "Mr. De La Cruz, do you recognize this weapon?"

"Yes, ma'am, it is my registered thirty-eight-caliber weapon."

"Let the record reflect exhibit C-three is entered into evidence." She held it in the air for all to see. "Mr. De La Cruz, did you pull this weapon out at any time during the course of the robbery?"

"Yes, ma'am," he said proudly. "When I was on the floor, I saw an opportunity when one of the gunmen had his back turned and made a move for my weapon, which I had stored in my ankle holster."

Ms. Hemmingway nodded. "Mr. De La Cruz, in your capacity

as security guard at the bank, were you paid as an armed or unarmed officer?" De La Cruz immediately knew where she was going with the question and was unable to answer it.

"Mr. De La Cruz, were you employed as an armed or unarmed officer at the First Bank of Savings?"

With much reluctance, he admitted, "Unarmed."

Ms. Hemmingway stared at the jurors and asked him as she continued to look at them, "So, you had an illegal weapon on you, is that right, Mr. De La Cruz?"

He put his head down and said, "Yes."

Ms. Hemmingway wasn't finished. "Let's go back to when you pulled the weapon out of your ankle holster. Were you still on the ground?"

"Yes." Deflated, he now decided to give short answers.

"Were you still next to the defendant when you reached for your weapon?"

"Yes."

Ms. Hemmingway decided to go for the jugular. "Mr. De La Cruz, you mentioned several times that you were sure the defendant and the armed suspects were in on the robbery together, correct?"

"One hundred percent sure."

"If you were one hundred percent sure that they were together, Mr. De La Cruz, why would you wait till the gunmen had their back turned to pull out your weapon, when you were next to their accomplice?"

He could not answer her question.

"Mr. De La Cruz, did you ever apply to become a New York City police officer?"

"Yes."

"Were you ever hired?"

"No, I was rejected because of medical reasons."

Ms. Hemmingway walked to her table and pulled out yet another document, entered it into evidence, and handed a copy to T. Bernard.

"This is the psychological evaluation of Mr. De La Cruz, which states that he was rejected by the police department because he suffered from homicidal tendencies and would be a liability to the department." Ms. Hemmingway held her copy in the air and said, "No more questions, Your Honor."

Chapter 40

On the second day of the trial, the arresting officers were called to take the stand. One by one, each gave testimony about how one suspect got away but they'd captured three running out of the bank.

A federal agent even testified how they'd considered bringing an indictment against Ceasar Barker because they believed that he was in on the robbery, but there had not been enough evidence to do so. And there was still the question about the one hundred and thirty thousand dollars that had been unclaimed and was ultimately entered into evidence and used against Clyde because Ceasar had originally said that he was holding it in a safe deposit box for his brother.

Since T. Bernard saw that the case was slipping away from him, he decided to throw the unclaimed money into the story so a federal IRS claim could be made against Clyde just in case things didn't work in favor of the prosecution. Keyshia had not figured on this and quickly made plans to offset it.

After the agent testified about the money, Ms. Hemmingway called to the stand Mr. Johnson Gadson, better known as "Pops," from Johnny's Ice House.

"Mr. Gadson, do you know the defendant, Clyde Barker?"

"Yes, ma'am, he's been working for me since he was a boy."

"And what is it that you do?"

"Oh, I run Johnny's Ice House, delivering ice to the businesses in the area."

"Sounds like hard work."

"It is, 'cause my back is killing me." All the jurors laughed at the elderly man's joke.

"What were Mr. Barker's wages at the time?"

Pops frowned and said, "Who?" She pointed at Clyde, and he said, "Oh, you talking 'bout Rocco." He said excitedly, "I paid him 'bout twenty-five dollars a day."

She nodded and said, "Well, Mr. Barker had over one hundred thousand dollars deposited in a bank. Would you know how a person who only earns twenty-five dollars a day could possibly obtain that kind of money?"

"I thought it was one hundred and thirty thousand dollars."

"How did you know the exact amount, Mr. Gadson?" asked Ms. Hemmingway.

"Because that's the amount we won together in Atlantic City gambling."

"So, you are saying you two won the money together gambling? Do you have any proof of that?"

Pops smiled. "Sure do." He reached into his pocket and

pulled out hotel invoices, restaurant bills, and store receipts. "The boy even took me to a concert that night to see Lyfe Jennings, who happens to be one of my favorite singers now." Pops pulled out two concert ticket stubs and smiled.

"Why would you only now make a claim on the money?"

Pops put his head down and said, "Well, to be quite honest, I thought he took the money and skipped town. I was so hurt because I trusted him out of all the boys who worked for me. But I was recently contacted and notified that he didn't skip out on me, he was arrested and the money was confiscated. I could care less about the money; just knowing he didn't steal from me makes me happy. Rocco has been one of the most honest young men I met in my ninety-one years. I may look old and broke, but my estate is worth over two million dollars, and I told him long ago that he can come to me and I'll give him anything he wants. Hell, I was giving him half the money we won gambling, so why would he want to rob a bank?"

The trial was winding down, and everything was looking good for Clyde. The time had come for Martha to testify. Since she was due to testify on Clyde's behalf, she had been restricted from sitting in on the proceedings until now.

"The defense calls Ms. Martha Woods to the stand."

Martha was led to the bench aided by a cane as the bailiff helped her to her seat. He swore her in and she sat down. Ms. Hemmingway asked her a barrage of questions about what kind of person Clyde was, if he had ever been in trouble, and his character in general. After Ms. Hemmingway finished asking her questions, T. Bernard was up to ask his own questions.

"Hello, Ms. Woods. How are you today?"

She smiled lightly and said, "I'm just fine, thank you."

"Good, good. I just have a few questions to ask you, Ms. Woods, okay?"

She nodded.

"I understand that you raised Ceasar Barker, Sonny Barker, and the defendant, Clyde Barker, since they were toddlers when their mother fell ill, is that correct?"

Martha smiled and nodded. "Yes, me and their mother was best friends growing up, and when that tragic incident happened, I took all three boys in and raised them."

T. Bernard smiled and said, "Wow, that's very noble of you, taking them in like that."

She nodded. "Oh, that's the least I could do. Like I say, me and their mother was closer than sisters, so them boys was like my own family, and I was always taught to take care of family."

T. Bernard paused as if searching for the right words and then asked, "What happened to their mother to cause them to live with you for so many years?"

Martha put her head down as if she were hurting to think about what occurred and said, "She was shot."

"By whom, Ms. Woods?"

She lifted her head up and said, "By her husband, the boys' father." Suddenly she began to cry. The entire courtroom seemed saddened by the revelation.

T. Bernard reached inside his suit jacket and pulled out a handkerchief and handed it to her. He gave her a moment to settle down, then asked, "Ms. Woods, can you tell us where their father and mother are right now?"

Martha wiped her eyes and said, "Their father is still in prison somewhere for the shooting, I believe, and Cathy, that's their mama's name, is still in a nursing home. They say she is catatonic, like a zombie. She's been like that ever since."

"Ms. Woods, we are going to move on, and I'm going to ask

you some questions about yourself, okay?" She nodded confidently, and T. Bernard went in for the kill. "What was your part in the bank robbery, Ms. Woods?"

The entire courtroom gasped, and Ms. Hemmingway jumped to her feet and yelled, "Your Honor, I object!"

The judge pounded his gavel and said with aggravation in his tone, "Sustained! Sidebar, Mr. Williams!"

Ms. Hemmingway and T. Bernard Williams walked to the judge's bench. The judge said through gritted teeth, "Mr. Williams, you better have a damn good reason to accuse Ms. Woods of bank robbery or I will personally see that you are disbarred."

"Your Honor, Ms. Woods is a convicted felon and had been involved in several federal-related bank felonies. I also have strong evidence that Ms. Woods is connected to this bank robbery and have a witness who will support that."

"But, Your Honor," Ms. Hemmingway protested, "Ms. Woods is not on trial here today, and it would be unfair to the entire case if she is brought into the proceeding at this stage."

"Your Honor, Ms. Woods is a defense character witness. I have every right to explore her character and ask her questions about her background. It isn't my fault that the defense did not do their homework and investigate their witnesses. Your Honor, this witness is a convicted felon who robbed banks and is here to testify about the character of a defendant that she has a connection to on a bank robbery charge."

The judge absorbed the argument and conceded, "Ms. Hemmingway, you opened the door for her to be questioned, and I'm overruling the objection."

"Thank you, Your Honor," T. Bernard said with a smile, and they both returned to their respective tables. T. Bernard pulled out a document and entered it as evidence. "Ms. Woods, I ask you again, what was your role in the bank robbery on April 10, 1981? And remember you are under oath."

Martha looked desperately at Ms. Hemmingway and toward the judge for help but received none.

"Can you answer the question, Ms. Woods?"

"I had nothing to do with no bank robbery," she said nervously. She had walked right into T. Bernard's web.

"How about the bank robbery you participated in in 1981, Ms. Woods? Can you tell us about that?"

It was if a dagger had stabbed Martha in the heart as she looked toward Clyde and his lawyer for some sort of support. T. Bernard smelled blood.

"Your Honor, in my hand I hold an indictment dated April 10, 1981, *United States v. Martha Woods*, charged with federal bank robbery, 18 USC Section 2113 (a)."

Normally, Ms. Hemmingway would have objected to such actions, but she thought this information might work in her client's favor. T. Bernard walked over to the defense table and handed her a copy.

"Your Honor, please enter this into evidence as J-six," he said as he continued. "Ms. Woods, I ask you once again, what role did you play in the bank robbery on May 16, 2001, at the First Bank of Savings?"

Martha grew angry. "I don't know what it is you talkin' about," she spat.

"Come on, Ms. Woods, isn't it more than a coincidence that all three brothers, one who worked at the bank where the other two brothers showed up, are charged with robbing that same bank?" Martha was boiling, and her eyes began to widen from the pressure. "I ask again," T. Bernard said twelve inches from her face, "what was your role in this bank robbery, Ms. Woods?"

"I fuckin' told you I ain't have shit to do with it!" T. Bernard had stripped away the innocent-looking caretaker role that she was displaying and exposed her for who she really was.

He stared at her with malice and said, "Your, Honor, I'm temporarily finished with this witness until after I call a corroborating witness to testify about Ms. Woods's connection to the crime and her character."

The judge stared at T. Bernard Williams and looked over to the defense. "Any cross, Ms. Hemmingway?"

"No, Your Honor, the defense has no questions."

"Ms. Woods, you are remanded to the courtroom until such time as witness examinations are heard."

"Thank you," said T. Bernard. "The government would like to call to the stand Sonny Barker."

Keyshia and Ceasar held each other's hands tightly as they sat in the rear of the courtroom and watched three federal officers escort Sonny inside the courtroom. His hands and ankles were shackled and he took short, choppy steps. Even though he wore gray prison coveralls, they could see that Sonny had packed on at least thirty pounds of solid muscle since the last time they'd seen him. Keyshia and Ceasar watched Sonny's girlfriend, Cheryl, wave wildly at him from the second row. She was still riding his bid out with him after all these years and was excited to see him.

They placed him in the witness chair and swore him in, but Sonny refused to raise his right hand as the bailiff asked. Keyshia noticed that Sonny wore a coffi on his head, which symbolized that he was now a Muslim. He had mentioned in his letters that he was studying the religion but hadn't said that he'd made the commitment yet. Sonny looked around the courtroom and spotted his girlfriend, Ceasar, Keyshia, and Martha. Though he was happy to see all of them, it seemed that he refused to crack a smile—a permanent mask that he'd acquired in prison.

"Good afternoon, Mr. Barker." Sonny remained silent and simply glared at him. T. Bernard cleared his throat and contin-

ued, "Mr. Barker, you have been found guilty on federal bank robbery charges and are currently serving time at Leavenworth federal prison, is that right?" Sonny remained silent.

T. Bernard looked at the judge, who said, "Mr. Barker, answer
his question or you will be charged with contempt of court."

Sonny tossed the judge daggers with his eyes, wanting so
badly to curse him out, but he looked at his little brother's pleading eyes and then at his girl's and answered, "Yes."

T. Bernard got straight to the point. "Do you know a Martha
Woods?"

Sonny sneered at him and said, "Yes."

T. Bernard walked over to his table. "Did she participate in
any part of the bank robbery that took place at the First Bank of
Savings in Harlem on May 16, 2001, Mr. Barker?"

Sonny jumped to his feet and yelled, "Fuck you, son of a
bitch!" and tried to leap over the bench at T. Bernard, but he was
quickly subdued by the court officers. Clyde, Sonny's girlfriend,
Keyshia, and Ceasar all covered their eyes. Martha was the only
one in the courtroom smiling. The judge banged his gavel and ordered that the witness be removed from the courtroom and stated
that questioning would be continued via closed-circuit television, then he called for a thirty-minute recess.

Deflated, Ceasar said, "Keyshia, I told you Sonny wasn't
going to say anything against Martha. He'd rather die before he
does that. When they call me to the witness stand, I'm gonna tell.
I've got to get my brother off."

Keyshia took a deep breath and knew that Ceasar was right.
The only way Clyde was going to get off was if one of the people
who took part in the robbery testified against Martha; and seeing
how violent Sonny became, she knew he wouldn't rat on her. But
she didn't want to see Ceasar go to jail because she knew the
brothers wouldn't want that and that Ceasar wouldn't be able to
make it in jail. She thought fast and decided to speak to T.

Bernard and ask him not to call on Sonny yet but instead to call on the witness who was supposed to be called last.

When everyone came back from recess, the court technicians had cable wires and cameras set up by the witness bench. Five minutes later the bailiff yelled, "All rise!"

"Please be seated," said the judge as he sat down.

The bailiff said, "Everything is set up, Your Honor."

"The witness room?" he asked.

"Yes, Your Honor."

"Okay," said the judge. "Mr. Williams, are you ready to resume questioning of Mr. Sonny Barker?"

"Yes, Your Honor, but I'd like to call another witness first."

The judge looked at the defense table and asked, "Defense, do you object to having the prosecution call another witness?"

"No, Your Honor."

"Fine," said the judge. "Mr. Williams, you can call your next witness." The video's red light suddenly came on as the technician swiveled the camera toward the witness door. Everything was being broadcast via closed-circuit television to a TV monitor that Sonny would be watching.

T. Bernard smiled and walked to the middle of the courtroom and said in a dramatic fashion, "The United States now calls Mrs. Catherine Barker to the stand."

Clyde, Ceasar, and Martha suddenly sat up in their seats as they watched the bailiff escort the boys' mother from the witness chamber. Martha looked as if she were seeing a ghost.

Ceasar looked at Keyshia, speechless. All the jurors watched as Mrs. Barker took tentative, fragile steps toward the witness seat. Clyde looked back at Keyshia, who was in tears as she gave her man a nod. The bailiff asked her to lift her hand, and she struggled to raise it, and he aided her by lifting it up for her.

"Do you swear to tell the truth, the whole truth, so help you God?" asked the bailiff.

Mrs. Barker nodded slowly and said almost in a whisper, "I do."

Clyde could not hold back his tears. This was the first time in his entire adult life that he'd ever heard his mother's voice and it pierced his heart. He could hardly contain himself as he wiped away his tears. He had to fight to keep from running over to his delicate mother and giving her a hug.

The bailiff helped her to her seat and walked away. She looked around the courtroom and saw Clyde and smiled.

T. Bernard approached her and asked, "How are you today, Mrs. Barker?"

She gave him a tremulous smile and said, this time a little louder, "I'm okay."

He smiled. "Good. Mrs. Barker, I'm going to be asking you a few questions, okay?" She nodded, and he continued, "Do you know why you are here today?"

"Yes," said Mrs. Barker. "My sons are in some kind of trouble and I'm here to help them."

T. Bernard smiled and nodded. "Do you know which of your sons are in trouble?"

She turned her head toward Clyde and said, "My youngest child, Clyde, right there, and my second son, Sonny." T. Bernard thanked her as he looked at the jurors' bewildered eyes.

Suddenly, Mrs. Barker recognized a familiar face, and her lips instantly began to curl and her brows began to turn downward. T. Bernard decided to take advantage of the precious moment.

"Mrs. Barker, do you know a Ms. Martha Woods?" Martha was nervous and refused to raise her head.

Mrs. Barker's eyes were like a razor as she stared at her former best friend. "Yes, I know her."

"When did you first meet Ms. Woods?"

"We were from the same projects, and we met when we was fourteen years old," she said, never taking her eyes off Martha.

"Are you and Ms. Woods still best friends, Mrs. Barker?"

"No!" she said flatly.

T. Bernard looked at the jury and walked closer to where Martha sat to ensure everyone knew where she was when he asked his next question. He gestured to where she sat and asked, "May I ask you, Mrs. Barker, when was the last time you saw Ms. Woods?"

The entire courtroom became silent as all eyes watched her stare at Martha with disgust. "The last time I saw her was when she shot me in the face!"

The courtroom erupted as Martha cried hysterically, "She's crazy! She's crazy! She doesn't know what she's talking about! Her husband shot her, not me!"

Both Ceasar and Clyde could no longer contain themselves as they jumped up and cursed at Martha.

The judge banged his gavel and called the court to order and threatened, "Young man in the rear, if you don't remain silent and sit down, I will have you removed from my courtroom. And Ms. Hemmingway, that goes for your client, also, so I suggest you keep his mouth shut and tell him to stay in his seat!" The judge saved his last remark for Martha. "Ms. Woods, if I even hear so much as a peep from you again, I will have you locked up for contempt of court—so sit down and shut up!"

It took another five minutes for the courtroom to come back to order, and then T. Bernard resumed his line of questioning.

"Mrs. Barker, according to the police report dated February 3, 1983, your husband, Mr. Lamont Barker, was charged with attempted murder for shooting you. Are you saying this is incorrect?"

"Yes," she said quickly. "My husband didn't shoot me, she did!"

"Can you tell us what happened that night to cause her to shoot you, Mrs. Barker?"

She nodded and spoke with anger as she recalled the fateful night that changed her family's lives.

"I had just come home from working overtime at my job at the telephone company." She paused and stared at Martha before continuing. "Martha had just gotten out of prison for getting mixed up in a bank robbery or something with her boyfriend. Since she ain't had nowhere to go, I let her stay with me and my family for a while until she got a job and an apartment. Like I said, I came home from working overtime and walked to the kids' room to check on them. They were all asleep. Then I walked toward my bedroom and heard a moaning sound." She paused and put her head down. T. Bernard asked her if she was okay, and she nodded.

"I walked slowly to the room and opened the door, and I saw Martha on top of my husband." All the jurors tossed Martha an evil glare as she continued, "I cut on the light and she hopped off the bed and put on the housegown she had dropped on the floor. My husband didn't move, and that's when I realized he was passed out." She turned to T. Bernard and confessed, "Back then my husband had a drinking problem and would pass out like that all the time. I turned toward Martha and told her to get her stuff and get out of my house. She was crying and saying she was sorry, but I wanted her out! The next thing I knew and last thing I remember was seeing her raise her arm with a black pistol in her hand and then everything went black."

Martha saw every eye was on her and could no longer take the heat of the stares and stood up and said angrily, "I don't have to listen to this anymore. She's sick in the head, delusional!" She made her way toward the aisle, but the judge ordered his bailiff to stop her.

"Get your fucking hands off of me!" she cried.

Two more officers detained her by putting her in handcuffs, and they all surrounded her as they put her back into her seat.

"I have no more questions, Your Honor!" said T. Bernard as he nodded to Mrs. Barker.

"Any cross, Ms. Hemmingway?"

"No, Your Honor," said Ms. Hemmingway.

Mrs. Barker walked slowly over to Clyde's table, and he jumped to his feet and gave the mother he never knew a hug and held on to her for dear life. Ceasar approached the front and joined brother and mother in a hug as they all cried together. A bailiff came out of the witness door and whispered in T. Bernard's ear and passed him a note. T. Bernard read it and said to the judge anxiously, "Your Honor, I would like to call Sonny Barker back to the stand!"

"I was going to call a recess. How long is this going to take?"

T. Bernard said, "Your Honor, I assure you it won't be long."

The judge nodded and told his bailiff to fetch the witness.

When the three officers walked in with Sonny this time, they no longer had to manhandle him to his seat. Sonny's entire demeanor seemed to have changed. He no longer had a mean scowl on his face but instead wore a humble, happier look as he searched around and spotted Ceasar sitting in the front row with their mother. Tears came to Sonny's eyes when he saw his mother wave to him. He wiped his eyes and waved back.

T. Bernard walked directly to where Sonny sat and asked, "Are you ready, son?" Sonny looked at Martha, and his face turned sour. He turned back to T. Bernard and nodded.

Sonny went on to answer every question that he was asked, and when he got to the part about how he got into a life of crime, he explained, "I was about thirteen when I did my first major robbery. It was a numbers spot in my neighborhood."

T. Bernard nodded. "You were very young. How did you pull it off?"

"I had somebody on the inside who worked there, and all I had to do was point a gun around and they put all the money in a bag."

"Who was that inside person, Sonny?"

Sonny turned and looked directly at Martha and pointed. "It was her, Martha Woods. She worked there at the time."

There were a few gasps.

"Where did you get the weapon to rob the place, Sonny?"

"Martha gave it to me."

"Did she set you up with any more robberies after that?"

"Yes," Sonny said casually.

"How many others?"

"I don't know. I lost count."

"How did she get you these robberies?"

Sonny paused and then said, "She would scope the places out and find out where the weak points were and devise a plan with the best time and way I should do it."

"Did you like doing these dangerous holdups?"

Sonny thought about the question. "At the beginning, I was scared to death and used to tell her I didn't want to do it any- more."

"What did she do?" asked T. Bernard as he walked toward the jurors' railing.

"She would call me names."

"What kind of names?"

"She would say I was soft, a sissy, and that I was a punk son of a bitch like my father. If that didn't work, she would cry and say that she didn't have any money to feed us and that me and my brothers would starve if I didn't do anything. I couldn't see my brothers starve, so I would give in." T. Bernard watched as every juror gave Martha a malicious glare.

"Sonny, was Martha Woods in any way involved with the bank robbery that happened at the First Bank of Savings in Harlem?"

"Yes, she was the one who set everything up. She even made sure that my older brother, Ceasar, who worked at the bank, wouldn't be at work that day so he wouldn't recognize me." T. Bernard looked at the jurors and was satisfied he'd done his job. He nodded to Sonny and said, "Thank you, Mr. Barker."

The judge said, "Cross, Ms. Hemmingway?"

"Just one question, Your Honor," she said as she walked to Sonny. "Mr. Barker, did your younger brother, Clyde, have anything to do with the robbery at the First Bank of Savings?"

"No, he didn't! We didn't even know he was going to be in the bank. That was the reason I didn't want my other brother, Ceasar, to be at work that day, so he wouldn't be in harm's way! If I knew Clyde was going to be there, I would have never done it."

"Thank you, Mr. Barker. Good luck with your future."

"Your Honor," T. Bernard said, "the government rests!"

Ms. Hemmingway said, "Your Honor, the defense requests an immediate dismissal in response to the testimony of Sonny Barker."

While Ms. Hemmingway knew that her motion would probably be denied, she wanted to reinforce in the jurors' minds that the defense had done some damage during cross-examination.

"Motion denied," said the judge.

Ms. Hemmingway smiled and said, "Then the defense rests, Your Honor."

Mrs. Barker stayed overnight with Keyshia, her grandson, and Ceasar, and for the first time in over twenty years, Ceasar felt as if he had a family. For any child, not having his mother in his life can cause irreparable emotional and psychological damage. Because he was never fully nurtured, he would always search for love, pleasure, and security. Many would always find their needs unfulfilled and would seek comfort and solace in codependency— through drugs, alcohol, sex, or crime. But none of these methods are enough to fill the void within. But the ones who get beaten enough, humiliated enough, and pained enough may come to believe that only they and God could ever make them whole, if they only searched within.

The next morning, they all arrived at court bright and early for the closing arguments and jury deliberation. By eight forty-five, the courtroom was packed, and Ceasar and his mother and his young nephew sat in the front row. Keyshia stayed in the back to ensure no conflict of interest would enter the equation and ruin things for Clyde. When Clyde was finally brought out, he smiled immediately when he saw his family gathered together directly behind him, including his mother and his son.

Finally, at nine-ten, the Honorable Theodore S. Denton exited his chambers and entered the courtroom.

"All rise for the Honorable Theodore S. Denton!" shouted the bailiff. All the spectators rose to their feet.

"Take your seat," muttered the judge. He surveyed both defense and prosecutor tables and bellowed, "Bring the jurors out." The bailiff retreated through the witness chambers and brought out the twelve jurors. In single file they walked to their assigned seats, with apparent readiness to get the trial over with and go about their lives. Once they were all seated, the judge cleared his throat and greeted them.

"Good morning, ladies and gentlemen of the jury. Today you will hear the closing arguments. The government will present the first closing argument and may reserve time for rebuttal. The defense will then present its closing argument, and after all rebuttals are rendered, you will be instructed to go to a room, where you will begin deliberation, weighing evidence and testimonies that you heard. Do you understand?" Each juror nodded.

"Mr. Williams," yelled the judge, "is the government ready to proceed with its closing argument?"

T. Bernard snapped to his feet like a heavyweight boxer during rounds and said loudly and crisply, "Yes, Your Honor, the government is ready!"

"Proceed," said the judge.

T. Bernard walked toward the jurors as if he were contemplating the precise words to say. He stopped directly in front of the jury's railing, wrapped his arm around his chest, and began rubbing his chin. It was so silent that you could hear a pin drop when he said softly, "Ladies and gentlemen, I have to admit to you today that this has been one of the most emotional and gut-wrenching trials that I have ever had to prosecute in my eight years working for the government. Like you, I'm touched and saddened when I hear about the tragic unfairness that is inflicted upon families, but I must tell you that the courtroom is not the place to right personal injustices. We truly have to look past the evil that men do, the evil that women do, in order to get through the reasons that we are all brought together here today, and that is to serve justice for a crime that had been committed by Clyde Barker. As much as we want this to be a perfect ending where the family is reunited and lives happily ever after from now on, we know that isn't reality. Reality is living on life's terms no matter what we have been through in our lives, and that's what makes us civilized and that's what keeps us safe—if not, there would be anarchy! If a person was beaten as a child, he or she doesn't have the right to beat others because he or she got beaten. If a person was hated as a child, that doesn't give him the right to hate the world. Clyde Barker is that child and didn't deserve the way life turned out for him, but that doesn't give him the right to commit an atrocious crime and blame it on his upbringing."

T. Bernard went into a tirade that would have made any preacher proud as he masterfully mesmerized the jurors. He went on for another fifteen minutes until finally he finished and thanked the jurors.

"Ms. Hemmingway, your closing argument," said the judge.

Ms. Hemmingway stood at her table as if she, too, were searching for the right words to say. She lifted her head and said, "Ladies and gentlemen, if you remember from the opening argument, I promised you that I would not insult your intelligence. I think I've kept my promise. I told you that I would prove to you that my client was in the wrong place at the wrong time and, yes, a victim of circumstance. I think I did that. Now I stand before you today, after three days of testimony, evidence, and facts that prove beyond an inkling of doubt that my client, Clyde Barker, is innocent—and I think . . . no, I *know* I proved that! The government proved nothing. Absolutely nothing. Their handling of the case has been a miscarriage of justice, and no doubt, the judge will remind you of the burden of proof. This is not a civil trial. We require high levels of proof, ladies and gentlemen. Surely you must have doubts, and if you have even one doubt—just one!" Mrs. Hemmingway looked every one of the jurors in their eyes before continuing. "Then by law, you must bring back a not guilty verdict and reject any misguided interpretations which point to guilt." She paused and walked over to Clyde. "Contrary to popular belief, we do not want your vote simply because you feel sorry for our client, who was wrongfully accused. We want your vote because he is one hundred percent innocent." She walked quickly over to the jury and raised her voice as if her life depended on them hearing her. "The time has come for you to decide, and the choice may not be as difficult as you might think. If you are not one hundred percent sure, you must return a verdict of not guilty."

• • •

The jury had deliberated for only three hours when the bailiff called the courtroom to order. Keyshia was so nervous that she broke her rule and edged closer to the front row. Like clockwork, the judge came lumbering out of his chambers and up to his bench. He shuffled some paperwork and looked at his bailiff. Electrified silence engulfed the courtroom at that moment as Ceasar hugged his mother with one arm and bit his fingernails with the other.

"I have been informed that the jury has reached a verdict. Is that correct, Mr. Bailiff?"

"Yes, they have, Your Honor."

"Okay, then. Mr. Bailiff, would you seat the jury."

It took the bailiff three minutes to bring out the jury, but to Keyshia it seemed like an eternity. The door finally opened, and as if it were déjà vu, Keyshia began to grow sick to her stomach. She looked at her man looking defenseless as two federal officers moved to flank him. She suddenly felt an urge to hug him. It was as if Clyde had felt her pain—he turned around, smiled, and whispered, "Body language."

Keyshia thought he was going mad until she looked at the faces and eyes of the passing jurors and began to smile herself. Ceasar stared horrified at Clyde smiling back at Keyshia and at her smiling at him. He saw no humor in what was going on at the moment. All the jurors finally took their seats.

"Ladies and gentlemen of the jury," said the judge, "have you reached a decision?"

"Yes, sir, we have," answered the jury forewoman.

The bailiff walked over to the forewoman, who handed the decision to the bailiff, who then handed it to the judge. The judge took the note and studied it, showing no emotion.

The judge looked at Clyde and said, "Will the defendant please rise." The judge handed the note back to the bailiff, who returned it to the jury forewoman.

"Please read the verdict, Madam Forewoman," the judge announced.

The forewoman looked at Clyde and unfolded the paper. "As to the charge of federal bank robbery, we find the defendant, Clyde Barker, not guilty!"

Clyde jumped to his feet and ran straight to his mother and child and hugged them tightly.

His mother held her son's face, looking at him tearfully. "I missed you, son," she said.

Clyde blinked back tears and said, "I missed you, too, Mama!"

All the jurors watched the family reunion through their own tears as they hugged one another, knowing that they had served justice and that it was all worth it. Even T. Bernard Williams had a hard time keeping himself from growing emotional as he sat back in his chair and considered himself a winner because he'd gotten a bigger fish in the process—Martha Woods, who was behind bars because of contempt of court charges, compliments of the judge.

After Clyde hugged his family and his lawyer, he looked around for his baby—Keyshia. Then he spotted her where she stood, teary-eyed and unable to move. He handed his son to his brother and walked slowly over to his woman. Keyshia burst into tears and ran into her man's arms. Clyde wrapped his arms around her as she buried her head in his chest and she cried like she'd never done before. Even Ms. Hemmingway found it hard to control her emotions; she fought to hold back her tears but lost.

"I missed you, baby. I missed you so much!" Keyshia said.

"I missed you, too," said Clyde as he wiped away her tears. "I'm going home now, and I'm never going to leave you again."

She looked up at him and said, "You promise?"

He nodded and said, "I promise," and kissed her hard.

When they pulled apart, Ceasar handed his nephew back to

Clyde, and the three of them, mother, father, and son, were finally together in freedom, for the first time.

When they looked up, T. Bernard was standing across from them with a grim, dumbfounded look on his face. The entire family, as well as Ms. Hemmingway, waited for him to lash out at them for the deception that had been pulled on him.

Finally he said, "Ms. Simmons, I want you to take a week off to spend with your family, and I'll see you back at work first thing Monday morning." He smiled widely and walked toward the doorway. Then he stopped and said, "Oh yeah." He reached into his jacket pocket and pulled out a slip. "This is the claim number for you to retrieve the money that the government confiscated. You must claim it within fourteen business days." He smiled again and said, "I'll put in the paperwork for it to be released when I get back to the office."

Keyshia, Clyde, and Clyde, Jr. walked over to Ms. Hemmingway.

"Ms. Hemmingway," Keyshia said humbly, "I . . . I don't know how to thank you for—"

Ms. Hemmingway cut her off. "You can thank me by passing the bar exam and doing legal service from time to time after you become a lawyer for people who have been unjustly convicted."

Keyshia smiled and said she would.

Clyde approached her and thanked her also. "Ms. Hemmingway, I just want to thank you for believing in me. I don't know how to ever repay you for giving me back my life and my family."

She nodded and said, "You just did, and that's more than enough." He hugged her, and she joked before she walked out of the courtroom, "You just stay away from those banks."

As they prepared to leave the courtroom, they began to look around for Clyde, Jr. He was in the well of the courtroom, playing a friendly game of cops and robbers with the bailiff.

"Bang! Bang! Bang!" little Clyde said to the bailiff as he shot him with his fingers as though he had a gun.

The bailiff fell to his knees playfully as if he'd been shot and said, "Oh no! You got me! The cop always gets the bad guy in the end!"

Little Clyde became furious with the officer and said at the top of his lungs, "I wasn't playing no cop, I was playing the bad guy!" and shot him two more times for good measure.

Keyshia and Clyde looked at each other, shook their heads, and said at the same time:

"Body language!"

Chapter 41

Shortly after the trial, Keyshia took emergency leave from school and her job to go down south to Charleston. Clyde and Clyde, Jr. went along with her when they received news that her daughter's father had died from an apparently self-inflicted gunshot wound to the head. He was found in his bedroom by Pastor Baker, the same pastor who had replaced him. Two weeks earlier, he had sent his daughter, Christina, to stay with her grandmother, Keyshia's mother. The circumstances surrounding the suicide were still under investigation, because neighbors had reported that they saw a young woman enter the house the same day. It turned out that the woman in question was one of his victims from the past, and she had been extorting him for years, threatening to go to the police if she wasn't given her money on a weekly basis. She told the police that on her last visit, he'd informed her that he would no longer be paying her, and as usual, she threatened to go to the police and left. She said she never had any intention of going to the police in the first place. After being questioned, she was asked if she had any remorse, and she told them she had none.

Keyshia's mother was given temporary custody of Christina until Keyshia petitioned the courts for her and her daughter's DNA and shortly after that was granted full custodial rights to her daughter. Keyshia and Clyde attended the funeral in support of Christina, who took her father's passing very hard, but in time she adapted to her newfound family setting with her mother, stepfather, and younger brother, Clyde. It was also about that time that Keyshia found it in her heart to forgive the man who had nearly ruined her life.

The very next summer, Keyshia, Clyde, Christina, and Clyde, Jr. attended the Simmons family reunion once again. Hundreds of family members attended that day, even more than Keyshia remembered from the last time. The day was festive as the family danced, hugged, and filled their stomachs with food. Then suddenly the music was halted as Keyshia's mother got up to speak into the microphone.

"Could I have everyone's attention for a moment, can I have your attention?"

Everyone stopped what they were doing and turned their attention toward Mrs. Simmons. "I'd like to thank everyone for coming to this year's Simmons family reunion, and I hope everyone is having a good time." Everyone responded by clapping and whistling as she continued, "At this time, I's like to ask my eldest daughter, Keyshia, to come to the front and announce some good news. Where is Keyshia?" she said as she surveyed the yard. "Where you at, baby? Come on up," she repeated.

Everyone started clapping again as they looked around for Keyshia. Clyde and both the children escorted her to the front as the clapping grew louder. A little embarrassed, Keyshia walked up to her mother, who gave her a hug and a kiss and handed her the microphone. Clyde was smiling widely as he nodded approval.

"Thank you, everyone, thank you." Keyshia blushed and continued as everyone grew silent, "I would like to let everyone know that as of last week, I passed the New York State Bar exam and I am now a lawyer." Everyone's eyes and mouths opened wider as they gave her a huge round of applause. Keyshia nodded and thanked everyone and continued, "At this time, I'd like to thank a few people. First, I'd like to thank my two children, Christina and Clyde." She beamed down upon them. "You two are my absolute joy and happiness. You are the reason that I strived to become who I am." Keyshia stared into Christina's eyes. "Mommy hasn't always been in your life, but I promise you, from this day on, that there is not a power, an entity, a force on this earth . . ." Keyshia paused as if she were losing her breath and then continued, "that will ever, ever keep you apart from me again." She nodded and smiled at her children, then turned her attention to Clyde. "And to the love of my life, my boyfriend, Clyde." Keyshia paused again as she searched the heavens for the right words. "You are the air that I breathe, the light of my life, and the reason I'm still living." Her lips began to quiver as she fought back the tears. "You picked me up when I was nothing and loved me when I never knew how to love myself. You made feel like I was beautiful when I thought I had no beauty at all. You saved me, and I love you to death, boy."

Clyde was at a loss for words as he tried to fight back his tears. Keyshia blew him a kiss, then turned her attention to her mother. "And to my mother." It was so unexpected, her mother put her head down as her palms began to sweat. "I learned that a mother was supposed to do everything in her power to protect her child."

She paused and stared at her mother for a moment and then continued, "A mother is supposed to never let her child go no matter what happens. But my mother did. For a long time I used to ask God, why did He allow me to be taken from my family, and I cursed Him when He never gave me an answer, I resented Him and my mother for a long time."

Her mother put her head down until Keyshia said, "I thought like that for a long time, until the same thing happened to me." It was so silent at that moment, one could hear the gnats flying. "See, I realize that a real mother is someone who is so strong that she is willing to do anything to ensure that her baby is safe. A real mother is someone who would sacrifice everything just so her baby would have a chance in life, even if it means giving them to someone who can do a better job at the time." Keyshia looked at her daughter. "See, I could have come to Charleston a long time ago and gotten custody of my daughter, 'cause I knew the law and that's what I do, but I never did, because just like my own mother, I'm a real mother and I was willing to sacrifice everything, even if it meant not having her, to ensure that she was happy, safe, and had a chance in life." Mother and daughter stared deep into each other's eyes for a moment. "Mommy, I love you."

Her mother was speechless as she tried to say *I love you* back, but she couldn't find the words, so they just embraced and cried in each other's arms.

The entire family began clapping as the two pulled away and wiped their eyes. Clyde was right beside Keyshia and gave her a loving tight hug. Clyde pulled away and took her by the hand and walked her to the middle of the crowd and said, "My beloved Keyshia, you brought me to Charleston, South Carolina, to meet your family, and your little sister, Kenya, asked me at the dinner table was I ever going to marry her sister. You remember?" Keyshia nodded as Clyde continued, "I told her that when the time is right, I was gonna bring her back to Charleston." Clyde looked around the yard and said, "Well, we in Charleston. I also told her that when I did, I was going to give you the biggest diamond ring I could find." He reached in his pocket and pulled out a ring box and opened it. Keyshia's hands flew to her mouth in shock. "I said that when that time come, I'm gonna ask you in front of your entire family"—he fanned his hand around the entire yard and continued—"then I said I was gonna get down on one knee." Clyde got down on one knee. "And ask the loveliest, most beautiful woman on the face of the earth, will she marry me?" Clyde stared deeply in her eyes and asked, "Keyshia Simmons, will you marry me?"

Everyone held their breath until Keyshia nodded and and said, "Yes, I will marry you."

There was a loud eruption of jubilation as Clyde put the ring on her finger and stood up and gave her a long kiss. They looked into each other's eyes, and Clyde said, "I love you, girl."

Keyshia returned the favor and said, "I love you more, boy."

Epilogue

Keyshia and Clyde got married that fall in Charleston, with over two hundred family members and friends in attendance, including Clyde's mother. Ceasar was Clyde's best man, Clyde, Jr. was the ring boy, and Christina was the flower girl. Keyshia went on to become a successful attorney with the same company she'd started with, which eventually became Hemmingway, Adorno, Shaw, and Barker. Clyde landed a job with the Department of Sanitation and is currently a supervisor in Brooklyn, and both Clyde and Keyshia have been happily married ever since, devoting all their off time to their two children.

Clyde's father was released from prison almost immediately after T. Bernard Williams had him exonerated from his prison sentence. Three years later, he settled with the city for a huge lawsuit for unlawful imprisonment. He was represented by his daughter-in-law's firm, of course, and he and his wife bought a one-family house in Long Island. Every Sunday without fail, all the brothers and their families meet up at their parents' house for Sunday dinner.

Ceasar got into corporate banking and married one of his co-workers, and they now have five kids and counting.

Sonny got out of prison two years after Clyde was released and went on to become a devout Muslim and is happily married to his longtime girlfriend, Cheryl, and they also have two kids.

Martha Woods was sentenced to five years in prison for her crimes. A year into her sentencing, she had a heart attack and died in her sleep.

Clyde once again needed a favor from his good friend Mike, only this time he had to go see him in person. He was doing a two-year sentence in Green Haven for a parole violation. They talked for nearly two hours, and then Clyde wished him luck and departed. Before Clyde left he filled up Mike's commissary account and promised to keep it filled until he got out. When Mike got back to his yard, he made several inquiries about an inmate named Omar Jackson. It didn't take him long to find him and put out the word that they had a rapist in the house. Two months after that, he was given the name Omara, after he was gang-raped by over eight inmates. He is now the property of a Spanish inmate named Alito and regularly walks around wearing tight prison greens and cherry Kool-Aid as lipstick.

About the Author

TREASURE E. BLUE was born and raised in Harlem. He formerly worked with the New York Fire Department as a supervising fire inspector in the Bronx. He now devotes himself full-time to writing and promoting his novels.

treasureeblue@yahoo.com